PRAISE FOR
Microserfs

"A funny and stridently topical novel. . . . Douglas Coupland continues to register the buzz of his generation with a fidelity that should shame most professional Zeitgeist chasers."

—Jay McInerney, *New York Times Book Review*

"The consistently au courant author Douglas Coupland (*Generation X*) has cooked up a timely group of successful, code-crunching twentysomethings, disgruntled with their round-the-clock hours at Microsoft. [Coupland's] real fun is in [his] frequent and rapidly fired pop culture references that span the seventies, eighties, and nineties." —*Entertainment Weekly*

"Like Steven Spielberg and Bret Easton Ellis, other masters of the everyday surface of things, Coupland's got the brand names, the speech habits, and the litter of nerd life nailed cold."

—*San Francisco Chronicle*

"*Microserfs* is a study in transformations, especially the personal epiphanies that are much better than a pulse to tell whether someone is actually living. . . . An accurate look at a thriving subculture." —*Boston Globe*

"A hilarious, intimate look at the way high technology is transforming American life—for better and for worse."

—*People*

microserfs

ALSO BY DOUGLAS COUPLAND

FICTION

Generation X
Shampoo Planet
Life After God
Girlfriend in a Coma
Miss Wyoming
All Families Are Psychotic
Hey Nostradamus!
Eleanor Rigby
JPod
The Gum Thief

NONFICTION

Polaroids from the Dead
City of Glass
Souvenir of Canada
School Spirit
Souvenir of Canada 2
Terry

microserfs

by

douglas coupland

HARPER  PERENNIAL

NEW YORK • LONDON • TORONTO • SYDNEY • NEW DELHI • AUCKLAND

Chapter 1 of this book appeared in modified form in the January 1994 issue of
Wired magazine.

This book may contain small factual errors. To help debug future versions, please
note any glitches and send them to the author c/o the Publisher: HarperCollins
Publishers, 10 East 53rd Street, New York, NY 10022. Many thanks to those read-
ers who have sent in corrections to date. These corrections have been incorporated
wherever possible.

A hardcover edition of this book was published in 1995 by HarperCollins Publishers.

P.S.™ is a trademark of HarperCollins Publishers.

FIRST HARPER PERENNIAL EDITION PUBLISHED 1996, REISSUED IN 2008.

The Library of Congress has catalogued the hardcover edition as follows:

Coupland, Douglas.
    Microserfs / Douglas Coupland. — 1st ed.
        p.   cm.
ISBN 978-0-06-039148-5
I. Title.
PS3553.O855M53   1995
813'.54—dc20   95-11472

ISBN 978-0-06-162426-1 (pbk.)

08 09 10 11 12 ID/RRD 10 9 8 7 6 5 4 3 2 1

thanks:

John Battelle
Elizabeth Dunn
Ian Ferrell
James Glave
James Joaquin
Kevin Kelly
Jane Metcalfe
Judith Regan
Louis Rossetto
Nathan Shedroff
Michael Tchao
Ian Verchere

Contents:

1
Microserfs

This morning, just after 11:00, Michael locked himself in his office and he won't come out.

Bill (Bill!) sent Michael this totally wicked flame-mail from hell on the e-mail system—and he just whaled on a chunk of code Michael had written. Using the *Bloom County*-cartoons-taped-on-the-door index, Michael is certainly the most sensitive coder in Building Seven—not the type to take criticism easily. Exactly why Bill would choose Michael of all people to whale on is confusing.

We figured it must have been a random quality check to keep the troops in line. Bill's so smart.

Bill is wise.

Bill is kind.

Bill is benevolent.

Bill, Be My Friend . . . *Please!*

Actually, nobody on our floor has ever been flamed by Bill personally. The episode was tinged with glamour and we were somewhat jealous. I tried to tell Michael this, but he was crushed.

Shortly before lunch he stood like a lump outside my office. His skin was pale like rising bread dough, and his Toppy's cut was dripping sweat, leaving little damp marks on the oyster-gray-with-plum highlights of the Microsoft carpeting. He handed me a printout of Bill's memo and then gallumphed into his office, where he's been burrowed ever since.

He won't answer his phone, respond to e-mail, or open his door. On his doorknob he placed a "Do Not Disturb" thingy stolen from the Boston Radisson during last year's Macworld Expo. Todd and I walked out onto the side lawn to try to peek in his window, but his venetian blinds were closed and a gardener with a leaf blower chased us away with a spray of grass clippings.

They mow the lawn every ten minutes at Microsoft. It looks like green Lego pads.

Finally, at about 2:30 A.M., Todd and I got concerned about Michael's not eating, so we drove to the 24-hour Safeway in Redmond. We went shopping for "flat" foods to slip underneath Michael's door.

The Safeway was completely empty save for us and a few other Microsoft people just like us—hair-trigger geeks in pursuit of just the right snack. Because of all the rich nerds living around here, Redmond and Bellevue are very "on-demand" neighborhoods. Nerds get what they want when they want it, and they go psycho if it's not immediately available. Nerds overfocus. I guess that's the problem. But it's precisely this ability to narrow-focus that makes them so good at code writing: one line at a time, one line in a strand of millions.

When we returned to Building Seven at 3:00 A.M., there were still a few people grinding away. Our group is scheduled to ship product (RTM: Release to Manufacturing) in just eleven days (Top Secret: We'll never make it).

Michael's office lights were on, but once again, when we knocked, he wouldn't answer his door. We heard his keyboard chatter, so we figured he was still alive. The situation really begged a discussion of Turing logic— could we have discerned that the entity behind the door was indeed even human? We slid Kraft singles, Premium Plus crackers, Pop-Tarts, grape leather, and Freezie-Pops in to him.

Todd asked me, "Do you think any of this violates geek dietary laws?"

Just then, Karla in the office across the hall screamed and then glared out at us from her doorway. Her eyes were all red and sore behind her round glasses. She said, "You guys are only encouraging him," like we were feeding a raccoon or something. I don't think Karla ever sleeps.

She harrumphed and slammed her door closed. Doors sure are important to nerds.

Anyway, by this point Todd and I were both really tired. We drove back to the house to crash, each in our separate cars, through the Campus grounds—22 buildings' worth of nerd-cosseting fun—cloistered by 100-foot-tall second growth timber, its streets quiet as the womb: the foundry of our culture's deepest dreams.

There was mist floating on the ground above the soccer fields outside the central buildings. I thought about the e-mail and Bill and all of that, and I had this weird feeling—of how the presence of Bill floats about the Campus, semi-visible, at all times, kind of like the dead grandfather in the *Family Circus* cartoons. Bill is a moral force, a spectral force, a force that shapes, a force that molds. A force with thick, thick glasses.

I am danielu@microsoft.com. If my life was a game of *Jeopardy!* my seven dream categories would be:
- Tandy products
- Trash TV of the late '70s and early '80s
- The history of Apple
- Career anxieties
- Tabloids
- Plant life of the Pacific Northwest
- Jell-O 1-2-3

I am a tester—a bug checker in Building Seven. I worked my way up the ladder from Product Support Services (PSS) where I spent six months in phone purgatory in 1991 helping little old ladies format their Christmas mailing lists on Microsoft Works.

Like most Microsoft employees, I consider myself too well adjusted to be working here, even though I am 26 and my universe consists of home, Microsoft, and Costco.

I am originally from Bellingham, up just near the border, but my parents live in Palo Alto now. I live in a group house with five other Microsoft employees: Todd, Susan, Bug Barbecue, Michael, and Abe.

We call ourselves "The Channel Three News Team."

I am single. I think partly this is because Microsoft is not conducive to relationships. Last year down at the Apple Worldwide Developer's Conference in San Jose, I met a girl who works not too far away, at Hewlett-Packard on Interstate 90, but it never went anywhere. Sometimes I'll sort of get something going, but then work takes over my life and I bail out of all my commitments and things fizzle.

Lately I've been unable to sleep. That's why I've begun writing this journal late at night, to try to see the patterns in my life. From this I hope to establish what my problem is—and then, hopefully, solve it. I'm trying to feel more well adjusted than I really am, which is, I guess, the human condition. My life is lived day to day, one line of bug-free code at a time.

The house:

Growing up, I used to build split-level ranch-type homes out of Legos. This is pretty much the house I live in now, but its ambiance is anything but sterilized Lego-clean. It was built about twenty years ago, maybe before Microsoft was even in the dream stage and this part of Redmond had a lost, alpine ski-cabin feel.

Instead of a green plastic pad with little plastic nubblies, our house sits on a thickly-treed lot beside a park on a cul-de-sac at the top of a steep hill. It's only a seven-minute drive from Campus. There are two other Microsoft group houses just down the hill. Karla, actually, lives in the house three down from us across the street.

People end up living in group houses either by e-mail or by word of mouth. Living in a group house is a little bit like admitting you're deficient in the having-a-life department, but at work you spend your entire life crunching code and testing for bugs, and what else are you supposed to do? Work, sleep, work, sleep, work, sleep. I know a few Microsoft employees who try to fake having a life—many a Redmond garage contains a never-used kayak collecting dust. You ask these people what they do in their spare time and they say, "*Uhhh*—kayaking. That's right. I kayak in my spare time." You can tell they're faking it.

I don't even do many sports anymore and my relationship with my body has gone all weird. I used to play soccer three times a week and now I feel like a boss in charge of an underachiever. I feel like my body is a station wagon in which I drive my brain around, like a suburban mother taking the kids to hockey practice.

The house is covered with dark cedar paneling. Out front there's a tiny patch of lawn covered in miniature yellow crop circles thanks to the dietary excesses of our neighbor's German shepherd, Mishka. Bug Barbecue keeps his weather experiments—funnels and litmus strips and so forth—nailed to the wall beside the front door. A flat of purple petunias long-expired from neglect—Susan's one attempt at prettification—depresses us every time we leave for work in the morning, resting as it does in the thin strip of soil between the driveway and Mishka's crop circles.

Abe, our in-house multimillionaire, used to have tinfoil all over his bedroom windows to keep out what few rays of sun penetrated the trees until we ragged on him so hard that he went out and bought a sheaf of black construction paper at the Pay N Pak and taped it up instead. It looked like a drifter lived here. Todd's only contribution to the house's outer appearance is a collection of car-washing toys sometimes visible beside the garage door. The only evidence of my being in the house is my 1977 AMC Hornet Sportabout hatchback parked out front when I'm home. It's bright orange, it's rusty, and damnit, it's *ugly*.

SATURDAY

Shipping hell continued again today. Grind, grind, grind. We'll never make it. Have I said that already? Why do we always underestimate our shipping schedules? I just don't understand. In at 9:30 A.M.; out at 11:30 P.M. Domino's for dinner. And three diet Cokes.

I got bored a few times today and checked the WinQuote on my screen—that's the extension that gives continuous updates on Microsoft's NASDAQ price. It was Saturday, and there was never any change, but I kept forgetting. Habit. Maybe the Tokyo or Hong Kong exchanges might cause a fluctuation?

Most staffers peek at WinQuote a few times a day. I mean, if you have 10,000 shares (and tons of staff members have way more) and the stock goes up a buck, you've just made ten grand! But then, if it goes down two dollars, you've just lost twenty grand. It's a real psychic yo-yo. Last April Fool's Day, someone fluctuated the price up and down by fifty dollars and half the staff had coronaries.

Because I started out low on the food chain and worked my way up, I didn't get much stock offered to me the way that programmers and systems designers get stock firehosed onto them when they start. What stock I do own won't fully vest for another 2.5 years (stock takes 4.5 years to fully vest).

Susan's stock vests later this week, and she's going to have a vesting party. And then she's going to quit. Larger social forces are at work, threatening to dissolve our group house.

The stock closed up $1.75 on Friday. Bill has 78,000,000 shares, so that means he's now $136.5 million richer. I have almost no stock, and this means I am a loser.

News update: Michael is now out of his office. It's as if he never had his geek episode. He slept there throughout the whole day (not unusual at Microsoft), using his *Jurassic Park* inflatable T-Rex toy as a pillow. When he woke up in the early evening, he thanked me for bringing him the Kraft products, and now he says he won't eat anything that's not entirely two-dimensional. "Ich bin ein Flatlander," he piped, as he cheerfully sifted through hard copy of the bug-checked code he'd been chugging out. Karla made disgusted clicking noises with her tongue from her office. I think maybe she's in love with Michael.

More details about our group house—Our House of Wayward Mobility.

Because the house receives almost no sun, moss and algae tend to colonize what surfaces they can. There is a cherry tree crippled by a fungus. The rear verandah, built of untreated 2x4's, has quietly rotted away, and the sliding door in the kitchen has been braced shut with a hockey stick to prevent the unwary from straying into the suburban abyss.

The driveway contains six cars: Todd's cherry-red Supra (his life, what little there is of it), my pumpkin Hornet, and four personality-free gray Microsoftmobiles—a Lexus, an Acura Legend, and two Tauri (nerd plural for Taurus). I bet if Bill drove a Shriner's go-cart to work, everybody else would, too.

Inside, each of us has a bedroom. Because of the McDonald's-like turnover in the house, the public rooms—the living room, kitchen, dining room, and basement—are bleak, to say the least. The dormlike atmosphere precludes heavy-duty interior design ideas. In the living room are two velveteen sofas that were too big and too ugly for some long-gone tenants to take with them. Littered about the Tiki green shag carpet are:

• Two Microsoft Works PC inflatable beach cushions
• One Mitsubishi 27-inch color TV
• Various vitamin bottles
• Several weight-gaining system cartons (mine)
• 86 copies of *MacWEEK* arranged in chronological order by Bug Barbecue, who will go berserk if you so much as move one issue out of date
• Six Microsoft Project 2.0 juggling bean bags
• Bone-shaped chew toys for when Mishka visits
• Two PowerBooks

- Three IKEA mugs encrusted with last month's blender drink sensation
- Two 12.5-pound dumbbells (Susan's)
- A Windows NT box
- Three baseball caps (two Mariners, one A's)
- Abe's Battlestar Galactica trading card album
- Todd's pile of books on how to change your life to win! (*Getting Past OK*, *7 Habits of Highly Effective People* . . .)

The kitchen is stocked with ramshackle 1970s avocado green appliances. You can almost hear the ghost of Emily Hartley yelling "Hi, Bob!" every time you open the fridge door (a sea of magnets and 4-x-6-inch photos of last year's house parties).

Our mail is in little piles by the front door: bills, Star Trek junk mail, and the heap-o-catalogues next to the phone.

I think we'd order our lives via 1-800 numbers if we could.

Mom phoned from Palo Alto. This is the time of year she calls a lot. She calls because she wants to speak about Jed, but none of us in the family are able. We kind of erased him.

I used to have a younger brother named Jed. He drowned in a boating accident in the Strait of Juan de Fuca when I was 14 and he was 12. A Labor Day statistic.

To this day, anything Labor Day-ish creeps me out: the smell of barbecuing salmon, life preservers, Interstate traffic reports from the local radio Traffic Copter, Monday holidays. But here's a secret: My e-mail password is *hellojed*. So I think about him every day. He was way better with computers than I was. He was way nerdier than me.

As it turned out, Mom had good news today. Dad has a big meeting Monday with his company. Mom and Dad figure it's a promotion because Dad's IBM division has been doing so well (by IBM standards—it's not hemorrhaging money). She says she'll keep me posted.

Susan taped laser-printed notes on all of our bedroom doors reminding us about the vesting party this Thursday ("Vest Fest '93"), which was a subliminal hint to us to clean up the place. Most of us work in Building Seven; shipping hell has brought a severe breakdown in cleanup codes.

Susan is 26 and works in Mac Applications. If Susan were a *Jeopardy!* contestant, her dream board would be:

- 680X0 assembly language
- Cats
- Early '80s haircut bands
- "My secret affair with Rob in the Excel Group"
- License plate slogans of America
- Plot lines from *The Monkees*
- The death of IBM

Susan's an IBM brat and hates that company with a passion. She credits it with ruining her youth by transferring her family eight times before she graduated from high school—and the punchline is that the company gave her father the boot last year during a wave of restructuring. So nothing too evil can happen to IBM in her eyes. Her graphic designer friend made up T-shirts saying "IBM: Weak as a Kitten, Dumb as a Sack of Hammers." We all wear them. I gave one to Dad last Christmas but his reaction didn't score too high on the chuckle-o-meter. (I am not an IBM brat—Dad was teaching at Western Washington University until the siren of industry lured him to Palo Alto in 1985. It was very '80s.)

Susan's a real coding machine. But her abilities are totally wasted reworking old code for something like the Norwegian Macintosh version of Word 5.8. Susan's work ethic best sums up the ethic of most of the people I've met who work at Microsoft. If I recall her philosophy from the conversation she had with her younger sister two weekends ago, it goes something like this:

"It's never been, 'We're doing this for the good of society.' It's always been us taking an intellectual pride in putting out a good product—and making money. If putting a computer on every desktop and in every home didn't make money, we wouldn't do it."

That sums up most of the Microsoft people I know.

Microsoft, like any office, is a status theme park. Here's a quick rundown:

- Profitable projects are galactically higher in status than loser (not quite as profitable) projects.
- Microsoft at Work (Digital Office) is sexiest at the moment. Fortune 500 companies are drooling over DO because it'll allow them to downsize

millions of employees. Basically, DO allows you to operate your fax, phone, copier—all of your office stuff—from your PC.

• Cash cows like Word are profitable but not really considered cutting edge.

• Working on-Campus is higher status than being relegated to one of the off-Campus Siberias.

• Having Pentium-driven hardware (built to the hilt) in your office is higher status than having 486 droneware.

• Having technical knowledge is way up there.

• Being an architect is also way up there.

• Having Bill-o-centric contacts is way, way up there.

• Shipping your product on time is maybe the coolest (insert wave of anxiety here). If you ship a product you get a Ship-It award: a 12-x-15-x-1-inch Lucite slab—but you have to pretend it's no big deal. Michael has a Ship-It award and we've tried various times to destroy it—blowtorching, throwing it off the verandah, dowsing it with acetone to dissolve it—nothing works. It's so permanent, it's frightening.

More roommate profiles:

First, Abe. If Abe were a *Jeopardy!* contestant, his seven dream categories would be:

• Intel assembly language
• Bulk shopping
• C++
• Introversion
• "I love my aquarium"
• How to have millions of dollars and not let it affect your life in any way
• Unclean laundry

Abe is sort of like the household Monopoly-game banker. He collects our monthly checks for the landlord, $235 apiece. The man has millions and he rents! He's been at the group house since 1984, when he was hired fresh out of MIT. (The rest of us have been here, on average, about eight months apiece.) After ten years of writing code, Abe so far shows no signs of getting a life. He seems happy to be reaching the age of 30 in just four months with nothing to his name but a variety of neat-o consumer electronics and boxes of Costco products purchased in rash moments of Costco-scale madness ("Ten thousand straws! Just think of it—only $10 and I'll never need to buy straws ever again!") These products line the walls of his room, giving it the feel of an air-raid shelter.

Bonus detail: There are dried-out patches of sneeze spray all over Abe's monitors. You'd think he could afford 24 bottles of Windex.

Next, Todd. Todd's seven *Jeopardy!* categories would be:
- Your body is your temple
- Baseball hats
- Meals made from combinations of Costco products
- Psychotically religious parents
- Frequent and empty sex
- SEGA Genesis gaming addiction
- The Supra

Todd works as a tester with me. He's really young—22—the way Microsoft employees all used to be. His interest is entirely in girls, bug testing, his Supra, and his body, which he buffs religiously at the Pro Club gym and feeds with peanut butter quesadillas, bananas, and protein drinks.

Todd is historically empty. He neither knows nor cares about the past. He reads *Car and Driver* and fields three phone calls a week from his parents who believe that computers are "the Devil's voice box," and who try to persuade him to return home to Port Angeles and speak with the youth pastor.

Todd's the most fun of all the house members because he is all impulse and no consideration. He's also the only roomie to have clean laundry consistently. In a crunch you can always borrow an unsoiled shirt from Todd.

Bug Barbecue's seven *Jeopardy!* categories would be:
- Bitterness
- Xerox PARC nostalgia
- Macintosh products
- More bitterness
- Psychotic loser friends
- Jazz
- Still more bitterness

Bug Barbecue is the World's Most Bitter Man. He is (as his name implies) a tester with me at Building Seven. His have-a-life factor is pretty near zero. He has the smallest, darkest room in the house, in which he maintains two small shrines: one to his Sinclair ZX-81, his first computer, and the other to supermodel Elle MacPherson. Man, she'd freak if she saw the hundreds of little photos—the coins, the candles, the little notes.

Bug is 31, and he lets everyone know it. If we ever ask him so much as "Hey, Bug—have you seen volume 7 of my *Inside Mac*?" he gives a sneer and replies, "You're obviously of the generation that never built their own motherboard or had to invent their own language."

Hey, Bug—we love you, too.

Bug never gets offered stock by the company. When payday comes and the little white stock option envelopes with red printing reading "Personal and Confidential" end up in all of our pigeonholes, Bug's is always, alas, empty. Maybe they're trying to get rid of him, but it's almost impossible to fire someone at Microsoft. It must drive the administration nuts. They hired 3,100 people in 1992 alone, and you know not all of them were gems.

Oddly, Bug is fanatical in his devotion to Microsoft. It's as if the more they ignore him, the more rabidly he defends their honor. And if you cherish your own personal time, you will not get into a discussion with him over the famous Look-&-Feel lawsuit or any of the FTC or Department of Justice actions:

"These litigious pricks piss me off. I wish they'd compete in the market-place where it really counts instead of being little wusses and whining for government assistance to compete. . . ."

You've been warned.

Finally, Michael. Michael's seven *Jeopardy!* categories would be:
- FORTRAN
- Pascal
- Ada (defense contracting code)
- LISP
- Neil Peart (drummer for Rush)
- Hugo and Nebula award winners
- Sir Lancelot

Michael is probably the closest I'll ever come to knowing someone who lives in a mystical state. He lives to assemble elegant streams of code instructions. He's like Mozart to everyone else's Salieri—he enters people's offices where lines of code are written on the dry-erase whiteboards and quietly optimizes the code as he speaks to them, as though someone had written wrong instructions on how to get to the beach and he was merely setting them right so they wouldn't get lost.

He often uses low-tech solutions to high-tech problems: Popsicle sticks, rubber bands, and little strips of paper that turn on a bent coat hanger frame help him solve complex matrix problems. When he moved offices into his new window office (good coder, good office), he had to put Post-it notes reading "Not Art" on his devices so that the movers didn't stick them under the glass display cases out in the central atrium area.

SUNDAY

This morning before heading to the office I read an in-depth story about Burt and Loni's divorce in *People* magazine. Thus, 1,474,819 brain cells that could have been used toward a formula for world peace were obliterated. Are computer memory and human memory analogous? Michael would know.

Mid-morning, I mountain-biked over to Nintendo headquarters, across Interstate 520 from Microsoft.

Now, I've never been to the South African plant of, say, Sandoz Pharmaceuticals, but I bet it looks a lot like Nintendo headquarters—two-story industrial-plex buildings sheathed with Death Star–black windows and landscape trees around the parking lot seemingly clicked into place with a mouse. It's nearly identical to Microsoft except Microsoft uses sea foam-green glass on its windows and has big soccer fields should it ever really need to expand.

I Hacky Sacked for a while with my friend, Marty, and some of his tester friends during their break. Sunday is a big day for the kids who man the PSS phone lines there because all of young America is out of school and using the product. It's really young at Nintendo. It's like the year 1311, where everyone over 35 is dead or maimed and out of sight and mind.

All of us got into this big discussion about what sort of software dogs would design if they could. Marty suggested territory-marking programs with piss simulators and lick interfaces. Antonella thought of BoneFinder. Harold thought of a doghouse remodeling CAD system. All very carto-graphic/high sensory: lots of visuals.

Then, of course, the subject of catware came up. Antonella suggested a personal secretary program that tells the world, "No, I do not wish to be pet-ted. Oh, and hold all my calls." My suggestion was for a program that sleeps all the time.

Anyway, it's a good thing we're human. We design business spread-sheets, paint programs, and word processing equipment. So that tells you where we're at as a species. What is the search for the next great compelling application but a search for the human identity?

It was nice being at Nintendo where everybody's just a little bit younger and hipper than at Microsoft and actually takes part in the Seattle scene. Everyone at Microsoft seems, well, literally 31.2 years old, and it kind of shows.

There's this eerie, science-fiction lack of anyone who doesn't look exactly 31.2 on the Campus. It's oppressive. It seems like only last week the entire Campus went through Gap ribbed-T mania together—and now they're all shopping for the same 3bdrm/2bth dove-gray condo in Kirkland.

Microserfs are locked by nature into doing 31.2-ish things: the first house, the first marriage, the "where-am-I-going" crisis, the out-goes-the-Miata/in-comes-the-minivan thing, and, of course, major death denial. A Microsoft VP died of cancer a few months ago, and it was like, you weren't allowed to mention it. Period. The three things you're not allowed to discuss at work: death, salaries, and your stock options.

I'm 26 and I'm just not ready to turn 31.2 yet.

Actually, I've been thinking about this death denial business quite a bit lately. September always makes me think of Jed. It's as if there's this virtual Jed who might have been. Sometimes I see him when I'm driving by water; I see him standing on a log boom smiling and waving; I see him buckaroo-ing a killer whale in the harbor off downtown while I'm stuck in traffic on the Alaskan Way viaduct. Or I see him walking just ahead of me around the Space Needle restaurant, always just around the curve.

I'd like to hope Jed is happy in the afterworld, but because I was raised without any beliefs, I have no pictures of an afterworld for myself. In the past I have tried to convince myself that there is no life after death, but I have found myself unable to do this, so I guess intuitively I feel there is something. But I just don't know how to begin figuring out what these pic-tures are.

Over the last few weeks I've been oh-so-casually asking the people I know about their own pictures of the afterworld. I can't simply come right out and ask directly because, as I say, you just don't discuss death at Microsoft.

The results were pretty dismal. Ten people asked, and not one single image. Not one single angel or one bright light or even one single, miserable barbecue briquette. Zero.

Todd was more concerned about who would show up at his funeral.

Bug Barbecue told me all this depressing stuff, of how the constituent elements of his personality weren't around before he was born, so why should he worry about what happens to them afterward?

Susan changed the topic entirely. *("Hey, isn't Louis Gerstner hopeless?")*

Sometimes, in the employee kitchen, when I'm surrounded by the dairy cases full of Bill-supplied free beverages, I have to wonder if maybe Microsoft's corporate zest for recycling aluminum, plastic, and paper is perhaps a sublimation of the staff's hidden desire for immortality. Or maybe this whole Bill thing is actually the subconscious manufacture of God.

After Nintendo I mountain-biked around the Campus, delaying my venture into shipping hell. I saw a cluster of Deadheads looking for magic mushrooms out on the west lawn beside the second-growth forest. Fall is just around the corner.

The trees around Campus are dropping their leaves. It's been strange weather this spring and summer. The newspaper says the trees are confused and they're shedding early this year.

Todd was out on the main lawn training with the Microsoft intramural Frisbee team. I said hello. Everyone looked so young and healthy. I realized that Todd and his early-20s cohorts are the first Microsoft generation—the first group of people who have never known a world without an MS-DOS environment. Time ticks on.

They're also the first generation of Microsoft employees faced with reduced stock options and, for that matter, plateauing stock prices. I guess that makes them mere employees, just like at any other company. Bug Barbecue and I were wondering last week what's going to happen when this new crop of workers reaches its inevitable Seven-Year Programmer's Burnout. At the end of it they won't have two million dollars to move to Hilo and start up a bait shop with, the way the Microsoft old-timers did. Not everyone can move into management.

Discarded.

Face it: You're always just a breath away from a job in telemarketing. Everybody I know at the company has an estimated time of departure and they're all within five years. It must have been so weird—living the way my Dad did—thinking your company was going to take care of you forever.

A few minutes later I bumped into Karla walking across the west lawn. She walks really quickly and she's so small, like a little kid.

It was so odd for both of us, seeing each other outside the oatmeal walls and oyster carpeting of the office. We stopped and sat on the lawn and talked for a while. We shared a feeling of conspiracy by not being inside helping with the shipping deadline.

I asked her if she was looking for 'shrooms with the Deadheads, but she said she was going nuts in her office, and she just had to be in the wild for a few minutes in the forest beside the Campus. I thought this was such an unusual aspect of her personality, I mean, because she's so mousy and indoorsy-looking. It was good to see her and for once to not have her yelling at me to stop being a nuisance. We've worked maybe ten offices apart for half a year, and we've never once really talked to each other.

I showed Karla some birch bark I'd peeled off a tree outside Building Nine and she showed me some scarlet sumac leaves she had found in the forest. I told her about the discussion Marty, Antonella, Harold, and I had been having about dogs and cats over at Nintendo's staff picnic tables. She lay down on the ground and thought about this, so I lay down, too. The sun was hot and good. I could only see the sky and hear her words. She surprised me.

She said that we, as humans, bear the burden of having to be every animal in the world rolled into one.

She said that we really have no identity of our own.

She said, "What is human behavior, except trying to prove that we're not animals?"

She said, "I think we have strayed so far away from our animal origins that we are bent on creating a new, supra-animal identity."

She said, "What are computers but the EveryAnimalMachine?"

I couldn't believe she was talking like this. She was like an episode of *Star Trek* made flesh. It was as if I was falling into a deep, deep hole as I heard her voice speak to me. But then a bumblebee bumbled above us and it stole our attention the way flying things can.

She said, "Imagine being a bee and living in a great big hive. You would have no idea that tomorrow was going to be any different than today. You could return to that same hive a thousand years later and there would be just the same perception of tomorrow as never being any different. Humans are completely different. We assume tomorrow is another world."

I asked her what she meant, and she said, "I mean that the animals live in another sense of time. They can never have a sense of history because they can never see the difference between today and tomorrow."

I juggled some small rocks I found beside me. She said she didn't know I could juggle and I told her it was something I learned by osmosis in my last product group.

We got up and walked together back to Building Seven. I pushed my bike. We walked over the winding white cement path speckled with crow shit, past the fountains, and through the hemlocks and firs.

Things seem different between us now, as if we've somehow agreed to agree. And God, she's skinny! I think I'm going to bring her snacks to eat tomorrow while she works.

I hope this isn't like feeding a raccoon.

Worked until just past midnight and came back home. Had a shower. Three bowls of Corn Flakes and ESPN. My weekends are no different than my weekdays. One of these days I'm going to vanish up to someplace beautiful like Whidbey Island and just veg for two solid days.

Todd is compressing code this week and as a sideline invented what he calls a "Prince Emulator"—a program th@ converts whatever you write into a title of a song by Minnesotan Funkmeister, Prince. I sampled it using part of today's diary.

A few minutz 18r I bumpd in2 Karla walkng akros the west lawn. She walkz rEly kwikly & she'z so smal, like a litl kid.

It wuz so odd 4 both uv us, C-ng Ech uthr outside the otmeel walz + oystr karpetng uv the ofiss. We stopd & s@ on the lawn + talkd 4 a wile. We shared a fElng uv konspiraC by not B-ng inside helpng with the shippng dedline.

I askd hr if she wuz lookng 4 shroomz with the Dedhedz, but she sed she wuz going nutz in hr ofiss, & she just had 2 B in the wild 4 a few minutz in the 4St B-side the Kampus. I thot this wuz such an unuzual aspekt uv hr prsonaliT, I mEn, B-kuz she'z so mowsy + indorzy lookng. It wuz good 2 C hr & 4 once 2 not hav hr yellng @ me 2 stop B-ng a noosanss. We'v wrkd mayB 10 officz apart 4 half a yEr, + we'v nevr once rEly talkd 2 Ech uthr.

I showd Karla sum brch bark I'd pEld off a trE outside Bildng 9 & she showd me sum skarlet soomak lEvz she had found in the 4St. I told hr about the diskussion MarT, AntonLa, Harold, + I had B-n havng about dogz & katz ovr @ Nin-10-do'z staf piknik tablz. She lA down on the ground + thot about this, so I lA down, 2. The sun wuz hot & good. I kould only C the sky + hear hr wrdz. She srprizd me.

She sed th@ we, az humnz, bear the brdn uv havng 2 B evry animl in the wrld rold in2 1.

She sed th@ we rEly hav no identiT uv our own.

She sed, "Wh@ iz human B-havior, X-ept tryng 2 proov th@ w'r not animalz?"

She sed, "I think we hav strAd so far awA from our animal originz th@ we R bent on kre8ng a noo, soopra-animal idNtiT."

She sed, "Wh@ R komputrz but the EvryAnimalMashEn?"

I kouldn't B-lEv she wuz talkng like this. She wuz like an episode uv *Star Trek* made flesh. It wuz az if I wuz falng in2 a dEp, dEp hole az I hrd hr voiss speak 2 me. But then a bumbl-B bumbld abuv us & it stole our a10nshun the wA flyng thngz kan.

She sed, "Imagin B-ng a B + livng in a gr8 big hive. You would hav no idea th@ 2morow wuz going 2 B any difrent than 2dA. You kould retrn 2 th@ same hive 1,000 yearz latr & ther would B just the same prception uv 2morow az nevr B-ng any difrent. Humanz R kompletely difrent. We asoom 2morow iz anuthr wrld."

I askd hr wot she ment, + she sed, "I meen th@ the animalz liv in anuthr sens uv time. They kan nevr hav a sens uv history B-kuz they kan nevr C the difrenss B-twEn 2dA & 2morow."

I juggld sum smal rokz I found B-side me. She sed she didnt kno I kould juggl + I told hr it wuz sumthing I lrnd by ozmosis in my last produkt groop.

We got up & walkd 2gethr bak 2 Bildng 7. I pushd my bike. We walkd ovr the windng wite Cment path spekld with krow shit, past the fountunz, + thru the hemlokz & frz.

I reread the Prince Version and realized th@ after a certain point, real language decomposes into encryption code; Japanese.

%43]505)%1$])3D=%5D526524Y'0T]24D5#5$Q954Y&3U(@$)$#L!PZ</
4,!,6D9UBPEE0^Y82AE$UT!R0,$$G[X91_^F@0(#B.&!@*4_TOTK#]TJ
M#BM>)\^(B\0!P825!+DUI8W)O<V]F="!86EL+DYO=&4,0!)&@#$"P'/#
@$<P"?V0$(&"49&!!N$("LKBBD/BSQ1D!H+P3%!4<FEX4F%B8FET%1
R:7A286)B:7186]L+FO;0(!"S!$(@DMTY$Q,T1A/PJ@!+L@>$P0L!4<FE
X4F%B8FET#!4,0!XS!$P%1R:7A286)B:7186]L+FO;0'@",$%4TU44"$*$
*$(0#@X,C1"S1%#1$,3$X!!3$)",CP!$'0V!"@"$$@$+0%1O;2!3=VEF="!
A;F0@A($$A=F5S(&]F($UE<WA9VEN9R#8:.:7)E+BXN8/06P.R@<(!\#@!1
"LP!%0$@,#@,,H'"?X$0K,10$!"8!"$X.#(T0C<T13T0S1#1#$Q.#1&0SP04$$$
P,#1"0C(P,,1!P$$D87D!(#!<L(P"PI8$$.000$N]%5FY42AF=_G5BY0(!40!%0
$U3.DLY354+T!3DE.12])04Y&L5P"P!8+%$!D!X'P!!0%U,'@?#$$OV\]34E#
4D]33T94+V]U/4%04%,M5T=!+!+VN/5)E8VEP:65N=',',O8VX];:6%N9P&$$*
5%8;P#0Y<!X"!!90%E/54A!5D5!3$Q42$5)3D9/25%3E142$5,2514Y$4T
%45$%,2U)534]24U1(15!23T),14U)4T%435ED0[64]505)%1$])3D=%5D5
26524Y'0T]24D5#5$Q954Y&3U(@$$)$#L!PZ</4,!,6D9U2%DI9\"@$/A4"I
P(8V@*P/!$970Q!=P"@P!0#XUK!K0"@$S(/?#0;P(,X<#Q1.Y!K!S=&5MH
#^?OJ",)\)V0*"H0+Q6^*0P"%D(8("V^9EYB'0,0==@@&@;;,NA8($D@$$$,"X@
5%T;H6P$5"?!!D!"!A@P59!L:RYR=01@^QO0'(1PV"8!;P&=!M>1TB8.R!
YM$"$*@M$$$*P&D;,&10"X!G'2;('(>>1N0(,,,%H@08W1L;'DN"H4*A54;X0@
=2IN'8!E(BL&X,B$,N,T,T'T>0=="(@(1$D(@*"!!109@70:04;W,))7!T)P9!=6(M0
3YTWE$L8#^DD@"!!PAR$'8%l!L2AA:V$D4#,P,0(BD$,$A`U1*G3H=V\J(::P)
$("5Q&F4T&@$?D?D>0<%!G\F4<A&9I$!%0'F!'[#!T$$+4QQN97AT)00(/<%H!
!U'S)W#_%0"20&T#O@=A\24Q([,&!N87MR:%5$"(%$$_@_+2R!^^B(<%(
P$2QS(:$$Q00@;AAP9AV!!!%;%A9&LL"UP8P=!;IL208GIU!4!I!4@H>1"X!C_
PI#;K;6P,0""."^:Q]P%X((<"0)!Z98\D(2)'0&EG;@>^S!!!2;$#!C'(C41N#*
GLD=LDZP7P32AA$'#!U)V7L?\OVRIF!"E\#'A'!^MPGP_23>2l/0R=@27P
X"(.\V@2B,O#H&8+8>)6!'ZL4@:&]O:!R)BT*L(P<RR8$$2T[CAL""Q!4!
&,Z(<"@@_P!P+78$!!l!"!B&Y+Y!0!A<"5@1,Z$E<1N2,I'_&!!$$G@'
(B7!!R8!B)F\G=O\?03L#$"!<"^%%$204_S")*L2WQ/6(HPB#".%F))%F+3+
P;7!U,VC_%Z!<0@8,;;:D!V!2NM<&\Q\5#__G86X<@!P:M],<#Y!'%$QX"_
=!^P*%+_+X(;;DD3A.S@1[Q2@,,ILO\$@4XP2O4?(0.@0%]!;1R]D@@IDW
=4+2&Y$?L"K"_QV1.&E74")<'"7H!LA&Y/_,!+PR1021<4;P2,\,?\H84!3H
(=81MC+9(M4020]U6Q,XJL&=93=A/_([/\ST"G11!(#H;@"8!2(0N_FL@P
@K"&M80/P&Y%T/\>,36R*$MP,0*0R$$%$$+2?RE74(D$$!*P_PB0C5<&%$\\
F!$9!K)!?T^9)*JT"!7+\Al(]ET1LP4@8Y\;LA:;@0CN@1LA0T0X!KTK4"
[$6@1O@T2(&$$/U"$$6Y:<@_@"XJU&&!3Z+/+•+Y%68FOJ!1!G:#MAU+_
!@G<!M@7R,M83DR952TOD<@"A(8(8+%3T3+!!"AM$$?\'0!^085$$,B"@

MONDAY

Dad got fired! Didn't we see that one coming a mile away. This whole restructuring business.

Mom phoned around 11:00 A.M. and she spent only ten minutes giving me the news. She had to get back to Dad, who was out on the back patio, in shock, looking out over Silicon Valley. She said we'll have to talk longer tomorrow. I got off the phone and my head was buzzing.

The results came in from the overnight stress tests—the tests we run to try to locate bugs in the code—and there were five breaks. Five! So I had my work cut out for me today. Nine days until shipping.

Right.

I telephoned Susan over in Mac Applications. The news about Dad was too important for e-mail, and we had lunch together in the big cafeteria in Building Sixteen that resembles the Food Fair at any halfway decent mall. Today was Mongolian sticky rice day.

Susan was hardly surprised about IBM dumping Dad. She told me that when she was briefly on the OS/2 version 1.0 team, they sent her to the IBM branch in Boca Raton for two weeks. Apparently IBM was asking people from the data entry department whether they wanted to train to be programmers.

"If they hadn't been doing boneheaded shit like that, your dad would still have a job."

I've been thinking: I get way too many pieces of e-mail, about 60 a day. This is a typical number at Microsoft. E-mail is like highways—if you have them, traffic follows.

I'm an e-mail addict. Everybody at Microsoft is an addict. The future of e-mail usage is being pioneered right here. The cool thing with e-mail is that when you send it, there's no possibility of connecting with the person on the other end. It's better than phone answering machines, because with them, the person on the other line might actually pick up the phone and you might have to talk.

Typically, everybody has about a 40 percent immediate cull rate—those pieces of mail you can delete immediately because of a frivolous tag line. What you read of the remaining 60 percent depends on how much of a life you have. The less of a life, the more mail you read.

Abe has developed a "rules-based" software program that anticipates his e-mail preferences and sifts and culls accordingly. I guess that's sort of like Antonella's personal secretary program for cats.

After lunch, I drove down 156th Avenue to the Uwajimaya Japanese supermarket and bought Karla some seaweed and cucumber rolls. They also sell origami paper by the sheet there, so I threw in some cool colored papers as an extra bonus.

When I got back to the office, I knocked on Karla's door and gave her the rolls and the paper. She seemed glad enough to see me (she didn't scowl) and genuinely surprised that I had brought her something.

She asked me to sit in her office. She has a big poster of a MIPS chip blueprint on her wall and some purple and pink flowers in a bud vase, just like Mary Tyler Moore. She said that it was kind of me to bring her a Japanese seaweed roll and everything, but at the moment she was in the middle of a pack of Skittles. Would I like some?

And so we sat and ate Skittles. I told her about my dad and she just listened. And then she told me that her own father operates a small fruit cannery in Oregon. She said that she learned about coding from canning lines— or rather, she developed a fascination for linear logic processes there—and she actually has a degree in manufacturing processes, not computer programming. And she folded one of those origami birds for me. Her IQ must be about 800.

IQs are one of the weird things about Microsoft—you only find the right-hand side of the bell curve on-Campus. There's nobody who's two-digit. Just one more reason it's such a sci-fi place to work.

Anyway, we started talking more about all of the fiftysomethings being dumped out of the economy by downsizing. No one knows what to do with these people, and it's so sad, because being 50 nowadays isn't like being 50 a hundred years ago when you'd probably be dead.

I told Karla about Bug Barbecue's philosophy: If you can't make yourself worthwhile to society, then that's your problem, not society's. Bug says people are personally responsible for keeping themselves relevant. Somehow, this doesn't seem quite right to me.

Karla speaks with such precision. It's so cool. She said that everyone worrying about rioting senior citizens is probably premature. She said that it's a characteristic of where we are right now on computer technology's ease-of-use curve that fiftysomethings are a bit slow at accepting technology.

"Our generation has all of the characteristics needed to be in the early-adopter group—time for school and no pesky unlearning to be done. But the barriers for user acceptance should be vanishing soon enough for fiftysomethings."

This made me feel better for Dad.

Michael came by just then to ask about a subroutine and I realized it was time for me to leave. Karla thanked me again for the food, and I was glad I had brought it along.

Caroline from the Word offices in Building Sixteen sent e-mail regarding the word "nerd." She says the word only came into vogue around the late '70s when *Happy Days* was big on TV—eerily the same time that the PC was being popularized. She said prior to that, there was no everyday application for the word, "and now nerds run the world!"

Abe said something interesting. He said that because everyone's so poor these days, the '90s will be a decade with no architectural legacy or style— everyone's too poor to put up new buildings. He said that code is the architecture of the '90s.

I walked by Michael's office around sundown, just before I left for home for a shower and a snack before coming back to stomp the bugs. He was playing a game on his monitor screen I'd never seen before.

I asked him what it was and he told me it was something he had designed himself. It was a game about a beautiful kingdom on the edge of the world that saw time coming to an end.

However, the kingdom had found a way to trick God. It did this by converting its world into code—into bits of light and electricity that would keep pace with time as it raced away from them. And thus the kingdom would live forever, after time had come to an end.

Michael said the citizens of the kingdom were allowed to do this because they had made it to the end of history without ever having had the blood of war spill on their soil. He said it would have been an affront to all good souls who had worked for a better world over the millennia not to engineer a system for preserving finer thoughts after the millennium arrived and all ideologies died and people became animals once more.

"Well," I said after he finished, "how about those Mariners!"

Oh—Abe bought a trampoline. He went to Costco to stock up on Jif, and he ended up buying a trampoline—14-x-14-foot, 196 square feet of bouncy aerobic fun. Since when do grocery stores sell trampolines? What a screwy decade. I guess that's what it's like to be a millionaire.

The delivery guys dropped it off and around midnight we set it up in the front yard, over the crop circles, chaining one of the legs to the front railing. Bug Barbecue is already printing up a release he's going to make Abe have all the neighbors with kids sign, absolving Abe of any blame in the event of an accident.

TUESDAY

Woke up super early today, after only four hours' sleep, to a watery light outside. High overcast clouds. Through my window I saw a plane fly over the house, headed into SeaTac, and it made me remember when 747s first came out. Boeing had a PR photo of a kid building a house of cards in the lounge up in the bubble. God, I wanted to be that kid. Then I got to wondering, Why am I bothering to get up? What is the essential idea that gets me out of bed and through the day? What is it that gets anybody out of bed? I figure I still want to be that kid building a house of cards in a 747.

I sandpapered the roof of my mouth with three bowls of Cap'n Crunch—had raw gobbets of mouth-beef dangling onto my tongue all day. It hurt like crazy, and it made me talk with a Cindy Brady lisp until late afternoon.

Spent two hours in the morning trapped in a room with the Pol Pots from Marketing. God, they never stop—like we don't have anything better to do eight days before shipping. Even the bug testers. Like, we're supposed to see a box of free DoveBars and say, "Oh—it's okay then—please, please waste my time."

I think everyone hates and dreads Marketing's meetings because of how these meetings alter your personality. At meetings you have to explain what you've accomplished, so naturally you fluff up your work a bit, like pillows on a couch. You end up becoming this perky, gung-ho version of yourself that you know is just revolting. I have noticed that everybody looks down upon the gung-ho type people at Microsoft, but nobody considers themselves gung-ho. They should just see themselves at these meetings, all frat-boy and chipper. Fortunately, gung-ho-ishness seems confined exclusively to marketing meetings. Otherwise I think the Campus is utterly casual.

Oh, and sometimes you get flame meetings. They're fun, too—when everyone flames everyone else.

Today's meeting was about niggly little shipping details and was numbingly dull. And then, near the end, a Motorola pager owned by Kent, one of the Marketing guys, went off on top of the table. It buzzed like a hornet and shimmied and twitched across the table in a dance of death. It was mesmerizing, like watching a tarantula scamper across the table. It killed all conversation dead. Killed it right on the spot.

My smiling-muscles hurt as a result of the meeting. On top of my Cap'n Crunch mouth. A bad mouth day.

I called Mom right after the meeting and Dad answered the phone. I heard Oprah on in the background, and I didn't think that was a good omen. Dad sounded upbeat, but isn't that a part of the process? Denial? I asked him if he was watching Oprah and he said he had only come into the house for a snack.

Mom came on the phone on the extension, and once Dad was off the line, she confided that he barely slept the night before, and when he did, he made haunted moaning noises. And then this morning he dressed, as though headed to the office, and sat watching TV, being eerily chipper, refusing to talk about what his plans were. Then he went out into the garage to work on his model train world.

I learned a new word today: "trepanation"—drilling a hole in the skull to relieve pressure on the brain.

Karla came into my office this morning—a first—just as I was logging onto my e-mail for the morning. She was holding a big cardboard box full of acrylic Windows coffee mugs from the company store in Building Fourteen. "Guess what everyone in the Karla universe is getting for Christmas this year?" she asked cheerfully. "They're on sale." There was a pause. "You want one, Dan?"

I said that I drink too much coffee and colas, and that I'm a colon cancer statistic just waiting to happen. I said I'd love one. She handed it to me and there was a pause as she looked around my office: an NEC MultiSync monitor; a Compaq workhorse monitor; a framed Jazz poster; a "Mac Hugger" bumper sticker on my ceiling and my black-and-white photo shrine to Microsoft VP Steve Ballmer. "The shrine started as a joke," I said, "but it's sort of taking on a life of its own now. It's getting scary. Shall we worship?"

It was then that she asked me, in a lowered tone, "Who's Jed?"

She had seen me keyboard in my password—like HAL from *2001*.

And so I closed the door and told her about Jed, and you know, I was glad I was able to tell someone at last.

Mid-afternoon, Bug, Todd, Michael, and I grabbed some road-Snapples in the kitchen and headed over to pick up some manuals at the library, out behind the Administration building. It was more of a fresh-air jaunt than anything else.

It was raining quite heavily, but Bug pulled his usual stunt. He made us all walk through the Campus's forest undergrowth instead of simply taking the pleasant winding path that meanders through the Campus trees—the Microsoft path that speaks of Ewoks and Smurfs amid the salal, ornamental plums, rhododendrons, Japanese maple, arbutus, huckleberry, hemlock, cedars, and firs.

Bug believes that Bill sits at his window in the Admin Building and watches how staffers walk across the Campus. Bug believes that Bill keeps note of who avoids the paths and uses the fastest routes to get from A to B, and that Bill rewards these devil-may-care trailblazers with promotions and stock, in the belief that their code will be just as innovative and dashing.

We all ended up soaking wet, with Oregon Grape stains on our Dockers by the time we got to the library, and on the way back we read the Riot Act and said that Bug had to stop geeking out and learn to enculturate, and that for his own good he should take the path—and he agreed. But we could see that it was killing Bug—literally killing him—to have to walk along the path past where Bill's office is supposed to be.

Todd toyed with Bug and got him going on the subject of Xerox PARC, thus getting Bug all bitter and foaming. Bug is still in a sort of perpetual grief that Xerox PARC dropped the football on so many projects.

And then Michael, who had been silent up to now, said, "Hey—if you cut over this berm, it's a little faster," and he cut off the path, and Bug's eyes just about popped out of his head, and Michael found a not bad shortcut. Right outside the Admin Building.

I realize I haven't seen a movie in six months. I think the last one was *Curly Sue* on the flight to Macworld Expo, and that hardly counted. I really need a life, bad.

It turns out Abe has entrepreneurial aspirations. We had dinner in the down-stairs cafeteria together (Indonesian Bamay with frozen yogurt and double espresso). He's thinking of quitting and becoming a pixelation broker—going around to museums and buying the right to digitize their paintings. It's a very "Rich Microsoft" thing to do. Microsoft's millionaires are the first generation of North American nerd wealth.

Once Microsofters' ships come in, they travel all over: Scotland and Patagonia and Thailand . . . *Condé Nast Traveler*-ish places. They buy Shaker furniture, Saabs, koi, Pilchuck glass, native art, and 401(k)s to the max. The ultrarichies build fantasy homes on the Sammammish Plateau loaded with electronic toys.

It's all low-key spending, mostly, and fresh and fun. Nobody's buying crypts, I notice—though when the time comes that they do, said crypts will no doubt be emerald and purple colored, and lined with Velcro and Gore-Tex.

Abe, like most people here, is a fiscal Republican, but otherwise, pretty empty-file in the ideology department. Vesting turns most people into fiscal Republicans, I've noticed.

The day went quickly. The rain is back again, which is nice. The summer was too hot and too dry for a Washington boy like me.

I am going to bring in some Japanese UFO-brand yaki soba tomorrow and see if Karla is into lunch. She needs carbs. Skittles and aspartame is no diet for a coder.

Well, actually, it is.

A thought: Sometimes the clouds and sunlight will form in a way you've never seen them do before, and your city will feel as if it's another city altogether. On the Campus today at sunset, people were stopping on the grass watching the sun turn stove-filament orange through the rain clouds.

It's just something I noticed. It made me realize that the sun is really built of fire. It made me feel like an animal, not a human.

Worked until 1:30 A.M. When I got in, Abe was down in his microbrewery in the garage, puttering amid the stacks of furniture handed down by parents—stuff too ugly to meet even the minimal taste standards of the upstairs rooms, the piles of golf clubs, the mountain bikes, and a line of suitcases, perched like greyhounds awaiting the word GO!

Bug was locked behind his door, but by the smell I could tell he was eating a microwaved Dinty Moore product.

Susan was in the living room asleep in front of a taped *Seinfeld* episode.
Todd was obsessively folding his shirts in his room.

Michael was rereading *The Chronicles of Narnia* for the 87th time.

A nice average night.

I went into my room, which, like all six of the bedrooms here, is filled up almost completely with a bed, with walls lined with IKEA "Billy" bookshelves and stereo equipment, jazz posters and Sierra Club calendars. On my desk sits a Sudafed box and a pile of stones from a beach in Oregon. My PC is hooked up by modem to the Campus.

Had a Tab (a Bill favorite) and some microwave popcorn and did some unfinished work.

WEDNESDAY

Well, it would seem that Bug Barbecue's theory might be correct after all. Michael got invited to lunch today with (oh God, I can barely input the letters . . .) B-B-B-B-B-I-L-L!

The news traveled around Building Seven like lightning just around 11:30. Needless to say, we tumbled into Bug's office like puppies within seconds of getting word, tripping over his piles of soldering guns, wires, R-Kive boxes, and empty CD jewel boxes. Of course, he went mad with grief. We totally needled him:

"You know, Bug, the deciding factor must have been Michael's walking over that berm and making that incredible shortcut. I tell you, Bill saw Michael make that call of genius and now I bet he's going to give Michael his own product group. You shouldn't have listened to us, man. We're losers. We're going nowhere. Now, Michael—he's a winner."

Actually, the invitation probably had more to do with the code Michael wrote during the bunkering last Friday, but we didn't tell Bug this.

During the two hours Michael was away, time ticked by slowly. The curiosity was unbearable and we were all giddy and restless. We emerged from our offices into corridors of caged whimsy, amid our *Far Side* cartoons taped to windows, Pepsi-can sculptures taped to the walls, and inflatable sharks hanging from the ceilings, all lit by full-spectrum, complexion-flattering lighting.

We lapsed into one of our weekly-ish communal stress-relieving frenzies—we swiped sheets of bubble-pak from the supply rooms and rolled over them with our office chairs, popping hundreds of plastic zits at a go. We punished plastic troll dolls with 5-irons, blasting them down the hallway, putting yet more divots in the particle board walls and the ceiling panels. We drank Tabs and idly slagged interactive CD technology (Todd: "I used the Philips CDI system—it's like trying to read a coffee table book with all of the pages glued together.").

Finally Michael came back and walked past everybody, oblivious to the sensation of his presence, and entered his office. I walked over to his door.

"Hi, Michael." Pause. "So*ooooo* . . . ?"

"Hello, Daniel. I have to fly to Cupertino tonight. Some kind of Macintosh assignment they're putting me on."

"What was, well—*he*—like?"

"Oh, you know . . . efficient. People forget that he is medically, biologically, a genius. Not one ummm or ahhhh from his mouth all lunch; no wasted brain energy. Truly an inspiration for us all. I told him about my Flatlander flat-foods-only concept, and we then got into a discussion of beverages, which, as you know, tend to be consumed with a straw in a linear, one-dimensional (and hence not two-dimensional) mode. Beverages are a real problem to my new Flatlander dining lifestyle, Daniel, let me tell you.

"But then Bill—" (first name basis!) "—pointed out that one-dimensionality is perfectly allowable within a two-dimensional universe. So obvious, yet I hadn't seen it! Good thing he's in charge. Oh—Daniel, can I borrow your suitcase? Mine has all my old Habitrail gerbil mazes in it, and I don't want to take them out and then have to repack them all when I return."

"Sure, Michael."

"Thanks." He booted up his computer. "I guess I'd better prepare for the trip. Where did I store that file—you'd think Lucy Ricardo handled my information for me. Well, Daniel—we'll talk later on?" He looked for something underneath a cardboard box containing a '60s Milton-Bradley game of Memory.

He then looked up at me, gave me an 'I want to return to the controllable and nonthreatening world inside my computer' stare. You have to respect this, so the rest of the crew and I left him inside his office, clicking away on his board, knowing that Michael, like a young beauty swept out of a small Nebraska town by some Hollywood Daddy-O, was soon to leave our midst for headier airs, never to return.

Mom called. Dad stuff—after not sleeping all night again, he dressed for work and then went into the garage once more to work on his model trains. When she tries to talk about the firing, he gets all jolly and brushes it away, saying the future's just going to be fine. But he has no details. No pictures of what comes next.

Dad called. From his den. He wanted to know what the employment situation was like at Microsoft for someone like him. I couldn't believe it. So now I'm worried about him. He should know better. I guess it's shock.

I told him to relax, to not even try to think about doing anything for at least a few more days until the shock wears off. He acted all hurt, as if I was trying to get rid of him. He wasn't himself. I tried to tell him what Karla had told me, about fiftysomethings now just entering the ease-of-use curve with new technologies, but he wouldn't listen. It ended on a bad note, and this bugged me, but I didn't know one other practical thing I could say.

I went to Uwajima-Ya and bought some UFO yaki soba noodles, the ones that steep in hot water in their own little plastic bowl. Amid all the lunch-with-Bill foofaraw, Karla and I managed to eat together. I asked her what her seven *Jeopardy!* dream categories would be—I told her about everyone else's, and she considered these as she twisted the yaki soba noodles in the little plastic dish, and then she said "they would have to be:"

- Orchards
- Labrador dogs
- The history of phone pranks
- Crime novels
- Intel chips
- Things HAL says in *2001*, and
- My parents are psychopaths.

She then said to me, "Dan, I have a question about identity for you. Here it is: What is the one thing more than any other thing that makes one person different from any other person?"

I got all ready to blurt out an answer but then nothing came out of my mouth.

The question seemed so obvious to start with, but when I thought about it, I realized how difficult it is—and sort of depressing, because there's really not very much that distinguishes anyone from anyone else. I mean, what makes one mallard duck different from any other mallard duck? What makes one grizzly bear different from any other grizzly bear? Identity is so tenuous—based on so little, when you really consider it.

"Their personality?" I lamely replied. "Their, uhhh, soul?"

"Maybe. I think I'm beginning to believe the soul theory, myself. Last June I went to my ten-year high school reunion. Everyone's body had certainly aged over the decade, but everyone's essence was essentially the same as it had been when we were all in kindergarten. Their spirits were the same, I guess. Dana McCulley was still a phony; Norman Tillich was still a jock; Eileen Kelso was still shockingly naïve. Their bodies may have looked different, but they were absolutely the same person underneath. I decided that night that people really do have spirits. It's a silly thing to believe. I mean, silly for a logical person like me."

As reality returned in mid-afternoon, my "boss," Shaw, came in for a hand-holding session. Shaw is a set-for-lifer. If you had to kill off all of the program managers, one by one, he would be the last to go—he has fourteen direct reports (serfs) underneath him.

Shaw really wanted me to have a juicy problem so he could help me deal with it, but the only problem I could think of was how we're never going to make our shipping deadline in seven days, and with Michael gone, that's just more work for all of us. But this problem wasn't juicy enough for him, so he went off in search of a more exotically troubled worker.

Shaw is fortysomething, one of maybe twelve fortysomethings on the Campus. One grudgingly has to respect someone who's fortysomething and still in computers—there's a core techiness there that must be respected. Shaw still remembers the Flintstones era of computers, with punch cards and little birds inside the machines that squawked, "It's a living."

My only problem with Shaw is that he became a manager and stopped coding. Being a manager is all hand-holding and paperwork—not creative at all. Respect is based on how much of a techie you are and how much coding you do. Managers either code or don't code, and it seems there are a lot more noncoding managers these days. Shades of IBM.

Shaw actually gave me an okay review in the semiannual performance review last month, so I have no personal beef against him. And to be honest, this is still not a hierarchical office: The person with the most information pertinent to any decision is the one who makes that decision. But I'm still cannon fodder when the crunch comes.

Shaw is also a Baby Boomer, and he and his ilk are responsible for (let me rant a second) this thing called "The Unitape"—an endless loop of elevator jazz Microsoft plays at absolutely every company function. It's so irritating and it screams a certain, "We're not like our parents, we're flout-ing convention" blandness. One of these days it's going to turn the entire under-30 component of the company into a mob of deranged postal workers who rampage through the Administration Building with scissors and Bic lighters.

Checked the WinQuote: The stock was down 86 cents over the day. That means Bill lost $70 million today, whereas I only lost fuck all. But guess who'll sleep better?

We slaved until 1:00 A.M. and I gave Karla and Todd rides home, first making a quick run to Safeway for treats. At the cash register, while paying for our Sour Strings and nectarines, we got into the usual nerd discussion over the future of computing.

Karla said, "You can not de-invent the wheel, or radios, or, for that mat-ter, computers. Long after we're dead, computers will continue to be devel-oped and sooner or later—it is not a matter of if, but when—an 'Entity' is going to be created that has its own intelligence. Will this occur ten years from now? A thousand years from now? Whenever. The Entity cannot be stopped. It will happen. It cannot be de-invented.

"The critical question is, Will this Entity be something other than human? The artificial intelligence community admits it has failed to produce intelligence by trying to duplicate human logic processes. AIers are hoping to create life-mimicking programs that breed with each other, simulating millions of years of evolution by cross-breeding these programs together, ultimately creating intelligence—an Entity. But probably not a human entity modeled on human intelligence."

I said, "Well, Karla, we're only human—we can only know our own minds—how can we possibly know any other type of mind? What else could the Entity be? It will have sprung from our own brains—the initial algo-rithms, at least. There's nothing else we could be duplicating except the human mind."

Todd said that the Entity is what freaks out his ultra-religious parents. He said they're most frightened of the day when people allow machines to have initiative—the day we allow machines to set their own agendas.

"Oh God, I'm trapped in a 1950s B-movie," said Karla.

Afterward, once I was back in my room by myself, I got to mulling over our discussion. Perhaps the Entity is what people without any visions of an afterworld secretly yearn to build—an intelligence that will supply them with specific details—supply pictures.

Maybe we like to believe that Bill knows what the Entity will be. It makes us feel as though there's a moral force holding the reins of technological progress. Maybe he does know. But then maybe Bill simply provides a focus for the company when no other focus can be found. I mean, if it weren't for the cult of Bill, this place would be deadsville—like a great big office supply company. Which is sort of what it is. I mean, if you really think about it.

THURSDAY

Woke up at 8:30 and had breakfast in the cafeteria—no crunchy cereals for the next week, thank you.

Over oatmeal, Bug and me were looking at some of the foreign employees—from France, or something—who were smoking outside in the cold and rain. Only the foreign employees smoke here—and always in sad little groups. Smoking's not allowed inside anywhere. You'd think they'd get the message.

We decided that the French could never write user-friendly software because they're so rude—they'd invent a little icon for a headwaiter that, once clicked, made you wait 45 minutes for your file. It's no surprise that user-friendliness is a concept developed on the West Coast. The guy who invented the Smiley face is running for mayor of Seattle—for real. It was in the news.

Mom phoned the minute I entered my office. She visited the garage this morning—a hot, dry Palo Alto morning with white sunlight screaming in through the cracks around the garage door—and there was Dad again in his blue IBM business suit and tie, standing in the center of his U-shaped, waist-high trainscape with just one dim light shining from the ceiling above, pushing his buttons and making the trains shunt and run and speed through mountains and over bridges.

Mom decided that enough was enough, that Dad really needed somebody to talk with—someone to listen to him. She pulled up one of the old Suzy Wong bamboo cocktail bar stools left over from the basement renovation, put aside her usual lack of enthusiasm for his model trains, and talked to Dad about them, like it was show-and-tell time.

"The model train setup has expanded since you were here last, Danny," she told me. "There's a complete small town now, and the mountains are steeper and he's put more of those little green foam trees on them. It's like Perfectville, the town where everybody's supposed to grow up. There's a church now—and a supermarket and boxcars—he even has little drifters living inside the boxcars. And there's—"

There was a pause.

"And what, Mom?"

Still more silence.

"And—oh, Danny—" This was not easy for her to say.

I said, "And what, Mom?"

"Danny, there is a small white house on the top of the hill overlooking the town—apart from the rest of the landscape. So amongst my other questions I asked him, 'Oh, and what's that house there?' and he said to me, without breaking his pace, 'That's where Jed lives.'"

We were both quiet. Mom sighed.

"How about I come down to Palo Alto tomorrow?" I said. "There's nothing pressing here. Lord knows I have enough time owing to me."

More silence. "Could you, honey?"

I said, "Yes."

"I think that would be good."

I could hear their fridge humming down in California.

"There's so many consultants on the market right now," Mom said. "People always say that if you get downsized you can become a consultant, but your father is 53, Dan. He's not young and he's never been competitive by nature. I mean, he was at IBM. We really just don't know what is going to happen."

I called a travel agent in Bellevue and VISA'd a ticket to San Jose. I skipped e-mail and tried to focus on the overnight stress tests, but my mind was blanking. Two code breaks overnight—so close to shipping and we're still getting breaks!

I tried roaming the corridors for diversion, but somehow the world was different. Michael was in Cupertino (with my luggage); Abe wasn't in his office—he'd bailed out for the day and gone sailing in Puget Sound with some Richie Rich friends; Bug had gone into a crazy mood since breakfast and had a "Get Lost" Post-it note on his door; and Susan was at home for the day preparing for the Vest Fest. And the one other person I wanted to see, Karla, wasn't in her office.

I was leaning over the rails of the central atrium, looking at the art displays in the cases and the spent nerds flopped out on the couches below, when Shaw walked by. I had to be all hearty and rah-rah and perky about the shipping deadline.

Shaw said that Karla was away with Kent doing a marketing something-or-other, and the thought flashed through my head that I wanted to kill Kent, which was irrational and not like me.

The day then degenerated into a "Thousand Dollar Day." That's what I call the kind of day where, even if you tell all the people you know, "I'll give you a crisp, new thousand-dollar bill if you just give me a phone call and put me out of my misery," even still, nobody phones.

I only received eighteen pieces of e-mail, and most of them were bulk. And the WinQuote only went up and down by pennies. Nobody got rich; nobody got poor.

The rain broke around 3:00 and I walked around the Campus feeling miserable. I looked at all the cars parked in the lot and got exhausted just thinking about all the energy that must have gone into these people choosing *just the right car*. And I also noticed something Twilight-Zoney about all the cars on Campus: None of them have bumper stickers, as though everyone is censoring themselves. I guess this indicates a fear of something.

All these little fears: fear of not producing enough; fear of not finding a little white-with-red-printing stock option envelope in the pigeonhole; fear of losing the sensation of actually making something anymore; fear about the slow erosion of perks within the company; fear that the growth years will never return again; fear that the bottom line is the only thing that really drives the process; fear of disposability . . . God, listen to me. What a downer. But sometimes I think it would be so much easier to be jerking espressos in Lynwood, leaving the Tupperware-sealed, Biosphere 2-like atmosphere of Microsoft behind me.

And this got me thinking. I looked around and noticed that if you took all of the living things on the Microsoft Campus, separated them into piles, and analyzed the biomass, it would come out to:
- 38% Kentucky bluegrass
- 19% human beings
- .003% Bill
- 8% Douglas and balsam fir

- 7% Western red cedar
- 5% hemlock
- 23% other: crows, birch, insects, worms, microbes, nerd aquarium fish, decorator plants in the lobbies . . .

Went home early at 5:30 and nobody was there. Susan had two card tables unfolded in the otherwise empty dining room area, awaiting their snacks. Abe had loaned Susan his sacred Dolby THX sound system for the party plus his two Adirondack chairs made from old skis. The place still looked a bit bare.

It was like The Day Without People.

Around dark, things started hopping. Abe returned from sailing and cranked up old Human League tunes, to which he sang along from the shower. Susan returned with bags of food from the caterers that I helped her carry in and set up: pasta puttanesca, Thai noodles, calzones, Chee-tos, and gherkins. Bug and some of his bitter, nutcase friends arrived with a wide selection of beer, and they were in good moods, sitting around playing peanut gallery to *Hard Copy* and *A Current Affair*, being amusing and eating half of Susan's party food while she was dressing.

By 8:00, other guests began arriving, bringing bottles of wine, and by 9:00, the house, which not two hours previously had been a pit of gloom, was brimming with good cheer and U2.

Around 9:30, Susan was talking with her friends, telling them that she'd vested just in the nick of time—"I've been switching from a right-lobe person to a left-lobe person over the past 18 months, and I couldn't have gone on coding much longer. Anyway, I think the era of vesting is coming to a close." The phone in my room rang just then. (We have nine lines into our house. Pacific Bell either loves us or hates us.) I excused myself to answer it.

It was Mom.

Apparently Dad had just flown up to Seattle from Palo Alto on impulse. She'd just gotten in from her library job and had found the note on the door. I asked what time his flight landed and she told me he was arriving at the airport as we spoke.

So I went and sat on the curb outside the house. It was a bit chilly and I was wearing my old basketball varsity coat. Karla walked up the hill from her place, said hello, and sat down beside me, carrying a twelve-pack of beer that seemed enormously large for her small arms. From my body language she knew that everything wasn't okay, and she didn't ask me anything. I simply said, "My Dad's just flown up here—he's come unglued. I think he'll be arriving shortly." We sat and looked at the treetops and heard the wind rustle.

"I heard you were in a marketing discussion all day with Kent," I said to her.

"Yeah. It was unproductive. Pretty numbing. He's a creep."

"You know, I've been going through the whole day wanting to bludgeon him."

"Really?" She said. She looked at me sideways.

"Yeah. Really."

"Well now, that's not too logical, is it?"

"No."

She then held my hand, and we sat there, together. We drank some of the beer she had brought and we said hello to Mishka the Dog, who cruised by to visit then went for a nap under the trampoline. And we watched the cars that pulled up to the house, one by one, waiting for the one car that would contain my father.

He arrived not too long afterward, in a rental car, piss drunk (not sure how he swung that), looking tired and scared, with big bags under his eyes, and a bit deranged.

He parked with a lurch right across the street from us. We sat and watched as he sucked in a breath and leaned back on the seat, his head slumped forward. He then turned his head toward us and through the open window said, a bit bashfully, "Hi."

"Hi, Dad."

He looked back down at his lap.

"Dad, this is Karla," I said, still seated.

He looked at us again. "Hello, Karla."

"Hi."

We sat on our opposite sides of the road. Behind us, the house had become a thumping shadow box of festivity. Dad didn't look up from his lap, so Karla and I stood up and walked over to him, and as we did, we saw that Dad was clutching something tight in his lap, and as we approached, he clutched it tighter. It seemed as though he was afraid we might take away whatever it was, and as we neared, I realized he was holding Jed's old football helmet, a little boy's helmet, in gold and green, the old school colors.

"Danny," he said to me, not to my face, but into the helmet which he polished with his old man's hands, "I still miss Jeddie. I can't get him out of my mind."

"I miss Jed, too, Daddy," I said. "I think about him every day."

He held the helmet tighter to his chest.

"Come on, Daddy—let's get out of the car. Come on into the house. We can talk in there."

"I can't pretend I don't think about him anymore. I think it's killing me."

"I feel the same way, too, Daddy. You know what? I feel as if he's alive still, and that he's always walking three steps ahead of me, just like a king."

I opened the door and Karla and I both supported Dad on either side as he clutched the helmet to his chest, and we walked into the house, his appearance generating little interest in the overall crowd. We went into Michael's room, where we placed him on the bed.

He was ranting a bit: "Funny how all those things you thought would never end turned out to be the first to vanish—IBM, the Reagans, Eastern bloc communism. As you get older, the bottom line becomes to survive as best you can."

"We don't know about that yet, Daddy."

I pulled off his shoes, and for some time Karla and I sat beside him on two office chairs. Michael's machines hummed around us and our only light source was a small bedside lamp. We sat and watched Dad filter in and out of consciousness.

He said to me, "You are my treasure, son. You are my first born. When the doctors removed their hands from your mother and lifted you up to the sky, it was as though they removed a trove of pearls and diamonds and rubies all covered in sticky blood."

I said, "Daddy, don't talk like that. Get some rest. You'll find a job. I'll always support you. Don't feel bad. There'll be lots of stuff available. You'll see."

"It's your world now," he said, his breathing deepening, as he turned to stare at the wall that thumped with music and shrieks of party-goers. "It's yours."

And shortly after that, he fell asleep on the bed—on Michael's bed in Michael's room.

And before we left the room, we turned out the light and we took one last look at the warm black form of my father lying on the bed, lit only by the constellation of red, yellow, and green LEDs from Michael's sleeping, dreaming machines.

2
Oop

Rained all day (32mm according to Bug). Read a volume of *Inside Mac*. Drove over to Boeing Surplus and bought some zinc and some laminated air-safety cards.

TUESDAY

Went into the office and played Doom for an hour. Deleted some e-mail.

Morris from Word is in Amsterdam so I asked him to try out the vegetarian burger at a McDonald's there.

There were soggy maple leaves all over the Hornet Sportabout this afternoon. The orange colors were dizzying and I must have looked like such a space case staring at the car for fifteen minutes. But it felt so relaxing.

Susan was talking about art today, about that surrealist guy who painted little businessmen floating through the sky and apples that fill up entire rooms—Magritte. She said that if Surrealism was around today, "It'd last ten minutes and be stolen by ad agencies to sell long-distance calls and aerosol cheese products." Probably true.

Then Susan went on to say that Surrealism was exciting back whenever it happened, because society had just discovered the subconscious, and this was the first visual way people had found to express the way the human subconscious works.

Susan then said that the BIG issue nowadays is that on TV and in magazines, the images we see, while they appear surreal, "really *aren't* surrealistic, because they're just random, and there's no subconsciousness underneath to generate the images."

So this got me to thinking . . . what if machines *do* have a subconscious of their own? What if machines right now are like human babies, which have brains but no way of expressing themselves except screaming (crashing)? What would a machine's subconscious look like? How does it feed off what we give it? If machines could talk to us, what would they say?

So I stare at my MultiSync and my PowerBook and wonder . . . *"What's going through their heads?"*

To this end, I'm creating a file of random words that pop into my head, and am feeding these words into a desktop file labeled SUBCONSCIOUS.

Cleaned out the kitchen cupboards. Read the phone book for a while. Read a *Wall Street Journal*. Listened to the radio.

Karla's been living here three weeks and I'm not sure I'm not going to screw things up. It's all so new. She's heaven. Imagine losing heaven!

Personal Computer
I am your personal computer

Hello

Stop
Being
Carbon

CNN
LensCrafters
magnetic ID card
instant noodles
dodecahedron

666
airbag
employee number
birth
ATM

Lawry's Garlic Salt

808 Honolulu
503 Klamath Falls
604 Victoria

702 Las Vegas
206 Tacoma
916 Shasta

oatmeal
cherry flavored antacids
holodeck
Sierra
NCC-1701
Schroder Wagg/London

laxatives
Rubbermaid
Courtyard Marriott
Big Gulp
liquid money
Rank Xerox

WEDNESDAY

Todd and I tied our "Ship-It" awards to a rope behind my AMC Hornet Sportabout hatchback wagon and dragged them for an hour around the suburbs of Bellevue and Redmond.

Net result: a few little nicks and scratches. They are awesomely indestructible.

I try to imagine someone or some new species in fifty million years, unearthing one of these profoundly unbiodegradable little gems and trying to deduce something meaningful about the species and culture that created it.

"Surely they lived not for the moment but for some distant time—obviously a time far, far beyond their own era, to have created such an astounding artifact that would not decay."

"Yes, Yeltar, and they inscribed profound, meaningful, and transcendent text inside this miraculously preserved clear block, but alas, its message remains forever cryptic:"

EVERY TIME A PRODUCT SHIPS,
IT TAKES US ONE STEP CLOSER TO THE VISION:
A COMPUTER ON EVERY DESK AND IN EVERY HOME.

Dad phoned to ask me how to hook up a modem. He's joining the Net now.

For three days last month he ended up on the green velveteen living room couch, sleeping endlessly. Or else he'd come sit with me in my office while we finished debugging for shipping. He seemed to like that. But he was so *fragile*, and when Karla and I drove him out to SeaTac airport he sat in the backseat, rattling like a stack of Franklin Mint souvenir plates.

Mom keeps sending me clippings about the information superhighway and interactive multimedia. She clips things out of the *San Jose Mercury News* (her librarian's heart). This highway—is it a joke? You hear so much about it, but really, what *is* it . . . slide shows with music? Suddenly it's *all* over the place. EVERYWHERE.

Morris e'd me back from Amsterdam:
>**I tried one and they're not very good, so don't romanticize them. They have a curry taste, and they're full of frozen *peas* (of all things). More importantly, by eating "burgers," aren't you just still buying into the "meat concept." Tofu hot dogs are merely an isotope of meat.**
>**If you yourself are a vegetarian, but still dream of burgers, then all you really are is a cryptocarnivore.**

Went to Nordstrom's. Watched *Wings* on The Discovery Channel.

Bug sulks in his room all day, listening to Chet Baker, restoring his antique Radio Shack Science Fair 65-In-One electronic project kit, and memorizing C++ syntax. Susan house hunts. Todd lives at the Pro Club gym. Abe has been reassigned to a subgroup in charge of designing a toolbar interface. *Whooo-ee!*

I think Abe's being punished for going sailing that day with his friends during the week we were all in crunch mode. We don't see him much—he's back in Microsoft time/space again. He gets home late, feeds his neon tetras sprinkles of ground-up, freeze-dried poor people, chides us all for not exhibiting more enterprise, and then sleeps.

2:45 A.M. Drove into Seattle tonight with Todd in separate cars. Todd scored at The Crocodile and at the moment he and his "date," Tabitha from Tukwila, are in his room getting acquainted.

Bug is here in the living room watching "Casper the Friendly Ghost" cartoons on the VCR, "looking for subtext." I can't believe it, but I'm getting into it, too. (*"Wait, Bug—rewind that back a few seconds—wasn't that a Masonic compass?"*) Karla was asleep ages ago. She stayed home and watched *The Thornbirds* on the VCR with Susan. ("It's a *girl* thing. Scram.") Karla has an unsuspected fathomless capacity for sleep of which I am most envious.

Continued adding to my computer's subconscious files.

Welcome to Macintosh   Carl's Jr.

Gore-Tex®   gray metallic Saabs

Barry Diller KISS

mini-bars   frequent flyer points
ads for pearls   Oscar de la Renta
outer space   minimum wage

manufacture
dungeons

magazine scent strips   flame broiled
Bell Atlantic   switchbox
phone jacks   the DMV
F-16   MiG-29
Calvin Klein   Han Solo
bourgeois decay images   Download
Upload   Drive
Sparkletts   Tori Spelling

Advil Kotex

Rosslyn   Langley
You jerk   Lee Press-ons

THURSDAY

I went to the library and looked up books on freeway construction—the asphalt and cement kind—Dewey Decimal number 625.79—and there haven't been any published on the subject for two decades! It's bizarre—like a murder mystery. It's as if the notion of freeway construction simply *vanished* in 1975. Sizzler titles include:

> *Bituminous Materials in Road Construction*
> *Surface Texture Versus Skidding*
> *Engineering Study: Alaska Highway*
> *Better Concrete Pavement Serviceability*
> *Vehicle Redirection Effectiveness of Median Berms and Circles*

Actually, there weren't all too many books *on* freeways ever published in the first place. You'd think we'd have whole *stadiums* devoted to the worship of freeways for the amount of importance they play in our culture, but no. Zip. I guess we're overcompensating for this past shortcoming by our current overhyping of the InfoBahn—the I-way. It's emerged from nowhere into this big important thing we Have to Know About.

I have borrowed, among others, the seminal work on the subject: *Handbook of Highway Engineering* (1975), by Robert F. Baker, editor; Van Nostrand and Reinhold Company. It'll help melt away my lax days before I join a new product group.

We ripped away some wallpaper in the kitchen by the fridge and found that underneath the various stratum of paper (daisies; Peel n' Stick peppermills), in condition just as fresh as the day they were written, the words:

> *one mellow day*
> *June 6, 1974*
> *I'm long gone but my idea of peace now remains with you*
> *d.b.*

Hippie stuff, but I lost my breath when I read the words. And I felt like for a moment that maybe an idea is more important than simply being alive, because an idea lives a long time after you're gone. And then the feeling passed. And we found all of these old, early 1970s Seattle newspapers behind a wallboard. The prices back then . . . cheap!

At the Bellevue Starbucks, Karla and I discussed the unprecedented success of Campbell's Cream of Broccoli Soup. On a napkin we listed ideas for new Campbell's soup flavors:

> *Creamy Dolphin*
> *Lagoon*
> *Beak*
> *Pond*
> *Crack*

Note: I think Starbucks has patented a new configuration of the water molecule, like in a Kurt Vonnegut novel, or something. This molecule allows their coffee to remain liquid at temperatures *over* 212° Fahrenheit. How do they get their coffee so *hot*? It takes hours to cool off—it's so hot it's undrinkable—and by the time it's cool, you're sick of waiting for it to cool and that "coffee moment" has passed. At least Starbucks doesn't stink like sweet coffee-flavoring chemicals . . . like the way you'd expect a Barbie doll's house to smell.

Saw a documentary about the commodities market. Read some books that were lying around. Watched some old 1970s TV shows later. I remembered an old Nova episode in which German hackers published a secret document, and some Ph.D.[3] hippie geek from UC Berkeley tracked them down with a baited document. Was this hippie geek tricked into trapping one of his own kind by the NSA or some other such organization? Ethics.

Then I started to think about those old Time-Life books with such all-embracing names like, "The Elements," and "The Ocean," and of how the information in them never really goes out of date, whereas the computer series books date within minutes: *"Most 'personal computers' now contain devices called 'hard drives' capable of storing the equivalent, in some cases, of up to three college textbooks."*

Felt a bit random.

*Capture
specific
functions*

Microsoft Navajo

NASA   **Kristy McNichol**
Flesh-eating bacteria   **Lance Kerwin**
Arthur Hiller   **skateboard**

trail mix   *job description*
PERL   *toner cartridge*

very   *a lot*
really   ## *ummm . . .*

Martin-Marietta

FRIDAY

Susan and Karla came into the living room when I was reading the *Handbook of Highway Engineering*, and they both flipped out. They totally grokked on it. We kept on *ooh*ing and *ahhh*ing over the book's beautiful, car-free on-ramps, off-ramps, and overpasses—"So clean and pure and undriven."

Karla noted that freeway engineers had their own techie code words, just as dull and impenetrable as geek talk. "Examples: subgrades, partial cloverleaf interchanges, cutslopes, and TBMs (Tunnel Boring Machines) . . ."

"They even abused three-letter acronyms," said Karla, who also decreed that Rhoda Morgenstern would have dated a freeway engineer back in the 1970s. "His name would have been Rex and he would have looked like Jackson Browne and would have known the compressive strength range of Shale, Dolomite, and Quartzite to the nearest p.s.i. x 10^3."

I am really terrible at remembering three-letter acronyms. It's a real dead zone in my brain. I still barely can tell you what RAM is. Wherever this part of the brain is located, it's the same place where I misfile the names and faces of people I meet at parties. I'm so bad at names. I'm realizing that three-letter acronyms are actually *words* now, and no longer simply acronyms: ram, rom, scuzzy, gooey, see-pee-you. . . . Words have to start somewhere.

Karla told me about when she was young. About how she remembered "trying to make—no, not make, *engineer*—Campbell's Vegetable Soup from scratch—chopping up the carrots and potatoes to resemble machine-cut cubes—getting the exact number of lima beans per can (4).

"I grew up with assembly lines, remember. My favorite cartoon was always the one with the little chipmunks stuck inside the vegetable canning factory. I used to guess at the spices, too. But in the end it never worked because I didn't use beef stock or MSG."

Random day. Fed on magazines for a while. Radio. Phone call from Mom, and she talked about traffic.

Industrial Light & Magic
jump
hit

We're just friends
run
multi-user dungeon

Ziggy Stardust
SkyTel paging
FORTRAN
IKEA

Wells Fargo
Safeway
hummingbird
I am an empath

4x4
Death Star

Kung Fu
platform

oligarchy
Highway 92
Deuteronomy
Staples
Pearle Express

Kraft singles
cordless
brain ded
Silo
an executive lifestyle

Maybelline

implicator

Insert
Font

Format
Tools

SATURDAY

Oh God.

I knew I'd do something. Karla's on the warpath because I forgot our one-month anniversary. *Doh!* She gave me until bedtime tonight to remember, but I still forgot, so now she's not speaking to me. I tried to tell her that time isn't necessarily linear, that it flows in odd clumps and bundles and clots. "Well, *err, um*—what exactly *is* a month, Karla? Ha Ha ha."

"I don't know about *you*, Dan," she interrupted, "but *I* programmed *my* desktop calendar to remind *me*. Good night." [Insert one frosty glare here. A bored yawn; a bedroom door nudged closed with little baby toes.]

It's nice to see this romantic side to Karla's personality—an unexpected bonus—but still, nobody likes THE COUCH. And so now after weeks of blissful insomnia-free sleep, I'm yet again PowerBooking my daily diaries here on the acid green couch in a big big way.

Comely superstar Cher hawks cosmetics on late-nite TV. Mishka is also spending tonight in the living room and she is making foul smells indeed. At least it's raining out—buckets—and the weird too-hot summer is over.

Tomorrow I will program my desktop computer to remind me of every one of our anniversaries, monthly or otherwise, until the year 2050.

Actually, we *all* have so much free time now. Karla, Todd, Bug, and I sit around awaiting our next product group assignment, feeling deflated and just plain exhausted. We forget about clock- and calendar-type time completely.

Today, while raking the front lawn, Todd said, "Wouldn't it be scary if our internal clocks weren't set to the rhythms of waves and sunrise—or even the industrial whistle toot—but to *product cycles*, instead?"

We got nostalgic about the old days, back when September meant the unveiling of new car models and TV shows. Now, carmakers and TV people put them out whenever. Not the same.

$\mathbf{Y}$es, Karla moved in a month ago. We're an item.

Todd, Abe, and I lugged her "ownables" from her geek house down the street up to our own geek house at the top of the cul-de-sac: futon and frame . . . cluster o' computers . . . U-Frame-It Ansel Adams print . . . and dumped it all into Michael's empty room. And then, once she installed herself in our house (*"Think of me as a software application"*) she announced that she was an expert in (*thank you, Lord* . . .) shiatsu massage!

$\mathbf{M}$om phoned this afternoon. Out of the proverbial blue she said to me, "The house! The soil up in the hills is settling and the roof's rotting. The door and windows need replacing. I just *stand* here and feel the money being sucked out of my body. At least we had the foresight to buy it when we did. But all my librarian's salary goes into the house. The rest goes to Price-Costco."

Money.

I changed the subject. "What did you have for dinner?"

"Those pre-formed pork by-product patties. And ramen noodles. Like the food you kids eat when you do your coding all-nighters."

It was a "Listening-Only" call.

"I know, Mom. How's Dad doing?"

"Prozac. Well . . . something *like* Prozac. At least he doesn't obsess on the garage anymore. He goes out in the morning I-don't-know-where looking for work. Let's not get into it. God, I wish I drank."

Life is stressful in Palo Alto. I send Dad $500 every month. It's all I can spare on the 26K I make here ([$26,000 / 12] - taxes = $1,500).

It was a really bad phone call, but Mom just needed to vent—she has so few ears in her life who will listen. Who really ever does, I guess?

$\mathbf{M}$ichael never *did* return from Cupertino.

Rumor had it *Bill* had Michael secretly working on a project called Pink, but nothing ever came of the rumor.

A delivery firm specializing in high-tech moves carted Michael's things to Silicon Valley. His pyramid of empty diet Coke cans—his suitcase-worth of Habitrail gerbil mazes—his collection of C. S. Lewis novels. Gone.

Fun fact: We found about 40 empty cough syrup bottles in the cupboard—Michael is a Robitussin addict! (Actually, he bulk-buys knockoff house brands—he's a "PayLess Tussin" addict.) The world never ceases to amaze.

It's late at night. Basketball on TV; computer and fitness mags everywhere. Let me talk about love.

Do you remember that old TV series, *Get Smart*? You remember at the beginning where Maxwell Smart is walking down the secret corridor and there are all of those doors that open sideways, and upside down and gateways and stuff? I think that everybody keeps a whole bunch of doors just like this between themselves and the world. But when you're in love, all of your doors are open, and all of *their* doors are open. And you roller-skate down your halls together.

Let me try again. I'm not good at this.

Karla and I fell in love somewhere *out there*—I think that's the way it happens—*out there*. The two of you start talking about your feelings and your feelings float outside of you like vapors, and they mix together like a fog. Before you realize it, the two of you have become the same mist and you realize you can never return to being just a lone cloud again, because the isolation would be intolerable.

Karla and I would talk about computing and coding. Our minds met out in the crystal lattice galaxy of ideas and codes and when we came out of our reverie, we realized we were in a special place—*out there*.

And when you meet someone and fall in love, and they fall in love with you, you ask them, "Will you take my heart—stains and all?" and they say, "I will," and they ask you the same question, and you say, "I will," too.

There are other reasons Karla's lovable, too, reasons not so poetic, but just as real. She's like a *friend* to me, and we have all of these common interests—"mind meld"—whatever. I can discuss computers and Microsoft and that part of our lives—but we also have esoteric conversations that have nothing to do with tech life. I've never really had a friend this close before.

And there's the nonlinear stuff: Karla's intuitive and I'm not, yet she's still on my frequency. She understands why yaki soba noodles in a plastic

UFO-shaped container from Japan are intrinsically glorious. She scrunches up her forehead when she knows she's not explaining an idea as clearly as she knows she can, and she gets frustrated.

Anyway, I want to remember that love *can* happen. Because there is life after not having a life. I never expected love to happen. What *was* I expecting from life, then?

As I type this in, I feel small arms around my neck and a kiss on my jugular and I don't know, but I think I may be forgiven. I hope so because my forgetting the anniversary thing was an honest mistake. I'm new at this love thing.

Sierra Nevada Pale Ale
Cedars Sinai

starburst explosion
Gak

UNDO
Ctrl Z
Ctrl Z
Ctrl Z

Phoenix
Cleveland
Luis Vuitton
Kalashnikov
Waxahachie

LA Lakers
San Antonio
bubble economy
Creamsicles
Livermore

the place for ribs

Taylor Sequences
frog

Bleeding eyeliner
Colossal

SUNDAY

Todd's obsessing on his body big-time these days. This afternoon he came in late from the gym and sat on the living room Orlon carpet flexing his arm and staring at his muscles as they bulged—buff and bored. His biggest project at the moment is making pyramids out of his empty tubs of protein supplements with their gold labels that resemble van art from the 1970s. Why do nerds make pyramids out of everything? Imagine Egypt!

The Cablevision was out for some reason, and Todd was just lying there, flexing his arms on the floor in front of the snowy screen. He said to me, "There has to be more to existence than this. *Dominating as many broad areas of automated consumerism as possible*'—that doesn't seem to cut it anymore." Todd?

This speech was utterly unlike him—thinking about life beyond his triceps or his Supra. Maybe, like his parents, he has a deep-seated need to believe in something, anything. For now it's his bod . . . I *think*.

He said, "What we do at Microsoft is just as repetitive and dreary as any other job, and the pay's the same as any other job if you're not in the stock loop, so what's the deal . . . why do we get so *into* it? What's the engine that pulls us through the repetition? Don't you ever feel like a cog, Dan? . . . wait—the term 'cog' is outdated—a *cross-platform highly transportable binary object*?"

I said, "Well, Todd, work isn't, and was never *meant* to be a person's whole life."

"Yeah, I know that, but aside from the geek-badge-of-honor stuff about doing cool products first and shipping them on time and money, what else *is* there?"

I thought about this. "So what is it you're really asking me?"

"Where does *morality* enter our lives, Dan? How do we justify what we do to the rest of humanity? Microsoft is no Bosnia."

Religious upbringing.

Karla came into the room at this point. She turned off the TV set and looked at Todd square in the eyes and said, "Todd: you exist not only as a member of a family or a company or a country, but as a member of a *species*—you are human. You are part of *humanity*. Our species currently has major problems and we're trying to dream our way out of these problems and we're using computers to do it. The construction of hardware and software is where the species is investing its very *survival*, and this construction requires zones of peace, children born of peace, and the absence of code-interfering distractions. We may not achieve transcendence through computation, but we *will* keep ourselves out of the gutter with them. What you perceive of as a vacuum is an earthly paradise—the freedom to, quite literally, line-by-line, prevent humanity from going nonlinear."

She sat down on the couch, and there was rain drumming on the roof, and I realized that there weren't enough lights on in the room and we were all quiet.

Karla said, "We all had good lives. None of us were ever victimized as far as I know. We have never wanted for anything, nor have we ever lusted for anything. Our parents are all together, except for Susan's. We've been dealt good hands, but the *real* morality here, Todd, is whether these good hands are squandered on uncreative lives, or whether these hands are applied to continuing humanity's dream."

The rain continued.

"It's no coincidence that as a species we invented the middle classes. Without the middle classes, we couldn't have had the special type of mind-set that consistently spits out computational systems, and our species could never have made it to the next level, whatever that level's going to be. Chances are, the middle classes aren't even a *part* of the next level. But that's neither here nor there. Whether *you* like it or not, Todd, you, me, Dan, Abe, Bug, and Susan—we're all of us the fabricators of the human dream's next REM cycle. *We* are building the center from which all else will be held. Don't question it, Todd, and don't dwell on it, but never ever let yourself *forget* it."

Karla looked at me. "Dan, let's go out and get a Grand Slam Breakfast. I have $1.99 and it's burning a hole in my pocket."

Susan taped the following clipping from the *Wall Street Journal* to her door (which won't be hers much longer—she's moving soon): Sept. 3, 1993, a little while ago. The clipping was about the Japanese rainy season that started this year in June, and never ended:

> *A typhoon flooded the moats of Japan's imperial palace in downtown Tokyo. Imperial carp fled their home for the first time and flopped in knee-deep waters covering one of Japan's busiest intersections.*

Susan's "totally right-lobe" now.

I tried to find her and ask her what she meant with the article, but she was out on Capitol Hill getting pixclated with her no-doubt right-lobed grunge buddies.

Susan quit the day after she vested and began "running with the wolves"—or so she announced to all of us the morning after her Vest Fest. She unveiled her new image as we were sitting in front of our Mitsubishi home entertainment totem, eating our last few boxes of Kellogg's Snak-Paks with plastic spoons, deconstructing old *Davey and Goliath* cartoons, and trying to figure out how/if to wake up my Dad, who. was still passed out on Michael's bed.

Susan's previous image—Patagonia-wearing Northwest good girl—had been shed away for a radicalized look: bent shades, striped Fortrel too-tight top, Angela Bowie hairdo, dirty suede vest, flares, and Adidases.

"Wow," said Bug. "What a *stud*."

She stormed past us, stopped at the top of the stairs, said, "*Fuck it*. I'm tired of being Mary Richards. I'm off to hold up a 7-Eleven," and then clomped down to the driveway.

I think she expected us to be a bit shocked, but you know, it's actually really great when a person reinvents themself. We finished our Froot Loops and soy milk.

Todd came up to me later tonight and said, "Dan, I wouldn't fuck around so much if I could meet somebody like Karla." This freaked me out and I got this awful feeling that I think is jealousy, but I can't be sure, because it was a new feeling, and nobody ever tells you what feelings are supposed to be like. But Todd saw this and said, "That's not what I meant, Dan. I'm not gonna *jump* her. Gimme *some* credit. But man, where do you *find* someone like her?"

"Yeah, she's something else," I said blandly, masking my interior burn.

"She's so smart, but not just coding-smart. She thinks like a preacher, but not a by-the-books preacher. She be*lieves* in something."

Watched an old documentary about NASA. Then afterward I saw this documentary about how codfish have been gill-netted into extinction in Newfoundland in Canada, so I went out to Burger King to get a Whaler fishwich-type breaded deep-fried filet sandwich while there was still time.

I think I'm going to keep my diary more regularly now. Karla got me to thinking that we really *do* inhabit an odd little nook of time and space here, and that odd or strange as this little nook may be, it's where *I* live—it's where I *am*.

I used to always think I had to have a reason to record my observations of the day, or even my emotions, but now I think simply being alive is more than enough reason. Unshackled!

UV rays

. . . arms armor ammo health

Brillo	backlit Plexiglas
Chicken Marsala	N x S x T

WW3

Tetris

Tonopah, Nevada	cat food
locate the source of urges	System Seven

Woodside	8
Los Altos Hills	17
San Jose	32
Space Cruiser	487

Superstar

Fear Uncertainty Doubt
Crashed in a cornfield

COBOL

Steak house
Calorie factory

Format?

Reject?

MONDAY

*M*elrose Place night tonight. We double-clicked onto the "BRAIN CANDY" mode. We're all addicts.

We like to pretend our geek house is actually *Melrose Place.*

Tonight Abe said, "I wonder what would happen if we all started randomly going nonlinear like the show's characters. What would happen if our personalities became divorced from cause and effect?"

"We could take turns going psycho," said Bug.

Susan, writing the words D-U-R-A-N/D-U-R-A-N on the proximal phalanges of her fingers, said, "You already *are* psycho, Bug. That doesn't count."

Susan read aloud bits from the *Handbook of Highway Engineering:*

"*'Improperly installed or unwarranted signals can result in the following conditions:*

>   —*Excessive delay*
>   —*Disobedience of the signal indications*
>   —*Use of less adequate routes to avoid the signal*
>   —*Increase of accident frequency . . .'*"

She paused and looked at the fire for a while. "I wonder if this guy is alive and if he's married?"

I called to see if Mom was feeling better, and she was. She's signed up for swimming classes at the local pool. But the big news occurred when Dad got on the extension line and shouted at me, "I'm employed!"

"Way to go, Dad. I told you something would come up. What are you going to be doing?"

"Oh—this and that. Michael is certainly one bright young fellow. Odd. But bright."

"You're working for *Michael*?"

"I certainly am."

"At Microsoft?"

"No, he's starting something else, a new company."

"He IS? What are *you* working on there?" (**Shock**)

"And he's living in one of the spare bedrooms—can you believe it?"

(*Good God!*) "Yes, I can. And your *job description?*"

"Here, your mother wants to speak to you . . ."

Mom chatted about being relieved with Dad's salary *plus* rent money flowing in. But the job description never arrived. Nor any clue about this mysterious new company.

We have a new word for vaporware: Sea Monkeys, as in, "ScriptX is really Sea Monkeys!"

Susan said, "Remember when you were a kid and sent away for that little nuclear family with Dad wearing a crown and everything, and instead all you got was . . . *brine shrimp?*"

Reading a book about viruses. Went into Boeing Surplus again. It was Monday, so all the new magazines were in.

Karla and I were here in my room, lying on my bed—bare legs akimbo—and we made this really embarrassing observation that neither of us have tan lines—that we spent all summer in the crunch mode to meet shipping deadline.

Karla began talking all Star Trekky again—the best thing about her.

She said, "I don't believe human beings store memory in our brains exclusively—there simply aren't enough storage slots or interconnective possibilities. And so if not in the brain, then *where?* I concluded that another viewpoint on memory was to see our bodies as 'peripheral memory storage devices.'"

Hence, **bliss**, shiatsu.

"You know yourself, Dan, that every sitcom ever *broadcast* is stored in your brain—that's *terabits* of terabits of memory—as well as the details of Burt and Loni's divorce. Brains just don't have enough space to handle all these bits. And so I decided to learn shiatsu massage—as a means of thawing memory frozen inside the *body*."

I thought about this. The concept of body as hard drive seemed very plausible to me.

I couldn't believe we had been enemies for so long. Trek on, woman!

So Dad's working—for Michael. Michael is *hiring* people. That is so random. The world is indeed chaotic.

Space Needle   1962

Mattel
C+++++++++++
silver lens sunglasses   **Redmond**

Schaumburg, Ill.
Interstate 80/287, NJ
Dallas Galleria/LBJ Fwy.
Torrey Pines/UTC Sorrento Valley, Ca.
Metroplex/Irvine, Ca.
King of Prussia/Route 202

Tandy Corp., Fort Worth, Texas 76107

relentless . . .
crispy . . .

fluids . . .
200 years from now

Ebola Reston
Marburg   **Michelangelo**
Hepatitis non-A/non-B   **Machupo**
Ebola Zaire   **Rift Valley**
Sabia   **Hanta**

TUESDAY

A FedEx pack arrived today with letters for everybody: *Roommates@Geek House* followed by our postal address. Talk about news. Michael's offering *all of us* jobs at a start-up company he's assembled down in Silicon Valley.

Excerpts from Michael's letter:

> . . . People our age are abandoning the tech megacultures in droves, starting up their own companies, or joining small, content-based start-ups. There's a recruiting frenzy going on . . . multimedia craziness . . . and the big companies that aren't minting money are hemorrhaging brains. It's intellectual Darwinism.
>
> . . . The five of you are rudderless at the moment. Is now not the time to take a risk and jump into the future?
>
> . . . Some say that the world is visibly cleaving into a race of information Haves, and a race of information Have-Nots. Whatever. Let me simply say that history is happening, it's happening now and it is happening here, in Silicon Valley and in San Francisco.
>
> . . . Tell me, are you seriously going to be at Microsoft 20 years from now? 15? 10? 5? Or even 2 years? At what point do you decide that you have to take your own life into your own hands?

    . . . At the very least, you'll make an
okay salary if you work with me; at best,
you'll gain equity in something that might
become very valuable; I have an idea for a
product that I think will be very popular.
And wouldn't it be amusing for all of us
to be together again!
    . . . I must have your decisions imme-
diately. Do call.

                  Most definitely yours,
                          Michael

Michael has designed this amazing code and the *scary* part is completed already—the proprietary work that could only have sprouted from Michael's brain—Object Oriented Programming from another galaxy. And he's been doing it in his spare time—as a game called *Oop!*. He offered me a job coding, as opposed to just testing . . . who knows how long it'll take me to move up to coding at Microsoft?

He sent us a rough draft of a product description he's written plus ERS—Engineering Requirements Specifications. Herewith:

Oop!

Oop! is a virtual construction box—a bottomless box of 3D Lego-type bricks that runs on IBM or Mac platforms with CD-ROM drives. If a typical Lego-type brick has eight "bumps"; an *Oop!* brick can have from eight to *8,000* bumps, depending on the precision demanded by the user.

Oop! users can virtually fly in and out of their creations, *or* they can print them out on a laser printer. *Oop!* users can build their ideas on a "pad" or they can build their ideas in 3D space, a revolving space station; running ostriches . . . whatever. *Oop!* allows users to clone structures, and add these clones onto each other, permitting easy megaconstructions that use little memory. Customized **Oop!** blocks can be created and saved. The ratios and proportions of **Oop!** bricks can also be customized by the user in much the same way typefaces are scaled.

Imagine:

"Oopenstein"—flesh-like **Oop!** bricks or cells, each with ascribed biological functions that allow users to create complex life forms using combinations of single and cloned cell structures. Create life!

"Mount Oopmore"—a function that allows users to take a scanned photo, texture map that photo, and convert it into a 3D visualized **Oop!** object.

"Oop-Mahal"—famous buildings, preconstructed in **Oop!**, that the user can then modify as desired.

"Frank Lloyd Oop"—architectural **Oop!** for adults.

As **Oop!** users won't have the *actual* plastic blocks in their hands, **Oop!** generates new experiences to compensate for this lost tactility: feedback loops . . . hidden messages . . . or "rewards" for properly completing a kit; i.e., King Kong will climb up and down your Empire State Building and install the flag if you finish. **Oop!** comes equipped with "starter modules" such as houses, cat shapes, cars, buildings, and so forth that can be added on to or modified or finished in an unlimited number of colors or surfaces: slate, leopardskin, woodgrain, and so forth. **Oop!** structures can grow hair or plant life. **Oop!** structures can be distorted, stretched, morphed, or "Jell-O'd." **Oop!** users can dissolve the connection lines between bricks to create "solid" structures.

Oop! constructions can be saved in memory or they can be "destroyed" by:

"Los Angeles" (earthquake simulator)

"Pyro" (fire and melting)

"Ruins" (decay simulator: x-numbers of years of decomposition can be selected and simulated. Imagine your ranch house rotted into fragments and covered in kudzu or a variety of choking vines. Another idea: "Flood")

"Big Foot" (elder sibling emulator: kicks constructions into bits)

"Terror!" (a bomb explodes either inside or outside the structure)

As the Lego Generation ages (*and* as the **Oop!** product invariably grows more sophisticated), **Oop!** becomes a powerful *real-world* modeling tool usable by scientists, animators, contractors, and architects. Object-Oriented Programming design allows great flexibility for licensees to develop cross-platform software add-ons.

Build every possible universe with . . .
Oop!

We felt surreal from Michael's offer.

At sundown, we congregated in the living room, turned off the ESPN$_2$, cracked open two Safeway fire logs, and chewed over Michael's data, while Mishka chewed up a Windows NT box. We felt like a Magritte painting.

We talked some more, but the basic idea was clear. As Abe said, "It's virtual Lego—a 3-D modeling system with almost unlimited future potential."

"*Oop!* sounds too fun to resist—like that pile of FREE BIRD SEED in the old *Road Runner* cartoons," said Bug.

Susan said, "Maybe *Oop!* is Sea Monkeys. Maybe it seems unbelievably fun, but in the end winds up as a cruel, bitter letdown upon arrival."

"I doubt it," said Abe. "Michael's a genius. We all know that. And the ERS looked great."

"Just think," said Karla, "Lego can be rendered into anything, in 2 or 3 dimensions. This product has the possibility for becoming the universal standard for 3-dimensional modeling."

We silently nodded.

And we didn't talk much. We just looked into the flames and thought.

Mom called. She's learning the butterfly stroke—at 60!

Karla kept on talking about bodies, her obsession, tonight, about an hour ago before she fell asleep and I, as ever, remained wide-eyed and awake.

"When I was younger," she said, "I went through a phase where I wanted to be a machine. I think this is one of the normal phases that young people go through now—like *The Lord of the Rings* phase, the Ayn Rand phase—I honestly didn't want to be flesh; I wanted to be 'precision technology'—like a Los Angeles person; I listened to Kraftwerk and 'Cars' by Gary Numan."

(A concerned pause.) "Oh . . . is your foot twitching, Dan? Let me fix it for you . . . .

(*Insert foot massage here.*)

"That was a decade ago, and years have passed since I had had that particular dream of wanting to become a machine.

"Then four summers ago when I was visiting my parents down in McMinnville, I accidentally fell back into the body/machine dream.

"It was a summer day—too bright out—and I was walking amid the family's apple orchards and developed a brain-splitting, wasp's sting of a headache and became nauseous. I walked into the house and went into the basement to be cool, but I threw up on the cement floor next to the washer and dryer. I lost control of my left arm and then I passed out on top of a stack of laundry for three hours. Dad freaked out over the paralysis and drove me into the city and we did a brain scan to check for stroke damage or clots and stuff.

"They injected all sorts of isotopes into me and I found myself part of a literal body/machine system—being bodily radioactive—and inserted like a fuel rod into a body-scanning machine. I remember saying, to myself, 'So *this* is the feeling of being a machine.' I felt more curious about death than I felt afraid; I felt glad to be no longer human for a few brief minutes."

"Was there a blood clot?" I asked.

"No. Simple sunstroke. And the feeling of my being a machine evaporated quickly, too. But the whole incident made me decide to discover my body, *pronto*. Here," she said, scratching my tender inner forearms lightly with her fingernails, sending me into paroxysms of delight. "How does that feel?"

"*Glrmmph.*"

"Just as I thought. People who do repetitive work on keyboards tend to have highly erogenous forearms and shoulder cuffs. Now, you scratch *me*."

I did, and then we scratched forearms together, and I felt like the two of us were in a nature documentary on mating African veld animals.

"Of course," she said, "you'll have to learn *all* of this stuff, and you're going to have to reciprocate on *me*."

"Body 101—sign me up now."

"Daniel . . ."

"Yes?"

"Have you ever been held before?"

"You always ask me these embarrassing, left-field questions. What do you mean, have I ever been *held* before?"

"Exactly what I said. *Have* you?"

"Why, ummm . . ." I thought about it. "No."

"I thought so."

I realized that I envied Karla's way of just talking about whatever was on her mind. She's fearless, exploring her theories and neuroses with the conviction that self-knowledge will bring the solutions. The more I notice this, the more I admire this.

We did spoons for a while, and then she said, "I remember being young, in school, being told that our bodies would yield enough carbon for 2,000 pencils and enough calcium for 30 sticks of chalk, as well as enough iron for one nail. What a weird thing to tell kids. We should be told our bodies can transmutate into diamonds and wine goblets and teacups and balloons."

"And diskettes," I added.

Q: *If there were two of you, which one would win?*

Jeffersonian individualism
victim   **loser**
winner   **thief**

http://www.city.palo-alto.ca/

Lexus.cel phone.traffic.

My body type was in last year.

We can no longer create
the feeling of an era . . . of time being
particular to one spot in time.

WEDNESDAY

Bug ranted a bit about Lego in the afternoon while we ate Arrowroot cookies and bounced on the trampoline. The air was cold and our breath visible. We were all wearing laundry-day junk clothes and we looked like scarecrows flailing about. Why are we all so hopeless with our bodies?

Bug said, "You know what really depresses the hell out of me? The way that kids nowadays don't have to use their imagination when they play with Lego. Say they buy a Lego car kit—in the old days you'd open the box and out tumbled sixty pieces you had to assemble to make the car. Nowadays, you open the box and a whole car, pre-fucking-built, pops out—the car itself is all one piece. Big woo. Some imagination-challenger *that* is. It's total cheating."

I got to thinking of my own Lego superstitions. "When I was young, if I built a house out of Lego, the house had to be all in one color. I used to play Lego with Ian Ball who lived up the street, back in Bellingham. He used to make his house out of whatever color brick he happened to grab. Can you imagine the sort of code someone like that would write?"

"*I* used to build with mixed colors . . ." said Bug.

"What do I know?" I said, pulling my foot out of it.

Karla cut in, "I had this friend, Bradley, who had a major Lego collection and I'd cheat, lie, and steal to go to his house and play with it. Then one day Bradley's mother put his Lego in the bathtub to wash it off. It was never the same—diseased, sort of—stinking, like the water was turning into feta cheese inside the plastic tubes of the locking devices. I think his memories of Lego must be pretty different from my own."

Bug said, "For designing games, Lego makes a great quickie simulator for figuring out mazes for gaming levels."

"You've designed *games* before?" I asked.

"I've done *every*thing you can do on computers. I'm 31."

Maybe we underestimate Bug. When I stop and think about him, he's so full of contradictions—it's like there's one big piece of him, that if only I knew it, it would make sense of everything.

Since Michael's offers came in, we've all become really quiet, I've noticed. We're all mulling it over. Our doors are closed; phone calls are being made to the 415 and 408 area codes. Karla says we're all trying to figure out what we really need in life, as opposed to what we simply want.

A weird shiatsu moment: Karla focused on a piece of my chest, just above the Xyphoid Process (that weird thing in the middle of your ribs) and *bang* out of the blue I started bawling. I couldn't stop. So I guess I have memories hidden away that I don't think about.

1999: The people were lying on the ground.

Demonize the symbolic analysts.

You're smarter than TV.
So what?

Uranium and Beethoven.

Define random
MFD-2DD

Ezekiel
Sony

THURSDAY

A random sort of day.

Woke up late; went on a CD rampage at Silver Platters in Northgate; bacon burger at the IHOP. Karla taught me some shiatsu basics—pressure points and stuff. (*"Massage is a two way street, mister . . ."*

I've been with Karla way over a month now, and just when I think I'm starting to understand her, something happens that makes me realize I don' One truly weird thing about her is that she never calls her family or talks about them. All she'll say is that they're psychotic, as if everybody else's family *isn't.*

She's a good deflector. She structures conversations so that her family never arises. Like today, I brought up the subject of phoning her parents sim ply because it was Sunday (call me old-fashioned—or at least an AT&T consumer victim) and she said, "McMinnville, Oregon—area code 503."

"Huh?"

"North America is running out of area codes. There's only two or three left, and they'll be gone soon enough. Suburban Toronto, Ontario, just got 905. West Los Angeles got 310. Suburban Atlanta got 706. Faxes and modems are eating up phone numbers faster than anyone ever thought they'd be eaten up. We've exhausted our supply of numbers."

"Your point being . . . ?"

"Only one thing—*eight-digit phone numbers.* Disastrous, because all *new* phone numbers will be like those European numbers that are eight d long and impossible to remember."

Karla then discussed a theory called "Five plus-or-minus-two memory."

"Most humans can only remember five digits at most. Exceptional people can remember up to seven (Michael, incidentally knows π up to, like 2,000 digits). So the chances are that phone numbers will be broken up into four and four, for easier memorization," she announced confidently.

"So are you going to call your family, or what?" I asked.

"Maybe. But let me digress a bit. Here's something interesting . . . did you know you can figure out how important your state or province was circa 1961 by adding up the code's three digits? Zero equals 10."

"No."

"It's because *zeros* used to take forever to go around the little rotary dial—while *ones* zipped along quickest. The lowest possible code, 212, went to the busiest place, New York City. Los Angeles got 213. Alaska got 907. See my point?"

Karla always comes up with the best digressions. "Yes."

"Imagine Angie Dickinson in Los Angeles (213) telephoning Suzanne Pleshette in Las Vegas (702) sometime before the Kennedy assassination. She dials the final '2,' breaks a fingernail, and cusses a *shit* under her breath irritated at Suzanne for being in a location with a loser area code."

"How come you won't call your family?"

"Dan, let it rest."

Karla's learning things about me, too. Like the fact that I don't like shopping but I *am* a new product freak. Slap a "NEW" sticker onto an old product, and it's in my cart. The day they introduced Crystal Pepsi, I harassed the local Safeway manager almost daily until it arrived. I thought this new Pepsi was going to be like regular Pepsi, except minus the plutonium stuff that turns it brown. Then I tasted it—it was like 7-Up and Dr. Pepper and Pepsi and tap water all sort of randomly mixed and decolorized. *Downer!*

I guess Pepsi wishes they had John Sculley at the helm for *that* one.

Karla brought me a whole fun-pak of clear products—Crystal Close-up, All "free" detergent, Crystal Pepsi (I guess she didn't know my feelings about it), and Crystal Mint breath drops. In a universe parallel to ours, she no doubt brought me Crystal Bologna, too.

nCube computers simulating the Tokyo power grid

They left a dead escalator, chewed and torn lying on the pavement like a dead gray candy necklace.

Imagine:
In Florida the wind is rattling the chimes.
You look over the alligators and
the sea grass and water. There it *is:*
The rocket's burn. The best century ever.
We were *here*. But now it's time to go.

The past is a finite resource.

Shinhatsubai!

FRIDAY

Another Presto Log fire in the living room. Abe lectured us about his Theory of Lego. It felt like school.

"Have you ever noticed that Lego plays a far more important role in the lives of computer people than in the general population? To a *one*, computer technicians spent huge portions of their youth heavily steeped in Lego and its highly focused, solitude-promoting culture. Lego was their common denominator toy."

Nobody was disagreeing.

"Now, I think it is safe to say that Lego is a potent three-dimensional modeling tool and a language in itself. And prolonged exposure to any language, either visual or verbal, undoubtedly alters the way a child perceives its universe. Examine the toy briefly . . ."

We were riveted.

"First, Lego is ontologically not unlike computers. This is to say that a computer by itself is, well . . . *nothing*. Computers only become something when given a specific application. Ditto Lego. To use an Excel spreadsheet or to build a racing car—this is why we have computers and Lego. A PC or a Lego brick by itself is inert and pointless: a doorstop; litter. Made of acrylonitrile butadiene stryrene (ABS) plastic, Lego's discrete modular bricks are indestructible and fully intended to be nothing except themselves."

We pass the snacks. "Soylent Melts": Jack cheese and jalapenos microwaved onto Triscuits.

"Second, Lego is 'binary'—a yes/no structure; that is to say, the little nubblies atop any given Lego block are either connected to another unit of Lego or they are not. Analog relationships do not exist."

"Monogamous?" asks Susan.

"Possibly. An interesting analogy. Third, Lego anticipates a future of pixelated ideas. It is digital. The charm and fun of Lego derives from reducing the organic to the modular: a zebra built of little cubes; Cape Cod houses digitized through the *Hard Copy* TV lens that pixelates the victim's face into little squares of color."

Karla and I discussed what we're planning to do. We don't have much time to choose; Michael needs a response by the end of this week. Michael is offering me a 24K salary plus 1.5 percent of EQUITY as opposed to my Microsoft 26K plus 150 shares vested over 3.5 years. Plus the opportunity to be a coder, and be closer to Karla on the food chain, and even best of all, the opportunity to be with Karla in the same product group again.

SATURDAY

It was another rainy night that called for a fire. We'd most of us spent the
day processing all of our new career option data.

We ran out of fire logs and had to light a *real* fire with flammables
culled from around the house: a Brawny paper towel carton full of junk mail
and bits of furniture too ugly to even throw out. And then Bug found a packaged fire log in the garage with (he read from the wrapping), "*'Realistic-
looking flames and colors'*—you can put *any*thing on a label and people will
believe it. We are one sick species, I tell you."

The fire was huge and felt religious, and triggered among all of us a discussion of our youthful pyromaniac tendencies. Our conversation became an
unexpected bonding experience for us. We talked about pipe bombs, M-80s,
Lysol spray can flame-throwers, sodium chunks borrowed from chem labs,
potassium nitrate melted together with sugar into smoke bombs, firecracker
bricks, MJB cans filled with gasoline into which lit matchbooks are tossed,
and methane bubbled through water mixed with Joy dishwashing liquid
("fiery bubbles of doom").

Question: Is there an *alt.pyro* on the Net? Probably. There's something
there for everybody.

Susan was able to dig up area code data from, of all places, Trieste, Italy—
on the Net. It turns out that North America is creating up to 640 new area
codes by allowing digits other than zero or one to go in the middle. So there
can be area codes like 647 and 329. With roughly eight million phone lines
possible per code, "That makes for roughly 5.1 billion new portals to fun."

Karla was relieved that we don't have to have eight-digit phone numbers, "at least until some new, as yet uninvented technology, eats up the old
ones again."

Then we digressed into a discussion of how the word "dialing" is itself such an anachronism—a holdover from rotary phones. "Inputting" would be more true. And who came up with the word "pound" for the "#" symbol. Wouldn't "grid" have been easier and more fun? I mean, *"pound"*

Or think of how dumb it is to say, *"I'm going to the record store."*

Technology!

You may have already won!

Technology of mythic strength given surrealistic applications.

Socially disengaged meritocratic elites.

Sporting goods stores always smell like the most advanced plastics.

Did the neutron bomb ever actually get built?

SUNDAY

Bug is going to accept Michael's offer. This is out of character, given that Bug worships *Bill* and the corporate culture of Microsoft so much. But he seems quite jolly and decisive about the move. I think the fact he was slated for transfer to the Converter Group in Building Seventeen, a notoriously glum Campus locale, added some *oomph* to his decision. Bug is a good debugger. That's how he got his name, so Michael's probably getting a good deal in hiring him. I *still* can't figure out why he never got stock options.

Todd, too, has decided to go, perhaps also propelled by his transfer into the OLE Group (*Olé!*), over in the Old Buildings.

This is the Object Linking and Embedding Group that writes code for an application allowing a user to drag part of, say, an Excel document into a Word document. About as much fun as it sounds.

Susan's accepting—and she's forking up some of her vesting money as seed capital for a larger equity stake—and she's clinching the title of Creative Director. "I'll be the Paul Allen of interactivit

Abe, however, is saying no. "What—you guys want to leave a sure thing?" he keeps asking us. "You think Microsoft's going to *shrink*, or are you nuts?"

"That's not the point, Abe."

"What *is* the point, then?"

"One-Point-Oh," I said.

"What?" replied Abe.

"Being One-Point-*Oh*. The first to do something cool or new."

"And so in order to be 'One-Point-Oh' you'd forfeit all of this—" (Abe fumbles for *le mot juste*, and expands arms widely to showcase a filthy living room covered with Domino's boxes, junk mail solicitations, Apple hard hats, three Federal Express baseball caps, and Nerf Gatling guns) "—*security?* How do you know you're not just trading places . . . coding like fuck every day except with a palm tree outside the window instead of a cedar?"

Karla reiterated what she said to Todd, about humanity's dreaming, but Abe is too scared, I think, to make the leap. He's too set in his ways. Repetition breeds inertia.

My computer's subconscious files continue still to surprise me. Who would have known that these are the words my machine wanted to speak? Well, actually, I *know* that it's *me* speaking through the computer, sort of like those really quiet guys who go all nuts when you give them a wooden puppet—ventriloquists—and these aspects of their personalities you didn't even know existed start screaming out.

MONDAY

Abe has actually provoked Karla and me into deciding, *yes*. We both gave Shaw our two weeks' notices, and basically he said we might as well leave at the end of the week since we're not currently "with project."

With start-ups: you get a crap shoot at mega-equity but more importantly, it's true, you *do* get a chance to be "One-Point-Oh." To be the *first* to do the *first* version of something.

We had to ask ourselves, "*Are you One-Point-Oh?*"—the answer is what separates the Microserfs from the Cyberlords.

But beyond this there's what Karla said—about being human, and the dream of humanity. I get this little feeling that we can all of us speed up th dream, dream in color, dream in volume, and dream together down south. We can, and *will*, fabricate the waking dream.

THURSDAY
Later that week

Preparing for this weekend's yard sale, I found a half-pound lump of hamburger meat in the garage that had been sitting in a Miracle Whip jar for about four months—an experiment I had forgotten about. The meat was still kind of pink, with gray fuzz growing on it. "A test to see if the beef industry pumps up cattle with preservatives," I told Karla.

She looked at the jar. "Your brain," she said dismissively, "during the last half-year here at Microsoft."

Mom phoned. She sounds so much better now that the economic stress is off her and that she's exercising. After a short while I got to asking what it i that Dad does for Michael exactly—"So what's Dad's *job*, Mom?"

"Well, I'm not sure. He's never here. He's driving with Michael up and down the Peninsula . . . picking things up. Fixing up the office, I think."

"Carpentry?"

In a whisper: *"It keeps him out of my hair all day. And he seems happy to be needed."* Resumption of normal tone: "So when will we be seeing you down here?"

"Next week."

My body: Today I've been feeling angry all day, and I have to get it off my chest. I went to Microsoft for the last time to clean out my office. Our section, having recently shipped, was unusually empty, even for a Sunday. I was all alone there for the first time, *ever*, I think.

I got to thinking of my cramped, love-starved, sensationless existence at Microsoft—and I got so pissed off. And now I just want to forget the whole business and get on with living—with being alive. I want to forget the way my body was ignored, year in, year out, in the pursuit of code, in the pursuit of somebody *else's* abstraction.

There's something about a monolithic tech culture like Microsoft that makes humans seriously rethink fundamental aspects of the relationship between their brains and bodies—their souls and their ambitions; things and thoughts.

Maybe if this thing with Karla hadn't started I never even would have noticed—I'd have accepted my sensory-deprivation lifestyle without a second thought. She's helping me get closer to getting a life—and having a . . . *personality.*

I erased the office voice mail message that has served me well for the past six months:
"Thank you for phoning the powerful Underwood personal messaging center.
>   Press *one* for Broyhill furniture
>   Press *two* for STP, the racer's edge
>   Press *three* for the roomy, affordable Buick Skylark
>   Press *four* for Rice-A-Roni, the San Francisco treat
>   Press *five* for Turtle Wax
>   Press *six* for Dan
>   Press *pound* to repeat this menu."

Shaw, of all people, came in, and he made this awkward little speech about how he was going to miss me, but I just wasn't in the mood. Shaw, ever the Boomersomething, says that he never got into Lego when he was a kid. "Too 1950s for me. I liked Kenner's modular skyscraper kits. *'If it's from Kenner, it's fun . . . SQUAWK!'*"

Shaw *did* point out that now that we're off Microsoft's e-mail system, we're going to get to invent new log addresses.

I think when people invent their Net log names, they reveal more about themselves than their given names ever reveal. I'm going to have to choose my new name carefully.

I figure there must have been a time in the past, like the year 1147, when there was a frenzy of family-naming—*Smith* and *Goodfellow* and *Green* and stuff—not unlike the current self-naming frenzy spawned by the Net. Abe says that within 100 years, many people will have abandoned their pre-millennial names and opted for "Nettier" names. He says it'd be inspiring to see people use other letters of the keyboard in their names, like %, &, ™, and ©.

Susan asked me later how I ended up at Microsoft in the first place. I told her, "No big surprise: I was 22 . . . it seemed like a studly thing at the time. Microsoft got what it wanted and I got what I wanted, so all's fair and no regrets."

I asked her: She said it was to get away from her parents and having to visit either of them because they were both trying to rip apart her loyalties in some nasty custody war.

"I wanted to go to a place where loyalty wasn't an issue. *Ha!* I wanted to not have a life because life back East sucked big time. So I made the choice to come here—we *all* made the choice to come here. Nobody was holding a carbine up to our temples. So us crabbing about our zero-life factors isn't up for debate, really. Yet do you remember, Dan—do you remember ever *having* a life? Ever? What is a life? I think I once had one—or at least dreamed of having one—and now with going to *Oop!*, I kind of feel like I have a hope of life again."

I said I remembered having a life, back with Jed and being a kid, and Susan said being a kid counted as life only sort of. "It's what you do after you're a kid when life counts for real."

I said, "I think I have a life now. With Karla, I mean. "

She said, "You guys really like each other, don't you?"

And I said—no, I whispered—"I love her."

I've never told anyone that yet—except Karla. It felt like I jumped off a steep cliff into deep blue water. And then I wanted to tell everybody.

More body talk: Karla believes that human beings remember *everything*. "All stimulation generates a memory—and these memories have to *go* somewhere. Our bodies are essentially diskettes," she says. "You were right."

"Lucky for *me*," I reply, "my own memories tend to get stored in my neck and shoulder blades. My body has never felt so . . . *alive*—I wasn't even aware I *had* one until you woke it up today. Life's too good."

Sometimes I think my subconscious has bad days, and I can't believe how mundane the stuff that I write into the file is. But isn't that the deal with a person's subconscious . . . that it stores all the things you aren't noticing visibly?

I'm driving up Interstate 5. It is raining and I remember I have to pick up paper towels and decaffeinated coffee at Costco.

And how did you feel about that?

Mom . . .
Dad . . .

I'm okay. I am not being starved, or beaten, or unnecessarily frightened.

Dropshadow lettering
Granite backgrounds
Hand
Held
Game
This is the end of the Age of Authenticity.

Oracle　　　　　　　　　　　**Ampex**
NeXT　　　　　　　　　　　　**Electronic Arts**

SATURDAY

Garage sale day.

It was a real "Zen-o-thon"—we decided the time had arrived to shake ourselves of all our worldly crap and become minimalists—or at least try starting from scratch again—more psychic pioneering.

"This is so 'Zenny,'" Bug said happily, as some poor cretin purchased his used electric razor (ugh!) as well as his collection of Elle MacPherson merchandise.

Also for sale:

- Japan Airlines inflatable 747
- official Hulk Hogan WWF focus-free 110 signature camera
- antique Ghostbuster squeeze toys
- Nick the Greek professional gambling home board game
- Ping-Pong table
- shoe box full of squirt guns
- blenders (2)
- vegetable juicer
- dehumidifier
- unopened cans of aerosolized cheese food product
- M. C. Escher pop-up books
- far too many Dilophosaurus figurines
- huge Sony box full of collected Styrofoam packing peanuts and packing chunks from untold assorted consumer electronics

The big surprise? Everyone sold everything—*everything*—even the box of Styrofoam. Bug's right: We're one sick species.

And my car sold, too—in a flash, to the first person who came around to look at it. *Wayne's World* did wonders for the secondary market of AMC products.

Actually, the Hornet was such a bucket I was surprised it sold at all. I was worried I'd have to drive it south. Or abandon it somewhere.

Now I am virtually possessionless. Having nothing feels liberating.

National Enquirer:

"Loni's Diary Rips Burt Apart"

He threatened her with a gun in jealous rage
He locked her out of her honeymoon suite
He hid vodka in water bottles

PLUS: Burt: "I wanted to ditch her at the altar."
Exclusive interview on his tell-all book

I do not want this to be me.

SUNDAY

Today we left for California and Karla did her first major flip-out on me. I suppose I was being insensitive, but I think *she* overreacted by far. In packing her Microbus, she buried all of the cassettes we were going to be using for the trip deep inside the bowels of luggage. I said, "God, how could you be so *stu*pid?"

Then she went crazy and threw a toaster oven at me and said things like, "Don't you *ever* call me stupid," and "I am *not* stupid," and she piled into the van and drove off. Todd was standing nearby and just shrugged and went back to bungeeing his Soloflex on top of his Supra. I had to take off in the Acura and catch up with her down by the Safeway, and we made up.

Karla said good-bye to her old geek house's cat, Lentil, named as such because that's how big its brain is. Nerds tend to have cats, not dogs. I th this is because if you have to go to Boston or to a COMDEX or something, cats can take care of themselves for a few days, and when you return, they'll probably remember you. Low maintenance.

Bug was like a little kid, all excited about our "convoy" down to California and was romanticizing the trip already, before we'd even left. The worst part was, he had his ghetto blaster on and was playing that old '70s song, "Convoy," and so the song was stuck in our heads *all*d

Cars for the trip:

Me:	Michael's Acura
Karla:	her Microbus
Todd:	his Supra
Susan and Bug:	their Tauri with U-Haul trailers

Todd said that our "car architecture" for our journey is "scalable and integrated—and fully modular—just like Apple products!"

Somewhere near Olympia, Bug's car rounded a bend and it was so weird— gravity pulled me into an exit off-ramp. And then everyone else trickled in, too. Served him right for lodging the virus of that dopey song in our heads. It was like in third grade, when you ditch someone. It just happens. Humans are horrible.

Then we all felt really horrible for ditching Bug, and we went out chasing him, but we couldn't find him and I got a speeding ticket. Karma.

I-5 is a radar hell.

During a roadside break I asked Karla why she didn't want to go visit her parents in McMinnville, but she said it was because they were psychotic, and so I didn't press the matter.

The Microbus is covered in gray bondo with orange bondo spots all over it. We call it The Carp.

We found Bug south of Eugene. He didn't even know about the ditch, so now all of us have a dark secret between us.

Along I-5, just outside a suburb of Eugene, Oregon, there were all of these houses for sale next to the freeway, and they were putting these desperate signs up to flog them: IF YOU LIVED HERE, YOU WOULD BE HOME RIGHT NOW. Karla honked the horn, waved out the window of the Microbus and pointed at the sign. Convoy humor.

We made this rule that we had to honk every time we spotted road kill, and we nearly burned out our horns.

On a diner TV set we saw that in Arizona, the eight men and women of Biosphere 2 emerged into the real world after spending two years in a hermetically sealed, self-referential, self-sufficient environment. I certainly empathized with them. And their uniforms were like *Star Trek*.

We switched vehicles and I drove Karla's Microbus for a while, but the Panasonic rice cooker in the rear filled with rattling cassette tapes drove me nuts. It was buried too deeply inside the mounds o' stuff to move, so around Medford we switched vehicles again.

We crossed the California border and had dinner in a cafe. We talked about society's accelerating rate of change. Karla said, "We live in an era of no historical precedents—this is to say, history is no longer useful as a tool in helping us understand current changes. You can't look at, say, the War of 1709 (I made this date up, although no doubt there probably *was* a War of 1709) and draw parallels between *then* and *now*. They didn't have Federal Express, SkyTel paging, 1-800 numbers, or hip replacement surgery in 1709—or a picture of the entire planet inside their heads."

She glurped a milkshake. "The cards are being shuffled; new games are being invented. And we're actually *driving* to the actual card factory."

Psychosis! We were discussing Susan's new image at dinner, when I told Karla about this really neat thing Susan's mother did when Susan was young. Susan's mother told Susan that she had an enormous IQ so that could never try and pretend she was dumb when she got older. So because of this, Susan never *did* feign stupidity—she never had any fear of science or math. Maybe this is the roots of her whole Riot Grrrl transformation.

On hearing this news, Karla went *nuts*. It turns out that Karla's parents always told *her* that she was stupid. Everything in life Karla had ever achieved—her degrees and her ability to work with numbers and code, had always been against a gradient of her parents saying, "Now why'd you want to go filling your head with that kind of thing—that's for your brother *Karl* to do."

"Karl's nice, and we like each other," Karla said, "but he's a total 100—center of the bell curve and no way around it. My parents drove him crazy expecting him to be a particle physicist. All Karl wants to do is manage a Lucky Mart and watch football. They've always refused to see us as we are."

Karla was off and running:

"Here's an example—once I went home to visit and the phone was broken, so I began fixing it, and Dad took it away and said, 'Karl should give that a try,' and Karl just wanted to watch TV and couldn't fix a phone if it spat on him and so I was screaming at my Dad, Karl was screaming at my Dad, and my Mom came in and tried to discuss 'women's things' and drag me into the kitchen. Meatloaffuckingrecipes."

Karla was just fuming. She can't bring herself to forgive her parents for trying to brainwash her into thinking she was dumb all her life.

Later, we got too bagged to drive, so we pulled into a Days Inn in Yreka. During a pre-bedtime shiatsu break we started talking about *Spy vs. Spy*, that old comic in *Mad* magazine, and how the very first time you read it, you arbitrarily chose either the black Spy or the white Spy and you voted for your color choice unflinchingly for the remaining period of your *Mad* magazine-reading phase.

I always voted for the black Spy; Karla voted for the white. Silly, but for a moment we had a note of genuine tension.

Karla broke the tension. She said, "Well, it's at least binary, right?" And I said, "Yes," and she said, "Are we geeks, or *what?*"

(Insert one more foot massage here.)

Even later on, Karla spoke to me again. "There's more, Dan. About the stupid business. About the sunstroke."

I wasn't surprised to hear this. "I figured as much. So . . . you want to tell me?"

The stars outside the window were sort of creamy, and I couldn't tell if I was seeing clouds or the Milky Way.

"There was a *reason* I was back at the house a few years ago . . . the time I had the sunstroke episode."

"Yeah?"

"Let me put this another way. Remember back up at Microsoft when you brought me the cucumber roll . . . just out of the blue like that?"

"I remember."

"Well—" (she kissed my eyebrow) "—it's the first time I can remember ever *wanting* to really eat, in like ten years." I was quiet. She continued talking: "Back when I had my sunstroke episode, I hadn't eaten in so long and I weighed about as much as a Franklin Mint figurine. My body was starting to die inside and my parents were worried that I'd gone too far, and I think I even scared my*self*. You think I'm small *now*, Buster, you'd better see . . . well you *won't* because I destroyed all photos . . . pictures of myself taken during my 'phase' as my parents call it."

She was fetal and I had my left hand underneath her feet and my right on top of her head. I cupped her closer and pressed her against my stomach and said, "You're *my* baby now: you're a thousand diamonds—a handful of lovers' rings—chalk for a million hopscotch games."

"I didn't want to do what I was doing, Dan—it just happened. My body was the only way I could get my message across and it was such a bad message. I crashed myself. In the end, it was work that saved my life. But then work be*came* my life—I was technically living but without a life. And I was so *scared*. I thought that work was all there was ever going to be. And oh, God, I was so *mean* to everybody. But I was just running so scared. My parents. They just won't accept what was going on with me. I see them and I want to starve. I can't let myself see them."

I put my forearm in the crook of her knees and pulled her as tightly together as she could go. Her neck rested on my other arm. I pulled the blankets over us, and her breath was hot and tiny, in little bursts like NutraSweet packets.

"There's just so much I want to forget, Dan. I thought I was going to be a READ ONLY file. I never thought I'd be . . . interactive."

I said, "Don't worry about it, Karla. Because in the end we forget everything, anyway. We're human; we're amnesia machines."

It's late and Karla's asleep and blue by the light of the PowerBook.

I'm thinking of her as I input these words, my poor little girl who grew up in a small town with a family that did nothing to encourage her to use her miraculous brain, that thwarted her attempts at intelligence—this frail thing who reached out to the world in the only way she knew, through numbers and lines of code in the hope that from there she would find sensation and expression. I felt this jolt of energy and this sense of honor to be allowed entrance into her world—to be with a soul so hungry and powerful and needful to go forth into the universe. I want to feed her.

I . . .

There's this term used in computers, where you try and squish something into another operating system holus-bolus, and the results are not always effective. The term is called "spooging." An example might be, "Consumer don't know it, yet, but Microsoft is going to spooge a lot of the interface of Word for Windows into the Word for Mac 6.0 version, and rumor has it the new Mac version will operate slow as a glacier, too, because of it—it's too nonintuitive for the Mac-user."

I say this because I think I'm about to spooge here, but I can't think of any other way to express what I feel.

For starters, it was funny, but after Karla told me about her and her family some more, about her eating problems, now a thing of the past, we got into a discussion of what may be the ultimate question: Is our universe ultimately digital or analog?

After this, as I said, Karla fell asleep, but I couldn't sleep myself. What else is new?

I remembered something Antonella from Nintendo once told me about her job at a day-care center, about storytelling to kids—about how the stories the children liked the best were the ones in which the characters fled their old planets amid great explosions, leaving everything behind them to start a new world.

And then I remembered this book-writing program my mom told me about from someone in her library. The big deal in book writing is to quickly establish at the very beginning what it *is* that the characters want.

But *I* think that the books I really enjoy are the ones in which the characters realize, only in the end, what it was that they secretly wanted all along, but never even knew. And maybe this is what life is really like.

Anyway, I have spooged. Good night little PowerBook—my world will shortly end for today, as will the universe, whether digital or analog—with sleep.

Personal Computer

Stars

drinking glasses wrapped in tissue paper

burnt arborite

dial telephones

```
010010010010000001101000011001010110000101110010011101000001000000
100110001101001011100110110000100100000010000110110111101101101 01
110000011101010111010001100101011100100111001100001101000011 01000
011010000110100001101000011010000110101010100011010000110100010111
001100100000011010010111001100100000001101101011110010010000001100
011011011110110110101110000011101010111010001100101011100100000110
101010100011010000110010101110010011001010010010000000110000101110010
011001010010000001101101011000010110110110011110010010000001101100 0
110100101101011011001010010000001101001011101000001011000000110101
100010011101010111010000100000011101000110100001101001011100110 01
000000110111101101100110010100100000011010010111001100100000 0110
110101101001011011100110010100101110000011010100110101111001 00100
000011000110110111101101101011100000111010101110100011001010 111001
000100000011010010111001100100000011011010111100100100000011 00010
011001010110011011101000001000001100110011100100110100101100 1010
110111001100100001011100000110101001001011101000001000000110 100101
110011001000000110110101111001001000000110110001101001011001 10011
001010010110000011010100100100100000011011010111010101011100110 111
010000010000001101101011000010111001101101110100001100101011 1001000100
000011010010111010000101100001000000110000101110011001000000 10010
010010000001101101011101010101110011011011101000010000001101 1010110000
101110011011101000110010101110010001000000110110101111100100100000
011011000110100101100110011000100101000101110000011010101011101101 0010
111010001101010001101111011101010101110100001000000110110101 10010100
101100001000000110110101111001001000000110001101101111011110110110101011
100000111010101110100011001010111001000100000011010010111001100100
000001110101011100110110010101101100110001101010111001101110011001 01
110000011010101011011010100101101010001101000011011110110110101011101
000010000001101101011110010010000001100011011011110110101110110101110 0
001110101011101000110010101110010011000100101100010000001001001001 00000
011000010110110100100000011101010111001101100101011010010110100001001010
111001101101100110010111000001101010010010010000001101101011101 01010
110011011110100001000000110101011100110110011001011110100001101 01011
110011011110100001000000111010101110011011010100100100000001101101011
110010010010000001100011011011110110110101110000011101010111010001100110
010101110010000001110101011001000010000001110100011001010111001101110001
101010111010101110100011001010111001001101111011010110100001 001010
110110111101101101010111110101110101110101110100011001010111010011010
110001010110010111001001101111011010110100001101101011110010010010000001100110
100101011011010111010111001001101111011010010010000001100101011011010110111001
```

```
0100101110011001000000011101000111001001111001011010010110111001
1001110010000000111010001101111001000000110101101101001011011000
1101100001000000110110101100101001011100000110101001001001000000
0110110101110101011100110111010000100000011011110110101011101001
0110001101101111011011010101100000111010101110100011001010010000
0011010000110100101101101001000000011000100110010101100110011011
1101110010011001010010000000110100001100101001000000110111101110
1010111010001100011011011110110110101110000011101010111010001100
1010111001100100000011011010110010100101110000011010100100100100
0000011101101101010010110110001101100001011100001101010000010011
0010101100110011011110111001001100101001000000100011101101111011
0010000010110000100000010010010010000000111001101101110110010101
1000010111001000100000011101000110100000110100101110011001000000
1100011011100100110010101100101011001000010111000001101010010011
0111100100100000011000110110111101101101011000011101010111010100
0110010101110010001000000110001011011100110010000010000000110110
1011110010111001101100101011011000110011000100000011000010111000
1001100101001000000110010001100101011001100110010101101110011000
1000110010101110011001110011001000000110111101100110001000000111
0100011010000011010010111001100100000001100011011011110110101011
0111001110100011100100111100100101110000011010101110110010010100
1000000110000101110010011001010010000001110100011010000011001010
0100000011011010110000101110011011011101000110010101110010011100 11
0010000001101111011001100001000000110111110111010101110010001000 0
0011001010110111001100101010110101011011100100101110000011010101
1011001010010000001100001011100100110010010010000001110100011010
0000110010101001000011001010010011000001101001011000010000001110100
0110100001100101011100100110010010010000001101001011100110010000 0
0011011100110110111100100000011010101101110011001010010110101111 00
1001011000000110101110001011100000110100001101000011010000110100 00
1101010101000110100101101110011011110110110101110000011101010111 010
1000011010001101000011010010111001100100000001100011011011110110 1010
1101110011101000111001001111001001011100000110101011101100100101 00
1000000110000101110010011001010010000001110100011010000011001010 01
0000001101010110000101110011011011101000110010101110010011100110 01
0010110000001101011100010111000001101000011010000110100001101000 0110
1010100010110100101101110011011110110110101110000011101010111010 1000
11010001101000011010010111001100100000011101000111001001111010011 1001
```

3
Interiority

We took a few hours off to attend a Halloween barbecue at the chic San Carlos home of *Oop!*'s president and CEO, Ethan, Mr. "Let's-Ship-Units!"

Also in attendance were a crew of Apple workers Ethan is scanning for "hireability."

The evening was a typical geek get-together, and conversation stayed along conventional lines: the Menendez brothers, consumer and military aviation, and hiring/firing gossip. But the mood was also tinged with an atypical moroseness: Crunchy Frog jokes blended with tales of fiscal woe. Apple people are all trying to get laid off so they can get the layoff financial package—so everybody's trying to be as *useless* as possible. It's a shock, let me tell you. And they're all frightened the PowerPC's going to bomb and they're worried about the Newton—and they're frightened they might merge with Motorola or IBM and lose their identity, and—*gosh*, they have a lot to worry about, it seems.

"It's all so . . . anti-*coding*," said Todd, dressed as Atlas. (Speedo swimsuit and a globe tied to his shoulder. Show-off.) "It's the total opposite of Microsoft. It's not the way, you know, we've been raised to think about Apple."

"Hey, Pal—just goes to show you what happens without a Bill to whip people into shape," said Ethan, dressed as "Money"—his face painted green underneath a green George Washington wig that was actually a rented Marilyn Monroe wig misted with green hair spray. "Without a charismatic at the helm, you're history."

Apple *is* kind of depressing, we agreed dispiritedly. Not at all what we expected, but we bravely try and Keep the Faith. We're trying to find somebody to give us an Apple campus tour.

*No*body rules here in the Valley.

No Bills.

It's a bland anarchy. It takes some getting used to.

Ethan, *Oop!*'s president, is somewhat evil. Well . . . a*mus*ingly evil. Smarmy? Perhaps *that's* the right word. White-toothed and always impeccably dressed, he's what Karla calls a "killer nerd." For some reason, he's paying a lot of attention to me and keeps giving me all sorts of confidant-type information. I'm not sure whether to be flattered or to consult an exorcist.

Sitting next to a burning Tiki torch spiked into the ground, beneath an orange tree, Karla said to me, "You know, Ethan's been a millionaire and filed for Chapter Eleven three times already—and he's only *33*. And there are *hun*dreds of these guys down here. They're immune to money. They just sort of assume it'll appear like rain."

While decoding Ethan's existence we were removing stray grass seeds from each other's *Clockwork Orange* thug costumes. I said, "There's something about Ethan that's not quite oxymoronic, yet still self-contradictory— like an 18-wheeler with *Neutrogena* written on the side—I can't explain it. The whole Silicon Valley is oxymoronic—geeky and rich and hip. I'm undecided if I even *like* Ethan—he's definitely not *one of us*. He's a different archetype."

Inspired by Ethan's costume, we discussed money. We decided that if the government put Marilyn Monroe on a dollar coin, it would be popular enough to succeed. "And if they want to replace the five-dollar bill with a coin," said Susan, approaching us from the hibachi, "they can use Elvis."

Susan didn't go out of her way to dress up this year and came as a biker chick. She was miffed at discovering that the assembly language programmer from General Magic she'd been chatting up all night was married. She swigged Chardonnay from a bottle, yanked an unripe orange from a tree, and said, "You guys are talking about Ethan? Being with Ethan is kind of like, *well* . . . like when you're sleeping with somebody who doesn't know what to do in bed but who thinks they're really hot stuff—and they're rubbing one part of your body over and over, thinking they've found your 'Magic Spot' when all they're doing, in fact, is annoying you."

Susan and Ethan never agree on anything, but it's not sexy disagreeing. It's just disagreeing.

There was a pause as the party slowed down, and Karla said, "Isn't it weird, the way Michael arrived without a costume, but he still looks like he's in costume?" She was right. Poor unearthly Michael.

Ethan was telling us the story of how he hooked up with Michael, how they met shortly after Michael's mystery trip to Cupertino, at the Chili's restaurant on the Stevens Creek Boulevard strip—a few blocks away from Apple—a tastefully landscaped four-lane corridor of franchised food and metallically-skinned tech headquarters.

"Michael was inking out all of the vowels on his menu," Ethan reminisced fondly, sitting down with us under the tree. "He was *'Testing the legibility of the text in the absence of information,'* as I was later informed. And when I saw him order a dozen tortillas, some salsa, and a side of Thousand Island dressing, I *knew* there had to be something there. How *rrrr*right I was."

"Michael is going to be your mother lode for the mid-1990s?" Susan asked ingenuously.

"Well, Miss Equity—for *your* sake, you'd better hope so."

We went in the house to warm up. Ethan's living room is painted entirely in white enamel, and lining the ceiling's perimeter are a hundred or so 1970s Dirty Harry bank surveillance cameras whirring and rotating, all linked to a wall of blue-and-white, almost-dead TV sets. A surveillance fantasy. "I used to date an installation artist from UC Santa Cruz," is all Ethan says about his art.

His house is small, but I think he enjoys being able to tell people he lives in San Carlos. San Carlos, just north of Palo Alto, is called Nerd Hill. The big problem in San Carlos is, apparently, *deer*—which eat all the rose shoots and the young tree buds. "There's this guy there who sells bottled mountain-lion urine he collects at zoos. You spritz the stuff around the yard to scare the deer away. It's like, 'Hey, pal—check out the cougar piss!'" Ethan held up a small, clear-yellow vial. "I'm investing in a biotech firm that tricks *e. coli* bacteria into manufacturing cougar pheromones."

Ethan is so extreme. He has this Patek Phillipe watch, which cost maybe ¥2,000,000 (purchased at Tokyo's Akihabara district, the nirvana of geek consumption, with all signage apparently in Japanese, English, and Russian). He says that every time he tells the time, he's amortizing the cost.

"Well, I'm down to $5.65 a glance, now. If I check the time every hour from now to the year 2023, I'll be down to a dime per look."

Ethan's nine blender settings are labeled with little LaserWriter labels in 7-point Franklin Gothic:

> 1) Asleep
> 2) In-flite movie
> 3) Disneyland at age 25
> 4) Good $8.00 movie
> 5) IMAX with Dolby
> 6) Lunch w/ D. Geffen and B. Diller
> 7) Disneyland at age 10
> 8) Aneurysm
> 9) Spontaneous combustion

Ethan's dandruff is truly shocking, but you know, life isn't like TV commercials. Karla and I spent thirty minutes trying to think of tell-your-friend-he-has-dandruff scenarios that wouldn't insult him, and in the end, we couldn't. It's so odd, because every other aspect of his grooming is so immaculate.

3:10 A.M. Just got back from Ethan's party. We're "flying to Australia" tonight—that's our in-house code word for pulling an insane, 36- to 48-hour coding run in preparation for a meeting Ethan has with venture capitalists.

E-mail from Abe:

You actually left.
I never thought that could happen. How could you have left Microsoft so EASILY!?!? It's such a good set up. The stock's supposed to split in Spring.
Who's yourBill?
I'm putting word out on-wire at Microsoft to locate new roomates, but still it feels pretty strange to be without rfoomates. A whole month now! I'm writing my ad for the inhouse BBS:

"SPACE!...
Not your final frontier in this instance, but there's lots of it here and its not a bad deal: Redmond, 5 minutes from Microsoft. Live in regal early 1970s splender. Dolby THX sound. Adirondack style chair made from old skis. Trampoline. Own bathrooom. Pets okay.
$235.00"

BTW: Did you know that Lego makes a plastic vacuum cleaner shaped like a parrot to pick up stray Legos??

SUNDAY

Ethan and I drove around Silicon Valley today looking at various company parking lots to see whose workers are working on a Sunday. He says that's the surest way to tell which company to invest in. *"If the techies aren't grinding, the stock ain't climbing."*

Karla doesn't like my being friends with Ethan. She says it's corrupting, but I told her not to worry, that I spent all of my youth in front of a computer and that I'll never catch up to all the non-nerds who spent their early twenties having a life and being jaded.

Karla says that nerds-gone-bad are the scariest of all, because they turn into "Marvins" and cause problems of planetary dimensions. Marvin was that character from Bugs Bunny cartoons who wanted to blow up Earth because it obscured his view of Venus.

Oh—earlier today, driving up Arastradero from Starbucks, the sunset was literally almost killer.

It was all we could do not to crash the car looking at the pinks and oranges. And the view from Mom and Dad's house on La Cresta Drive was staggering: from the San Mateo bridge to the north, practically down to Gilroy in the south. The Alameda Mountains were seemingly lit from the inside, like beef-colored patio lanterns, and we even saw a glint from the observatory atop Mount Hamilton. And the dirigible hangar at Moffet Naval Air Station looked as if the Stay-Puft marshmallow giant was lying down to die. It was so *grand*.

We sat there on the sagging cedar balcony to watch the floor show. The balcony sags because the sugary brown soil underneath all these older ranch houses is settling; floors bump; doors don't quite close true. We threw chew toys to Misty, Mom's golden retriever that she bought two years ago secondhand. Misty was supposed to be a seeing-eye dog, but she failed her exam because she's too affectionate. It's a flaw we don't mind.

It was just a nice moment. I felt like I was home.

Karla also keeps a diary, but *her* entries are so brief. For example, she showed me a sample entry for the entire trip to California, all she wrote was: *Drove down to California. Dan drew a robot on my place mat at lunch in south Oregon and I put it in my purse.* That was *it*. No mention of anything we talked about. I call it Reduced Instruction Set Computation diaries.

MONDAY

Karla and I took an R&R break and drove 40 miles up to one of the Simpsons bars in the City—the Toronado, where they play *The Simpsons* every Thursday night. Except I realized it was Monday, so no Simpsons. I can never get the dates right anymore. But soon enough they'll be syndicated on the junky stations every night until the end of the universe, so I suppose I'll survive.

We took the wrong off-ramp (a deadly mistake in San Francisco—they STILL haven't rebuilt after the 1989 quake; the 101/280 connector links are so unbelievably big and empty and unfinished) and we got lost. We ended up driving through Noe Valley by accident—so pretty. Such a VISION, this city is. I suppose the City is putting all its highway-building energy into building the mention-it-one-more-time-and-I'll-scream information superhighway.

Speaking of the information superhighway, we have all given each other official permission to administer a beating to whoever uses that accursed term. We're so sick of it!

On the mountain coming in from the airport they have what has to be the world's ugliest sign saying, SOUTH SAN FRANCISCO, THE INDUSTRIAL CITY, in huge white letters up on the mountainside. You just feel so sorry for the mind set that would treat a beautiful mountainside like it was a button at a trade convention.

"If they changed it to POSTINDUSTRIAL city, it *might* be meaningful," said Karla.

Anyway, we couldn't find the bar and wound up in a coffeehouse somewhere in the Mission District.

San Francisco is a weird tesseract of hipness: lawyers don tattoos and listen to the Germs' first album. Everyone here is so young—it's like Microsoft that way—a whole realm composed of people our own age. Because of that, there's an abundance of dive bars, hipsterious coffeehouses, and cheap-eats places. It's a big town that feels like neighborhoods: a municipal expression of Local Area Networks.

And I must admit I'm impressed by the level of techiness—people here are fully jacked in. Should some future historian ever feel the need to duplicate an SF coffee bar circa The Dawn of Multimedia, they will require the following:

- thrashed PowerBooks covered with snowboarding and Chiquita banana stickers
- a bad early 1980s stereo (the owner's old system, after he upgraded his own personal system)
- used mismatched furniture
- bad oil paintings (vaginal imagery/exploding eyes/nails protruding from raw paint)
- a cork bulletin board (paper messages!)
- sullen, most likely stoned, undergrads
- multi-pierced bodies
- a few weird, leftover 1980s people in black leather coats and black-dyed hair
- nightclub flyers

Parking in San Francisco is a nightmare. There *are* no spots. We decided that the next time we came we'd bring our own spots with us. We decided to invent portable, roll-up spots, like those portable holes they use in cartoons. Or maybe a can of spray-on parking spot remover to get rid of other cars. It's crazy there, that way. Just crazy. In the end we said a prayer to Rita, the pagan goddess of parking spots and meters. We shot out beams of parking karma into the hills ahead of us. We were rewarded with fourteen luxurious feet of car space. Rita, you kooky goddess you!

Learned a new word today: "interiority"—it means, *being inside somebody's head.*

Michael has a new obsession: he sits on the patio beside the pool and watches the automated Polaris pool-sweeper scrape decomposed eucalyptus leaves off the pool's bottom. The pool sweeper looks like R2D2 as it hobbles about its duties, and I think they're becoming best friends.

Oh—we have this Euroneighbor named Anatole. He started dropping by when he found out there were other nerds in the neighborhood. As he used to work at Apple, we don't mind his presence as much as we would otherwise. He's a repository of Apple lore (gossip ahoy!). He's a real turtlenecker—one of those French guys who'd be smoking in the rain up at Microsoft.

He said that it was at Clinton's congressional speech when John Sculley sat next to Hillary Clinton that everybody realized Apple was way out of control. Personally, I thought it was glamorous. Then he hit us with a bombshell, which was that Apple never had a contingency plan in the event that they lost the Look & Feel suit. They totally *believed* they were going to win. Maybe the PowerPC will save them. We warned Anatole not to discuss Look & Feel with Bug, but he said they'd already discussed it and that Bug had seemed bored by it. Bug's forgetting his roots! California's turned him mellow.

Also, Anatole says nobody's simply *at* Apple; they're *still* at Apple. It would appear that none of what we hear matches the One-Point-Oh, Gods-in-the-Clouds mental pictures we have of the company. But like most gossip, it merely makes us want to be closer to the core of the gossip itself. We're all drooling for a chance to visit Apple, except a chance never seems to appear. Anatole is useless in this regard. We think he burned some bridges before he left—expense report fudging?

And of course Anatole is a genius. In the Silicon Valley the IQ baseline (as at Microsoft) *starts* at 130, and bell-curves quickly, plateauing near 155, and only *then* does it decrease. But the Valley is a whole multi-city complex of persnickety eggheads, not just one single Orwellian technoplex, like Microsoft. As I said—it's sci-fi.

Bug accidentally used the term *information superhighway*, and so we were able to administer a beating.

TUESDAY

Our money situation is tight.

Trying to find money through venture capital is a long, evil, conflictual process full of hype and hope. If I have learned anything here, it's that snagging loot is the key struggle and obsession of any start-up. Fortunately for us, Michael and Ethan have agreed that the best thing to do is to be an R&D company (research and development) and get another company to "publish" our products. That way we don't have to hire our own sales and marketing people, or shell out the enormous amounts of money it takes to market software. We still need funding to build the product, though.

Susan's freaking out worse than anybody. Maybe that's why she and Ethan disagree on everything. He always says everything's "fabulous," while she fumes.

Today Ethan called Silicon Valley "the 'moniest' place on earth," and he's probably right. Everything in this Valley revolves around $$$ . . . EVERYTHING. Money was something you never had to think about at Microsoft. I mean, not that Microsofters don't check out WinQuote daily, but *here*, as I have said, there's this *endless,* boring, mad scramble for loot.

For financial reasons, we have to work at Mom and Dad's place, until we're flush with VC money.

We work at the south end of the house in a big room that was supposed to be the rumpus room, back during the era when society still manufactured Brady children. It has been completely converted into the tasteful carnage of our "Habitrail 2." We call it Habitrail 2 because it's a big maze, because its ventilation hinges on the anaerobic, and because paper is *ev*erywhere, just like gerbils nesting inside a Kleenex box. Michael has installed his own two pet gerbils, "Look" and "Feel," inside his astoundingly large yellow plastic Habitrail kit, which encircles the office . . . decades' worth of collecting. We get to hear Look and Feel scampering about endlessly while we work. Karla likes the Habitrail setup because it reminds her of the old cartoon with the chipmunks trapped inside the vegetable factory. She and Michael are continually adding on to it. It's their common bond.

At a glance around the Habitrail 2, there are Post-it notes, photocopies, junk mail, newspapers, corporate reports, specs, printouts, and litter, plus thumbed-to-exhaustion copies of *Microprocessor Report, California Technology Stock Letter, Red Herring, Soft•Letter, Multimedia Business Report, People*, and *The National Enquirer*. You get the feeling that if you only reached into this paperstorm you could withdraw a strand of six pulsating rubbery pink gerbil babies. Paperless office . . . *ha!*

There is a billiard table covered with SGIs, MultiSync monitors, coding manuals, printouts, take-out food boxes, coils, cables, dry-erase pens, and calculators. Over by "The Dad Bar" (diamond tufted leatherette; *"Tee Many Martoonies"*-style knickknacks) there are compiler manuals, more monitors, and an EPROM chip toaster stacked alongside cases of Price-Costco diet Cokes and fruit leather whips. (*My* workspace, I am pleased to say, is spotless, and my barely scratched Microsoft Ship-It Award rests proudly underneath a Pan-Am 747 plastic model.)

Needless to say, *Far Side* cartoons are taped *everywhere*. I think techies are an intricate part of the life cycle of *The Far Side* cartoon, the way viruses can only propagate in the presence of host organisms. Susan says, "We are only devices for the replication of *Far Side* cartoons." Now that's *one* way of looking at humanity.

And of course there are two long couches for those flights to Australia.

Mom is happy to have our pittance of rent money, and my commuting time is ninety seconds, as I live with Karla in one of the guest bedrooms.

The main drawback about the Habitrail 2 is the ventilation, which *could* be better. Todd calls it *"hamper fresh."* We'd keep the sliding door leading into the backyard open more often, but Ethan doesn't want dust and insects infecting our technology. Or Mom's golden retriever, Misty.

Habitrail 2 also features:

- 4-fingered cartoon gloves
- ubiquitous Nerfiana
- 24 Donna Karan coffee mugs (long story)

- a decaf coffee tin labeled "666"
- GoBot transformer-type toys
- Glass beads at the door, like the ones Rhoda Morgenstern had
- herbal tea packets and tea-making apparatus
- several Game Boys
- three 4'-x-8' dry-erase wall boards
- a diet 7-UP pyramid
- an extensive manga collection
- T2 spin-off merchandise
- one Flipper thermos

We inhabit our workstations daily for a minimum of 12 hours. We use brown and white plastic folding patio chairs, so our backs are completely shot. So much for ergonomics. (Thank God for shiatsu.) There's the occasional Homer Simpson *"doh!"* punctuating the air when someone's cursor bleeps, or the occasionally muttered *piss* and *crap*. No one can agree on music, so we play none. Or use Walkmans.

We're doing a Windows version and a Mac version of *Oop!*. And Michael's drafted the coolest ERS for the graphics, AI, interface, and maybe sound. Just *killer* stuff, all patentable. Michael needs *us* to bring his vision to life. Our jobs are:

Michael: Chief Architect. He has the overall vision. He also writes the core engine that drives the graphics and modeling algorithms. He rules the engineers—us.

Ethan: President, CEO, and Director of Operations. His job is to find investors to fund us, find a company to publish and distribute our products, and to run the business day-to-day. Most companies have a CFO, but we can't afford one, so Ethan does the bill-paying, accounting, taxes, equipment-buying, and all that stuff.

Bug: In charge of database and file I/O (Input/Output). It's how *Oop!* stores information to and from the hard drive; it's really complicated, and the kind of thing Bug loves.

<u>Todd</u>: He is "Ditherman"—working on the graphics engine and printer driver. All of the graphics need to be converted into an output format in order to be printed by a printer.

<u>Me and Karla</u>: We're working on the cross-platform class library so *Oop!* will run on both Mac and Windows. I'm Windows lead, she's the Mac lead.

<u>Susan</u>: She's the User-Interface Designer; in charge of the look-and-feel, the graphics, all that. She's the U-I police keeping me and Karla's code in sync.

Mom has a collection of rocks. This sounds weird, and it really *is* weird. She has this small pile of rocks on the patio that just sits there. I ask Mom why she likes them, and she says, "I don't know, they just seem special."

So is this something that might lead to her requiring medication? I mean, they're not even nice-looking rocks. I keep looking at them and try and see what she sees, and I can't.

As stated, Karla and I are working on the same things, just in different formats. She's Mac, I'm Windows.

"Entirely appropriate," says Karla, "because Windows is more male, and Mac is more female."

I felt defensive. "How so?"

"Well, Windows is nonintuitive . . . counterintuitive, sometimes. But it's so MALE to just go buy a Windows PC system and waste a bunch of time learning bogus commands and reading a thousand dialog boxes every time you want to change a point size or whatever . . . MEN are just used to sitting there, taking orders, executing needless commands, and feeling like they got such a good deal because they saved $200. WOMEN crave efficiency, *elegance* . . . the Mac lets them move within their digital universe exactly as they'd like, without cluttering up their human memory banks. I think the reason why so many women used to feel like they didn't "understand computers" was because PCs are so brain-dead . . . the Macintosh is responsible for upping not only the earning potential of women but also the feeling of mastering technology, which they get told is impossible for them. *I* was always told that."

Remember at the very end of *Soylent Green* where Charlton Heston screams, *"Soylent Green is people!!!!"*? Well, I had that same sort of feeling today when Anatole began telling us about working life down at Apple . . . *"Apple is Microsoft!!!"* He told us that the moods on the two "campuses" are almost exactly the same, and that the two corporate cultures, although they purport to be the opposite of each other, are actually about as different as Tide and Oxydol.

Anatole was hanging around all day today and on the drywall he made this big list of similarities and differences between Apple and Microsoft. Herewith:

Microsoft	Apple
waiting for stock to vest	*trying to get laid off*
"the Campus"	"the Campus"
make money	*"1.0" sensibility*
Microsoft Way	Infinite Loop
Bill	*(no longer any equivalent)*
Apple envy	Microsoft envy
boring buildings/good art	*good buildings/art a sideline only*
better cafeterias	better nerd toys
soccer field	*sculpture garden*
I-520	I-280
Intel	*Motorola*
average age: 31.2	average age: 31.9
gray Lexus	*white Ford Explorer*

not wild at creating new things but good on follow-through	good at creating new things but not wild on follow-through
no one ever gets fired	*no one ever got fired . . . until the layoffs started*
wacky titles on business cards	*wacky titles on business cards*
eerie, *Logan's Run*-like atmosphere	eerie, *Logan's Run*-like atmosphere
uneasy IBM symbiosis	*uneasy IBM fusion*
13,200 employees	14,500 employees
people hired in 1991–92 being shuffled around	*people hired from colleges in 1988–89 being turfed*
stock set to split	stock price at cash liquidation value of company; now's the time to buy!

*S*till no tour of the Apple facilities, I note.

Today was one of those days where it was warm if you were standing in the sunlight, but the moment you left it, you froze.

I saw doves and I thought they were rocks, but they were

asleep. My breath made them stir, **and the rocks**
took flight, **the earth**
exploding . . . and my only thought was that

I wanted you to see them, too

The man from **Whirlpool** came to fix the

washer today, and he found Black Widow spiders nesting

underneath its **broken engine**, and

he showed me the web, and I found myself thinking of catch-

ing you, **biting you**, spinning you within my

limbs and setting you free

Don't tell me this isn't true.

Tell me you feel this fire.

Oxydol   *throw cushion*
Revell   *binder paper*
makeover   *lipstick*

WEDNESDAY

Down at the library, Mom made up a list of "deer-proof" plants for Ethan. She got it from *Sunset's Western Garden Book*. Mom loves Ethan. He's a go-getter.

During lunch, as Ethan, Todd, and I drove in Karla's Carp through the Carl's Jr. drive-thru, Ethan gave us an inspirational chat. "Guys, the *last* thing we want," he said, "is to seem to be hurting for money. Venture capitalists like to see stability first. Only then will they come in with cash."

Todd expressed some disappointment that *Oop!* was, in fact, quite desperate for money, in spite of Michael's and Susan's infusions.

He replied, "Todd: fate hands you opportunities for a while, and if you don't take them, Fate says to itself, 'Oh I see—this person doesn't *like* opportunities,' and stops giving them to you."

I notice that *I* had to pay for the Western Burgers and fries and diet Cokes.

"Think of money this way," he went on, "take an initial sum and teach it to multiply itself, the way you copy-and-paste text to multiply it. *Never* think of money in terms of numbers. Only think of money in terms of other things. For example: two weeks of bug-checking equals a Y-class ticket to Boston. That sort of thing. If you think of money simply as numbers then you're doomed."

Ethan then fed a used Band-Aid from his index finger to a seagull squatted on a landscaped berm beside the road, and Todd and I lost our appetites. We gave Ethan our meals and dropped him off at his dermatologist's office.

*M*elrose Place night. One hour of work-free bliss and catcalls as the six of us monopolize the living room TV. It's better than the Academy Awards—and every week, too. Added bonus: *90210* as an hors d'oeuvre.

Susan noted tonight that the computers in Billy's office aren't connected to, or plugged into, anything. But this just made the show even better.

Todd chugged Snapples. He calls them "Workahol."

We all made fun of the commercial for Mentos mints, saying "Mentos" all night with a goofy European accent. *"Mentos."* It's so dumb.

This is embarrassing to admit, but I *still* don't really know what Dad *does* for Michael. I am amazed that I can be this clueless, but all either of them will say is that he's working on our final corporate space in downtown Palo Alto. But can we af*ford* this? I thought we were hurting for money. I am going to try and sleuth out what he's doing. Whatever it is, it's totally sucked up all of his model train-making energy. He doesn't go near the garage any-more.

I told Karla what Ethan said at lunch, about teaching money to multiply itself. She said Ethan's talking "bollocks." I asked her what that word meant, and she said she wasn't sure—it was a term from the punk rock era. "Something to do with anarchy and safety pins." We're going to e-mail someone in England and find out what it means.

THURSDAY

Today we were talking about the name of our corporation. It's so boring—
E&M Software. Obviously, that's Ethan and Michael, and it *is* their company, but Michael said if we had a better idea we could change it. Since we
haven't shipped anything yet anyway.

Over the day, we wrote our suggestions on our code-blemished dry-
erase wall. This is a really common thing down here: dry-erase boards covered in name suggestions. Here are some of our own:

"Cybo"

"GeekO"

"1410 C°" (Michael suggested this—it's the melting point of silicon.)

"@" (My suggestion. Susan said the name sounded too skateboardy,
and Ethan said that somebody's probably already used it, anyway.)

"Clean Room" (Abe's e-mail suggestion and my favorite—Lego was
always hell to clean up.)

"Dead Pixel"

"Xen" (Pronounced "Zen." Half the companies down here have an X in
their name.)

"InfiniToy"

"Bottomless Box"

"Dangerously Overcrowded Electrical Outlet"

"Box of Oily Rags"

"Dream Enabling Technologies" (Ethan suggested this to a chorus of
gagging noises.)

"WaferMap" (Suggested by Susan, but then immediately nixed by her
as "Too 1981," but Michael liked the idea of InterCapping—mixing capital
letters in with lowercase letters.)

Something **"European"** (Karla: "Americans can only digest one new
extremely weird European word every two years. It's a fact. My proof:
Nadia Comaneci, Häagen-Dazs, and *Fahrvergnügen.* We can become this

year's scary European word.") Everybody agreed in principle, but nobody knows any other languages besides computer languages, except Anatole, but he's like the wacky upstairs neighbor from a sitcom, and not a part of our core team, so the idea died.

"Cher" or "Sting" (Ethan suggested something one-syllable. So we asked which syllable in particular, and he blanked. "Ummm . . ." doesn't count.)

":•)" (Mom wrote this one, saying, "They're called *emoticons*—I read about them in *USA Today*. They're like sideways happy faces." We all ganged up on her: "We *hate* those things!" Everyone except for Bug who, as it turns out, loves them. And then Susan 'fessed up that she liked some of them. And then Todd. And then Karla. I guess emoticons are like *Baywatch*—everyone says they don't watch it, but they really do.

Mom, the librarian, said: "Just *think* of how confused librarians would be! I mean, what would they *file* it under? Diacritical marks are extraordinarily confusing." I was pleased to note this anarchical streak in her. "We could call the emoticon, ;•), 'WINK'"

Ethan asked what keyboard character the "nose" was, and Michael quickly replied, "It's a dingbat—OPTION-8 on a Mac keyboard using Word 5.1. PCs use the asterisk."

"Interiority" (The winner, and my suggestion. Prize: a Nerf Gatling gun.) So now we're making *Oop!* an Interiority product.

Housing update: Bug and Susan now live 40 miles north in San Francisco. They drive the 280 against the rush-hour traffic, it's not too bad.

Susan lives in the sumptuous 2-bedroom apartment next door to Bug's seedy bachelor "bedsitter." We gloated at their decision to live next to each other, but Susan told us to stop smirking like dungeonmasters. "Don't think I don't know what I'm in for. I warned Bug that if I smell even *one* of his crappy little Dinty Moore meals through the walls, I'm going to get him evicted." Susan just doesn't want to admit she doesn't want to be alone. She acts all tough and wolfwoman, but it's all bark. Michael lives in the other spare room down the hall from me and Karla. More to the point, he announced he's moving to a personalized 1-800 number. That's where he *really* lives—1-800land. Todd's renting a room in a geek house—Stanford grad students—near the Shoreline exit off the 101 in order to be closer to the Gold's Gym. He lives at the gym. It's lots of EZ-to-access free sex. Abe is still in Redmond. We miss him, but then we do talk to him daily over e-mail. Probably more than we did when we were there.

I yawned too loudly this afternoon, and Susan said, "Don't you *ever* sleep, Dan?"

Karla, hearing this, said, "She's right, Dan—you're insomniacal again. So, what's the deal?"

I admitted the truth—that I was having bad dreams. Not insomnia, but bad dreams, which is different. I said it's just a patch, and it'll probably pass. I also told them that for the time being, when I go to sleep, I try not to have any dreams at all—"as a precautionary measure."

"You mean you can turn your dreams off, just like that?" Susan asked.

I said, "A little bit. A nightmare doesn't count as sleep, so I don't get any real rest. I wake up even more tired."

Michael overheard this and said, "But that's so inef*fic*ient!"

He told me of how his real life and his dream life are becoming pretty much the same. "I *must* come up with a new word for what it is that goes on inside my head at night. The delineation between awakeness and asleepness is now marginal. It's more like I'm running 'test scenarios' in my head at night—like RAND Corporation military simulations."

Count on Michael to find a way to be productive, even while sleeping.

E-mail from Abe:

Fast food for thought: Do you know that if you feed catfish (America's favorite bottom feeder) nothing but leftover grain mash they endup becoming white-meat filet units with no discernible flavor (marine or otherwise) of their own? Thus they beocome whatever coating you apply to them (i.e. Cajun, xesty cheddar, tangy ranch) They're the most postmodern creatiures on earth... metaphores for characters on Merlrose Place...or for coders with NO LIFE.

Found out what bollocks means, from a Net user at a university in Bristol. Those Brits are a cheeky lot! It means, "balls"!

FRIDAY

Abe e-mailed from Redmond. He finally fessed up to something that I've known a long time—that nobody really *knows* where the Silicon Valley is—or *what* it is. Abe grew up in Rochester and never came west until Microsoft.

My reply:

Silicon Valley

Where/what is it?
Its a backward J-shaped strand of cities, starting at the
south of San Francisco and looping down the bay, east of
San Jose: San Mateo, Foster City, Belmont, San Carlos,
Redwood City, Menlo Park, Palo Alto, Los Altos, Mountain
View, Cupertino, Sunnyvale, Saratoga, Campbell, Los
Gatos, Santa Clara, San Jose, Milpitas and Fremont. I used
a map for this.

They dont actually MANUFACTURE much by way of silicon
here anymore...the silicon chip factories are mostly a
thing of the past...it's no longer a cost effective thing to
do. Chips are printed and etched here but the DIRTY stuff
is offshored. *CLEAN* Intellectual properties are created
here now, insted.

Palo Alto:

Population: 55,900
Size: 25.9 square miles

I used to live here when Iwent to Stanford, so I know it pretty well.

Palo Alto is half bedroom suburb, half futuristic 1970s science fiction movies starrring Charlton Heston. It has lush trees, relatively fear-free schools, and only a few malls. Its real estate was the first in America to hyperinflate, back in the 1970s.

The *BIG* thing about Palo Alto is that, as a city, it designs tons of incredibly powerful and scary shit inside its science parks, which are EVERYWHERE.

The science parks are these clean boxes set atop eerie, beatifully maintained lawns that have never felt the crush of a football. There's this senssation that something weirds going on, but you can't articulate it, because the weirdness is 9too deep.

Once you leave the Camino Real, the main strip, the city becomes deadly quiet, exept for the occasionnal BMW, Honda or truck carrying 50-foot lengths of PVC tubing encasement for optical fibers.

I broke down and asked Dad today, "Dad, what exactly are you doing for Michael?" and he said, "Well, Daniel, I haven't really signed a nondisclosure form on the subject, but I *did* promise Michael I'd keep it top secret until it was time to reveal."

Gee, thanks.

Susan and Ethan are actually united on an issue—a local crusade against leaf blowers—the gas-fired kind. The noise from them is, I have to agree, something shocking. They phoned Palo Alto City Hall and got some poor civil servant on the line and harangued them. Ethan screamed, "After a certain point, decibels turn into BTUs. We're *melting* here." Susan phoned up and screamed, "Is Palo Alto Spanish for leaf blower? Ban these things NOW!"

It's fun to watch your friends get random. Especially when they're ragging on something that's a direct metaphor for their personalities.

I have noticed that on TV, all of these "moments" are sponsored by corporations, as in, *"This touchdown was brought to you by the brewers of Bud Lite,"* or *"This nostalgia flashback was brought to you by the proud makers of Kraft's family of fine foods."*

I told Karla, "I'm no sci-fi buff, but doesn't this seem like a dangerous way to be messing with the structure of time—allowing the corporate realm to invade the private?

Karla told me about how the city of Atlanta was tampering with the idea of naming streets after corporations in return for paying for the maintenance of infrastructure: "Folgers Avenue; Royal Jordanian Airlines Boulevard; Tru-Valu Road."

"Well," I said, "streets have to get names *somehow*. The surnames Smith, Brown, and Johnson probably looked pretty weird when they first started, too."

Karla said, "I think that in the future, clocks won't say three o'clock anymore. They'll just get right to the point and call three o'clock, 'Pepsi.'"

During tonight's massage lesson, Karla said, "Remember living in that enormous furniture-free rancher up in Redmond with all the rain clouds and everything? It feels like a long time ago. I sort of miss it."

I said nothing. I don't miss it. I prefer the chaos of *here* to the predictability of . . . *there*.

My body felt like overcooked spaghetti after tonight's session. *Yeah!*

I tried Ethan's theory about copy-and-pasting. I was mesmerized by the results—think and grow rich:

money money money money money money money money money money
money money money money money money money money money money
money money money money money money money money money money
money money money money money money money money money money
money money money money money money money money money money
money money money money money money money money money money
money money money money money money money money money money
money money money money money money money money money money
money money money money money money money money money money
money money money money money money money money money money
money money money money money money money money money money
money money money money money money money money money money
money money money money money money money money money money
money money money money money money money money money money
money money money money money money money money money money
money money money money money money money money money money
money money money money money money money money money money
money money money money money money money money money money
money money money money money money money money money money
money money money money money money money money money money
money money money money money money money money money money
money money money money money money money money money money
money money money money money money money money money money
money money money money money money money money money money
money money money money money money money money money money
money money money money money money money money money money
money money money money money money money money money money
money money money money money money money money money money
money money money money money money money money money money
money money money money money money money money money money
money money money money money money money money money money
money money money money money money money money money money
money money money money money money money money money money
money money money money money money money money money money
money money money money money money money money money money
money money money money money money money money money money
money money money money money money money money money money

money money money money money money money money money money
money money money money money money money money money money
money money money money money money money money money money
money money money money money money money money money money
money money money money money money money money money money
money money money money money money money money money money
money money money money money money money money money money
money money money money money money money money money money
money money money money money money money money money money
money money money money money money money money money money
money money money money money money money money money money
money money money money money money money money money money
money money money money money money money money money money
money money money money money money money money money money
money money money money money money money money money money
money money money money money money money money money money
money money money money money money money money money money
money money money money money money money money money money
money money money money money money money money money money
money money money money money money money money money money
money money money money money money money money money money
money money money money money money money money money money
money money money money money money money money money money
money money money money money money money money money money
money money money money money money money money money money
money money money money money money money money money money
money money money money money money money money money money
money money money money money money money money money money
money money money money money money money money money money
money money money money money money money money money money
money money money money money money money money money money
money money money money money money money money money money
money money money money money money money money money money
money money money money money money money money money money
money money money money money money money money money money
money money money money money money money money money money
money money money money money money money money money money
money money money money money money money money money money
money money money money money money money money money money
money money money money money money money money money money
money money money money money money money money money money

I stared at an entire screen full of these words and they dissolved and lost their meaning, the way words do when you repeat them over and over—the way *anything* loses meaning when context is removed—the way we can quickly enter the world of the immaterial using the simplest of devices, like multiplication.

SATURDAY

Poor or not, life has become coding madness all over again—except *this* time we're killing ourselves for our*selves*, instead of some huge company to whom we might as well be interchangeable bloodless PlaySkool figurine units. We began coding the day after we arrived. Michael's code is elegant stuff—really fun to tweak. And there's certainly lots *of* it. No shortage of work here. And there's so much *planning*, and we all have our milestone charts pasted up on our booth walls.

And once again, work is providing us with a comforting sense of normalcy—living and working inside of coding's predictably segmented time/space. Simply grinding away at something makes life feel stable, even though the external particulars of life (like our paychecks, our office, and so forth) are, at best, random.

Bug has surprised us with his untapped talent for generating gaming ideas and coding short cuts. Ethan called him a Burgess Shale of untried ideas. He's blossoming—at 32!

Michael has an office more or less to himself, behind the bar, and walled off with sound baffles. He shares it with Ethan, who visits only twice a day for "face-time": first to talk with Michael in the morning—and then once in the afternoon for a wrap-up. The downside of a closed door office is the overaccumulation of dead skin particles. With Ethan's dandruff, the floor looks like Vail, Colorado.

Not infrequently, Michael locks himself inside and geeks out on code. We call this bungee-coding. He always does his best work when he really geeks out. Nobody's offended—it's the way he is.

I asked *Mom* what she knew of Dad's work with Michael. She said it's Top Secret, but she gave me a clue: his fingers are all red and sore at night.

"Don't worry about it, Dan, he's happy, and so as long as the Feds aren't called in, let him be." So much for curiosity.

I tried looking at Mom's rock collection today. They continue to perplex me. Beauty is absolutely in the eye of the beholder.

Todd broke the 400-pound mark on the bench press today and celebrated by making protein drinks for everybody, but they had a rotting protein odor. We pretended to enjoy them, then formed tag teams running to the laundry sink to dump them.

I looked at Dad's hands and they are indeed all chafed and red.

Susan's dating some guy from Intel, but I don't think it's going to work, because Intel's corporate culture is so weird.

"They're like Borgs," says Susan. "They have one mind. They're like this sci-fi movie I once saw where if one child in a village learned something, all the other children learned it simultaneously. It's a hive mind. You get the feeling there's a sub-audible tape playing that says, *resistance is futile . . . you WILL assimilate . . .*" And then Susan got thoughtful and said, "The more I think about it, it's actually like Microsoft. In fact all huge tech firms are like Microsoft."

Went out for a drink with Ethan at the Empire Tap Room on Emerson Street. He said, "There is no center to the Valley in any real sense of the word. There is no one watching; it's pretty, but it's a vacuum; a kingdom of a thousand princes but no kings."

I know what he's talking about—the deficit of visionaries—the center-less *boredom* of Valley life. I mean, if I really think about it, Valley people work and sleep—work and sleep and work and sleep and somewhere along the line the dream border is blurred. It's as if there is a collective decision to disfavor a Godhead. It's not despair; they just want the Real Thing. The Beast.

And the penny pinching! The nondisclosure forms! The extreme wealth of the high-IQ'ed genetic gift baskets who won on the Punnet Square of life! I suppose this *is* the birthplace of the new postindustrial economy here amid the ghosts of apricot orchards, spinach farms, and horse ranches—here inside the science parks, industrial areas, and cool, leafy suburbs. Here, where sexy new technologies are being blueprinted, CAD'ed, engineered, imagineered, and modeled—post-machines making countless millions of people obsolete overnight.

Palo Alto is so invisible from the outside, but invisibility is invariably where one locates the ACTION.

Worked until 3:30 A.M. Breezy night. Went for a walk down La Cresta Drive. So quiet. I got to feeling meditative. I felt as though my inner self was much closer to the surface than it usually gets. It's a nice feeling. It takes quiet to get there.

The **liquid engineers** left the pool heater on too long, and at night, **chlorine** vapors rose above the plant life of the planet, and I **imagined my flesh**, being inside the pool, being warm, and protected, feeling **gravity**, but able to mock it as I floated. Would you float with me now, if I asked you, would you jump in the pool and not even bother to **strip?** Could I strip you down, remove your clothing and we would fall inside the water together?

It scares me.

I don't want to lose you. I can't imagine ever feeling this strongly about anything or anybody ever again. **This was unexpected, my soul's connection to you.** You stole my loneliness No one knows that I was wishing for you, a thief, to enter my house of autonomy, that I had locked my doors but my Windows were open, hoping, but not believing, **you** would enter.

SUNDAY

Michael made us attend: "*Interactive Multimedia, Product Design, and the Year 2000.*" It was at a Hyatt or something down in San Jose. Michael wanted us to have "a good overview of the industry." We barely made it through the event.

The day after the seminar, I might add, Michael bought us all San Jose Sharks inflatable toys as penance. (The Sharks are *huge* here. I think I'm already beginning to bond with them.) If my ship comes in this year, I'm going to buy season's tickets for next year's games. Can't wait for the season.

I e-mailed my notes to Abe.

"29 Steps: My Trip
to the
Interactive Multimedia Seminar "
by Daniel Underwood

1)
Some people believe that the suspension of disbelief is destroyed by interactivity.

2)
The people who attend "Multimedia Seminars" aren't the same people who design games. Their shirts are ironed, they carry unscuffed leather attaché cases, they're infinitely earnest and they look like they work for Prudential-Bache and Kidder-Peabody. These suits are all bluffing now, but soon enough they'll "get it" and they will become "visionaries."

3)
Narratives (stories) traditionally come to a definite end (unlike life); that's why we like movies and literature—for that sense of <u>closure</u>—because they <u>end</u>.

4)

The stakes for multimedia *may* actually turn out to be embarrassingly small in the short run—like Milton Bradley, Parker Brothers, or Hasbro cranking out board game versions of *The Partridge Family*, *The Banana Splits,* and *Zoom.*

5)

With interactivity, one tries to give "the illusion of authorship" to people who couldn't otherwise author.

Thought: maybe the need to be told stories is like the need to have sex. If you want to hear a story, you want to hear a story—you want to be passive and sit back around the fire and listen. You don't want to write the story yourself.

6)

This *sick* thing just happened: I had this moment when I looked up and everyone had been picking at the baby zits on their foreheads and everybody's forehead was bleeding! It was like stigmata. So gross. Even Karla.

7)

"There's an endemic inability in the software industry to estimate the amount of time required for a software project." (*TRUE*!)

8)

Networked games, like where you have one person playing against another, are hot because you don't have to waste development dollars creating artificial intelligence. Players provide free AI.

9)

The 8 Models of Interactivity (as far as I can see)
i) The Arcade model
Like Terminator: kill or be killed.

ii) The Coffee Table Book model
Enter anywhere/leave anywhere; pointless in the end; zero replayability factor.

iii) The Universe Creation model
I built you and I can crush you.

iv) The Binary Tree model
Limited number of options; reads from left to right; tightly controlled mini-dramas.

v) The Pick-a-Path model
Does our hero smooch with Heather Locklear, or not—*you* decide! Expensive. Unproven entertainment value. Audiences don't pay money to *work*.

vi) RPGs (Role-Playing Games)
For adolescents: half-formed personalities roaming (in packs) in search of identity.

vii) The Agatha Christie model
A puzzle is to be solved using levels, clues, chases, and exploration.

viii) Experience Simulation models
Flight simulators, sport games.

10)
I wonder if we oversentimentalize the power of books.

11)
Studios in Hollywood are trying to sucker in writers by burying multimedia rights into the boilerplate of contracts. It's intellectual gill-netting. They say they've "always been doing it historically" . . . assuming "since July" means historically.

12)
The extraordinary cost of producing multimedia games theoretically is supposed to exclude little companies from entering the market, but it's the little companies, I'm noticing, that are coming up with all of the "hits." Hope for *Oop!*.

13)
Karla and I met this cool-looking woman at lunch, Irene, and so we had coffee with her before the afternoon session began. It turns out she's a makeup artist for multimedia movies, and she wants to get into production herself. Karla said, "Gee, you look really tired," and she said, "Oh—I've been working double shifts every day for two weeks."

So I asked her, "What kind of things are people filming for multimedia games?" and she said, "It's always the same . . . Sir Lancelot, Knights of the Round Table, thrones, chalices, damsels. Can't somebody come up with something new? My Prince Arthur wig is getting all tired-looking."

I suggested she use a Marilyn Monroe wig.

14)
Ideally in a game you have hardheaded adventures, but at the end you get a glimpse of the supernatural.

15)
In Los Angeles everyone's writing a screenplay. In New York everyone's writing a novel. In San Francisco, everyone's developing a multimedia product.

16)
There's a different mental construction in operation when you're playing tennis as opposed to when you're reading a book. With adrenaline-based competitive sports,

the thought mode is: *"I want to kill this fucker."* It's the spirit of testing yourself; accomplishment. You are *gripped*. <u>Suspension of disbelief is not an issue.</u>

17)

A multimedia product has to deliver $1 per hour's worth of entertainment or you'll get slagged by word-of-mouth.

18)

The great Atari gaming collapse of 1982 (**sigh** I remember it well).

19)

Games are about providing control for nine year olds . . . "the bigger and neater the entity I can control, the better."

20)

Multimedia has become a "packaged goods" industry now. The box copy is more important than the experience. But how do you write cool sexy box copy for a game like Tetris? You can't.

21)

Cool term: "<u>Manseconds</u>": (Ergonomic unit of measurement applied to keyboards, joysticks).

22)

"<u>Embedded intelligence</u>": (Intelligence buried in the nooks and crannies of code and storyboard design).

23)

Last year at a Christmas party up in Seattle, there were all these little kids—all highly sugared and on the brink of hysteria—but instead of screaming, they sat complacently by the TV playing SEGA games. The games were like "Child Sedation Devices." It was spooky.

Susan was there. She said, "Just think, in 50 years these same kids will be sitting at the switches of our life-support systems figuring out a way to play a game by biofeedbacking our failing EKGs. Me, I seem to remember that when I was younger, overly sugared brats were sent down into the basement to fend for themselves, like *Lord of the Flies*."

24)

How will games progress as 30somethings turn into 50somethings? (*"Cardigan: The Adventure"*)

25)

Flight Simulation games are actually out-of-body experience emulators. There must be all of these people everywhere on earth right now, waiting for a miracle, waiting to be pulled out of themselves, eager for just the smallest sign that there is something finer or larger or miraculous about our existence than we had supposed.

26)

"The replayability problem" (Engineering a desire for repetition).

27)

I think "van art" and Yes album covers were the biggest influence in game design.

28)

I wonder if I've missed the boat on CD-ROM interactive—if I'm too old. The big companies are zeroing in on the 10-year-olds. I think you only ever truly feel comfortable with the level of digitization that was normal for you from the age of five to fifteen. I mean sure, *I* can make new games *workable*, but it won't be a kick the way Tetris was. Or will it?

29)

In the end, multimedia interactive won't resemble literature so much as sports.

MONDAY

Random moment earlier tonight: out of the blue Todd asked everyone in the Habitrail 2, "When they make processed cheese slices that are only 80 percent milk, what's the *remaining* 20 percent made from?"

Michael replied *instantly*, "Why, nonmilk additives, of course."

Today we learned that Bug had a piece of shareware on his computer that installs wood paneling all over your Macintosh desktop—and he didn't even tell us! Grudgingly he gave us a download. "It's called *share*ware, Bug, not *hogware*."

So now we all have digitized wood paneling on our desktops. The rumpus room dream lives on inside our computer world.

Abe-mail:

I am going to RANT today. 2 things:
1)
The US Dollar is the working currency not only of the domestic econimy, but of nearly every other country on earth (minus Europe and Japan). That must count for somethin. It's obviously grossly undervalued. Why dows the Federal Reserve keep the value so low?

(*insert conspiracy theory here*)

And WHATS WITH THESE MUTUAL FUNDS AND PENSION FUNDS? I REFUSE to believe that money put into a bank in 1956 is *still* money in 1994.

1956 money may still techinically be "there" (wherever "there" is) – but it's undead money. It's sick. Evil.

I can't believe that *I*, of all people, am saying this, but there's soemthing obscene about money that sits inside a bank and collects interest for decades. "It;s hard at work," we're told . . .

OH RIGHT!

No, I think money is due for some sort of collapse. People are going to realixe that money has a half-life – a decade or so? and then it becomes perverse and random. Expecting a pension kids? Ha hah ha!

I'm feeling like Bug today.

2)
> Easter egg
> platform
> surfing
> frontier
> garden
> jukebox
> net
> dirty linen
> pipeline
> lassooo
> highway

We will have soon fully entered an era where we have creatted a computer metaphor for EVERY thing that exists in the real world.

Actually when you think about it , *everything* can be a metaphor for *anything*.

To quote YOU, Daniel: "I mean, If you realy think about it."

Abe has a friend in research who's working on "metaphor-backwards" development of software products. That is, thinking of a real-world object with no cyber equivalent, and then figuring out what that cyber equivalent should be. Abe's worried because at the moment he's working on "gun."

Thought: sometimes you accidentally input an extra digit into the year: i.e., 19993 and you add 18,000 years on to *now*, and you realize that the year 19993 will one day exist and that time is a scary thing, indeed.

Actually, I've noticed recently that conversations always seem to reach the point where everybody says they don't have any *time* anymore. How can time just . . . *disappear*? Early this morning I told this to Karla as we were waking up and she said she's noticed this, too.

She also said that everybody's beginning to look the same these days—"Everybody looks so Gappy and identical." She considered this for a second. "Everybody looks the same nowadays because nobody has the *time* to differentiate themselves—or to even shop."

She paused and looked up at the ceiling. "Your mother doesn't like me."

"How can you get so random out of nowhere? Of course she does."

"No. She doesn't. She thinks I'm a hick."

(Oh *God*—not this stupid stuff again.) "You two never talk, so how can you even *tell?*"

"So you *admit* she doesn't like me?"

"No!"

"We have to do something together. We have no shared experiences or memories."

"Wait a second—don't *I* count?"

"Maybe she sees me as stealing you."

"Mom?"

"Let's arrange a lunch. We've been here how long? And we've never even had a lunch out together."

"Lunch? That's not much."

"Memories have to begin somewhere."

Now that I think about it, Mom never comes over to our work area. Ever. And the two of them never really do chat. It occurs to me that I *should* have noticed, and I realize that I'm worried about it.

A crisis in my new-and-improved life.

We shot Nerf darts (Jarts) for a few hours this afternoon down in the backyard to allow the sunlight to reset our circadian rhythms. We drank Napa Valley Cabernet like we were Cary Grant and made Klingon jokes. We used Dad's Soviet binoculars to inspect the enormous blue "Jell-O cube" down in the Valley below—a.k.a. the Air Force Satellite Control Facility, at Onizuka Air Force Base in Sunnyvale.

A citrus tree was blossoming outside the house; the air was lemony fresh and smelled like an expensive hotel's lobby.

Ethan was, as usual, in a beautiful suit, like one of those suntanned Academy Awards guys. (But again, his dandruff!) He greeted us with, "Good afternoooon, my precious content delivery system."

We asked Ethan if he wanted to throw Jarts with us, but he said, "Love to, kids, but antidepressants make me photosensitive. Sunlight kills me. My retinas'll get etched like a microchip. You kids keep on playing. Sunlight is *good* for productivity." He and Dad then went into the kitchen to discuss psychopharmacology while Mom made us a tray of Dagwood sandwiches.

Ethan told me something really cool. He said that the reason lion tamers brandish chairs while cracking the whip is because the lions are mesmerized by all four points of the chairs' legs, but never all of them at the same time—their attention is continually distracted, and hence they are subdued.

Ethan talks so "big-time." I've never heard people talk this way before. Susan says he talks like characters in a miniseries.

I agree with Susan that Ethan is annoying, but it's hard to peg exactly why—there are all these little things that he does that just add up to ANNOYING. When I really think about it, I realize that if someone else did those things they probably wouldn't annoy me. It's just the way he *is*, all smarmy and fake genuine. Like he's always coming into the office and going up to me and saying, "How *are* you" in this concerned voice while looking deep into my eyes. *Retch.* Like he cares. And when I say, "Fine," he squeezes my shoulder and says, "No, really, how *are* you?" as though I wasn't really being honest. "I *know* you've been working hard." I never know what to say so I always just look back at my screen and keep on coding.

Another annoying thing he does is ask you something about what you're working on, and just as you start really talking about it, he takes over and somehow ties it into an anecdote about himself. Like I was telling him about the problems we were having deciding whether or not *Oop!* will have sounds or not, and how we're trying to calculate the extra memory space sound would occupy and whether or not having sounds adds enough value to justify the extra work. It was like Ethan was just waiting for a place where he could break in. He said, "Added value. What an arbitrary concept, since it's different for every person." He then launched into this story of holiday-ing in Bali, staying in little shacks at this super-resort called Amand-something which cost $400 a night which even had little slaves to do his bid-ding. In his mind it tied into the notion of "value-adding," but my question about sound and memory was lost.

I sure wish we had that Bali money back now.

One must grudgingly admit Ethan *does* seem to know a good deal about Valley business. Like many people in computers and gaming, he never went to college. He designed a game that sold millions in the Pong era, became a millionaire, went bust with Atari, became a millionaire again in Reagan's '80s with a SEGA-based something-or-other, went bust again, and now I guess he's going to become a multimillionaire in the Multimedia '90s.

His tech credentials are good, too. Somewhere amidst all the money he *did* manage to squeak in work with Xerox's El Segundo Lab and TRW in Redondo Beach.

I've never seen a stock get more attention than 3DO. Everybody's wonder-ing if they should invest in it. I mean, if we had money to invest. I must remember to drive by their parking lot some Sunday afternoon.

Karla asked Mom out to lunch and Mom balked at first—"I don't know how much time the Library can spare me for." That kind of thing. I mean, if someone wants to have lunch with you, they simply *don't* make pseudo-excuses like that.

But Karla wore her down, like someone who's been to Anthony Robbins lectures. The three of us are going to have lunch later this week, but I hope it isn't a grudge match.

I asked Michael what he wanted for his 25th birthday next week. His message flashed onto my screen at 2:40 A.M., from his office where he was working with the door shut:

>**Birthday:**
I want one of those keys you win in video games, that allows you to blast through walls and reach the next level — to get to *the other side*.

This is a particularly long message for Michael whose e-mail tends to be about three words long, normally. A carriage return, punctuation marks and everything!

Now that I've been thinking about it, I'm not sure what exactly *Oop!*'s money structure *is*. Wouldn't it be a sick joke if I got into something without understanding the financial underpinnings . . . if I hadn't even bothered to ask the questions I'm supposed to ask because I've never had to ask them before because I'd been coddled to death by benefits at Microsoft? *Naaaaah* . . .

There was a windstorm last night and a bunch of branches blew off the eucalyptus tree beside the garage. Around sunset Bug, Karla, and I pretended we were a trio of evil Finnish masseuses named Oola, swatting naughty victims with much vim. I've got mentholated scratches all over my arms.

Karla is preparing a list of subjects to discuss at lunch with Mom. I said, "Karla, this is a lunch, not a *meeting*." She wants to make a good impression so badly. I am surprised by how much that pleases me.

Michael is furious at Todd for taping over a VHS cassette of *Oop!* graphic animation that Michael had done as a demo for potential investors. Todd replaced it with *The Best of Hockey Fights III*.

Todd and Susan have the flu, so I guess we're all doomed for it now. And Ethan's been acting weird all week. Our bank account must be running on fumes again.

**unraveled brown
cassette tape
on the freeway**

Staples   **PIN number**
CK-one   **basketball hoop**

If we were machines, we'd

have the gift of being eternal and I want you to understand

TUESDAY

Everybody's flu-ridden today except for Ethan and me. Ethan asked me to accompany him up to Electronic Arts in San Mateo, and then down to a VC meeting out at the Venture Capital mall at the corner of the 280 and Sand Hill Road—in his ruby red Ferrari.

"The Ferrari is like a rite of passage here for new money. You buy one at 26, get it out of your system, flip it for a gray Lexus or Infiniti, and then you drive gray sedans the rest of your life. I keep mine because I can't afford anything else at the moment, and I can't afford the capital gains taxes if I sold it. I should get one of those 'DON'T LAUGH: AT LEAST IT'S PAID FOR' bumper stickers. Nobody would appreciate the irony that I'm holding on by my teeth."

We roared south past the rolling hills that oozed trees and fog. I looked down at the palm of my hand, slapped it, and said, "Hey, Ethan—I'm looking at my sympathy-o-meter, and the needle isn't moving."

"It's the *Valley*, pal—think *sideways*. This is the Lexus Freeway, the most scenic in America."

I told Ethan about the book on freeways I had read, Robert F. Baker's *Handbook of Highway Engineering*; Ethan in turn told me that 280—the Lexus Freeway—is also nicknamed the Mensa Freeway.

I looked in the glove compartment and there was a bottle of Maalox cherry. Ethan said, "I keep Maalox in the glove compartment of the car, and sometimes I swig it like a wino in parking lots before meetings. I once walked into this meeting with dried white Maalox powder caked on my lips and everybody thought it was coke or something. I told them it was Pixy Stix and they said, *oh, how cute*, but they still thought I was coked out. Man, if they only knew the *truth*—that a Pixy stick would burn a crater in my stomach like Mt. Saint Helens."

Then we got into a discussion about volcanoes, and the year Mt. Saint Helens erupted and that old guy who lived on top of the mountain, who was

all crotchety, and wouldn't leave, and everybody thought he was a real individual—and then he got creamed when the mountain blew. And this got me
thinking of all the people at IBM, and I got to thinking about Dad and . . .

This is my first-ever VC meeting. Ethan has attended hundreds of them
during his Valley career. Apparently, the Monday Partner's Meeting is a
Silicon Valley tradition, according to Ethan. They mostly occur up at the
venture capital "mall" at the corner of Sand Hill Road and Interstate 280.
Monday is when partners *agree to agree.* And Tuesday is when the decisions are acted upon.

Fifteen years in the business have loaned Ethan a rote tour-guidish quality. Humming up the 280, he further briefed me on the situation:

"Initial presentations are made by capital seekers. If their idea seems
promising, then there's a callback for a broader presentation—not unlike
Broadway.

"The 'VC team' by then will have run due-diligence checks—spoken
with insiders who have provided background on an idea—its suitability or
marketability—as well as checked the technical robustness of the idea.
Essentially, they must know *what is the significance or defensibility of the
technology underlying the idea?* What is the *overall viability of the idea?
What do you have that the others don't?* Is the *necessary technical acu-
men on the team?* Michael and I have been through this already. Today is
the callback.

"We passed all of the techie checks, but the VC firms aren't quite sure
about *Oop!*'s marketability. With round-one seed capital, all the risk is
ahead of you. Plus, software is a *consumer*, not a corporate business now—
it's 10,000 units off to CompUSA instead of one jumbo unit to Delta Airlines
or National Cash Register.

"This isn't good for us, because Silicon Valley firms have little or no experience with Procter & Gamble–style focus grouping, but they won't admit
it. So they pose as multimedia visionaries instead. They might as well be
slitting open a sheep and reading the entrails. It's a big exercise in chain-
yanking. Let the floor show begin!"

We arrived and got out of the car. "Ethan, here—some leaves have
fallen on your shoulder." I snowplowed away drifts of dandruff from his
suit. "There," I said, "all set."

Condensed Version . . .

Venture Capital Meeting (My First [and Last])

1)
Me:
(I'm dressed like an outpatient; these VC people are dressed like they're about to whisper a deal into David Geffen's left ear. Why didn't Ethan <u>dress</u> me properly? He began flaking the moment we walked in the doorway. His shoulders!)
"Hello."

2)
VC Woman with Barbra-Streisand-in-Concert Hairdo:
"Investors want to see a committed, marketing-sensitive visionary at the product's helm." (Who the heck is that . . . Michael? Marketing Sensitive?)

3)
Me:
(Nodding and seeming interested)
"Hmmm . . . ."

4)
A different VC with an eerie resemblance to Barry Diller:
"One of the main reasons people start companies is to control their environment and the people they work with."
Michael nods. Ethan agrees.

5)
Richie Rich Boomersomething with loud Hermès tie:
silence

6)
Barbra:
(earnestly)
"Is there—an opening for world class leadership in this product's area?"

7)
Barry:

"Start-ups appeal either to jaded cynics—because they know the way things really work—or to the totally naïve—because they don't. Which are you?"

8)
Ethan:

"We're that irreducible 5 percent of talented people—our culture's pearl divers."

9)
Young VC guy, who would be the same age as Rosemary's Baby:

"You'll need more than lots of pearl divers . . ." (smug titters) "You need focus groups. People surprise you. They tell you that what you thought was worth $99 is only worth $29."

10)
Barry:

Sugarishly: "We have to function as parents to new companies who are in the process of growing up."

11)
Hermès tie:

more silence

12)
Ethan:

"That's where *I* come in." (give prisoner last cigarette)

13)
Ethan:

(now on a roll)

"VC was in a lull until spring of 1992, and then came" [awed pause] "*convergence*. Unless there's a breakthrough hit, by 1997, multimedia is going to be a leper industry. We have the missing killer app right here."

14)
Barbra:
"Yes, but as a VC firm we like to feel we're *beyond* 'the hit thing' now. In general, we don't like small, technology-oriented companies. There's nothing the world wants as little as a new technology company. If you give a company $2 million, they'll spend it all and never ship a profitable product."

15)
Hermès tie:
noise of his silence equals noise of his tie

16)
Rosemary's Baby:
"With a round-one seed, all of the risk is ahead of you."

17)
Barry:
"Frankly, we're not totally convinced you have a crew that can market your product, that is, should it even make it past beta."

18)
Me:
(Detached metaphysical perspective: as we speak, the Stanford Linear Accelerator, a quarter of a mile south, running underneath the Mensa Freeway, is quietly blowing up atoms into quarks and bosons and leptons and Fruity Pebbles.) "Hmmm."

19)
Ethan:
"Frankly," (*Oooh—everybody's trying to compete with each other through overuse of the word* frank) "I have brought four products to market myself. Four very successful products. (Unspoken sentiment hangs in the air like dying fart: *"Yeah, but your companies all tanked within a year."*) "Our staff is so dedicated to the project they are working without pay until an alpha version is ready."

20)
Me:
(Inside thought balloon above my head as Ethan looks at me and gave me this big *You're-fucked-and-you-have-no-choice* smile, in front of all these suits): "What do you mean working without pay?"

21)
Me:
(Out loud)
"We have to have a product that works first, and we *can* take care of the business side, with your help . . ." (The *one* thing I say and it's obsequious and stupid. <u>Q</u>: Do I feel like a liability? <u>A</u>: Yes.)

22)
Hermès Tie:
"We'd like to help you . . . *mwah mwah mwah (Charlie Brown's Teacher noise)* . . . no infrastructure . . . *mwah mwah mwah* . . . no corporate plan for growth . . . *mwah mwah mwah.* . . ." (Pull trap door)

23)
Rosemary's Baby:
(Parting shot to me, in confidence, after the others have left—like he's really helping us out as he discreetly escorts me toward the Mission oak doorway):
"You probably wouldn't want to work for a VC-funded firm because in the end they'll just crack the whip and force you to ship, even if it's not entirely full-featured."

24)
Suits:
(I paraphrase)
"Please fuck off and die."

25)
Ethan:
"Dinner, dance, and a kiss at the door. So much for meeting number 216. Well, pal, there's a saying down in these parts: *twenty-four hours heals all wounds.*"

26)
FIN

I asked Ethan in the Ferrari on the way back to the office, "What do you mean we're working without pay?" and he said, "Well, technically, *yes*."

I flipped out: *"Yes ?!"*

Then he said, "Well, technically, *no*."

"Ethan, what the fuck is going on?" I asked.

"Don't be so petty bourgeois, Dan. Look at the big picture."

The Ferrari passed about eight cars in one fell swoop. I didn't want to look petty. "I'm *not* petty, Ethan, " I said.

"And I *am*?"

"That's not the issue."

"Stop being so linear about money. Be horizontal. It's all cool."

I asked Mom what she thought of Karla and she said she thought she was "delightful." Sounded a bit forced.

No flu symptoms yet.

WEDNESDAY

Lunch today.

Karla was draggy with the flu, but she forced herself to come. She, Mom, and I went to lunch at the Empire Grill and Tap Room. As we entered, there were two seeing-eye dogs and two blind masters standing near to each other. Within seconds, Mom was down on the floor chatting with the dogs. She then interrogated the dogs' owners: "Do you two hang around together a lot? Do your dogs get to visit each other? They would make good company for each other, you know." (My mother the matchmaker.)

The two owners laughed and said, "I should think so—we're married."

Mom exclaimed, "Oh—how wonderful—they can discuss their jobs with each other!" (Mom's a true Silicon Valley girl—she grew up here, down in Sunnyvale.) "Oh my, you *must* meet Misty—" and she raced out to the car to fetch Misty, and the three dogs were soon sniffing each other.

I was aching to get to lunch, but Mom and the two blind people were deep in DogTalk. I went out to Mac's and bought a copy of the *San Jose Mercury News*. When I returned they were still there, laughing. They exchanged cards, and afterward I asked Mom what they were laughing about, and she said, "We tried to think of the worst seeing-eye breed imaginable and we came up with the idea of the 'seeing-eye whippet,' prancing into traffic . . . isn't that a riot? Perhaps you could make a video game out of it, like that Pong game that was so much fun that Christmas years ago."

Mom, like most people her age, will know Pong as their sole video game experience. It's tragic.

At lunch, Mom preempted all other conversation starts by discussing Michael. "Sometimes I think that Michael is ummm—*autistic*." She blushed. "Oh, of course, what I mean to say is—well—have *you* noticed?"

"Michael's not like other people," I said. "He goes off into his own world—for days at a time sometime. A few months ago he locked himself into his office and we had to slide food under his door. And so he stopped eating any food that couldn't be slipped underneath a door."

"Oh, so that explains the Kraft cheese slices. Carton-loads."

Karla, still low energy from the flu, broke in: "You know, Mrs. Underwood, I think *all* tech people are slightly autistic. Have you ever heard about *dyspraxia*? Michael is an elective mute."

"No."

"Dyspraxia's like this: say I asked you to give me that newspaper. There's no reason on earth why you couldn't. But if you had dyspraxia, then you'd be blocked and you'd just sit there frozen. Dyspraxia is the condition where you become incapable of initiating an action."

"Then every*body* is dyspraxic, dear. It's called procrastination."

"Exactly. It's just that geeks are slightly more so than most people. Autism's a good way of focusing out the world to exclude everything but the work at hand."

I added that Michael was also the opposite of a dyspraxic, too. "If he has an idea, he acts on it. But he has to put the idea into action *immediately*— like this company—or with an elegant strip of code. He's a blend of the two extremes."

Karla added, "The doors in Michael's brain are wide open to certain things, while simultaneously nailed shut to all others. And we must admit, he *does* get things done. He has no brakes on certain topics. He's a true techie geek."

Mom looked askance.

I said, "You *can* say geeks now, Mom."

"Yes, well, you geeks are an odd blend of doors and brakes."

The discussion changed to the (groan) information superhighway. "Do you think libraries are going to become obsolete?" she said stirring her coffee and fearing for her job. "Books?"

Karla lapsed into a discussion of the Dewey decimal system and the Library of Congress cataloging system, which was numbing to say the least. Mom found herself begrudgingly getting very into the discussion of cataloging. Librarians love order, logic, and linearity.

In the end lunch was like a balloon with not enough helium in it to float—not enough helium in it to even puff it up, really. I think the dynamic of Mom and Karla's relationship has been set. At least they don't *hate* each other. Truthfully, I'm a little worried . . . why is Mom being like this?

Later on, I found myself being the only person working in the office. It was so strange, and I can't remember the last time this happened. Actually, I wasn't *totally* alone: Look and Feel were scurrying about inside their Habitrail. But other than that, I was alone. It was odd to be the only person in the office. I wished I could go to Kinko's and photocopy myself . . . be more productive.

Karla found this allergy medicine I've been taking and said, "*This* is what's been causing your nightmares." She could be right—I hope she is. I'm going to stop as of today.

THURSDAY

No nightmares last night.

FRIDAY

Again, no nightmares. Problem solved?

Misty came into our work space and barked at Look and Feel. Gerbils really stink. I'll be glad if we ever get out of this space.

SATURDAY

Karla and I were watching cartoons, and that old Warner Brothers cartoon came on with the frog that's buried in cement in the 1920s and comes alive and sings and dances, but only in front of one person. Karla looked at it and said, "That's me around your mother. I sit around and say '*ribbet*' around her, but I'm the dancing, singing frog around you."

Everyone is getting a cold and sounds nasal and scary. Todd said, "Man, you don't want to see the stuff coming out of my nose into the Kleenex. Eggs Benedict."

Thanks, Todd.

Look and Feel had babies! We think there are five, pink and plump, so we're going to call them Lisa, Jazz, Classic, Point, and Click. We hope they don't get eaten by their parents. We put raw hamburger into the Habitrail tubes to keep Look and Feel away from "the kids." The Habitrail is actually rather like *Logan's Run*. Imagine gerbils with little 1970s feathered hairdos!

I was up at Ethan's frighteningly chic house tonight (all those bank cameras) and told him about the other night, when I wished I could go to Kinko's and photocopy myself. He misunderstood me. I merely wanted to increase my productivity, but he thought I was getting all cosmic and wanted to discuss the universe, and this became a cue for Ethan to commandeer the conversation into his direction, as usual.

Ethan did the "Ethan Thing" and went off on a tangent about himself. He said, "I've already photocopied myself!"

He explained: "People tend to assume that as we get older, years naturally start feeling shorter and shorter—that this is 'nature's way.' But this is crap. Maybe what's *really* happening is that we have increased the information density of our culture to the point where our perception of time has become all screwy.

"I began noticing long ago that years are beginning to shrink—that a year no longer felt like a year, and that one life was not one life anymore—that "life multiplication" was going to be necessary.

"You never heard about people 'not having lives' until about five years ago, just when all of the '80s technologies really penetrated our lives." He listed them off:

> *"VCRs*
> *tape rentals*
> *PCs*
> *modems*
> *answering machines*
> *touch tone dialing*
> *cellular phones*
> *cordless phones*
> *call screening*
> *phone cards*
> *ATMs*
> *fax machines*
> *Federal Express*
> *bar coding*
> *cable TV*
> *satellite TV*
> *CDs*
> *calculators of almost other-worldly power that are so cheap*
>   *that they practically come free with a tank of gas."*

"In the information Dark Ages, before 1976, before all of *this*, relationships and television were the only forms of entertainment available. Now we have other things. Fortunately depression runs in my family."

"*Fortunately?*" I asked.

"Absolutely, pal. I couldn't figure out a way of rigging my brain to work in parallel instead of linear mode—and then they invented Prozac and all the Prozac isomers and *kablam!*—my brain's been like an Oracle parallel processing server ever since."

"I'm not sure I get this, Ethan."

"Prozac is great—and I think it goes beyond seratonin and uptake recep-
tors and that kind of thing. I think these chemicals physically *rewire* your
brain to think in parallel. It literally converts your brain from Macintosh or
IBM into a Cray C3 or a Thinking Machines CM5. Prozac-type chemicals
don't suppress feelings—they break them down into smaller 'feeling units,'
which are more quickly computationally processed by the new, parallel
brain."

"I think I need a second to digest this, Eth—"

"I *don't*. Linear thinking is out. Parallel is in."

"Explain to me more clearly—*how* does whatever you take affect your
time?"

"I remember once when I was majorly depressed for, like, six months.
When it ended, I felt like I had to make up for those six 'lost' months. Man,
depression *sucks*. So my logic is, as long as I'm not bummed, I'm not wast-
ing time. So I make sure I'm never bummed." He seemed quite happy to be
telling his theory.

"You know how when somebody says, 'Remember that party at the
beach last year?' and you say, 'Oh God, was that last *year*? It feels like last
month'? If I'm going to live a year, I want my whole year's worth of year. I
don't want it feeling like only one month. Everything I do is an attempt to
make time 'feel' like time again—to make it *feel* longer. I get my time in
bulk."

I left Ethan's thoroughly depressed, and not sure whether I still disliked
Ethan or just felt sorry for him. I e-mailed Abe with a synopsis of Ethan's
time theory, and he was online and answered me right away:

>**What would happen if TV caracters continued their theo-
retical lives in our linear time . . . Bob and Emily Hartley, in
their early 70s now, would be living in their brown apartment, wrinkled and childless. Or Mary Tyler Moore, now
60... surely bitter, alone, sterile . . .**

Prozac!

SpaghettiOs   **What's My Line**
Aspirin   **Jell-O simulator**
invasion   **Russian winter**

Q: What animal would you be if you could be an animal?

A: *You already are an animal*

SUNDAY

Ethan phoned me and asked me to come over to San Carlos. When I arrived, he was on a cordless phone in his kitchen, leaving me in his ultra-monitored living room reading his copies of *Cellular Buyer's Guide, Dr. Dobbs Journal, LAN Times*—and *Game Pro (#1 Video Game Magazine)*.

He came out of the kitchen wearing an Intel T-shirt—rare, as I've never seen him in anything but a shirt and tie in all the time I've known him. He was wearing jeans, too. "It's Friday—'jeans day,' pal," he said.

He then sat down on the couch beside me and there was this silence as he shuffled his coffee table magazines back into geometric orderliness after my perusal, and then he sat back on the white leather with his arm behind my back.

I pointed out that his copy of *Binary File Transfer Monthly* was possibly the most boring document I'd ever seen in my life. He said, "Well, what if it were *actually* a copy of *Penthouse Forum* letters encrypted as something so dull and opaque, that nobody would realize that it was something else. Imagine an encryption system that could reconfigure the words, *'I am a sophomore at a small midwestern college'* into *'Does not conform to ITCU Convention specifications for frequency ranges.'*" It'd be the biggest stroke of encryption genius since the U.S. military used Navajo Indians to speak freely over the radio about top secret operations."

He then became quiet and still, and the presence of his arm behind me was eerily warm. I stiffened my posture. The scenario felt so charged—the whole situation. I felt like a Yankee schoolteacher on a Hollywood casting couch. He said to me, "I have something important I have to ask of you, pal," and I thought, "Oh God—here it is . . . I'm going to get hit on."

He then removed his T-shirt, and I was trying to be cool about the situation, and I was truly freaking out as Ethan's not really my, *err*, cup o' tea. He was reading my mind and said to me, "Don't be a prig—I'm not gonna jump you, but I *am* going to ask you a favor."

"Oh?"

"Chill out, it's not *that* kind of favor." His missing T-shirt revealed a torso of average buffitude, "You can see, I'm no Todd," he said, and then he turned around, and I'm embarrassed to admit it, but I gasped. His rotation revealed his back covered in a matrix of bandages, dried blood and micropore tape, and it looked as if several soiled disposable diapers had been taped to his skin all higgledy-piggledy. "It's this . . . *these*."

I said, "Ethan, what the fuck is this all about? Did you have an accident? Jesus!"

"Accident? Who gives a shit . . . ozone . . . a bologna sandwich I ate in third grade . . . one hour too many in front of a Russian-built VDT. But it's a part of *me*, Dan . . . the damage . . . the whateverthefuck it is. It's moles gone bad. Maybe they're gone forever and, well, maybe they're not."

I was trying to look away, but he said, "That is so fucking insulting," and he jumped up and sat on the coffee table facing away from me, sticking the bandages in my face. I then looked and was mesmerized by this biomash of cotton, plastic, and body fluids barnacled to his skin. I didn't say anything.

"Dan?" he asked.

"Yeah . . ."

"You gotta remove them for me."

"Yeah?"

"There's nobody else who'll do it for me. You know that, Dan?"

"There's nobody?"

"Nobody."

I looked some more and he said, "Doc hacked 'em out of me like they were divots on the thirteenth fairway a week ago. And not one of you dumb bastards ever even bothered to ask why I was going to the dermatologist. Nobody asked and I had nobody to tell."

"Jesus, Ethan—we thought you were going to the dermatologist about your *dan*druff."

"I have dandruff?"

"It's, ummm, nothing out of the ordinary." I touched the bandages and they felt crackly, like Corn Flakes.

"You said I had dandruff?"

"Ethan. Discussing body malfunctions is like discussing salaries. You don't do it."

"Fine. Can you just remove them? They itch. They hurt."

"Yeah, of course."

He went into the kitchen and came back with a bottle of hydrogen per-oxide solution, rubbing alcohol, and old shirts cut into strips for rags. And so with him on the coffee table I removed chunk after bloody chunk, snipping away at his back and pulling scraps away, horrified at exactly how much of *him* had been removed.

We were talking. He said he can't believe how far dermatology has advanced in the past ten years. "They can practically put a small video cam-era inside your body and the doctor says to you, 'This is how your zit sees the world,' and they have a camera looking out from inside the zit."

I asked him what his prognosis was, and he said, "*Shhh*, pal—it's just the devil in me, but let's hope he's gone."

In the end, after all of the plastic, cotton, and dried blood and rags were gone, his back looked as though craters of the moon had been stitched together, violet and swollen. I used a small hair dryer and dried off the stitches, and when I turned off the hair dryer, the noise was somehow shock-ing, and Ethan still sat there, hunched and breathing, and I felt sorry for him, which is something I would never have thought imaginable toward Ethan. I said, "The devil in you, the devil in me," and I grabbed him as gingerly as I could from behind and he moaned, but it wasn't a sex moan, just the moan of someone who has found something valuable that they had thought was lost forever.

We lay down on the couch, me clasping his chest from behind, his breathing becoming deeper and slower, and he said, "You and Karla do that shiatsu stuff, right?"

"Yeah. We do. But you've got a few too many stitches for that at the moment." I told him a bit of Karla's theories of the body and memory stor-age. He laughed and said, "*Ow!*—Christ, stitches hurt," and then he said, "Well, if that's the case then think of me as a PowerBook dropped onto a marble floor from a tenth-story balcony."

I said, "Don't laugh at yourself. Your body is you, too." I felt like I had to heal here, or else something would leave Ethan forever, so I held him a bit tighter. "Karla told me that in other cultures, the *chest* is often thought of as being the seat of thought. Instead of slapping yourself on the forehead when you forget something, like a V-8, instead you slap yourself on the chest."

Ethan said, "I guess that if you start young enough, you could actually consider your *toes* as the seat of your thought. If you tried to remember something, you'd scratch your toe."

I said this is possible.

And then I simply held him. And then we both fell asleep, and that was six hours ago. And I have been thinking about it, and I realize that Ethan has fallen prey to The Vacuum. He mistakes the reward for the goal; he does not realize that there is a deeper aim and an altruistic realm of technology's desire. He is lost. He does not connect privilege with responsibility; wealth with morality. I feel it is up to me to help him become found. It is my work, it is my task; it is my burden.

I am Bill's machine

I may be the largest machine that will ever be built.
I may be the richest machine that will ever be built.
I may be the most powerful machine that will ever be built.

Raised with Cheerios and station wagons. Diagonal-slotted parking stalls of the Northgate mall.

As a child I once drove in a sedan's backseat along Interstate 5 and looking out the windows I saw my city beside the sea, dreaming in airplanes and wood; metal and rock ballads . . . better ways of living. *Golden sun falling on this city that wanted for more;* sailboats atop the golden water.

Pocket calculators   cheeseburgers
sneakers   Datsun

The challenge of newness

Saturday morning cartoons recycling programs crying Indians.

You think you can live without me, but just try.

You desire images of a better tomorrow;
I feed you these images.

You dream of a world in which your ego will not dissolve.

I am the architect of the arena.

Reconsider your notions of what you think will rescue you from a future sterilized of progress.

4
FaceTime

MONDAY

Everybody's decided what title to put on the business cards Susan designed.

> Bug: *"Information Leafblower"*
> Todd: *"Personal Trainer"*
> Karla: *"Who can turn the world on with a smile?"*
> Susan: *"Her name is Rio."*
> Me: *"Crew Chief"*
> Ethan: *"Liquid Engineer"*
> Michael: *"You're Soaking In It"*

We got in this discussion about the word "nerd." "Geek" is now, of course, a compliment, but we're not sure about "nerd." Mom asked me, "What, exactly, *is* the difference between a nerd and a geek?"

I replied, "It's tougher than it seems. It's subtle. Instinctual. I think geek implies hireability, whereas nerd doesn't necessarily mean your skills are 100 percent sellable. Geek implies wealth."

Susan said that geeks were usually losers in high school who didn't have a life, and then not having a life became a status symbol. "People like them never used to be rewarded by society. Now all the stuff that made people want to kick your butt at fifteen becomes fashionable when fused with cash.

You can listen to Rush on the Ferrari stereo on your way to get a good seat at
Il Fornaio—and wear Dockers doing it!"

Todd, not surprisingly, added, "Right now is the final end-stage when
God said the meek shall inherit the earth. Is it a coincidence that geek
rhymes with meek? I think not. A dipthongal accident."

Mom said, "Oh you *kids!* I guess I'm just not in the loop."

Being "in the loop" is this year's big expression. Only three more weeks
remain before the phrase becomes obsolete, like an Apple Lisa computer.
Language is such a technology.

Åll day Michael kept on humming a refrain from the Talking Heads song
"Road to Nowhere." I asked him to sing something a bit more uplifting. The
flu epidemic has left us all at low ebb. Or does Michael know something
about E&M Software that we don't? I dare not ask.

Pi fight! Late afternoon:

It turns out that Ethan knows pi up to 10,000 digits, just like Michael, so
the two of them sat there in the Habitrail and banged off strands of numbers,
like a Gregorian chant. In stereo—it felt religious. Work stopped dead and
we sat there listening.

"Four."	*"Four."*
"Seven."	*"Seven."*
"Zero."	*"Zero."*
"One."	*"One"*
"Eight."	*"Eight."*
"Three."	*"Three."*
"Eight."	*"Eight."*
"Nine."	*"Nine."*
"Zero."	*"Zero."*
"Three."	*"Three."*
"Four."	*"Four."*
"One."	*"One."*

Ethan has risen in our collective estimation considerably as a result.

I must add that Dad visits the Habitrail every single night, recharging Michael's Tang and bringing him serial volleys of snacks. *"Some fruit leather, Michael?—oh look—there's one blueberry strip remaining."* I'll say, "Hi, Dad," and he sort of turns around and stumbles for words and grunts, "Hi, Dan."

But then I suppose I *ought* to be grateful. Dad looks 1,000 percent better than he did up in Redmond—so long ago, it now seems. His hair's going white, though.

Also, Michael is using Jed's desk and lamp in his bedroom down the hall from my room. Mom and Dad moved all of Jed's things to Palo Alto when they moved, as though he was just away at school. I'm not even using *my* old lamp. Everyone else uses IKEA and lawn furniture.

I recognize that I'm avoiding something here: Michael using Jed's lamp. Dad hasn't mentioned Jed once since Michael moved in. Maybe that's what's bothering me. I'm in denial.

TUESDAY

The house down the hill from us burned down around two in the afternoon. *Fwoosh!* We all went out on the verandah and watched, drinking coffee and sitting on an old pool slide turned onto its side. Mom was loading up the car, but Dad said it was no big deal because the vegetation wasn't dry enough for "you know, another open-hills thing."

A pair of hawks nesting nearby were diving into the smoke plume. I guess there were mice and things running away. Like a buffet table for birds.

The first time I ever saw a house burn down was the first time I heard the English Beat version of "Tears of a Clown" on the radio, and the two memories are toasted onto each other in my head like an EPROM.

Memory!

Later, Michael and Dad and I were buying AAA batteries at the Lucky Mart down on Alma Street, a main corridor through Palo Alto, and then out in the parking lot Michael and Dad began waving at the CalTrain that was screaming northward up the tracks, headed into the Palo Alto station. Once it had passed I asked Michael, just by way of conversation, why it is that people wave at trains.

He said, "We wave at people in trains because their lives—their cores—are so intensely and powerfully reflected in the inexorable, unstoppable roaring dreams of motion and voyage and discovery, which trains embody. One can't help but admire the power and brutality and singularity of decision a moving train implies. Wouldn't you agree, Mr. Underwood?"

Does Michael practice these things? Where does he *get* them from? And wouldn't you just *know* Michael's a train nut like my dad.

I say "*Ummm . . .*" a lot. I mentioned this to Karla and she says it's a CPU word. "It means you're assembling data in your head—spooling."

I also say the word "like" too much, and Karla said there was no useful explanation for people saying this word. Her best guess was that saying "like" is the unused 97 percent of your brain trying to make its presence known. Not too flattering.

I think I'm going to try and do mental Find-and-Replace on myself to eliminate these two pesky words altogether. I'm trying to debug myself.

Karla is changing herself, too. She's becoming a womanly woman. She's growing her hair and trying to look like an adult. Right now she looks in between, as do most techies. Her skin certainly looks better. Actually, we *all* have better skin . . . except maybe for Ethan. California sunshine and an attempt to at least slightly cut the crap food seems to have positive epidermal results.

Smoother skin in seven days.

Karla drinks Ovaltine instead of coffee. She drinks it from her high school reunion mug. Her reunion actually *had* custom mugs, and this is so weird. Susan looked at the mug last week and asked, "Your high school reunion had horizontally cross-marketed merchandise tie-ins? Where'd you go to high school . . . Starbucks?"

Apparently there's some company in Texas that helps you market your reunion.

Beware of the corporate invasion of private memory.

Misty busted into my work space after all the fire engines and everything left, and pawed and slobbered all over me. She smelled like roses and topsoil, so I guess she was down in her special grotto in the lower yard.

Ethan came into the office shortly afterward trying to lug Misty out, but instead Misty barraged him with dirty fur and mouth goo, and I know Ethan enjoyed it. He said to her, "Quite often *I* feel like pawing and slobbering over people I like, too, but I never, of course, actually *do* it."

I told Ethan that I speak in an unrestricted manner to animals—things like, *aren't you just the cutest little kitty* . . . that kind of thing, which I wouldn't dream of doing to humans. Then I realized I wish I *could*.

Misty really would have made a terrible seeing-eye dog. She'd bound into traffic to greet truck drivers. Ethan lured Misty outside with a Cocoa Puffs promotional Frisbee, and then stood, wearing his sunglasses, beneath the balcony's shade and played with her a while. He didn't seem to mind the muck all over his Dolce & Gabbana three-piece.

Ethan just wants some company. He's spending far more time around the Habitrail these days since The Hug. We all hug Ethan a lot now because suddenly he's human and Karla held a small meeting the day after the bandage-removal episode and told us all we had to be extra kind to Ethan. I haven't mentioned it at all to Ethan though—too weird. Susan was in shock.

After a while Ethan and I went down to look at the rubble of the house below. Gone. *Fwoosh!*

Ethan said something provocative and left me dangling. He muttered something about "Michael's expensive little addiction," and I said "Robitussin? It's cheap," and Ethan said "Robitussin?" so I said, "Well, what did you mean then?" and he said, "Nothing." I hate it when people only open the floodgates a little bit, and then close it up again.

Oh—Ethan is trying to wean himself off cel phones. Good luck!

I heard a lovely expression today about brains—an ad for smart drugs touting *thicker, bushier dendrites.*

Moist little tumbleweeds blooming inside one's skull.

Susan was doing her biannual hard-drive cleanup, which is half chore/half fun—going on a deleting frenzy, removing all those letters that once seemed so urgent, that now seem pointless, the shareware that infected your files with mystery viruses and those applications that seemed groovy at the time.

Susan's own efforts *did* get me to do a brief cleanup of my own hard drive. I thought of Karla's equation of the body with the computer and memory storage and all of that, and I realized that human beings are loaded with germs and viruses, just like a highly packed Quadra—each of us are bipedal terrariums containing untold millions of organisms in various states of symbiosis, pathogenisis, mutualism, commensualism, opportunism, dormancy, and parasitism. We're like Pig Pen from Charlie Brown, enclosed in a perpetual probabilistic muzz of biology.

I posted a question on the Net, asking bioheads out there what lurks inside the human hard drive.

Michael and Dad were out in the backyard later on watching R2D2 clean out the pool. There was a fair amount of soot because of the fire.

Around midnight I was in the reflective mode and walked around the streets by myself. I felt as though I was walking around the neighborhood on *Bewitched*. "*Look*—it's Larry Tate driving a big, ugly mattress of a car! One great big honking *machine*."

I thought about the word "machine." Funny, but the word itself seems almost quaint, now. Say it over a few times: *machine, machine, machine*— it's so . . . so . . . *ten-years-ago*. Obsolete. Replaced by post-machines. A good piece of technology dreams of the day when it will be replaced by a newer piece of technology. This is one definition of progress.

machine machine machine machine machine machine machine machine
machine machine machine machine machine machine machine machine
machine machine machine machine machine machine machine machine
machine machine machine machine machine machine machine machine
machine machine machine machine machine machine machine machine
machine machine machine machine machine machine machine machine
machine machine machine machine machine machine machine machine
machine machine machine machine machine machine machine machine
machine machine machine machine machine machine machine machine
machine machine machine machine machine machine machine machine
machine machine machine machine machine machine machine machine
machine machine machine machine machine machine machine machine
machine machine machine machine machine machine machine machine
machine machine machine machine machine machine machine machine
machine machine machine machine machine machine machine machine
machine machine machine machine machine machine machine machine
machine machine machine machinemachine machine machine machine
machine machine machine machine machine machine machine machine
machine machine machine machine machine machine machine machine
machine machine machine machine machine machine machine machine
machine machine machine machine machine machine machine machine
machine machine machine machine machine machine machine machine
machine machine machine machine machine machine machine machine
machine machine machine machine machine machine machine machine
machine machine machine machine machine machine machine machine
machine machine machine machine machine machine machine machine
machine machine machine machine machine machine machine machine
machine machine machine machine machine machine machine machine
machine machine machine machine machine machine machine machine
machine machine machine machine machine machine machine machine
machine machine machine machine machine machine machine machine
machine machine machine machine machine machine machine machine
machine machine machine machine machine machine machine machine
machine machine machine machine machine machine machine machine
machine machine machine machine machine machine machine machine
machine machine machine machine machine machine machine machine
machine machine machine machine machine machine machine machine

machine machine machine machine machine machine machine machine
machine machine machine machine machine machine machine machine
machine machine machine machine machine machine machine machine
machine machine machine machine machine machine machine machine
machine machine machine machine machine machine machine machine
machine machine machine machine machine machine machine machine
machine machine machine machine machine machine machine machine
machine machine machine machine machine machine machine machine
machine machine machine machine machine machine machine machine
machine machine machine machine machine machine machine machine
machine machine machine machine machine machine machine machine
machine machine machine machine machine machine machine machine
machine machine machine machine machine machine machine machine
machine machine machine machine machine machine machine machine
machine machine machine machine machine machine machine machine
machine machine machine machine machine machine machine machine
machine machine machine machine machine machine machine machine
machine machine machine machine machine machine machine machine
machine machine machine machine machine machine machine machine
machine machine machine machine machine machine machine machine
machine machine machine machine machine machine machine machine
machine machine machine machine machine machine machine machine
machine machine machine machine machine machine machine machine
machine machine machine machine machine machine machine machine
machine machine machine machine machine machine machine machine
machine machine machine machine machine machine machine machine
machine machine machine machine machine machine machine machine
machine machine machine machine machine machine machine machine
machine machine machine machine machine machine machine machine
machine machine machine machine machine machine machine machine
machine machine machine machine machine machine machine machine
machine machine machine machine machine machine machine machine
machine machine machine machine machine machine machine machine
machine machine machine machine machine machine machine machine
machine machine machine machine machine machine machine machine
machine machine machine machine machine machine machine machine
machine machine machine machine machine machine machine machine
machine machine machine machine machine machine machine machine

Windows
Win7ows
cQndo#s
2ind5ws
&_s4Zaa
5@sFAz
cozrPa
Pzraoc
zocPar
aPzroc

WEDNESDAY

This morning I was sitting by the pool with Michael, watching him watch the R2D2 pool cleaner. I mentioned last night's machine/progress notion. He was eating a Snickers leftover from Halloween trick-or-treating, and said, "If you can conceive of humans developing a consciousness more complex than their own, then *BINGO,* you believe in progress whether or not you even think so."

So I guess I believe in progress.

Michael was staring into the clean blue fluid, an anti-Narcissus, and he twiddled his index finger in it. He said, "You know, Daniel, I wonder if, after all these years, I have been subliminally modeling my personality after machines—because machines never have to worry about human things— because if they don't get touched or feel things, then they don't know the difference. I think this is a common thing. What do you think?"

I said, "I think nerds secretly dream of speaking to machines—of asking them, 'What do you think and feel—do you feel like *me?*' "

Michael asked me, "Do you think humanoids—*people*—will ever design a machine that can pray? Do we pray *to* machines or *through* them? How do we use machines to achieve our deepest needs?"

I said I hope we do. He wondered out loud, "What would R2D2 say to me if R2D2 could speak?"

My brain is built of paths and slides and ladders and lasers and I have invited all of you to enter its pavilion. My brain, as you enter, will smell of tangerines and brand-new running shoes.

HELLO
My name is:
UNIX

Friend
or
Foe?

I went out shopping for memory this afternoon with Todd and Karla. I had to get a strip of 27512 EPROMs—at Fry's, the nerd superstore on El Camino Real near Page Mill Road. I had to grovel to Ethan for the petty cash; so degrading.

The Fry's chain completely taps into MSE: Male Shopping Energy. This is to say that most guys have about 73 calories of shopping energy, and once these calories are gone, they're gone for the day—if not the week—and can't be regenerated simply by having an Orange Julius at the Food Fair. Therefore, to get guys to shop, a store has to eat up all of their MSE calories in one crack-like burst. Thus, Fry's concentrates only on male-specific consumables inside their cavernous shopping arena, aisles replete with dandruff, bad outfits, and nerdacious mutterings full of buried Hobbit references.

Near the EPROM shelves, Karla, Todd, and I were marveling at the pyramids of Hostess products, the miles of computing magazines, the cascade of nerdiana lifestyle accessories: telecom wiring supplies, clips, pornography, razors, Doritos, chemicals for etching boards, and all the components of the intangible Rube Goldberg machines that lie just beneath the Stealth black plastic exterior of the latest $1,299.99 gizmo. The only thing they *don't* have is backrubs. Karla tried to find tampons and failed. *"Make mental note,"* she said, speaking into an imaginary Dictaphone machine, *"Fry's sells men's but not women's hygiene products."*

Shortly after, over near the model train mock-up of the Wild West "Canyon City" was when I suddenly saw this kid who looked *just* like my dear departed brother Jed. And that's when I, well, freaked out.

I stood frozen, and Karla was saying, *"Dan, are you okay?"* Then Todd walked by, and looked over toward where I was staring, and blurted out, *"Hey, Dan—that kid looks just like the kid in the pictures in your Dad's den."*

Karla then understood, and moved to stand in front of me, and Todd said, *"Uh oh . . ."* and headed off to the CD player aisle. Karla said, *"Dan, come on. Let's go."*

But I said, "That's *him*, Karla. I'm okay. But look at him. *That's* what he looked like."

We followed this döppel-Jed around, but it felt too weird stalking someone, so we stopped ourselves. I forgot my EPROMs, and we went and sat on a parking island outside.

Todd came out and said, "Sorry about that."

I said it didn't matter, but you know what Todd said? He said, "I think it *does* matter. And I *do* care. So can you please tell me? Sometimes I think you underestimate me, Underwood. So just give me a chance, okay?"

So we went to The Good Earth for turkey burgers and Smoothies (Todd's gym food) and I explained Jed to Todd. I think I do underestimate people. I don't know why I keep these things cramped up inside me. And I think Todd is a friend to call me on it.

Afterward I quietly went into Dad's den, closed the door behind me, and looked at Jed's old photo, in an oval frame, lost amid Dad's knicks and knacks. There he was as he always will be, slightly yellowed, forever twelve and forever smarter than me.

I guess I feel dumb in the same way Karla feels dumb. Except Karla really *is* smart compared to her family, and I really *am* dumb—compared to Jed. He wrote such lovely things when he was here—stories about air pilots working with scientists fighting to protect Earth from being stolen. Imaginative.

You just can't compete with the dead. It would be easier if I had another brother or a sister, but I was born after the Pill.

Anyway, this is all to say I went into the worst head space all afternoon, as though I'd taken eleven of those cold tablets containing both an upper and a downer to cancel out the mutual side effects. So I merely felt buzzed. Just like after too much coding.

Abe's e-mail is getting more frequent and more personal. I think he's losing it up at Microsoft. He doesn't like his new roommates and would seem to be missing us.

The 2 new roomates are both engaged to partner units and don't want to hang out. They're NEVER here.

I suppose there's nothing wrong with my not having a life. So many people no longer have lives that you raeally have to wonder if some new mode of existence is being created which is going to become so huge that it is no longer on the moral scale – simply the way people ARE.

Myabe thinking you're supposed to "have a life" is a stupid way of buying into an untenable 1950s narrative of what life *supposed* to be.
How do we know that all of these people with "no lives" aren't really on the new frontier of human sentience and perceptions?

I only need 2 hours of people a day. I can; get by on that amount. 2 hours of FaceTime.

I replied:
2 hours of FaceTime is not good enough Abe.

YOU are not a productmanager, and life is not a product . . . though wouldn't it be SO MUCH CLEANER AND EASIER were that so.

Nonetheless, this line of thinking reminds me of the URBAN LEGEND of a Japanese exchange student who thought he was saving money by eating nothing but Top Ramen noodles every day for a year, but he died of malnutrition before he graduatd.

After sundown, Karla and I went out to the garage to see Dad's model train world. Mom says he hasn't been in there at all since he began working with Michael—after returning from "his episode" up in Redmond. I guess this is a good sign—that he's stopped obsessing and is out in the world and doing new things.

Todd and Michael had plonked down two monitors right in the middle of the landscape directly atop a farm. They had arranged the small animals in small herds atop the monitors, which are coaxial'ed into the Habitrail. The monitors were displaying some Gouraud-shaded *Oop!* bricks, rotating them in 3D space. *Oop!* is looking really good, by the way. It looks fresh and modern, as if the future is being squeezed out of the monitor screens like meat from a hamburger grinder. Todd taped a note to one monitor saying, PLEASE GOD, LET RENDERING TIME GET CHEAPER AND FASTER.

Karla had brought along a feather duster and she dusted off the moun-

tains and the village and the little white house Dad built where Jed is supposed to live. I turned on the trains, and we watched them drive around,
through the towns, over the mountains, past the rotating building blocks, and
then we turned the trains off, and turned the lights out and left. Dad doesn't
seem to mind "us kids" stealing his world.

We call the two systems in the garage "Cabernet" and "Chardonnay."

Three other system units (two Quadras and a Pentium) are called
"Ogre," "Hobgoblin," and "Kestrel." Two file servers are called "Tootie"
and "Blair."

Our two printers are called "Siegfried" and "Roy," because they're all
shiny and plastic.

Our SGI Iris workstation running an old version of Vertigo software is
named, of course, "HAL."

I'm trying to end this day on an up note, but it's hard.

THURSDAY

Mom was cleaning out the spice rack in the kitchen. I watered her philo-dendron plant. She was really funny. She said she eats ripple chips for break-fast now. She says it's a bad habit and she's trying to break it and she blames "us kids"! She always says, *"You kids."* We like it, even though I think I stopped thinking of myself as a kid about four years ago. I don't mind responsibility. I guess that's why I don't mind the repetitive nature of com-puter work.

Boy did I get a response to my Net question about the organisms that lurk inside the human body. My Pig Pen theory was indeed confirmed: the aver-age human body contains 1 x 10^{13} cells, yet hosts *1 x 10^{14}* bacterial cells. Long, scary names:

> *Escherichia coli*
> *Candida albicans*
> *S. aureus*
> *Klebsiella*
> *Actinomyces*
> *Staphylococcus*

It really makes you take seriously all these articles in the news about old diseases becoming *new* diseases. I took so many antibiotics and sulfas for zits in my teens that I'm going to be felled by the first postmodern virus to walk down Camino Real. Doomed.

I mentioned all these microbes to Susan and I think she's going to become germ phobic. I could see it in her eyes. Fear.

Karla asked me what I thought of modern yuppie parents who smother their kids with attention and affection—those households where the kid rules and everything in the universe revolves around making sure they get touched enough by their parents.

I paused and tried to be honest and the answer blurted out: "Jealous."

Susan overheard and started singing "Cars," by Gary Numan, and we all started singing it. *Here in my car, I can only receive, I can lock up my doors . . .*

And then the moment passed. I e-mailed Abe on the subject, and he was online, so the response came back immediately:

I come from one of those "zero-kidney" families . . . we all made this agreement once . . . that if anybody else in the family needed a kidney it was going to be, "Well, sorry . . . Been nice knowing you."

I think that's why it's so hard for me to understand my body. Becauze our family was so zero-touch.

As I type, I'm bouncing my 11 pound ball of rubber bands contructed form my daily Wall Street Journal. It grows.

I learned a great new word today: "deletia." When you get an e-mail and reply to the sender, you simply obliterate everything they sent you and then, in small square brackets, write:

[deletia]

It stands for everything that's been lost.

Dad bought a P/S2 Model 70 computer just before he got fired. He stores it out in the garage with the train world. Locked deep inside the P/S2's brains memory are WordPerfect, a golf application, and some genealogical data he tried to assemble about our family, but which he abandoned after he finally realized that our family erased itself as it moved across the country.

FRIDAY

Dad mouthed a Michaelism today: "If you can conceive of humans developing a consciousness more complex than the human brain at some point, then, BINGO, you're a de facto believer in Progress."

My ears were burning when I heard him say this, and it was all I could do to not say, "That's Michael's quote." My ears were *red*.

E-mail from Abe:

Im re-reading all my old TinTin books, amd I'm noticing that there are all of these things absent in the Boy Detective's life . . . religion, parents, politics, relationship, communion with nature, class, love, death, birth . . . it's a long list. And I find that while I still love TinTin, I'm getting currious about all of its invisible content.

The Valley is so career-o-centric. So much career energy! There must be a 65-ton crystal of osmium hexachloride buried 220 feet below the surface of Menlo Park, sucking in all of the career energy in the Bay Area and shooting it back down the Peninsula at twice light speed. It's science fiction here.

Mom's signed up for a ladies 50-to-60 swim meet. It's next week.

Susan bought a case load of premoistened towelettes at Price-Costco. She's mad at the rest of the Habitrail because it's such a pigsty. She daintily wipes off her keyboard and screen and as she does so she says, "Man, I need a date, *bad*."

Karla's hair is down past her shoulders now. And she bought a dress with pink wildflowers on it, and it's funny, the way she's the same as ever, yet also reformatted, and it makes me look at her with a new fascination.

She's eating all sorts of food like a total person now and I've noticed that when I work on her body, she's just not as tense anymore. Everyone has a special place they store their tension (I'm on shiatsu duty), the same way everyone misspells the same words over and over. Karla stores her tension in her rhomboid muscles, and I remove it. This is making me feel good. That I can do this.

Daydream: today the traffic was locked on the 101. I saw visions of the Valley and snapped out of my daydream jealous of the future. I saw germanium in the groundwater and dead careers. I saw venture capitalists with their eyes burned out in their sockets by visions of money, crashing their Nissans on the 101—past the big blue cube of NASA's Onizuka Air Force Base, their windows spurting fluorescent orange blood.

SATURDAY

Bug's dream came true today. He got to visit Xerox PARC with a friend of a friend from Seattle. Back with us in the Habitrail, while arranging a handful of purple iceplant flowers nipped from the PARC's groundcover, he filled us in on details: "It's set in a purposefully blank location—they cover up all outside traces of civilization with berms and landscaping devices so you feel as if you're nowhere. Feeling like you're *somewhere* must be bad for ideas.

"Anyway, there's nothing but chaparral and oak trees on the hill to the west, and you feel like you're on a virgin planet, like the planets they visit on *Star Trek*. It feels really 'outposty.' But not scary, like you're in Antarctica. And the lobby—it's like a really successful orthodontist's waiting room in the year 2004. And guess what . . . I got to sit in the Bean Bag Chairs!"

An hour later we were all back at work, when apropos of nothing, Bug said, *"Ahem,"* called our attention, and announced that he's gay. How random!

"I've been 'inning' myself for too long," he said, "and now it's time to out myself. It's something you'll all have to deal with, but believe me, I've been dealing with it a lot longer than you."

It never even entered our heads to think Bug was anything except a sexually frustrated, bitter crank, which is not unusual up at Microsoft, or in tech in general. I think we all felt guilty because we don't think about Bug enough, and he *does* work hard, and his ideas really are good. But we're just so used to him being cranky it never occurred to us he had an interior life, too.

I asked him, "But what about the Elle MacPherson shrine, Bug?"

"Replaced. Marky Mark for the time being, but he's only a phase."

"Oh, Bug . . ." said Karla, "how long have you been deciding this?"

"Always."

"Why *now*?" I asked. "So late."

"Because now is when we all explode. We're like those seeds you used to plant on top of sterile goop in petri dishes in third grade, waiting to sprout or explode. Susan's exploding. Todd's going to explode. Karla's germinating gently. Michael's altering, too. It's like we're all seeds just waiting to grow into trees or orchids or houseplants. You never know. It was too sterile up north. I didn't sprout. Aren't you curious to know what you really are, Dan?"

I thought about it. It's not really something you think about.

"Now I can be *me*—I think," Bug said. "This is not easy for me. Let me repeat that—this is not easy for me."

"Does this mean you'll start dressing better? " asked Ethan.

"*Yes*, Ethan. Probably."

So that was that.

Maybe he'll be less cranky now. Karla and Susan said they were proud of Bug. I guess it did take guts. He's a late bloomer—that's for sure. And me? Am I curious to know what *I* really am? Or am I just so grateful to not be a full-scale, zero-life loser that it doesn't matter?

Bean bag chairs: how odd it is that they're still . . . I don't know . . . a part of the world.

Dad signed up for a night course in C++. He's going to make himself relevant.

Susan's sister sent her a bag of pot via FedEx. She wrapped it in magazine scent strips to foil FedEx dope dogs. What a good way to make those things do something useful.

Bug's right. We are all starting to unravel. Or sprout. Or whatever. I remember back in grade school, VCR documentaries on embryology, and the way all mammals look the same up until a certain point in their embryological development, and then they start to differentiate and become what they're going to become. I think we're at that point now.

SUNDAY

My sense of time perception has gone all screwy. Sundays always do that to me. One day is so much like every other day here, and yet every day is somehow different. I designed a little program that I click into every time I get an interruption—like a phone call or someone asks me a question—or I have to change a tape in my Walkman. My average time between interruptions is 12.5 minutes. Perhaps this is part of my time schism.

I mentioned these interruptions to Todd who said, "I'm still doing 18-hour days like up at Microsoft, except instead of doing just one thing, I'm doing a *hundred* different things—my job is so much better. More diversity. It's the diversity of interruptions . . . time becomes 'initiative driven' as opposed to passive."

He then added that in Christian eschatology ("the study of the Last Things") it is always made very clear that time and the world both end simultaneously, that there is no real difference between the two.

Then he panicked, worrying that he was doomed to turn into his parents, and roared off to the gym. He's doing upper body today. He alternates upper and lower body. He *never* sleeps. That's how he names his days: Upperbodyday; Lowerbodyday; Absday; Latsday . . . Sometimes I admire his single-minded drive to achieve muscular perfection, and sometimes I think he's a freak.

I read about fishermen off the Gulf Coast whose net, dragging the ocean floor, snagged a sunken galleon, and when the net was raised, a shower of coins fell on the ship's deck. Talk about a story to appeal to us here in the Valley!

Sent out my Christmas cards today—I went to McDonald's and got a stack of "JOIN THE FAMILY" job application forms and filled them out for everybody. The only remotely personal question the form asks is: Sports? Activities?

Here's what I wrote for everybody: *"Abe/Susan/Bug/Michael/etc . . . greatly enjoys repetitive tasks."*

"**G**eek party" night: it's kind of like if we were in Hollywood and going to an "industry party." That guy Susan met from General Magic had a party up at his place in the Los Altos Hills. All day at the office Susan and Karla talked about what they're going to . . . *wear.* It was really un-Karla, but I'm glad she's getting into her body and taking pride in it.

Susan's on the prowl, so she wants to look sexy, techie, "fun," and serious all at once. Good luck. She complains to Karla that "I've got period boobs . . . they feel like they're going to go on a lactating spree momentarily." She's so tell-it-like-it-is, but *Susan* . . .

Karla said, "Well, that could work to your advantage if you wear that Betsy Johnson dress."

"Excellent idea!" Susan was motivated.

At geek parties, you can sort corporate drones from start-up drones by dress and conversation. Karla and I stood next to two guys who work on the Newton project at Apple. They talked with unflagging enthusiasm about frequent flyer miles for about 45 minutes. They had a purchasable Valley hip. One guy had the mandatory LA Eyeworks glasses and a nutty orange vest worn over baggy jeans. The other guy had Armani glasses and a full Calvin Klein ensemble, but not a *matching* ensemble, mind you—"thrown together" in "that expensive way." You can't help but be conscious here of how much everything costs, and where it comes from.

Newton Guy One: I'm trying to make United Premiere Executive 100K. Are you 100K yet?

NG 2: Oh, yeah, right after Hanover this fall. And you'll never believe this—I was late for a flight the other day, and when the woman at the United counter pulled up my record, I looked at the monitor and my name was surrounded by DOLLAR SIGNS. How subtextual.

NG 1: Wow, great! (Obviously genuinely impressed) I think I *might* make it if they let me fly United to Japan the next two times. Fucking Apple Travel. I now have frequent flyer miles on Alitalia, Northwest, JAL,

Lufthansa, USAir, Continental, American, and British Air. I wish we flew Virgin Air . . . *that* would be the coolest.

NG 2: I like the toiletries case from British Air.

NG 1: They used to be cooler . . . all the stuff used to be from the Body Shop. But Virgin Air rules because you get your own video game monitor and you can play SEGA Games with other passengers.

NG 2: All over the plane? Or just business class?

NG 1: I don't know. Business class only, I think. I guess it would be cooler if you could play with the 13-year old kids back in coach . . . SEGA should send group testers on flights *and* do market research that way!
(Titters.)

Karla and I looked at each other and rolled our eyes, but were impressed. APPLE! NEWTON! JAL FIRST CLASS! I don't have frequent flyer miles on *any* airline.

Loser.

MONDAY

Anatole's Lexus has a vertical slot in its dashboard. It's a coffee cup holder that pops out and does this *flip-flip-flip* origami thing—*whoosh-whoosh-whoosh*—and becomes horizontal.

Karla and I went out around sunset and had coffees and sat in the car. This was the highlight of the day, so you can imagine how dull the day was.

Stocking stuffers: I bought these red "panic buttons" at Weird Stuff, the computer surplus store across from Fry's on Kern Street in Sunnyvale. It's a fake IBM button with adhesive tape on the back that you're supposed to tape on to your board and push whenever you're feeling "wacky."

I felt really sad for the panic buttons, because panic seems like such an outdated, corny reaction to all of the change in the world. I mean if you *have* to be negative, there's a reasonable enough menu of options available—dis-engagement—atomization—torpor—but *panic*? Corrrrrrny.

I mentioned to Abe about my lessons in shiatsu and the weird relationship people in tech firms can have with their bodies. He replied:

I know what you mean about bodeis. At Microsoft you pretend bodies dont' exist . . . BRAINS are what matter. You're right, at Microsoft bodies get down played to near invisibilty with unsensual Tommy Hilfiger geekwear, or are genericized with items form the GAP so that employees morph themelfues into those international symbols for MAN and WOMAN you see at airports.

Susan got a job offer from General Magic—that guy she chatted up at the Halloween party recommended her—and *Todd* got a job offer from Spectrum HoloByte. At first I couldn't imagine why—then he told us that

someone at the gym must have recommended him. It's occupational canni-
balism here. Both offers are tempting. But Susan's got too much money
stoked into the *Oop!* fire to leave, and Todd's simply too into it. But it's nice
to know that if *Oop!* flushes the toilet, there's a Plan B ready.

Oop! isn't about work. It's about all of us staying together.

TUESDAY

We ate lunch in Chinatown up in SF only today, and there were these paper birds strung from the ceiling and this little kid who wanted to touch the birds and his father lifted him up to touch them. I didn't realize, but I was staring at the whole thing the whole time, and zoned out of the conversation, and then I realized Karla was watching *me*.

Time time *time*. It's such a current subject. It's like money—if you don't have it, you think about it too much.

Karla's been thinking about time, too. Tonight during shiatsu training, with me flat on my stomach, my back and sides being poked and pummeled, her voice, disconnected from her body, informed me that in general, "One's perception of time's flow is directly linked to the number of connections one has to the outer world. Technology increases the number of connections, thus it alters the perception of having 'experienced' time.

"It's a bell-curve relationship. There's actually an optimum point at which the amount of technology one owns ex*tends* the amount of time one perceives or experiences.

"It's as if your brain holds a tiny, cashew-shaped thalamus going *tick-tick-tick* while it meters out your time dosage for you. There's a technological equilibrium point, after which, it's all downhill."

Abe e-mailed a response to my time stuff:

Once you've used your brain flat-out, you can't go into the SLOW mode. You can't drive an Infinite J-30 and then get downgraded to an Daewoo. Brains don't workd that way.

WEDNESDAY

This morning Dad was singing "Road to Nowhere." Michael is reprogramming my father. I have to figure out a way of dealing with this.

Whenever Anatole gets too European and insufferable—complaining too much, basically—we say to him, "Hey, Anatole, your turtleneck's showing." He doesn't get this particular joke. *"But I am not wearing a turtleneck . . ."*

Anatole told us this really great thing, how at Apple they used to have a thing called RumorMonger that allowed employees to anonymously input up to one hundred ASCII characters worth of gossip into the system. So Todd hacked together a quick in-house version for our network, called Rumor-Meister. It got *way* out of control almost immediately:

```
1) SUSAN SHOPS AT TARGET BUT PUTS HER STUFF IN
NORDSTROM BAGS
2) DANIEL SELLS HIS USED BOXERS VIA MAIL ORDER
. . . $5.00 PER DAY OF WEAR
3) BUG SWEATS TO THE OLDIES
4) DAN . . . THOSE DOCKERS . . . HIP!
5) TODD HAS SAGGY NIPPLES FROM TOO MUCH BODY
BUILDING THEY'RE CALLED 'BITCH TITS'
5) TODD WEARZ DEPENDS WHEN HE BENCH PRESSES
BECUZ UTHERWIZE HE'LL EVACUATE HIS BOWELS
ON THE BENCH
7) KARLA PAID TO SEE "THE BODY GUARD"
8) BUG LAUGHS AT GARFIELD CARTOONS
9) KARLA CAN'T ACCESSORIZE
10) SUSAN HAS COMBINATION SKIN
11) TODD SMOKES 'MORE' CIGARETTES
12) I CAN HEAR KARLA'S COLOSTOMY BAG SLOSHING
```

```
13)  ETHAN'S FERRARI IS A KIT CAR
14)  ETHAN BUYS TIRES AT SEARS
15)  BUG LOVES BARNEY
16)  KARLA THINKS SHE'S A SUMMER BUT SHE'S
REALLY A FALL
17)  BUG HAS 2 RAFFI CASSETTES
18)  DAN HAS A YANNI CD IN HIS CAR
19)  ETHAN'S VISA LIMIT IS $3,000
20)  SUZAN'Z BOYCRAZY SUZAN'Z BOYCRAZY SUZAN'Z
BOYCRAZY SUZAN'Z BOYCRAZY SUZAN'Z BOYCRAZY
21)  DAN: LISTERINE KILLS GERMS THAT CAN CAUSE
BAD BREATH
22)  DAN STILL LIVES WITH HIS MOTHER
23)  BUG SHOPS AT CHESS KING
24)  MICHAEL'S SHIRT SMELL LIKE GERBIL PEE
```

Todd quickly removed the program from the system.

Ethan had a time crisis. "I look at my Daytimer and see: CES in January, COMDEX in May, Tim's wedding in July, etc., and I realize the whole year is over before it's even begun. What's the point of it all? It's all of it so predictable."

Mom won a swim meet this afternoon, so we dug out the nickels from under the seat cushions and went out for a low-fat dinner to celebrate. She's so fit these days.

I was driving down from the 280, down Peter Coutts Road, up by Systemix, Wall Data, IBM, Hewlett Packard, and the *Wall Street Journal* printing plant—up where Dad used to work before he was rendered obsolete—and who should I see taking a stroll together but Dad and Michael! They were lost in discussion, their arms donnishly held behind their backs.

I pulled the car into a side street and ran out to join them. Upon hearing me yell their names, they turned around, absentmindedly interrupted, utterly unfazed at seeing me. I asked what they were doing and Dad said, "Oh, you know—just taking a stroll past the old hunting grounds" (IBM).

Cars hummed by. A tech firm's lawn sprinkler spritzed. I didn't know what to say, surrounded by all these blank buildings with glassed-out windows, these buildings where they make the machines that make the machines that make the machines.

I began walking up the hill with them and shortly we were in front of IBM. I felt humiliated for my father, because surely there'd be employees behind the reflecto windows saying, *"Oh look, it's Mr. Underhill stalking us. He must have really lost it."*

But Dad seemed unfazed. I said, "Dad, how can you even look at those people?"

He replied, "You know, Daniel, I have noticed that people are generally quite thrilled to have change enter their lives—disasters are weathered by people with a sturdiness that is often unlike their day-to-day personality."

Michael piped in, "Just think of the Mississippi River floods. All those people having barbecues up on their roofs, waving to the CNN helicopters— having a grand old time."

"Precisely," said Dad. "I've realized that people most dread the thought of actually initiating change in their lives and we old people are obviously the worst. It's hard coping with chaos and diversity. We old folks mistake the current deluge of information, diversity, and chaos as the 'End of History.' But maybe it's actually the Beginning."

This sounded like Michael-style words coming out of my father's mouth. *Brainwashed!*

He continued. "Old people have more or less dropped out of the process of creating old-fashioned-style history. We've been pushed to the side, and nobody's pointed out to us what we, the newly obsolete humans, are supposed to do."

"The only thing that is immune to change is our desire for meaning," added Michael, to my overweening annoyance.

We scurried across the street during a lull in the Lexuses, and began walking down the hill. "Don't ask *me* to explain this eight-jobs-in-a-lifetime reality we now inhabit. I could barely deal with the one-job-in-a-lifetime world," Dad said.

The sun was golden—birds swung in the sky. Cars purred at a stoplight. Dad looked so relaxed and happy. "I always assumed that history was created by think tanks, the DOE and the RAND Corporation of Santa Monica,

California. I assumed that history was something that happened to other people—out *there*. I never thought history was something my kid built in the basement. It's a shock."

I told him about the new word I'd learned, *deletia*, and Dad laughed. "That's me!"

We were soon down at El Camino Real. I had to go back to my car. I asked, "Are you guys driving? You need a ride anywhere?"

"We'll walk," said Dad. "But thanks."

"See you back in the Habitrail," said Michael.

Yeah. Right.

Karla was outside the house watering the herb garden with a can when I drove up. I told Karla that it was really unChristmassy of me, but I wanted to kill Michael.

"Michael? What on earth for?"

"He's . . ."

"Yes?"

"He's stealing my father."

"Don't be silly, Dan. It's in your head."

"Dad never talks to me. He's always with Michael. Shit, I don't even know what he *does* with Michael. They could be selling bomb implosion devices to the Kazakhs for all I know."

"Maybe they've become life-partners," said Karla.

"What?"

"It's a joke, Dan. Calm down. Get a grip on yourself. Listen to yourself. First of all, Michael couldn't shoplift a Nestlé's Crunch bar, let alone a parental unit. He's not the type. Has it ever occurred to you they might simply be friends?"

"He knows about Jed. He's trying to be Jed. And I can't compete."

"This is nonsense."

"Didn't I say that about you and your family?"

"But that's different."

"How?"

"Because . . . because it *is*."

"Good logic, Karla."

She came up to me. "Feel yourself—you're lucky you didn't get the killer flu. Your muscles are as rigid as a crowbar. You're making yourself sick thinking like this. Come on—I'll do your back. I'll talk you down from this."

As she plucked the knots from out of my body, removed the abandoned refrigerators and couches and sacks of garbage from underneath my skin, she talked in the way she does. She told me, "Bodies are like diskettes with tags. You click on to them and you can see the size and type of file immediately. On people, this labeling occurs on the face."

Prod, prod, rub, poke.

"If you know a lot about the world, that knowledge makes itself plain on your face. At first this can be a frightening thing to know, but you get used to it. Sometimes it can be off-putting. But I think it is only off-putting to people who are worried that they themselves are learning too much too quickly. Knowing too much about the world can make you unloving—and maybe unlovable. And your father's face is different now. He seems like a new man—different than when he first drove up to the old house in Redmond. However he may have changed, it's for the better. So don't lose sight of that."

Grudgingly: "All right."

If it weren't for Karla, sometimes I think I'd just implode.

FRIDAY, December 24, 1993

Software fun: Work crawled to a standstill today as Bug shared anagram software that spits out all the combinations of words you can make with your name. Michael was mad, because we lost several combined people-hours doing it. Everyone's faxing and e-mailing their relatives and friends their name-as-anagram for Christmas tomorrow. It's the low-budget gift-giving solution.

Everybody's also downloading shareware and scuttling about the valley cobbling together melanges of bootleg software programs to give as presents. We're all broke!

It seems everybody's trying to find a word that expresses more bigness than the mere word "supermodel"—*hyper model—gigamodel—megamodel*. Michael suggested that our inability to come up with a word bigger than supermodel reflects our inability to deal with the crushing weight of history we've created for ourselves as a species.

We got off work early (7:00) to shop, but we all came back in around 10:00 and started working again, until around 1:00. Slaves, or what?

Around midnight, December 25, Susan grunted, "*Uhhh*, Merry Christmas." We all reciprocated, and then went back to work.

Christmas Day, 1993

$\mathbf{W}$e sat inside and opened prezzies over coffee. Outside it was Richie Cunningham weather—like from *Happy Days* when Ralph Malph and Potsie come over and ding the doorbell, and they're wearing their varsity coats and they say, "Hello, Mrs. C." and the weather outside is . . . simply *weather.*

But where is everybody's family? Why isn't everybody with their *families*? Nobody went home. Bug still can't face his parents in Idaho; Susan either (her mother is in Schaumburg, Illinois; her father is in Irvine, down south); Karla—not likely. Only Anatole went to visit his parents, and then only because they're three hours north in Santa Rosa.

$\mathbf{A}$nyway, we're all so broke this year that we agreed not to buy anything expensive for anyone, and it was fun. Gag gifts. Christmas really brings out the geek in tech people:

- From Todd to Bug: a brown Wackenhut security baseball cap
- From Karla to me: the IBM PC version of *The $100,000 Pyramid*
- From me to Karla: a Hewlett-Packard calculator with jewels for buttons
- From Ethan to all of us: CandyCaller toy cellular phone filled with candies
- From Bug in all of our stockings: Dream Whip, nondairy whip topping
- From me to Karla: a Play-Doh fun factory insect-shaped insect extruding device ("Look—softer, less crumbly Play-Doh," she squealed.)
- From various people to various people: Ren & Stimpy screensavers ("Screensavers are the macramé of the '90s," Susan boldly exclaimed.)
- From Susan to all of us: HANDMADE Martha-Stewart-y gift bas-

kets, which made us all feel cheap. Michael asked her out-
right: *"Susan, where did you find the discretionary time to
assemble these?"* She looked guilty, and then told Michael to
piss off, and it was funny. Michael whispered to me:
*"Handmade presents are scary because they reveal that you
have too much free time."*

For some reason, everyone gave Susan premoistened towelette-related
products. It's one of those jokes that went out of control the way sometimes
things go out of control for no obvious reason. A spontaneous nonlinear
event. She received:

- 124 klear screen™ premoistened towelettes, "with love
  from Dan and Karla" (I also mailed Abe a bottle of
  Spray-N-Clean so he can remove the nasal encrusta-
  tions on his Mac screens)
- Celeste® sani-com 3205 premoistened towelettes specifi-
  cally targeted for consumer electronics mouthpieces—
  from Ethan. (*"'Cleans and freshens communications
  equipment.'* I stole a wad of them from business class
  on United last year.")
- "Pocket Wetty" brand premoistened towelettes from Japan,
  made by Wakodo KK. (¥ 145, thank you, Anatole.)

Everybody gave Mom a rock for Christmas and she said they were the best
presents she's ever had. Everybody tried to give her a really *good* rock. It's
so weird—everyone genuinely tried to find a cool rock.

Todd made a joke about Charlie Brown trick-or-treating and getting a
rock in his bag, and saying, *"I got a rock,"* but Mom didn't catch the media
reference.

Needless to say, there was much merchandise from Fry's:
- From me to Dad: a wall calendar with pictures of different model
  train sets for every month
- From Abe to Susan: Copy of Quicken, the oddly religious per-
  sonal/financial software program that has no option for roommates or other non–Cold War era sex/space-sharing alliances.

- From Susan to Todd: SIMMs (Macintosh memory modules: Single
  Inline Memory Modules)
- From everyone to everyone: Video and audio cables
- From Michael to Dad: an old-fashioned red Craftsman tool chest
- From Santa to all of us in our stockings: diet Cokes, Hostess prod-
  ucts, blank video tapes, and batteries!

Of course: minivan-loads of *Star Trek*kiana—

- three British import CDs of William Shatner karaokeing "Mr.
  Tamborine Man" (famous career mistake #487) as well as
  "Lucy in the Sky with Diamonds"
- *Starlog* magazine subscriptions
- bootleg galley proofs of the upcoming Gene Rodenberry biography
- *Next Generation* mouse pads
- photo glossies of Data, Riker, Deanna Troi, and Wesley from *Star
  Trek: The Next Generation*
- a plastic *Starship Enterprise* Control Center as well as a Franklin
  Mint *Starship Enterprise* replica
- a *Deep Space Nine* yo-yo, but no one has really clicked into *Deep
  Space Nine* yet, so it wasn't popular and sat on the coffee
  table

Overheard: *"It got rated four-and-a-half mice by* MacUser*!"*

Mom made a turkey for dinner, and wore pearls and hammed it up as a TV
mom. We all ate together in the "formal" dining room. Christmas is traditionally a bigger deal in our house, but we all see each other so much, it was
no big deal being together. We talked about Macs and product.

In the background the TV set was playing a *Wheel of Fortune* rerun, and
was making a *ding-ding-ding* sound. Mom asked, "What's that noise," and
Susan said, "Someone just bought a vowel."

Then the BIG surprise was that ABE appeared! Like something from a
Disney movie, right in the middle of dinner, in a white rental car, laden with
Sony products, bottles o' booze, and a big box with a spectacular bow on top
for Bug—a paper shredder from a surplus store. Bug was positively sniffling
with gratitude (*"It's the nicest present anybody's ever given me!"*) He spent

the rest of the afternoon wrapping newspapers and lighting flash bombs of the shredded remnants in the fireplace, ridding the Habitrail of several months and stratum of bedding material, and it looked quite presentable at the end of it.

After dinner we forced Abe into the van and drove him to 7-Eleven to buy him more Christmas presents, so he ended up with copies of *People*, microwaved cheeseburgers, Reese's Pieces, and string as gifts. I realized how much I liked Abe, but I wonder if I'd ever have recognized that if I had kept living in the group house. I think our e-mail correspondence has given us an intimacy that face-to-face contact never would have. Irony!

I almost made Dad a cardboard sign saying, "WILL MANAGE FOR FOOD" but then I felt like a bad, bad son, and then, like clockwork, I got to feeling depressed for fifty something's, imagining them standing at the corner of El Camino Real and Rengstorff Avenue holding up such a sign. And I can't believe Michael got Dad a nice tool kit for Christmas. How fucking thoughtful.

SUNDAY
December 26, 1993

All family'ed out.

Karla and I drove down the hill to Syntex, birthplace of the birth control pill, a little bit below Mom and Dad's house, down on Hillview Avenue—a 1970s utopian, *Andromeda Strain*ishly empty tech complex. We sat in the grass amphitheater by the leafless birch trees, looked at the sculptures from the sculpture garden, walked over the walkways and pretended we were Susan Dey and Bobby Sherman on a date, falling through a dark cultural warp, and landing inside the technological dream that underwrote the free-wheelin', swingfest TV-lifestyle of that era.

Syntex was the first corporation to invent the "workplace as campus." Before California high-tech parks, the most a corporation ever did for an employee was maybe supply a house, maybe a car, maybe a doctor, and maybe a place to buy groceries. Beginning in the 1970s, corporations began supplying showers for people who jogged during lunch hour and sculptures to soothe the working soul—proactive humanism—the first full-scale integration of the corporate realm into the private. In the 1980s, corporate integration punctured the *next* realm of corporate life invasion at "campuses" like Microsoft and Apple—with the next level of intrusion being that the borderline between work and life blurred to the point of unrecognizability.

Give us your entire life or we won't allow you to work on cool projects.

In the 1990s, corporations don't even hire people anymore. People become their own corporations. It was inevitable.

Karla and I felt like the last couple on earth, walking through the emptiness. We felt like Adam and Eve.

I told Karla that Ethan doesn't think biotech is such a hot investment because it's "too 9-to-5," and the workers follow non-techie time schedules, and their parking lots NEVER have cars in them on Sundays. Actually, to this day, Ethan is *still* trying to find a biotech firm with Sunday workers. He says that once he finds one, he'll be able to invest the farm, lie back, and retire. If only Ethan had something to invest!

Karla picked some iceplant flowers, the semiofficial plant of the high-tech world because it stabilizes hillsides so quickly. She said it's thornless-ness makes it "the Play-Doh" version of cactus.

We were being very freestyle. We discussed whether we should go try and crash into the research institute off the 280 where Koko the gorilla lives with her kitten. Karla said that the transdermal nicotine patch was invented just over the hill, on Page Mill Road, near the Interval Research Corporation headquarters. History! Then Karla suggested we visit Interval Research's campus and see what it's like: "If Syntex was the 1970s and Apple was the 1980s, then Interval is the 1990s."

Interval Research's headquarters were like a middle-class honeymoon hotel in Maui circa 1976, and slightly gone to seed, with *Gilligan's Island*-style lagoonlets between the buildings and a lobby with a vaguely medical/dental, is-this-where-I-drop-off-my-urine-sample? feel.

And (important) there were CARS in the parking lot, even on the Sunday after Christmas.

Karla said she knew this girl Laura who worked there, and so we checked, and she *was there*. We rapped on her window, overlooking the central courtyard's lagoon, and she looked up and came out and let us in. Laura has an IQ of 800, just like Karla. She invited us inside and we played pool at their pool table. The pool table is to the 1990s what PARC's bean bag chairs were to the 1970s.

Interval Research is so weird because nobody knows for sure what it is they really *do* there. They have stealth cachet. Laura does something on neural nets.

People project onto Interval's blankness either their paranoia or their hope. People always get emotional when you mention it. Interval was the think tank-slash-company Paul Allen from Microsoft started when he learned he had something terminal. His disease left after he founded it.

Interval's mandate is solely to generate intellectual properties, not to develop products—a heresy in Silicon Valley. If an idea is good enough, the unwritten concept is that there's an in-house VC dude in the form of Paul

Allen to foot the bill. No wonder people get jealous—imagine not having to struggle for start-up money—the intellectual freedom!

Abe is against the lack of gung-ho-ishness in pure research. He says Interval is an intellectual *Watership Down*. *We* have to remind him that since the government has pulled out of Big Science, *someone* has to do pure theoretical research. He grudgingly agrees.

Laura used to be at Apple's Advanced Technology Group, but left a year ago. When she started at Apple, they had a 3- to 7-year yield time for theoretical research; a project had to pay for itself from three to seven years after its start. In the early 1990s, the yield time dropped to one year—"Not one-point-oh enough," said Laura. "Here, it's 5- to 10-years' yield time. That's good."

We asked her what the difference was between Apple and Interval, and she said that Apple tried to change the world while Interval tries to *affect* the world. "We have a touchie-feelie reputation," she said, "probably because of Brenda Laurel's work in gender and intelligence, but believe me, it's *heaven* to be able to do pure math, theoretical software, or watch Ricki Lake if you need to." (I should add, Laura is a real pool shark. I pointed this out and she said, "Oh, it's only math.") Brenda Laurel is the woman responsible for research into how women interact with math. She's the Anti-Barbie.

"Staff here are a bit older, too," she said, "and people mostly only get in via recommendation. There's no snatch-the-pebble-from-my-hand koan routine for prospective employees. And there's no reporting tree. It's post-grad school, sort of. Everybody's supposed to be equal, too, but of course you have sub-equal and super-equal personalities. They fall into planet/moon relationships soon enough. But for the most part, we're all start-up types, ex-academic and ex-corporate types who want to keep the one-point-oh flame alive."

Laura cleaned up at pool. I felt goofy losing, the way you do with pool. Pool is like rollerblading: you have to pretend you're the cooly-wooliest person on earth, while you're quietly cringing inside.

Other techies came and went, and it felt refreshingly like a normal workday. Karla promised to fix Laura up with Anatole. Laura used to have a crush on him back at Apple. *L'amour, l'amour*. I was a little underwhelmed. I guess I was expecting them to be doing Tesla Coil experiments or building jets out of Mylar. Or 3,000-lb. onions being carried out of the parking lot with machine-gun totin' guards alongside the truck.

I said that since Anatole's friends were going to help us alpha test *Oop!*, maybe we could get her closer to Anatole if she wanted to help test. She agreed immediately. Talk about Tom Sawyer painting a fence white!

When we got home, Mom and Dad were just back from a bike ride along the Foothills Expressway. They were sweating, and Misty was licking them in pursuit of sodium. After this, they watched Martha Stewart tapes and felt guilty for not orchestrating their lives more glamorously.

Bug popped by en route to a party in San Jose. We told him about our trip to Interval and he told us that the replacement paradigm for Graphic User Interface was going to emerge from there, and that PARC's 1970s desktop metaphor work had become the "intellectual avocado-colored appliance of the computer industry."

"My, how fickle are our allegiances," said Karla.

"Oh come on, Bug," I said, "can't you be even a *bit* bitter about PARC anymore?"

"I can foam about PARC forever," said Bug, "or I can groove on the next PARC-like think tank. I choose to groove. Where's your mom, Dan? I brought her a rock she might like."

Bug is spending part of his off-time developing a traffic-monitoring routine for offices that allows office workers to minimize the number of times they bump into each other in the hallway. He was inspired by that cartoon character, Dilbert, who freaks out every time he has to walk down a hall with somebody else. "I mean, what's a person supposed to say, Kar? How often can a person regenerate fresh and witty banter each and *every* time they bump into a person? Oohhh . . . *nice carpeting.* Oohhh . . . *what an attractive Honeywell thermostat control switch next to the photocopier.* Human beings weren't de*signed* to bump into each other in hallways. I'm providing a valuable postindustrial service. Microsoft would have been heaven if my system had been operative and in place."

SATURDAY
New Year's Day, 1994

Abe left for SFO Airport and then we all went for a drive in the Carp—Karla, Ethan, Todd, Bug, and I.

We drove past the home of Thomas Watson Jr., 99 Notre Dame Avenue, San Jose, California. Watson steered IBM into the computer age—and was made prez of the company in 1952. In 1953 he developed the first commercial storage device for computers. He died on a New Year's Eve.

On the radio we heard that Bill got married, on Lanai in Hawaii, and we all screamed so loudly that the Carp nearly went off the road. And apparently Alice Cooper was there. So to celebrate we played old Alice Cooper tapes and purchased a "Joey Heatherton" fondue kit in a secondhand store and later on boxed it up to mail to Microsoft. They'll probably think it's a bomb.

"Ooh, Bill—please, please feed me another bite of hot, bubbly cheese cube," Susan whispered in a little girl voice in the backseat.

"I feel as though we're in a witness relocation program," said Todd. "You can leave Bill, but Bill will never leave *you.*"

We also went to "The Garage," the Tech Museum of Innovation in San Jose. We were expecting a Pirates of the Caribbean kind of exhibit, with bioanimatronic Deadheads hacking an Altair inside a re-created 1976 Sunnyvale Garage.

Instead there was a mock clean room, a Silicon Graphics 3D protein simulator, and a chromosome map in the biotechnology section:

Goiter:	bottom of gene pair no. 8
Epilepsy:	lower half of gene pair 20
Red hair color:	middle of pair 4
Albinism:	lower 11th pair

Karla said that a quarter of all pure white cats are deaf—that the trait of whiteness and the trait for deafness are entwined together, so that you can't have one without a possibility of the other.

This segued into a discussion of algorithm breeding that lasted well until we arrived in Berkeley where we went to a yuppie-style party at a college friend of Karla's. Ethan drank too much and told loud jokes, and the yuppies weren't happy. We had to take him into the backyard and cool him off. He said, "What's a bar bill but a surtax on reality." We're not sure if he has a drinking problem.

The music was Herb Alpert and Brazil 66. It could easily be your own parents' party, circa *Apollo* 9. Later, even though we all agreed not to, we ended up surrounding a Mac and oohing and aahing over a too-tantalizing piece of shareware.

Anecdote: We talked with Pablo and Christine, Karla's "we-have-a-life" friends who were having the party. I asked them, "Are you married?"

"Well," said Pablo, "we went down to Thailand and a guy in a yellow silk robe waved his hands around our bodies and . . ." Pablo paused. "You know, I suppose we don't really *know* if we're married or not."

"It was sort of Mick-and-Jerry," said Christine.

Later on, Pablo was telling this deep intimate story about how he found religion in the hinterlands of Thailand, and just at the most intense, quietest moment in the storytelling, Ethan walked into the kitchen, overheard a snatch of conversation, and said, "Thailand? I love Thailand! I'm dying to build a chain of resorts all over Thailand and Bali, kind of like Club Meds but a little more nineties. I'm gonna call them 'Club Zens,' right? 'Cause of the Buddhism thing. There's all kinds of statues and monuments over there I could use to make it look authentic—like you're in a monastery, but with booze and bikinis. Now that's nirvana! As soon as I make my next million . . ."

It was a very "Ethan" moment.

Oh—at the Museum in San Jose there was a pile of this stuff called aerogel—solid, yet almost entirely air. It seemed like thoughts made solid. It was so lovely.

Another "Oh"—Susan complains that Bug stays up all night shredding paper and the whirring of the rotors is driving her nuts.

NEW YEAR'S RESOLUTIONS

Me:	to penetrate the Apple complex
Karla:	undisclosed (doesn't want to jinx)
Ethan:	to slow down time
Todd:	visit junkyards more often, to bench 420, and to have a relationship
Susan:	to hack into the DMV and to have a relationship
Bug:	to overhaul his image and to have a relationship

680X0

a burning Lego Los Angeles	moon
880 Nimitz Freeway	Premium Saltine crackers
Control and the feeling of mastery	I Robot

The Apollo rocket designers and the NASA engineers of
Houston and Sunnyvale grew up in the 1930s and 1940s dreaming of Buck Rogers and the exoterrestrial
meanderings of *Amazing Stories*. When this aerospace
generation grew old enough, they chose to make those dreams
in metal.

TUESDAY
January 4, 1994

Woke up sick this morning—finally got the flu. I thought it might be a hangover, but no. In spite of the fact that I think I feel like death-on-a-stick, I want to write down what happened today.

First, Michael bounced through the sliding doors around noon in a shiny happy mood, and invited us all out to see our (game show tone of voice) . . . *new office!* Ethan sold his Ferrari to do the lease. "Farewell 1980s!" he said. (He drives a 1987 Honda Civic now. "I feel like I'm in high school.")

Uncharacteristically brash, he yelled, "Convoy! Everybody . . . down to our new office. You, too, Mrs. Underwood . . . we've been liberated from the Habitrail."

We stuffed ourselves into two cars and drove through the vine-covered suburbs and carefully mowed, Frisbee-free lawns of Palo Alto's tech parks, to Hamilton Street, a block south of University Street downtown. And it was there that we learned what Dad has actually been doing all this time.

As Michael opened a second-floor oak door, he said to me, in a voice intended to be heard by everybody, "I figured your father's talents as a model railroader might have translatable applications into our world here . . ."

The wet paint smelled like cucumbers and sour cream and made me a bit pukey, but the feeling passed as I saw what lay before us . . . the most sculptured environment I've ever seen—an entire world of Lego—hundreds of 50 x 50-stud gray pads on the floors and on the walls, all held in place with tiny brass screws. Onto these pads were built skyscrapers and animals and mazes and Lego railroads, sticking out of the walls, rounding corners, passing through holes. The colors were shocking; Lego-pure. A skeleton lay down beside a platoon of robots; cubic flowers grew beside boxcars loaded with nickels that rounded the blue railroad bends. There was a Palo Alto City

Hall—a '70s Wilshire modernist box—and there was a 747 and a smoking pipe . . . and . . . *everything in the world!* Pylons and towers of color, and dogs and chalets . . .

"I think your father should take a bow, don't you, Daniel?"

Dad, who was in the back tinkering with a castle, looked flustered but proud, and fidgeted with a stack of two-stud yellow bricks. This universe he had built was a Guggenheim and a Toys-R-Us squished into one. We were having seizures, all of us. Susan was livid. She said, "You spent my vested stock money on . . . *Lego?*" She was purple.

Ethan looked at me: "Michael's addiction."

I, too, was flubbered. In the magic of the moment I looked up into the corner—and I caught Mom looking, too—at a small white house in the far back corner, sprouting from a wall, with a little white picket fence around it, the occupant inside no doubt surveying all that transpired beneath its windows, and I said, "Oh, Dad, this is—the most *real* thing I've ever seen.*"*

And I wondered then, how do we ever know what beauty lies inside of people, and the strange ways this world works to lure that beauty outward?

What follows I will write only because it's what happened, and I'm sick, and I don't want to lose it—I might accidentally erase the memory. I want a backup.

What happened was that while everyone was *ooh*ing and *ahh*ing over the Lego sculptures (and staking out their new work spaces) the colors in front of my eyes began to swim, and everybody's words stopped connecting in my head, and I had to go down to the street for fresh air, and I wobbled out the door.

It was a hot sunny day—oh California!—and I walked at random and ended up standing on the blazing piazza of the Palo Alto City Hall, baked in white light from the suntanning cement, the civil servants around me buzzing in all directions, efficiently heading off to lunch. I heard cars go by.

My body was losing its ability to regulate its temperature and I was going cold and hot, and I wasn't sure if I was hungry or whether the virus had deactivated my stomach, and I felt like my system was getting ready to shut down.

I sat in this heat and light on the low-slung steps of the hall, feeling dizzy, and not quite knowing where I was, and then I realized there was somebody sitting next to me, and it was Dad. And he said, "You're not feeling very well, are you, son."

And I said, "Nnn . . . *no*."

And he said, "I was following you down the streets. I was right behind you the whole time. It's the flu, isn't it? But it's more than just the flu."

I was silent.

"Right?" he asked.

"Yeah."

"I'm a young man, Daniel, but I'm stuck inside this old sack of bones. I can't help it."

"Dad . . ."

"Let me finish. And so you think I'm old. You think that I don't understand things. That I never notice what goes on around me—but I *do* notice. And I've noticed that I'm maybe too distant with you—and that maybe I don't spend enough time with you."

"FaceTime," I said, regretting my bad joke as the words slipped out.

"Yes. FaceTime."

Two secretaries walked by laughing at some joke they were telling, and a yuppie guy with a stack of documents walked past us.

The inside of my head did a dip, like on a ride at Knott's Berry Farm. I found myself saying, "Michael's not Jed, Dad. He just *isn't*. And neither am I. And I just can't keep trying to keep up with him. Because no matter how hard I run, I'm never going to catch up."

"Oh, my boy . . ."

My head was between my legs at this point, and I had to keep my eyes closed, because the light from the piazza was hurting me, and I wondered if this was how Ethan's eyes felt on his antidepressant chemicals, and then I started thinking of a small plastic swimming pool Jed and I used to play in when we were babies, and I think my mind was misfiring. And then I felt my father's arms around my shoulders, and I shivered, and he pulled me close to him.

I was too sick, and Dad's words weren't registering. "You and your friends helped me once when I was lost. The whole crew of you—your casual love and help—saved me at a time when no one else could save me.

And now I can help *you.* I was lost, Daniel. If it weren't for you and your friends, I would never have found the green spaces or the still waters. My mind would not now be calm . . ."

But I don't remember what I said next. I have faint memories—my arms touching the warm cement—of a stop sign—of a sago palm branch brushing my cheek; my father's worried face looking forward right above my own; the clouds above his head; birds in the trees; my father's arms beneath me; depositing me within the Lego garden; my mother saying, "Dear?" and my father's voice saying, *"It's okay, honey. He just needs to sleep for a long, long time."*

5
TrekPolitiks

An earthquake hit Los Angeles at 4:31 this morning and the images began arriving via CNN right away. Karla and I stayed home to watch, and when Ethan, a Simi Valley boy, heard about it on the radio driving in from San Carlos, he ran right through our front yard's sprinkler to watch our TV. (His own Cablevision bill remains unpaid.) Damage seemed to be localized but extreme—the San Fernando Valley, Northridge, Van Nuys, and parts of Santa Monica and Pacific Palisades.

"The freeways!" moaned Ethan. "My beloved freeways—Antelope Valley, ripped and torn, the 405, rubble—the Santa Monica freeway at La Cienega—all collapsed."

We'd never seen Ethan cry. At the sight of some particularly devastated overpass, he told me, "I kissed my first date beside that off-ramp—we'd sit on the embankments and watch the cars go by."

Anyway, it really *did* make us sad to see all of this glorious infrastructure in ruins, like a crippled giant. We ate breakfast, leafed through the *Handbook of Highway Engineering* (1975), and watched all the collapsed structures.

Mom made us hot chocolate before she went to the library and then dropped us off at the office on her way. Ethan was a mess all day.

Dad quit his night course in C++ because all of the kids in his class were seventeen and they just stared at him and didn't think he could be a student because he was too old. The students were saying things to each other like, "If he comes too close to you shout, *'You're not my father!'* as loud as you can." Kids are so cruel.

So we're going to teach Dad C++ instead.

Random moment: This afternoon I was in the McDonald's on El Camino Real near California Street and they had this Lucite box with a slot on top where people put their business cards. It was *stuffed* with cards. Really *stuffed*.

But the weird thing was, I couldn't locate anything on the box saying what the cards were to be used *for*. So I guess it's just this human instinct to stick your business card in a slot. Like you're going to win . . . *what*—a free orange drink machine for your birthday party? I saw a woman's card from Hewlett-Packard and a card from some guy in Mexico saying "Graduate from Stanford Graduate School of Business." Here's this Stanford graduate at *McDonald's* putting his card in a box at random. I just don't understand people sometimes. Didn't he learn anything at Stanford?

Geek party tonight. Relief! Without geek parties, we'd never see anybody but OURSELVES, day in, day out. And the big news of the day was that Karla and I found a place to house-sit—it belongs to a woman who got the layoff package from Apple. We move in this weekend (yayyy!), and the move comes as some relief as the Karla/Mom not communicating thing is oddly wearing on all of us.

The party: It was in San Francisco (the "sit-*tay*," as now cooler-than-us-by-virtue-of-living-there Bug and Susan call it), in Noe Valley at Ann and Jorge's, Anatole's friends. Jorge's with Sun Microsystems and Ann's with 3DO. There were LARGE quantities of delicious, snobby San Francisco food, great liquor, industry gossip, and TVs displaying earthquake damage all over the apartment. Since us *Oop!*sters are all broke, we saved pots of money by not eating all day before the party. We never eat before geek parties.

In the moneyed world of Silicon Valley, nothing is uncooler than being broke. Karla and I were both curious to see how Ann and Jorge live. When we arrived, I was overwhelmed by the hipness factor. And where are the GEEKS? Everyone was dressed. . . . like *real people*. Where were the ironic fridge magnets? The futons? The IKEA furniture? The Nerf products? The house looked as though it had been made over by Martha Stewart. There were REAL couches, obviously purchased NEW, in red velvet with gold and silver silk throw pillows; Matisse-derived area rugs; little candles every-where; a REAL dining table with SIX chairs around it in its OWN ROOM with vases and bowls full of pine cones on the mantel. These people were like ADULTS . . . seamless!

Susan said they've merely disguised their evidence of not having a life: "I mean, it's like you go to somebody's house for Thanksgiving and they've spent eighteen hours covering the rooms with little orange squashes and quinces and crepe paper, and the meal is like Henry the Eighth, and you can't eat because you get this creepy sick feeling that the person who did the dinner has nothing else to do with their life. It's the dark side of *Martha Stewart's Living*."

Ethan said Susan still felt guilty for putting too much work and money into our gift baskets at Christmas.

I thought that overdecoration and nice houses might be the regional ver-sion of the never-used kayak in the garage up at Microsoft. But a darker thought emerged: these may possibly be techies who HAVE A LIFE, and they're upping the ante for the rest of us.

Susan, in spite of ragging on the decor with us, started fellating our hostess, Ann, over the subject of houses. They were talking about some expensive store in Pacific Heights where no doubt all of this furniture comes from.

Ann: "Fillamento, it's on Fillmore and Sacramento. They have the best stuff, I just got this amazing coverlet for our bed there. They had to special-order it from Germany, but it is so gorgeous . . . do you want to see it?"

Susan: "Of course!"

Off they went, comparing decor purchases. You'd never know that Ann used to be a chip designer.

The local rage is obscure, expensive premium vodkas—it's the litmus of cool at geek parties. Later on, Susan, Karla, and I were standing around drinking Ketel-1, when some guy who'd been checking Karla out came up and said, "Hi, I'm Phil, I'm a PDA."

PDAs are what Newton is—it's an acronym for Personal Digital Assistant.

"You look more analog than digital," Susan oh-so-wittily batted back at him.

"It stands for Peons Down at Apple!" Phil chortled, ignoring Susan, and zooming in on KARLA. It was really embarrassing, because Susan wasn't picking up on the fact that she was being ignored by Phil. Karla was grossed out by Phil, and I was on red alert about this big hulk zooming in on Karla. I inserted myself between him and Karla. "Maybe it stands for Public Display of Affection." I put my arm around Karla and introduced everybody.

Susan was laughing at Phil's jokes—she's so desperate for a dating architecture in her life, and when Phil turned around Karla mouthed the words: REMOVE HIM FROM MY LIFE to Susan, then grabbed my shoulder, and we went off to the den to marvel at the amount of *stuff* owned by our hosts. We felt like East Germans visiting West Germany for the first time. Phil, meanwhile, sensing defeat, finally noticed Susan, and began chatting *her* up.

For the next hour, we watched Phil regale Susan with exciting tales of product meetings, shipping deadlines, engineering crises, and code names for products.

I can't stop marveling at how *together* geeks are in the Valley. At Microsoft, there was no peer pressure to do anything except work and ship on time. If you did, you got a Ship-it Award. Easy. Black and White.

Here, it's so much more complicated—you're supposed to have an exciting, value-adding job that utilizes your creativity, a wardrobe from Nordstrom's or at the very least Banana Republic, a $400,000 house, a cool European or Japanese car, the perfect relationship with someone as ambitious, smart, and well-dressed as yourself, and extra money to throw parties so that the whole world can observe what a life you have, indeed. It makes me miss Redmond, but at the same time, it *is* kind of inspiring. I feel conflicted.

Even Michael noticed, with a rare lapse into pop culture: "Perhaps David Byrne was talking about the geeks inheriting the earth in that Talking Heads song, *'This is not my beautiful house! This is not my beautiful wife! My God! How did I get here?'*"

Bug talked to a guy who's a game producer at a company called PF

Magic. (What's up with all of these companies named "Magic"? Is it some New Age/George Lucas-type deal or *what*? Uniquely Northern Californian.) Bug thinks the guy might be gay, but it was hard to tell. "All the guys around here dress well enough to have their heterosexuality be suspect . . . it's not very helpful for me."

Bug has done a little damage himself over at the Stanford Shopping Center, as part of his new program to "become enculturated into my new lifestyle."

It would be so weird to all of a sudden have to take all of the myths and stereotypes and information about another kind of sexual orientation and somehow wade through them in order to construct yourself within that image. Susan's kind of doing it, too, but within heterosexuality—all of a sudden she's a Sexual Being, and I think she's having to learn as much about sex as Bug is, even though theoretically she's been heterosexual all her life.

Many geeks don't really have a sexuality—they just have work. I think the sequence is that they get jobs at Microsoft or wherever right out of school, and they're so excited to have this "real" job and money that they just figure that the relationships will naturally happen, but then they wake up and they're thirty and they haven't had sex in eight years. There are always these flings at conferences and trade shows, and everyone brags about them, but nothing seems to emerge from them and life goes back to the primary relationship: Geek and Machine.

It's like male geeks don't know how to deal with real live women, so they just assume it's a user interface problem. Not their fault. They'll just wait for the next version to come out—something more "user friendly."

Ethan got through to his parents on a cellular phone around sunset; he learned they were having the grandest of times, barbecuing burgers and corn on the front lawn, and meeting their neighbors for the first time in years. "Mom said the Ronald Reagan Library was untouched. Like I care."

I think he wanted more drama. I think he would have been happier to hear that his mother was pinioned beneath a collapsed chimney, trickling blood into the phone receiver held up to her ear by his father.

Todd didn't come to the party. He was out on an actual, real, genuine, not-fake, date-style DATE tonight.

I'm coming to the conclusion about the human subconscious . . . that, no matter how you look at it, machines really *are* our subconscious. I mean, people from outer space didn't come down to earth and make machines for us . . . *we* made them ourselves. So machines can only be products of our being, and as such, windows into our souls . . . by monitoring the machines we build, and the sorts of things we put into them, we have this amazingly direct litmus as to how we are evolving.

Champaign-Urbana

Her parents are engineers but that wasn't enough to keep them together.

Pull the wires from the wall

Chelyabinsk-70

TUESDAY

Shake-up: Todd has begun seeing a female body builder named Dusty, so I guess Armageddon can only be a little ways away. And here's the freaky part—Dusty codes! She's done systems for Esprit and Smith & Hawken. But she's the uncodiest female I've ever met.

"We met at the protein drink sales case at Gold's Gym," beamed Todd, showcasing Dusty, who emerged into our office like a Close Encounter of the Third Kind. "Dusty," Todd called, "strike the pose!" From offstage a ghetto blaster pumped out thwomping lipstick-commercial Eurodisco.

Dusty—late twenties or early thirties, with titanium hamstrings (and perhaps too much time spent in tanning booths) in ragged fringed hotpants and a ripped T-shirt commenced vogueing official International Bodybuilding Federation poses. We gaped openly. Such brazen posing!

Dusty then grabbed Misty, who Mom brought downtown and then promptly left with us while she did some shopping, and twirled her by the paws in circles above our office's Lego garden. All that was missing were popping flash bulbs and a smoke machine, and Misty, unused to being picked up in such a manner, was blissed and became Dusty's instant lifelong fan.

Dusty put down the now-dizzy Misty and said, "Yeah . . ." in a Chesterfields-smoked-through-a-tracheotomy-slit voice (Dusty gets her voice from barking out aerobics commands, which, Todd informs us, she teaches) ". . . all those big plastic tubs of branch-chain protein growth formula with gold lettering—Toddy and me were fighting for the last container of MetMax."

Their eyes met and they squeezed each other's hands—it's a good thing they like each other, because otherwise it would be like two monster trucks chewing each other up at the Kingdome.

Karla and Susan were being catty about Dusty:

Karla: "Dusty—sounds like the name of someone who rides in a radio station traffic news-copter."

Susan: "She looks like she just escaped from an Ice-Follies Smurfs-on-Ice mall show—tousled mall hair, spandex, and perky perma-smile."

Michael closed his door. He doesn't like this side of human nature, but later Karla said it's because he's attracted to super-strong women. "Trust me," she said. "I can tell these things."

Ethan is building a Lego freeway cloverleaf. Once it's finished, he's going to smash it and repair it. He's been horrified by the Northridge quake in Los Angeles. He's indeed a Valley boy.

At a Canon photocopy shop he enlarged a news wire photo of the collapsed Antelope Valley freeway to up to wall-sized and hung it in the office as a model to build from. I suppose he should have used the money to pay his CABLE BILL, but Karla thinks he likes to have an excuse to visit us more at the office.

Michael wisely allows no cable in the office and has forbidden us from playing *Melrose Place* and hockey fight dubs on the office VCR unit.

Ethan has already demolished the Wilshire Modernist block of the Palo Alto City Hall Dad constructed.

"Reconstruction is part of the plan," said Ethan, and Dad, although miffed, took pity on Ethan and decided not to get huffy.

We LOVE our new office and we no longer have to worry about rubbing our fingers on surfaces and finding accumulations of Ethan's dead scalp particles. Dad has a Dustbuster mounted on the wall. We also have SPACE.

Nobody scored last night. Susan got Phil's phone number and Bug got the PF Magic guy's number, even though he's not sure if he's straight or not. The 1990s!

Susan was a bit sheepish around me and Karla, because she *knows* Phil is a loser, and she *knows* that we know.

Tech moment: we have our own Internet domain and are subservient to nobody. Our house is wired directly to the Net with a mail-order 486 using

Linux on a 14.4 modem with a SLIP connection to the Little Garden (an Internet service provider down here). I am now daniel@oop.com.

"@" could become the "Mc" or "Mac" of the next millennium.

Surprise: Mom told me that Dad's been looking for work elsewhere—and that Michael knows about it. "He needs to be among his own kind, dear."

Actually, today was just a big waste of a day, work-wise. I didn't get anything done because I had too many interruptions. I'd start to do something, then I'd be distracted by something else, forget what I was doing in the first place, and then get so worried that I wasn't getting anything done, that it wrecked even *further* my ability to get anything done. Sometimes too much communication is too much communication. I *should* rent a *Nature* video and relax, but instead, tonight we rented *The Poseidon Adventure* and watched the ship turning upside down scene over and over about fifty times and then we rented *Earthquake* and watched LA dismantle itself about fifty times, frame-by-frame.

Mom was in the breakfast nook typing a letter to her sister on an IBM Selectric and we got into an argument about whether anybody made them anymore. Maybe in Malaysia.

WEDNESDAY

Dusty is now working with us! Michael hired her under the condition that she devote herself to the company and confine her body experimentation to off-hours—as well as to forgo aerobic instruction moonlighting altogether until shipping. "And *no* smart drugs!" said Michael. "Not that it's my business, but smart drugs turn people into Tasmanian Devils, not Einsteins."

"*Touché*, Michelangelo," said Dusty. "That's French for *meow*." She has a hard time calling anybody by their real name.

Dusty was trying on a new marigold yellow posing bikini she's hoping to wear in this Fall's Iron Rose IV Competition in San Diego. Dusty herself was the color of a roasted turkey.

Karla and Susan were once again certainly gaping. But in the end they broke down, approaching her, asking probing questions, touching her body like it was the monolith in *2001*. They've—*we've*—never seen such a hyper-articulated body before. It reminds me of the first time I ever saw an SGI rendering at full blast.

"Toddy" has bailed out of his geek house near the Shoreline off-ramp and has moved in with Dusty up in Redwood City. Eyebrows shot up at the news of such speedy cohabitation, and then Todd confessed he and Dusty had been seeing each other for MONTHS. How could he keep a secret like *that* in an office as small as ours?

Look and Feel escaped this afternoon from their newly reconfigured Habitrail and chewed up the caboose on Michael's Lego train. So they're on probation now.

All of us went to the Tonga Room at the Fairmont in San Francisco to celebrate Dusty's first day as our hacker, working with Michael. It was this incredible blowout, like in college. Dusty cut in front of all these people who were lined up to get in and then blithely waved us over to the table she'd procured. Cool! She's a bulldozer.

The Tonga Room is filled with rich dentists from Düsseldorf watching this *Gilligan's Island* fake Tiki raft float across an old swimming pool while fake thunder and rain roar, and a live band plays disco medleys. We ordered these ridiculous umbrella and fruit-wedge drinks with high centers of gravity, so every time somebody got up to dance (*Oye Como Va!*), all the drinks fell over and the waitresses just wanted to kill us. We had to switch tables three times because of the fruit pulp buildup, and the ochre tablecloths looked like swamps of barf.

Two things: Dusty said, "I put myself through school working as a waitress. The guys loved me. I brought them food and beer—and then I left them. Pigs."

Karla and Susan said, "Amen," much to my horror. They were all wearing those little drink umbrellas in their hair.

Michael noted that the Tonga Room uses a form of ice that is neither cubic nor slush-based: "Someone had better notify 7-Eleven immediately. It's a niche!"

Dusty gave Susan lessons in dating architecture: "Tech women hold all the cards, and they know it. Tech men outnumber tech women by about three to one, so the women can choose and discard mates at will. And let's face it, it's cool for a guy to be dating a tech chick."

I inwardly agreed with this. "Tech chicks" all seem so much wiser and mature than the guys (the Karla Attraction Factor) that I think they must get fed up. I overheard Susan and Karla complaining about tech guys at a geek party last month, and I started to feel a little insecure. Up at Microsoft, geeks looked exactly like what they were—nerds, misfits, Dungeons & Dragons players out on day pass. Down here in the Valley, these tech guys are good-looking—they can pass in the "normal" world without revealing their math team past. Whenever Susan and Karla started gushing over some cute guy, I started saying, "He's probably in MARKETING." It made me feel better.

Susan, nonetheless, wanted to know why she was having such a dating problem. Dusty said, "I think your problem is that you think everyone else is a freak except you, but everybody's a freak—you included—and once you learn that, the World of Dating is yours."

I thought Susan would go ballistic, but instead she agreed.

THURSDAY

Dad was out today—job hunting. Anywhere else on earth except here in the Valley he wouldn't have a chance, but here he *might* find something.

Bug is freaked out because Magic Eye stereograms, the black light posters of the 1990s, don't work with him. He's worried it's color-blindness linked, and he called the Garage Museum down in San Jose to see if it means something bad. He remembers those genetics charts they had there. "I'm stereogramatically blind!"

Ethan and I went out for a drink again. He was really swigging down the drinks, and so I asked him if it was smart to drink while taking antidepressants. He said, "Technically no, it's a pretty fuck-witted thing to do, but drinking allows me to take an identity holiday."

I asked him what this meant. He said that since the new isomers of antidepressants are rewiring his brain, and since he's becoming a new person because of it, every day he forgets more and more what the *old* person was who used to be.

"On the stuff I'm taking, booze never really makes you smashed," he said, "but it *does* allow me to remember the sensation of what *I* used to be and feel like. Just briefly. Life wasn't *all* bad back then. I'd never go back to it full time, but I *do* get nostalgic for my old personality. I imagine in a parallel-forked road universe there's a sad, fucked-up Ethan, achieving nothing, feeling cramped, and going nowhere. I don't know. Once you've experienced the turbo-charged version of yourself, there's no going backward."

He had another Wallbanger—"You know, pal—maybe I *should* de-wire myself. De-wiring would reconnect me to the world of natural time—sunsets and rainbows and crashing waves and Smurfs." He took a final sip. "*Nahhhh . . .*"

Susan caught a cold, "From having my panties systematically saturated with fruit pulp at the Tonga Room."

Tomorrow we move into our house-sitting house.

Before bed I told Karla about Ethan's identity holiday—of drinking to recapture the feeling of what your real personality used to feel like.

"It's all about identity," she said.

She said, "We look at a flock of birds and we think one bird is the same as any other bird—a bird unit. But a bird looks at thousands of people, at a Giants game up at Candlestick Park, say, and all they see is 'people units.' We're all as identical to them as they are to us. So what makes *you* different from *me*? Him from you? *Them* from *her*? What makes any one person any different from any other? Where does your individuality end and your species-hood begin? As always, it's a big question on my mind. You have to remember that most of us who've moved to Silicon Valley, we don't have the traditional identity-donating structures like other places in the world have: religion, politics, cohesive family structure, roots, a sense of history or other prescribed belief systems that take the onus off individuals having to figure out who they are. You're on your own here. It's a big task, but just *look* at the flood of ideas that emerges from the plastic!"

I stared at her, and I imagine she was assuming I was digesting—compiling—what she'd just told me, but instead, all I could think of, looking into her eyes, was that there was this entity—Karla—who was different from all others I knew because just under the surface of her skin lay the essence of herself, the person who thinks and dreams these things she tells to me and only me. I felt like a lucky loser and I kissed her on the nose. So that's *me* for the day.

Oh . . . I found a big stack of old *Sunset* magazines for sale in a second-hand shop. I bought them for Mom. She's a *Sunset* freak. Mom picked them up like they were feathers. She's strong now. She's all for Dusty developing her body. She and Dusty have been comparing notes. It's such a relief when your friends date cool people.

FRIDAY

A be:
Today I called 1-800 numbers and ragged on companies about therir products. I complsined to the Matell hotline (1-800-524-TOYS) that the new HotWhheels aren't as cool the ones I had when I wazs growing up. The only decent one they have is a Lexzus SC400. I've bought 3 of them (the toys), but be this as it may, Mattel is NOT exonerated. Where are the Bubble cars, may I ask? So this is my life, Dan. C'est la Vie.

Mattel karma! Susan came storming into the office late in the afternoon, having just visited a Toys-R-Us store in pursuit of a present for her niece. Susan was furious about Mattel products, too—in particular about Barbie dolls. As I was the only person in the office, I received the entirety of her postfeminist critique.

"The aisle—it was pink—I mean, the entire aisle was this shocking, moist, Las Vegas labia pink color, and it was a *big* aisle, Dan. Tens of thousands of Barbies gazing vapidly at me—this wall of mall hair—the aisle haunted with the ghostly sound of purged vomit yet to come—of unsustainable desire. Their necks thicker than their waists; sparkles; an incitement to eating disorders—"

Susan was just going on and on, so I used that tactic you use on little kids who won't stop crying—I simply changed the subject. I told her how weird it is to think that simply by walking down the wrong aisle at Toys-R-Us at the wrong moment in your child's development, you can forever screw up their future: "They have a whole aisle devoted to McDonald's restaurant products—french-fry making machines, burger makers, shake makers . . . Say you overlook the computer aisle and walk down the

McDonald's aisle instead—one tiny error and your kid's got a drive-thru headset surgically embedded in his cranium for the next seven decades.

"Toy stores are like *Brave New World*. Mom! Pop! Choose your aisle correctly. That's all I can say."

I later e-mailed this Huxleyan thought to Abe who replied:

1959
100th McDonald's: Fon du Lac, Wisconsin
1960
200th McDonald's: Knoxville, Tennessee
1964
Filet-o-Fish born
1966
First indoor-seating McDonald's: Huntsville, Alabama
1970
First McDonald's breakfast: Waikiki, Hawaii
1973
Quarter Pounder born
1975
Egg McMuffin born
1975
Twoallbeefpattiesspecialsaucelettucecheesepicklesonions-
onasesameseedbun
1983
McNuggets born

At the office we've decided that instead of Friday being jeans day, we'd have Boxer Shorts Day instead. It's way comfier, way sexier, and it's funny watching Michael admonish the male staff members, "Er . . . gentlemen: no units displayed if at all possible."

Dad came in to the office from job hunting around sundown. We made him a Cup O'Noodles and played some crank phone call tapes to cheer him up. Dusty tried to get him to wear a pair of striped boxers but Dad politely refused. Later on I went up to the house and helped him remove an old basketball hoop above the garage that's been there since the dawn of bell-bottoms. I fell and cut myself on some of Mom's rosebushes, and I know it's

corny, but I got to thinking, it's no surprise roses are the Official Flower
of Love.

My hard drive accidentally trashed today's file, so I include a snippet of
the trash here as a curiosity piece. Language!

A11111111t the office we"11ve decided that instead of Friday
F1111113636111136being jeans day, we"11111111113636373738d have Boxer
Shorts Day instead. It"111138383939404041414242434344444s way comfier,
way sexier, 1111and it"1111s funny watching Michael admonish the male staff
members, ""11114511111145454646474748111148848Please guys, no units displayed   if   at   all
possible.""11114949505051&f&v&w&x&z&Ä&ë&ì&∂&∆&¤&Ô' '4'O'S'['_'õ
' Ω' Ú * * " * t * | * } + + + L + h + v, , ?, ´ - 9 - a - } - Å - Ö - º - © - ≠ - º - » - Ã - ◊ - fl - „ -
ÂÒÛ. .?.G.O.S.T.b.|.~.Ñ.Ö.è.ê.í.ì.ú.ü.ß.Ø/ /
/S/b/c/d/e/Â/È000¥0ÿ˜Ù˝˝Ú˝Ú˝Ú˝Ú˝Ú˝Ú˝Ú˝Ú˝˝Ú˝ÙÚ˝Ú˝Ú˝Ú˝˝˝Ì˝˝Ì˝˝Ì˝Ì˝Á˝˝Ì˝Ì˝
˝˝Ì˝ÌÁÁÌ˝„˝„˝„˝„˝˝Ú˝Ú˝˝˝Ú˝˝Ú˝Ú˝\]c UÅVÅ]
`UÅcH]UÅ]c$\]c PR5151525253535454555556561111111111Dusty tried to get
him to wear a pair of striped boxers but Dad politely refused.

SATURDAY

Today was the day Karla and I finally moved into our (temporarily) own place . . . the Apple friend of Anatole who's going to Tasmania for eight months to study batik (she got the layoff package . . . it's like backward Microsoft) and so we're house-sitting for her. Like so many techie houses, it's big, sterile, stuffed with consumer electronics, and there's nothing on the walls and there are about six empty rooms lit by dozens of skylights. At least it's not one of these big Mediterranean 1980s stucco houses Susan calls "Drug Lord" houses—ostentatious stucco monuments with a Porsche 928-S parked out front.

Anyway, to remedy the house's sterility we're doing what Ethan did with his photo of the collapsed freeway overpass, and we're making photocopy blowups of cool images. We've made blowups of Barry Diller (inventor of the Movie of the Week back in 1973—in an office inside the ABC Entertainment Complex, Century City, Los Angeles, California) as well as a blowup of the ABC Entertainment Complex's twin towers.

I also enlarged an elegant *undamaged* California freeway cloverleaf from the seminal *Handbook of Highway Engineering*. And needless to say we did a double portrait of *BILL*. One right-side up—another upside down.

Ethan delivered to us a bottle of 1977 Cabernet as a housewarming present and said he felt jealous of our posters—the highest compliment, coming from him.

Todd and Dusty seem to have found soulmates in each other. They spend their precious few hours of post–code time discussing the vagaries of the New Human Body—in the office and at gym, deciding which mini-muscle needs alteration, discussing steroids as though they were Pez, and figuring out the mechanics of cosmetic surgery. They want to become "post-human"—to make their bodies like the Bionic Woman's and the Six Million Dollar Man's—to go to the next level of bodyhood.

Todd was in a chatting mode today—love's first sweep, and I know what it is—and he told me of how happy Dusty makes him feel, of how pretty he thinks she is, of how she seems to believe in something and to believe more than Todd believes. "It's as if all those one-night stands never mattered. Because all I care about is Dusty crushing my body (Have you ever done that Daniel . . . been crushed? God, is it sexy) and having her speak to me. Nobody's ever spoken to me before. I mean, not to *me*. I was always just a soul to be harvested or a human unit. But with Dusty I'm me, and I don't have to fake normality."

"That's how I feel with Karla," I said.

Todd said, "She pumps me. Love is just this great big pump."

Todd, on top of his coding work, is designing an *Oop!* Muscleman starter kit that will fold and mutate like a GoBot or a protein molecule into bulldozers, tanks, satellite stations, and Kalashnikovs. Michael thinks it'll be a big hit.

Michael is making each of us design an *Oop!* starter module so that we can utilize all segments of our brain aside from the cattle-blindered coding part of our brain. Michael is really such a slave driver. He squishes everything he can out of us. It's very Bill, so we can relate to it. I'm doing a space station.

Susan, among her many tasks—the main one of which is designing the *Oop!* user interface—is designing a dancing skeletons program. She has a burned-out Stanford medical grad student converting all human bones into *Oop!* bricks, which are in turn linked, like bones in the human body. But she's also having other animal skeletons digitized, and she's designing her program so that users can build new species. Flesh comes next.

Ethan is even developing a game—one where players train dolphins for the Department of Defense and he's designing *Oop!* weaponry and boats and submarines.

Karla's designing a vegetable factory in which small chipmunks trapped inside must run for their lives or end up diced ("God bless Warner Brothers"); Bug is designing a castle with dungeon, and I must say, it's good. He's come up with "torture nodes."

Michael wants *Oop!* users to be able to play Doom-like chase games throughout whatever we build, and is working to form an allegiance with a company up-Bay in San Francisco that provides a multiline server so that nerds in different area codes can game together.

Michael was on a rant, quite justified, I thought, about all of this media-hype generation nonsense going on at the moment. Apparently we're all "*slackers*." "Daniel, *who* thinks up these things?"

Michael pointed out that humans are the only animals to have generations. "Bears, for example, certainly don't have generations. Mom and Dad bears don't expect their offspring to eat different kinds of berries and hibernate to a different beat. The belief that tomorrow is a different place from today is certainly a unique hallmark of our species."

Michael's theory is that technology creates and molds generations. When technology accelerates to a critical point, as it has now, generations become irrelevant. Each of us as *individuals* becomes our own individual diskette with our own personal "version." Much more logical.

Mom couldn't get the garage door opener to work, so I fixed it for her. We took Misty for a walk along La Cresta. The stop sign at the corner of Arastradero was completely covered with Scotch tape, pieces of ribbon, and empty balloons from where people mark off birthday parties. It was funny.

Ethan's freeway is taking far longer to build than he anticipated and it "eats bricks like crazy."

I asked Dusty if she grew up with Barbie dolls and she said, "No, but indeed I rilly, *rilly* lusted after them in my heart. Hippie parents, you know. *Rill* crunchy. I had a Raggedy Ann doll made in, like, Sierra Leone. And all I *rilly* desired was a Barbie Corvette—more than life itself."

sigh

"So instead I played with numbers and equations. Some trade-off. The only store-bought toy I was ever allowed was a Spirograph, and I had to *beg* to receive it as a May Day present. And I had to pretend I wanted it because it was mathematical—so clean and solvable. But my parents were suspicious of mathematics because math isn't political. They're like, freaks."

Dusty's forearms resemble Popeye's. And they have pulsing veins that look like a meandering river. Ethan and I were talking, when he shouted across the room, "Jesus Christ, Dusty—I can take your pulse from over *here*."

I asked Karla if she grew up with Barbie dolls and she said (not looking up from her keyboard), "This is so embarrassing, but not only did I play with Barbies, but I played with them up until an embarrassingly late age—ninth grade." She then looked over at me, expecting reproach.

This *did* come as some surprise; I suppose it revealed itself on my face. She began typing again, and speaking over the clack of her fingers on the keyboard.

"But before you go and think I'm a lost cause, you should know that I gave my Barbie *ad*mirable pursuits—I took apart my brother's Hot Wheels and made a Barbie Toyota Assembly Plant, giving Barbie white overalls, a clipboard, and I provided jobs for many otherwise unemployed Americans." She paused and looked up from her keyboard. "God, no *won*der my parents refused to believe I was intelligent."

MONDAY

This afternoon while visiting Todd and Dusty's cottage in Redwood City, I tried to find a snack in their fridge.

Bad idea.

Pills, lotions, capsules, powders . . . anything except what normal human beings might call "food." There was a Rubbermaid container of popcorn. There was Turbo Tea, Amino mass, pure Creatine, Mus-L-Blast 2000+, raw chickens, Super Infiniti 3000, and chromium supplements as well as small bottles I thought it more polite not to inquire about.

I really have to wonder if Todd's doing steroids. I mean, he's just *not* physically normal. We're all going to have to face this.

Dusty was out at the Lucky mart buying bananas and kelp. I asked Todd, "Shit, Todd—what is it exactly you want your body to *do* for you? What is it your body's not doing for you now that it's going to do for you at some future date?" Not really Todd's sort of question.

"I think I want to have sex using a new body which allows me to not have to remember my ultrareligious family." Todd mulled this over. We looked around the apartment, strewn with hex dumbells and rubber flooring mats. "My body was just something I could believe in because there was nothing else around."

Susan was sulking about her dating architecture here in the Valley. Her fling with Mr. Intel ended long ago—she says Intel's culture is too macho to accept macho women. Phil the PDA was history eons ago. She kept talking about that Mary Tyler Moore episode where Mary tabulates the number of dates she's had over the span of her dating career and gets depressed. And then there was a big debate as we tried to remember if that was the episode where she began dating Lou.

Susan only seems to meet techies. ("Well, Sooz," says Karla, "you *do* spend almost all of your time in the Valley . . .")

"It's not just the techiness, Kar—it's that the number of flings I've had in my life now outnumbers the number of relationships. I've crossed a line."

Tonight she has a date with a Marina District tattoo artist, so we're all expecting her to show up tomorrow with a Pentium chip etched into her shoulder.

The thing about Susan is that she's making the leap into self-reconstruction so late in life. Her new dominant attitude comes from a genuine need, but it's so twisted by years of—I don't know exactly *what*. I don't know as much about Susan as I ought, I suppose. Her IBM upbringing and all of that. But the subject . . . how to broach it?

Ethan seems to have forgotten his partially completed freeway. We've nicknamed it the "Information Superhighway."

Susan reformatted and zinged-up Dad's resume on Quark. He used a (oh God . . .) *dot-matrix printer* to do his old resume. Mom's Selectric would have even been cooler.

This afternoon I mistakenly said Palo Alto was in the "Sili*cone* Valley," and Ethan snapped at me, "Sili*cone* is what they put inside of tits, Dan-O. It's Sili*kawn* . . ."

Boom! Dusty began telling us about her first breast implants at age 19, its subsequent failure, her litigation and her support groups—tales of black goo seeping from nipples, ". . . immunosuppressive globules of silicone gel migrating through my blood system, triggering this never-ending yuppie flu. It was awful. That's how I got into body manipulation and extreme health . . . because of the globules."

Yet again, the Dustmistress had us all riveted. Karla and Susan are now totally obsessed with Dusty's arms, which are like leather-sheathed steel cables from the Bay Bridge, all digitally animated like Spielberg dinosaurs. When she flexes her arms, you feel queasy—like you're going to be eaten. She says that because she has long arms, she has to work "harder to the power of three" to make them appear as proportioned as they would on a shorter woman. She's a calculus whiz.

The cattiness with Dusty ended quickly. Now they all like each other. Actually, I think it goes deeper than *"like"*—but where or how, I don't know.

Dusty's older than Todd by about five years. During a carbo-loading break later in the day, she started telling me and Karla all this personal stuff. It doesn't take much with Dusty. The distinction between herself and the public is muzzy.

"I made the switch and started liking younger guys about two years ago. The older ones kept getting all serious . . . and wanting to discuss marriage. The young kids are puppy dogs and when I want to get rid of them, I just start talking babies and before you know it they start giving me reasons why they have to hang out at their friends', and why they can't come over."

She found a piece of skin on her chicken breast and picked it off.

"I think that once I start having babies, I'm going to forget my body. But tell that to Toddy and you're dead meat. I think he's 'a keeper.' Remember— I can crush you into cat food with my thumb and index finger alone."

And she could!

Karla says that Dusty's freaked out that any baby she might have will be a freak because of the fantastic quantities of scary digestibles she's eaten over the years, on top of her implants and her flirtations with bulimia and extreme diets.

"She's done it all," says Karla, "steroids, uppers, downers, coke, poppers, Pritikin, Oprah . . ."

Went with Karla up to Mom and Dad's and helped them sort things out for recycling. When nobody was looking, I hucked some fallen tangerines at the Valotas' house down below ours. Mr. Valota is this Gladys-Kravitz-from-*Bewitched* type guy who somehow taps into all of the misinformation, apocrypha, and bad memes floating about the Valley and feeds them back to Mom in the aisles of Draeger's in Menlo Park. He's always saying discouraging things about *Oop!* to Mom. *Gee thanks, Mr. Valota.*

I liked hearing the tangerines go thunk as they hit the cedar shingles of his lanai. It's never the Mr. Valotas of this world whose houses burn down.

I was breathing really hard as I was carrying the Rubbermaid Roughneck containers to the end of the driveway. I hope nobody noticed that I'm way out of shape.

Abe's list of things to do on how to get a life:

1) Move out of a group house
2) Get involved in non-computer-related activities
3) Treat yourself to a bubble bath (I couldn't think of anything else)

TUESDAY

Dusty's twin sister, Michelle, came to visit. She's a collagen sales rep for a biotech firm near San Diego and like a plumper, less turbo-charged Dusty.

She ambled around the Lego garden for a while, watched us code, then yawned pointedly. After further multiple theatrical yawns, she then pulled two *Simpsons* dubs on VHS out of her purse and started watching them on the VCR, and one by one we melted away from our workstations and began watching along with her.

Michael arrived with Dad, found us recumbent and laughing, freaked out, and sent us back to work, sending Michelle packing on the CalTrain. Michael is now Bill!

Dusty said *Ciao*, and resumed tweaking her algorithms. Dusty's poor parents—all they wanted was a nice pair of folk-singing, shawl-knitting Leslie Van Houtens and Patricia Krenwinkels. Instead they got two lighter-complexioned Grace Jones replicants morphed together with a Malibu Barbie.

Date update: Susan is without a tattoo.

It turns out Dusty's an expert on, of all things, the Austro-Hungarian Empire (UC Santa Cruz undergrad). Talk about pure randomness. She did this to please her Leftoid hippie freak parents. ("It was an accelerated program that only took two years," she says. "Subjectivity is so much faster to scale.")

Discovering that Dusty was well informed about some calcified aspect of European history was like discovering—I don't know—like discovering that the happy face on the Kool-Aid pitcher is a cross-dresser. It's so *random*.

I mention this because tonight Todd and Dusty had dinner with a crew of moping ex-Marxist buddies of her parents over in Berkeley—all of them feeling left behind by the tide of history, singing freedom songs with a 5-stringed guitar; facial hair. That kind of stuff. There were probably lots of candles.

I think the religious feeling made Todd homesick for his religion-frenzied parents in Port Angeles. He returned to the office, brooded, and then he started to cry, then he went out on the lawn and didn't return for an hour.

Oh, and this afternoon I caught Ethan scrounging under the couch cushions, in pursuit of lost coins. The embarrassment!

WEDNESDAY

Big gossip—Todd has announced he's becoming a . . . *Marxist!* Of all things.

"Oh, Christ, Todd," said Ethan, "that's like announcing you're becoming Bugs Bunny."

Karla asked, "A Marxist? But Todd—the Wall came down in 1989."

"That doesn't matter."

"No, of *course* it doesn't," said Ethan.

"Arrogant bourgeois *cochon*," Todd slung back.

So anyway, Todd's found something external to believe in. I don't think it's a matter of dumbness or smartness, just his need to need, as ever.

Ethan was on the warpath: "If Todd expects us to treat him with some sort of respect just because he believes in some sort of outdated, cartoon-like ideology, he has *another* thing coming."

Ethan is being "reactionary" (Todd told me the word). But, as with any recent conversions to any new belief, Todd *does* exude a righteousness that is a touch off-putting, if not boring.

Michael said of the matter, "Everything else aside, his preaching interferes with his coding—as if bodybuilding didn't already use up enough of his brain's CPU. I think his parents being so religious and all, he has been trained with a deep need to follow."

Karla said, "Let's call them Boris and Natasha from now on."

Karla and I were both perplexed as we discussed the change in bed. "Where on earth did *politics* come from?" I asked. "Todd's gone from being historically empty to becoming a young post-Marxist, post-human code cruncher. Converted on the posing dais, I suppose."

"Red in his bed."

So who says people don't change?

Abe e-mailed from his mini-holiday in Vancouver:

I'm at the Westin in Vancouver. Room service asked me, inocently enough, "How many people will be eating?" and I replied, "2" , because I didn't want to seem like I was alone. Which I wwas.
How bad is this on a scale of one to ten?

My reply:

Abe . . . it's an *ELEVEN*

Dad got a callback from Delta Airlines for a job in their billing systems department. "It's tangential to high-tech—not really part of it—but . . ." Dad's interview is in two days. Bug and Dad went into town to get their hair cut together at one of those barber shops with a stuffed bass on the wall. Bug said it was like going to a Toppy's in Moscow.

Political nuttiness:

Todd: "Marxism presupposed that technology would never pass beyond a certain point . . . Marxism's 19th-century creation lends it an attractive distance in the postindustrial, late capitalist era."

Ethan: "There is more to prosperity than envy and redistribution."

Susan: "I'm *sure* the Hollywood unions are just waiting with bated breath for coding and multimedia production to unionize. What's it going to be—I write the code and then somebody from I.A.T.S.E. comes in and has to press the RETURN key?"

Me: "TIME OUT!"

   Politics only makes people cranky. There must be some alternative form of discourse. How is political will generated? Susan is embarrassed to be agreeing with Ethan over something. Normally they squabble over *every*thing.

Michael caught us playing Doom on the office operating system and flipped out . . . or rather, he deleted it from the system and gave me a lecture about lost people-hours when I later asked him to please reinstall it. In the end he did, because it would be catastrophic to worker morale to not be able to hunt and kill your co-workers.

"And Daniel, they have a new version called Doom II coming out in October, and rumor has it that pirated versions have a hard-drive-trashing virus, so all I ask is that you don't even con*sider* installing it."

Good luck.

Bug was so mad that he wanted to write a Marburg virus and stick it in Michael's machine, but this is just typical Bug ranting. The Marburg virus is so dangerous, it can't even be studied. Thirty-seven German laboratory workers died in conjunction with it.

THURSDAY

Todd called me a cryptofascist today.
In honor of this,
I'm formatting this particular paragraph
flush right.

Michael said something cool today. He said something remarkable and unprecedented has occurred to us as a species now—"We've reached a critical mass point where the amount of memory we have externalized in books and databases (to name but a few sources) now exceeds the amount of memory contained within our collective biological bodies. In other words, there's more memory 'out there' than exists inside 'all of us.' We've peripheralized our essence."

He went on:

"Given this new situation, the presumption of the existence of the notion of 'history' becomes not necessarily dead but somewhat *beside the point*. Access to memory replaces historical knowledge as a way for our species to process its past. Memory has replaced history—and this is not bad news. On the contrary, it's excellent news because it means we're no longer doomed to repeat our mistakes; we can edit ourselves as we go along, like an on-screen document. The transition from history at the center to memory on the periphery may prove to be initially bumpy as people shed their intellectual inertia on the issue, but the transition is an inevitability, and thank heavens we have changed the nature of change itself—the prospect of cyclical wars and dark ages and golden ages has never particularly appealed to me."

Finally:

"And the continuing democratization of memory can only accelerate the obsolescence of history as we once understood it. History has been revealed as a fluid intellectual construct, susceptible to revisionism, in which a set of individuals with access to a large database dominates another set with less access. The age-old notion of 'knowledge is power' is overturned when all memory is copy-and-paste-able—knowledge becomes wisdom, and creativity and intelligence, previously thwarted by lack of access to new ideas, can flourish."

I changed the subject to that of tickets to the upcoming Sharks game in San Jose.

FRIDAY

Todd apologized for calling me
a cryptofascist and called me "benignly centrist," instead.
The formatting for this paragraph is
obvious.

Dad had his interview with Delta. "An interview's an interview's an interview," he said. I think he just doesn't want to overly raise his hopes.

I later told Dusty Michael's theory of history being dead and she went goggle-eyed. Dusty said conspiratorially, *"Michael may be a crypto-Marxist."* (Oh God . . .) She kept blabbing, and it's so weird to see Dusty's mouth moving and genuine political words emerge. It just doesn't mesh with her computer image. I get the impression she should be discussing exfoliation or tanning factors instead, but then, bodies are political, too. Or so Dusty has informed the office.

I surprised Dusty. I said that, "Since Marxism is explicitly based on property, ownership, and control of means of production, it may well end up being the final true politik of this Benetton world we now live in." She said, "Hey, Danster—I underestimated you."

It was interesting to briefly enter the political realm—as such.

SATURDAY

Dusty made a "Bulimia Top Ten List." Dusty is so incredibly willing to discuss her body. She even confessed she had to become a big-time shoplifter to support her habit. "Hey babe—bulimia ain't cheap." Karla was, needless to say, silent on the subject.

Bulimia Top Ten List:

- several buckets of Häagen-Dazs strawberry
- two large spaghetti dinners
- large box of Godiva chocolates
- stack of eight grilled cheese sandwiches with ketchup
- entire cheesecake
- two dozen chocolate pudding cups
- four hundred grapes
- bucket of McDonald's french fries
- even larger box of Godiva chocolates
- largest box of chocolates in the universe

Dusty is designing a cosmetic surgery program for *Oop!* as her creative project. Basic body and facial structures are loaded into the system, and by sucking and implanting bricks in and out, *Oop!* users can reengineer whatever body shape they want.

Dusty's being stringent in using 100 percent genuine medical parameters, so even if you wanted to, you couldn't transform Arnold Schwarzenegger into Christy Turlington. "You can only max out the potential of what's already there. Users *must* know the body's limits."

She and Susan are sharing bone parameters from Susan's dancing skeletons product.

Speaking of Christy Turlington, I have noticed that a fair number of women seem to want to *be* her. In fact, I have noticed that if modern conversations don't switch to the disappearance of time, they shift to discussions of super-models. I guess supermodels are like geeks, but instead of winning the Punnet Square of brains, they won the Punnet Square of looks. It must be bizarre being fabulously good-looking. I mean, at least you can disguise brains.

Supermodel; Superhighway. *Coincidence?*

The Boris and Natasha nickname is really catching on. We actually use the names to their faces. I think they love it.

I keep forgetting Susan's rich, but she is. She came back from grocery shopping at Draeger's with edible flowers ($1.99 a tub) and Bear Head mushrooms ($19.99/lb.—they look like white coral). Karla and I buy noo-dle-helper-style boxed products at Price-Costco. We're going to have to start eating better. Food is too good here, and eating crap makes you feel like such an outsider in the Bay Area.

Rants are the official communication mode of the '90s.

Karla asked Dusty what she thought of Lego, and this triggered a mega-rant:

"What do *I* think of *Lego*? Lego is, like, Satan's playtoy. These seem-ingly 'educational' little blocks of connectable fun and happiness have irrev-ocably brainwashed entire generations of youth from the information-dense industrialized nations into developing mind-sets that view the world as uni-tized, sterile, inorganic, and interchangeably modular—populated by bland limbless creatures with cultishly sweet smiles."

("Minifigs" are what the tiny Lego people are called—Dusty must learn the correct terminology.)

"Lego is directly or indirectly responsible for everything from postmod-ern architecture (a crime) to middle class anal behavior over the *perfect lawn*. You worked at Microsoft, Dan, you know them—their *lawns* . . . you *know* what I mean.

"Lego promotes an overly mechanical worldview which once engen-dered, is rilly, rilly impossible to surrender."

"Anything else, Dusty?"

"Yes. Lego is, like, the perfect device to enculturate a citizenry intolerant of smell, intestinal by-products, nonadherence to unified standards, decay, blurred edges, germination, and death. Try imagining a forest made of Lego. Good luck. Do you ever see Legos made from ice? dung? wood? iron? and sphagnum moss? No—grotacious, or *what?*"

"Sure, Dusty, but what do you think of Michael's product idea—his coding?"

"It's rilly, rilly brilliant."

We've decided that we *must* have entertainment to break the monotony of coding and work.

We tried going to movies at the Shoreline Cineplex, but movies at a theater take FOREVER to watch—no fast forward. And VCR rental movies take forever to watch, even using the FFWD button.

Then Karla accidentally discovered this incredible time-saving secret—foreign movies with subtitles! It's like the crack cocaine equivalent of movies. We watched a Japanese movie—an artistic one, at that (Kurosawa's *No Regrets for Our Youth*)—in less than an hour. All you have to do is blast directly through to the subtitles, speed-read them, and then blip out the rest. It's so efficient it's scary.

"Why can't they subtitle *English* movies?" asked Karla. "I mean, they do books-on-tape for commuters. Subtitled English movies would fill a potentially big niche. No one has time anymore."

Mr. Ideology himself (Boris) walked in, and Ethan couldn't resist telling him that he'd run a search on Lenin on an on-line encyclopedia, and it turns out Lenin's name means nothing. "It's a made up name—like Sting—he just showed up at the dacha one morning and said, 'Call me Lenin.'"

Todd responded by saying, "Just goes to show you how he was postmodern a century ahead of his time."

Dusty was trying to tell us all about *"Mehrwert"*—surplus value per unit of time/labor: "A worker creates more value than that for which he is compensated. You know?"

Michael went purple, like a Burger King manager who hears one of his employees discuss unionization.

And then Karla screwed Michael's notions of production up even further by passing along a meme somebody spammed her on the Net that day, that any multiple of 6, minus one, is a prime number. Easy as this was to disprove, all work stopped immediately as everybody set out to prove its validity.

Todd pointed out something I thought was really true. He said that when future archaeolgists dig up the remains of California, they're going to find all of these gyms and all of this scary-looking gym equipment, and they're going to assume that we were a culture obsessed with *torture*.

Went for late coffee at the Posh Bagel on Main Street in Los Altos. The white lights in the trees were so pretty. Human beings can't be all *that* bad.

SUNDAY

Dusty is furious with *Todd*. She discovered a collection of cans of aerosol "religious sprays" he had hidden in his cupboard—like "Aerosol Stigmata" and "Santa Barbara in a Can." His mom sends them to him from Port Angeles. She buys them from a Catholic mail-order house in Philadelphia. It's so weird, but these sprays really exist.

Todd sulked: "She threw them out like time-expired antibiotics."

In order to foster a less combative working environment, Michael and I are trying to think of the most apolitical environment possible. We finally hit upon *Star Trek* as a zero-politics zone. So I introduced the notion of TrekPolitiks to the office.

Susan said, "Ever notice how, like, nobody ever goes *shopping* on *Star Trek*? They're a totally post-money society. If they want a banana they simply photocopy one on the replicator. Substitute Malaysia or Mexico for the replicator, and make Palo Alto the Bridge, and *bingo:* RIGHT NOW = STAR TREK."

It's true.

If you think about it.

I added, "Ever notice how they never have to report to anybody on *Star Trek*? No suits zoom in from Star Fleet Corporate and hold them fiscally responsible for frying a dilithium crystal doing doughnuts in the Delta Quadrant. Or Star Fleet Marketing, for that matter." (Pointed glares at Ethan.)

Karla likes the notion of TrekPolitiks. "Left vs. right is obsolete. Politics is, in the end, about biology, information, diversification, numbers, numbers, and numbers—all candy coated with charisma and guns."

Karla like myself is of the new apolitical pick-and-choose style of citizen. I think politics is soon going to resemble a J. Crew catalogue more than some 1776 ideal. If somebody wants to run for office, they had better be able to explain why they want to run for office. Wanting to be a candidate seems, in itself, reason for exclusion.

Dusty said, "Thomas Jefferson never anticipated Victoria's Secret catalogues and media-induced social atomization. Just think—we're rapidly approaching a world composed entirely of jail and shopping." She paused to consider this, said, "Gro*ta*cious!" then she went for a jog.

Dad had his second callback from Delta.

Karla apparently noticed my breathing the other day when I was carrying the trash cans to the end of the driveway. She has decided I should start going to the gym. "You have to add more megs to your hard drive. I'm going, too." She's right—we both need meat on us—excuse me—we both need more *crystal lattice* added on to our drives.

Every time I look at Karla, she changes and changes, and now I realize other men are looking at her and this makes me have to look at myself, and what I see is sort of scrawny. Suddenly Karla can date higher on the geek food chain than me if she wants to—she can date all the Phils-from-Apples of this world—she has entered the realms of buffness and cleft chins. I care about being with her too much to lose her to a . . . Phil unit. To lose her ever, to anyone. I can't imagine losing her. I must make myself stronger. I must build a better me. I must become the Bionic Man.

It turns out that if you tape TV shows that are close-captioned, you CAN have English language subtitles. Our entertainment universe has multiplied itself!

MONDAY

Susan told us today what our characters and powers would be if we were on *Star Trek*:

Michael:
Disembodied neocortex afloat inside a tank of nutrient-bearing solution; has ability to see back and forth in time; communicates via LEDs and a synchronized swim team of hybridized dolphins living in a satellite-linked inlet on the Goa Coast.

Todd:
Repairer of broken machines; has tools instead of fingers; regulation hunk required by TV network to stimulate sales of tie-in merchandise; able to telepathically determine sexual coefficient of alien beings; skin can turn to gold by beaming himself to the planet TanFastic.

Karla:
Crew Biologist; able to camouflage feeling with scientific theories; superior intelligence allows for dominance over all males or spore-bearing entities.

Me:
Token earthling; prey to foibles and pratfalls of all humanity (*thanks* Susan).

Bug:
Feathered creature picked up in sympathy from a collapsing Throm Nebula; most likely to say uncon-

trolled, angry things about fellow cast and crew
members to *Entertainment Tonight* years after the
series ends up in syndication . . . lack of Screen
Actors Guild residuals plus an addiction to cosmetic
surgery will provide an impetus.

Susan herself:
Priestess of the Right Lobe; erotic female interest
demanded by TV networks; will devour males if
overly excited; designs castles while sleepwalking;
flawless plastic skin; thighs conceal bevatron guns.

Dusty:
Bionic creature from a destroyed Valley planet; disci-
plinarian; feeds on X rays; arms contain snakes that
will fight her wars.

Ethan:
Bearer of the Dark Force; can transmute feces into
uranium; owns hyperspace cruiser that can vanish
and reappear at any moment across time, space, and
money.

Abe:
Wise hermit cast adrift on asteroid for thousands of
years; has developed odd code languages for everyday actions; lonely but not bitter; his heart is cryogenically frozen, and he must search the universe
pursuing the Thawer.

Went to the gym for the first time today and my body feels like an East
German Trabant car running on linseed oil crashing into a stack of burning
televisions. The pain!

Susan's going psycho over an asthmatic Detroit car artist named Emmett
who Michael brought in to do drawings and storyboards. ("We run a very

disciplined little software shop," says Ethan. "Detroit really knows how to crack the whip!")

I think it would be a very scary thing at this point in Susan's sexual radicalization to be the subject of her infatuation. Good luck, Emmett.

Oh—Emmett's last name is—*Couch*—isn't that a hoot! And his big personal beef is Japanese animation. He says that SEGA and Nintendo are responsible for the "subtle but massive Hello-Kittification of North American animation. You can kiss our Hanna-Barbera heritage good-bye." How can anybody take this so seriously?

Emmett has 4,000 manga comics from Japan. They're so violent and dirty! The characters all look as if they're saying unbelievably important things—talking to God and the Wizard of the Universe—but when you translate them, all they're really doing is making belching noises. Susan has discovered in these manga a rich source of fashion ideas.

The more we realize our Lenin jokes rankle Todd, the more the Lenin jokes grow out of control. Even Mom got into the act and made "Lenin's Face" cookies, dropping them into the office on her way to work. We told Todd to close his eyes and touch them and describe their texture—"kind of leathery—kind of dry—kind of . . . chewy—kind of like . . ." (opens his eyes).

Ethan: "An embalmed syphilitic tyrant?"

"You assholes! Oh, sorry, Mrs. Underwood."

I learned a new expression today: "protein window." Todd told it to me.

Apparently, after you bodybuild, you have a two-hour time window in which your body can suck up amino acids. This is your protein window. I was talking to him and he said, "Man, I'd like to talk some more, but my protein window is closing," and he ran off to the kitchen and ate a chicken. What a decade this is.

I forgot to eat while my protein window was open. Maybe that's why I'm in pain.

Abe mail:
In the future all planets will have roman numerals after their names and have one or two sylable names that sound like Dupont carpet material from 1966. . . Norlon IV . . . Erthrea IX . . . Gil II

Bug has joined a "Lego Bobsledding Team" and has plummeted to a new nadir of Nerddom. It's over in Berkeley—they use Mattel Hot Wheels tracks, bet with Monopoly money, have megaphones and everything. Lego trophies, too.

Todd called me "decadent" today—this, after *he* discussed protein windows! I couldn't believe it. He said I was decadent because I was eating Lucky Charms. He said they were "symptomatic of a culture in decline—sucrose hysteria, you know."

I said, "But Todd, Lucky Charms were invented during the *Johnson* Administration. Society couldn't have been more anti-decline than it was then. Guns and butter . . . I can't believe I'm even talking to you seriously about this. This is silly beyond belief."

Anyway, that was the seed notion. Karla and I wrote a big list of "decadent cereals" on the office dry-erase wall:

CAP'N CRUNCH:
Reason this cereal is decadent:
a) Colonialist exploiter pursues naïve Crunchberry cultures to plunder. b) Drunkenness, torture, and debauchery implicit in long ocean cruises.

SUGAR FROSTED FLAKES:
Reason this cereal is decadent:
Silky throated military-industrial complex spokestoad "Tony the Tiger" exploits the need of the undereducated underclass for a paternalistic, Reagan-like figure. A cautionary tale of the perils of not indoctrinating at the crèche level.

TRIX:
Reason this cereal is decadent:
Well-meaning rabbit, "Trix," kept in continual state of malnutrition/subservience by dominant children of the parasitic bourgeoisie. "Silly rabbit, Trix are for kids" can only be construed as a call to class warfare.

LUCKY CHARMS:
Reason this cereal is decadent:
Man with no known adult friends lures children into forest for purpose of nutritional (ideological) seduction. Sprightly twinkle motif on packaging (putatively an allusion to "flavor") are, in fact, metaphors for soul-deadening sucrose.

RICE KRISPIES:
Reason this cereal is decadent:
Snap, Krackle, and Pop thinly veiled emblems for the Trilateral Commission.

COCOA PUFFS:
Reason this cereal is decadent:
"I'm cuckoo for Cocoa Puffs," the demented cackle of Sonny the Cocoa Puffs bird/spokesmuppet, is resonant with the insanity inherent in the needless enslavement of the proletariat.

COUNT CHOCULA—FRANKENBERRY:
Reason this cereal is *not* decadent:
Gay relationship offers an excellent role model for this new era of diversity. Witty vampire motif plays on never-ending struggle of the oppressed to topple the ruling classes.

On the same theme, from Abe:
I have settled up on the calorie delivery system of choice: Stouffer's home sytle fish fillet with macaroni and chees. Microvaves in six minutes; 430 caloreis. Eat two of them and you don't have to think of food for 5 hours. Beverage: Tang.

Do you like the Airbus A300?

TUESDAY

Dad got the Delta job! "My boss is 32 and a little prick if you ask me, but I'm in the real world now." He starts next week. We offered to take him out to dinner, but he and Mom took a taxi down to Il Fornaio in Palo Alto. They wanted to get pissed. My parents!

We had this competition inside the office to come up with alternative solutions as to what to do with what is (to the Russians) the increasingly embarrassing and willfully nondecomposing body of Vladimir I. Lenin. The suggestions:

SUSAN:
   "Put Lenin in a tuxedo and use him as a seat filler at the Academy Awards. At the Oscar ceremonies they have this big holding pen full of attractive people in gowns and tuxes and whenever the Academy gives away the awards for achievement in sound and everyone flees into the lobby, seat fillers are zoomed in so that the cameras scanning the audience won't register any vacant seats. When Daniel Day-Lewis has to go to the bathroom, the cameras could zoom in and see a picture of Sigourney Weaver sitting next to . . . *Lenin*!"

DUSTY:
   "The Reagans would, like, probably rilly enjoy having Lenin in their billiard room in Santa Barbara. They could put him inside a fake suit of armor (which they no doubt already own) and then when Henry Kissinger came over, Nancy could say, "Ooh, *Henry*—who do you think we have here tonight with us," and she could *skreeeek* open the little faceplate and there would be—*Lenin*!—and they could all giggle."

BUG:

"The Lenster's dead, but that doesn't mean he can't endorse products, does it? At the very least, Benetton could fit him into one of their sweaters. That's a two-page magazine spread right there. Revlon? Len Babe must look like hell after all these years. Maybe Clinique has some nice, youthful goo they could slap onto his face—a makeover! Makeovers are *the* official art form of the 1990s, you know."

Dusty tried to get us to do aerobics in mid-afternoon, but all she got were six insolent stares. She, like, jogs to Oakland during her lunch hour or something. People in the Bay Area are so ext*reme*.

Ethan is getting involved in an Antarctic banking scheme: *"No regulation!"* I bet if the Chicago futures market started selling plutonium futures, Ethan would be in like spit.

Look and Feel and the gerbil babies make a real racket now. The way they race around the office . . . it's as if the walls are alive.

It turns out that *three* of us visited the Gap independently of each other today, and when we found out, we got spooked, and we analyzed the Gap, trying to make ourselves feel better about our vague mood of consumer victimization.

Susan says the Gap is smart because they cut it both ways: "Kids in Armpit, Nebraska, go into a Gap with pictures in their heads of Manhattan, Claudia Schiffer, and the Concorde, while kids in Manhattan go into the Gap with a picture in their head of Armpit, Nebraska. So it's as though Gap clothing puts you anywhere except where you actually *are*."

Bug said that the Gap is good "because you can go into a Gap anywhere, buy anything they sell, and never have to worry about coming out and looking like a dweeb wearing whatever it was you bought there."

Susan responded that the only problem now is that everybody shops at the Gap (or an isotope of the Gap) and so everybody looks the same these days. "This is such a punchline because diversity is supposed to be such a hot modern issue, but to look at a sample crowd of citizens, you'd never know it."

I figured that Gap clothing is what you wear if you want to appear like you're from nowhere; it's clothing that allows you to erase geographical differences and be just like everybody else from anywhere else.

Dusty agreed, saying this is good in that it spoke vaguely of social democratic notions, promoting the illusion of a unified, consensual monoculture, "But it's maybe li'l bit sad, because this is *all* that democracy's rilly been reduced to: the ability to purchase the illusion of cohesive citizenry for $34.99 (belt included)."

We also figured that Gap clothing isn't about *place*, nor is it about *time*, either. Not only does Gap clothing allow you to look like you're from nowhere in particular, it also allows you to look as though you're not particularly from the *present*, either. "Just look at the recent 'Khakis of the Dead' campaign," said Bug. "By using Balanchine and Andy Warhol and all these dead people to hustle khakis, the Gap permits Gap wearer to dissociate from the *now* and enter a nebulous *then*, wherever one wants *then* to be in one's head . . . this big place that stretches from Picasso's '20s to the hippie '60s."

Todd wasn't there, so we didn't bother asking if Lenin wore khakis.

Karla pointed out that there are more Gaps than just the Gap. "J. Crew is a thinly veiled Gap. So is Eddie Bauer. Banana Republic is owned by the same people as the Gap. Armani A/X is a EuroGap. Brooks Brothers is a Gap for people with more disposable income whose bodies need hiding, upscaling, and standardization. Victoria's Secret is a Gap of calculated naughtiness for ladies. McDonald's is the Gap of hamburgers. LensCrafters is the Gap of eyewear. Mrs. Fields is the Gap of cookies. And so on."

Susan said that the unifying theme amid all of this Gappiness is, of course, the computer spreadsheet and the bar-coded inventory. "A jaded cosmopolite in the Upper West Side buys an Armpit, Nebraska–style worker's shirt (in 'oatmeal') and Gap computers" (doubtless buried deep within a deactivated NORAD command center somewhere in the Rockies) "instantaneously spew out the message to Asian garment manufacturers, *'Armpit worker shirts are HOT.'* Likewise, an agrarian soul out there in Armpit, pining away for a touch of life away from the silo, buys an oxford cloth buttondown shirt at the local Gap, and computerized Gap-funded looms in Asia retool for the preppie revival."

Bug said that, "Deep in your heart, you go to the Gap because you hope that they'll have something that other Gap stores won't have . . . even the most meager deviation from their highly standardized inventoried norm becomes a valued treasure. It's like when you go into a McDonald's and they're test-marketing Lamb McNuggets, or something, and you know that it's an experiment."

Ethan broke in and agreed wholeheartedly: "Last December at the Eaton's Centre in Toronto I purchased a 'GP 2000' Commander Picard–like red-and-black sweatshirt that I have yet to see in a Gap anywhere else. Was this a test-marketing of a new line that tanked, or a marketing SKU that simply bombed? I ask *you*."

Then Michael pointed out that a few years ago there was a minor furor over the ethics of Dairy Queen, who sent their franchisees hamburger patties that were pseudo-randomly shaped, with little bumpies around the patty's edges, so that burger's consumer would feel more as though they were having a "handmade" burger. "In this same spirit, one wonders if the Gap randomly assigns nonstandardized clothing items to its various outlets so as to simulate the illusion of regional variety."

To break the trance that was forming, I shouted, *"Gap check!"* and everyone in the office had to guiltily 'fess up to the number of Gap garments currently being worn. Karla, the only Gap-free soul, for the remainder of the day wore the smug, victorious grin of one who has escaped the hungry jaw of bar-code industrialism. We Gap victims, on the other hand, fast-forwarded to an entirely McNuggetized world of dweeb-free, standardized consumable units.

We got back to work, and Dusty got to thinking "It would appear that to be a dweeb becomes a political statement—a means of saying that 'I choose not to ally myself with the dark forces of amoral, transnational, bar-coded, GATT-based trade practices.'"

"So let's be dweebs," I said.

"But *how* to be a dweeb, then, Dan?"

"Well, you could maybe *make* your own clothes," said Bug, but we all said, "Naaaahhh . . ." if for no other reason than the fact that nobody has free time these days.

"You could buy clothing that predates computerized inventorying," suggested Susan, but then Bug replied that you'd become a retro fashion victim.

In the end, we all figured that the only way to be a dweeb was to have your mother buy your clothes for you at, like, Sears or JC Penney.

Or have Michael buy them.

Susan couldn't be less subtle about her entrancement with Emmett if she tried. And Emmett's so thick, he misses every clue. It's a wonder humans ever manage to propagate.

Today for Susan it was hotpants and a *Barbarella* mesh top with plastic hoop earings and a *Valley of the Dolls* wig. She was like a 1967 *Life* magazine cover. This outfit, coupled with the day's warm weather, Todd's working shirtless, and with Dusty's rehearsing Iron Rose IV competition practice sessions (Karla and Susan learning the poses)—the office now reeks of sex. This is not natural!

WEDNESDAY

Abe:
Someone scrawled on the bathroom cubicle floor here:

MATES = BRAKES
Below it someone else wrote:
OVERWORK = POLYGAMY

MICROSOFT! You know how it is here – singles overwork to make themselves shine, but the *Marrieds* become the managers, and move up the ladder more quickly, Elearnor Rigbies need not apply.

Got yesterdays faz. [*I'd faxed along the instruction kits to a Lego 9129 Space Station Kit.*] **I think yours was the first fax I've had in years. Faxes are like email from 1987. Thanks.**

Susan walked in tonight after dinner clutching a handful of crappy little objects: a bent fork, a bruised apple, a Barbie's head, and the plastic top from a Tylenol container. She laid them out in a row on the floor and asked Todd, "Hey, Todd, what's *this*?"

We all looked at this sad little row of debris and none of us had a clue.

Todd said, "I dunno."

She said, "It's a Russian garage sale."

We all said, "*Ooooh* . . ." expecting Todd to freak out, and he *did* get huffy.

"I know, I know," she said preemptively, "the Russians are supposed to be our friends now. But face it, Todd—they'll *never* get it right. Capitalism is something that's ingrained in you from birth. There's more to developing a market economy than pulling a switch and suddenly being a capitalist overnight. As a child you need to read about Lucy's 5-cent psychiatry booth in Charlie Brown; game shows; mailing away for Sea Monkeys—it's all a part of being 'encapitalized.'"

She removed the Barbie head from the lineup of objects: "Probably too good."

Later on, Susan and Karla were cackling together. I asked them what about and they shot guilty looks at each other.

"Barbies," said Karla.

Susan added, "It's like every girl I know did all this incredibly sick sex shit with their Barbies, and in the end the head and/or limbs would fall off and you'd have to hide her but your Mom always found the dismembered Barbie and would say, 'Gee, honey—what happened to Barbie?'"

"Oh God—you'd just be *dying* of shame, remembering the debauch that landed her in the degraded state."

(More cackling.)

"I remember when my Barbie discovered my brother's G.I. Joe's," said Karla. "Talk about a spree. She was in fragments within an hour."

"Oh my God—me too!" said Susan.

"Hair gone, too?"

"Yup."

I was feeling a bit excluded and cut out discreetly, leaving more cackles in my wake. How can the two of them *both* have done the exact same things?

My body no longer kills me when I come back from the gym. However, I had a moment of total humiliation today: theoretically my ideal body weight is 172 pounds and I weigh 153 lbs. The woman at the gym calibrated my fat/water/meat/bone ratios, made an inward gasp and I asked her what was wrong. She said (after a tentative, you-have-cancer pause), "You're what's technically known as a *'thin fat person.'*"

It was so degrading. Not only am I skinny, but what meat I *do* possess isn't meat at all, but lard. I have to burn that off before I can even begin beefing up. I don't even deserve the honor of calling myself carbon-based, let alone silicon-based—maybe I'm based on one of those useless elements like boron that don't do anything.

I'm not telling Karla about *this* one.

THURSDAY

Word leaked out at the office that I'm a thin fat person (the gym lady blabbed to Todd) and I had to endure a barrage of crude jokes at my expense for 14 hours. Todd pulled me aside and gave me a canister of amino acids and a pep talk.

Dad started work today at Delta. He popped into the *Oop!* office to show his face on the way back. Susan, Bug, and Michael pleaded for some access into the Delta system or at least something they could start to hack with. Michael wanted to add ten million frequent flyer points to his account: "I want to fly to the South Pole, first class, Saudi Airlines, with a sleeper seat, and Reuben Kincaid sleep goggles made of passenger pigeon breast feathers."

Across the street from our house, these little kids were having a tiny garage sale: a single, spine-worn copy of *Cosmopolitan*, two filthy Big Bird toys, a paperback of *Future Shock*, and a cowboy boot remover. It was so depressing—and eerily similar to Susan's joke about Russian garage sales. Karla said, "Susan's right. The Russians'll never catch up."

Ethan, over for a visit, said, "*Au contraire*, pal, they'll probably outlap us shortly."

Dusty was barfing all over the office sink when I came in this morning. She said she'd been working out too hard at the gym.

Abe:
My magnetic card keys fucked upa nd I couldn't get into the building and I gfelt like I'd stopped existing

FRIDAY

Todd burst in this morning: "I'm a Maoist now!"

The rest of us are so numb from politics now we couldn't even muster up the will to shoot him a yawn.

"You *do* know the three forms of Communism, don't you?"

"No, Todd. But I'm *sure* you'll let us know."

"Oh good . . .

"First, there's Marxist Leninism.

"Second, there's Stalinism—well, actually, Stalinism is an *application*, not an operating system. I mean, if you want to wipe out 40 million people, you install Stalinism on your hard drive. It's like a political ebola virus."

Susan likened the Stalinist purges to those at IBM.

"Finally, there's Maoism. Maoism is about the total elimination of all culture. Anything that smacks of culture is bad. Everything from cocktail umbrellas up to Mozart. It all has to go."

I said, "That's dreadful, Todd—culture is *everything*. Without culture we're nothing. You're telling me you'd have all existing Bob Newhart reruns de*stroyed*?"

"Bob Newhart romanticizes decadent, self-absorbed bourgeois liberal therapeutic culture. It is redeemable only in that therapy repudiates the Church."

"Sounds like a pretty chuckle-free universe to me," said Karla.

"More to life than chuckles, Kar," said Todd, frappéing a can of Del Monte pineapple and some form of protein powder in the office blender. "It's obvious—culture must perish."

"Why?" I asked.

"I'm not sure. Just that it must. I'm working on that one. Oh look—there's Dusty down on the street—we're off to our posing seminar. Gold's just had new daises delivered. Ciao, comrades."

Glurp. Guzzle. Chug. Slam.

"Be sure and flex one for me."

"Can't those two just *code*?" moaned Michael in a rare show of feeling.

So now the Gang of Two (Boris and Natasha no more) are onto their next political kick.

Abe:
Went into Microsoft. Spent most of the morning entering my old vynyl records into a database Iv'e built. Filemaker Prod by Claris gets to Track my CHS tape collection..

Questions: Can you gusess what this is by the ingeredients?

SD Alcobol
Water
Tween 20
Glycerine
Flavor
Sodium Sacchharine
FD&C Blue №1
"Made in USA"

Keep guessing. I'll give you the answer later. [*Answer: Ice Drops icy-mint breath freshener.*]

Dusty was telling us later on all of this cool body stuff: about an aerobic drug, RPO, that enhances the body's ability to metabolize oxygen. Rumor has it a French bicycling team all died of heart attacks using it. And she discussed how too many steroids make women grow hair and can make users "acromegliac"—their craniums distort.

Oh—Dusty barfed up whole Lake Superiors of muck all morning. I wonder what's up with *that*.

Some new diet regime, doubtless.

Ethan says Type-A personalities have a whole subset of diseases that they, and only they, share, and the transmission vector for these diseases is the

DOOR CLOSE button on elevators that only get pushed by impatient, Type-A people. Ethan pushes these buttons with his elbow, now. I'm starting to worry about all of us.

In the spirit of Ethan's neurosis, we made a drywall list of keyboard buttons we would like to see:

> PLEASE
> THANK YOU
> FUCK OFF
> DIE
> OOPS . . . MY MISTAKE
> DO SOMETHING COOL AND SURPRISE ME

Later, everyone got in a debate over whether or not Fisher Price's minifigs were cooler than Lego's. The debate went onto the drywall:

FISHER PRICE minifigs versus LEGO minifigs

Fisher Price Minifigs:

Plus:	limbless figures give children a feeling of helplessness
Minus:	faces resemble those of beloved but unfunny cartoon characters in *FamilyCircus*

Plus:	generic, Gap-like outfits
Minus:	height/weight-disproportionate bodies imply eating disorders: bad role model for millennial youth yearning to be functional

Lego Minifigs:

Plus:	interchangeable, unisex hairdos
Minus:	clawlike hands are scary and potentially traumatizing

Plus:	bodies can be incorporated into architecture
Minus:	bad fashions

Dad hates his boss, "the 32-year-old prick." "He's a humorless Total Quality Management freak who uses Anthony Robbins pep talks to motivate me into learning humiliatingly simple input codes. Hell, I'm younger than him in everything but body."

Dad's only one-third the way up the food chain in his division at Delta, and it must be really degrading for him. Mom said, "I know your father wanted a job badly, but maybe this isn't his cup of tea. Can't you people teach him C++ a bit faster?" We had to tell her that learning doesn't scale. But the idea of Dad being a hip and with-it coder is one that appeals to all of us in the office. Who knows where this will lead.

FRIDAY
(one week later)

Dad quit his job. He showed up at the office around two in the afternoon to tell me. Michael promptly gave him some C++ manuals and put him in an empty chair in the corner and said, "Time to learn for real, Mr. Underhill."

Mom was P-I-S-S-E-D off. But even still, she knew the Delta thing was going nowhere. She figures Dad's just caught in this weird demographic glitch: too young to retire; too old to learn new tricks. She figures Dad's around for the long haul, so she told Dad two new rules she's made up for day-to-day living:

    1) I'm never making you lunch.
    2) You're never allowed to come shopping with me.

Other changes: the Gang of Two traipsed in this morning. "We have ceased being Maoists. We are now ideologically basing ourselves on Product Theory."

Being numb from all of their flip-flop—and from extreme politics in general—once again nobody bothered to look up. "Gee kids, that's nice. See *Star Trek* last night?"

Todd added, "The modern economy isn't about the redistribution of wealth—it's about the redistribution of *time*."

His eyeballs were rolling inside his head with pleasure. "Instead of battling to control rubber boot factories, the modern post-Maoist wants to battle for *your* 45 minutes of daily discretionary time. The consumer electronics industry is all about lassoing your *time*, not your money—that time-greedy ego-part of the brain that wants to maximize a year's worth of year."

"But that," I said, "is exactly what *Ethan* believes."

Silence.

Ethan shot me a self-satisfied glance, and the ex–Gang of Two went to work without much ado.

"Really," said Michael, "I hope this here is the end of politics."

Karla said to me later on, "Did you know that Michael spends one hour a day on e-mail talking to someone named BarCode who lives in Waterloo, Ontario, Canada? Has he ever mentioned this to you?"

"Michael discussed his interior life?"

Todd overheard and added, "You know, if I read *one more* article about cybersex I am going to explode," to which Dusty said, "Now, Toddy, if you shoot one more vial of 'roids you *will* explode." Which shut him up.

But Todd's right. The media has gone berserk with Net-this and Net-that. It's a bit much. The Net is cool, but not *that* cool.

I thanked Michael for being nice to my Dad, letting him hang around the office and that kind of stuff, but Michael said, "Nice? I suppose so. But once he gets the basics down, he'll make an excellent representative for *Oop!*, don't you think? All that silver hair, and best of all, no *dan*druff."

Two pounds of solid rippling muscle gained this week! Maybe. It could have been my extended visit to the water fountain before the weigh-in that tilted the scales upward.

I had to drop off some diskettes at Todd and Dusty's tonight. I walked up to the house and through the main window I could see Todd slathering Dusty with barbecue-tinted goo as she was standing on a posing dais in front of a full-length mirror, happy as a clam. He was brushing Dusty's tummy; I peeked through the bougainvillea, thought twice about interrupting their ritual, and drove into the flower-scented, gasoline-powered California night.

SATURDAY

Karla and Dusty disappeared around ten this morning, returning around noon, with Dusty blubbering and her words spilling out of her—to Todd and to everybody else in the office—that she's pregnant.

"Oh fuck," said Dusty, "I've done so much weird shit to my body that I'll birth a *grapefruit*." She was howling. She was a real mess.

We made the usual "Version 2.0" jokes you have to make whenever a techie gets pregnant, and cooled her down. Ethan called a doctor friend on his cellular phone and bullied him out of his golf game and made him give Dusty a pep talk. And we all had to promise to come to the ultrasound with her. Todd bailed out and visited the gym all afternoon.

It was actually a lovely, lovely day and the sun was hot and we walked down the streets, and the colors were so exotic and bright and the air so quiet and we felt alive and living.

MONDAY

"The petty bourgeois ideal of withdrawal into Jeffersonian autonomy is no longer sustainable in a simultaneous, globalized environment with the asynchronous, instantaneous transfer of capital from one cashpoint to another."

"Just piss off and get into the car, Dusty."

Karla and I drove with Dusty to her clinic in Redwood City. She's so convinced her baby is going to be a grapefruit. I foresee seven and a half more months of extreme anxiety and ultrasounds. On the way out she said, "It's leaving me, you know."

"*What*'s leaving you, Dusty?"

Dusty was looking out the back window of the van. "Ideology. Yes—I can feel it leaving my body. And I don't care. And I don't miss it."

We drove a while—caught all the red lights—they were doing construction on Camino Real. At stoplight number seventeen, Dusty turned around, looked out the Microbus's rear window one final time, and whispered, "Bye."

She then turned to Karla and roared, "Off to Burger King, *now*! Three fishwiches, double tartar sauce, large fries, and a Big Gulp–type beverage. Are you with me, kids? I'm rilly, *rilly* hungry, and if you tell Todd we went to Burger King, I'll grind you *both* into Chicken McNuggets."

"Revolutionary, babe. We are *there*. Whalers ahoy!"

Poor Todd—"Pops"—he was in a daze all day, and vanished off to the gym around six. I went out the door to follow him because maybe he needed to talk, but instead of going to get into his Supra, he walked down the street, and so I walked behind him, wondering what it must be like to be hit with the notion of spawning. He then surprised me a few blocks later by entering a small Baptist church. I waited a minute and then I followed him into the church, feeling the small *whoosh* of cool interior air on my face, and I walked down the center of the aisle and sat next to Todd who was praying in a pew. He looked up at me and I said, "Hi," and sat down next to him.

He wasn't sure what to do with his hands. I hummed, "*Stopped into a church . . .*"

He said, "Huh?"

I said, "'California Dreaming' . . . the song."

He said, "Right."

I said, "Here's a deal: I'm going to sit right here, right beside you, and I am going to dream. And you . . . well . . . why not continue praying?"

"*Right*," he said.

And he prayed and I dreamed.

Oh—Ethan finished his freeway.

6
Chyx

From behind the fabric-covered disassemblable wall partitions of our office I heard Emmett mumble to Susan: *"Hey, Sooz—want to go out tonight?"*

"I don't know, Emm . . ."

"Hey, it'll be great. We can listen in on cellular calls with my Radio Shack Pro-46 scanner—I altered its megahertz range with a soldering gun— or maybe listen to some crank calls I have on tape—hack a few passwords. Grab some calzones . . ."

Susan played it cool: "Uh huh—I'll, umm, think on it."

But the *moment* Emmett was out of sight, Susan instant-mailed Karla and they scurried down to the street for a debriefing, Susan's hoop earrings jangling like Veronica Lodge's tambourine. Karla told me afterward that Susan said it was the best date proposal she'd ever had. "Dream date!"

No conversation is private in our small office, and every day I listen in on what is becoming a female bond-o-thon.

Today, however, Karla, Susan, and Dusty really broke through a wall into a new level. It started out simply enough, with all of us discussing the way that food products in recent years have been cloning themselves out into eighteen versions of themselves. For example, old Coke, new Coke, diet

Coke, old Coke without caffeine, new Coke without caffeine, Coke with pulpy bits, Coke with cheese . . . We tried to figure out the roots of product multiplication and we decided it was peanut butter manufacturers who decades ago invented chunky and smooth versions of themselves.

Then things went out of control. Karla suddenly remembered to tell Susan about how Fry's doesn't sell tampons, and Susan got angrier and angrier, and the conversation became entirely tamponic.

"I don't know why they *don't* sell them. If nothing else, they're so damned expensive the profit margin must be like 1,000 percent."

She phoned to fact-check that Fry's indeed did not sell them.

Karla said, "This woman Lindy that I met at last week's geek party works at Apple, and *she* told *me* that in all of the women's bathrooms there they have these clear Lucite dispensers of tampons that are *free*. Now *that's* corporate intrusion into employee's lives that I could live with."

They all agreed *tampons gratis* are the acme of hip.

"Apple must be run by a woman," said Dusty. "Maybe it is and they're hiding it to stay on good terms with the Japanese."

Karla said, *"Wha . . . ?"* and Dusty replied, "Oh, come *on*, babe, Japanese businessmen are notoriously adverse to accepting authority from women, no matter how powerful they are in their American companies."

Conversation lapsed into a discussion of Apple's charisma deficit crisis, but then soon enough returned to tampons, and for me it was *so* embarrassing, like watching *Mutual of Omaha's Wild Kingdom* with your mom, and suddenly a Summer's Eve commercial comes on, and Mom scurries out of the room and you're not sure why you're supposed to be embarrassed, only that everybody *is*.

Karla said, "But the bad thing about the free tampons at Apple is that they're Playtex, not O.B."

All three in unison: *"Designed by a woman gynecologist . . ."*

Susan said, "Playtex suck because they just get longer, not wider . . . When I bleed, it's not a vertical thing . . . it's 360 degrees. And it's so freaky because when you put it in, it's this innocuous little lipstick size, and then when you take it out there's this long cotton *rope* at the end of the string! I'm afraid it's going to hook my uterus and I'll accidentally drag it out!"

Todd sent me an instant mail, which blinked on my screen, saying, *I can't believe what I'm hearing.*

Dusty said, "O.B.'s rock! But I guess not every powerful female executive is comfortable enough with her body to put her finger (fake '50s house-wife voice) *you know where.*"

They all laughed ironically.

Susan said, "I think that the lamest excuse women use about why they don't use O.B. is because they don't want their *index finger* to get dirty . . . I mean whenever you pay for something with a dollar bill your hand gets filthy, but does that stop them from making purchases with dollar bills?"

"They need to make tampons for those 'chunky' days . . . 'light' days panty-liners blow!" said Karla.

This is obviously a universal tampon concern judging by the enthusiasm that ensued.

Todd instant-mailed me, *Women have *chunky* days? Are guys supposed to know this stuff? I am experiencing fear.*

I was trying to think of a "guy" equivalent of chunkiness, but I couldn't, and meanwhile, the three of them just kept rocking on, and Todd, Bug, and I just buried our heads deeper into our work areas.

Dusty said, "*Gawd* . . . I was rilly, *rilly* freaked out the first time I had chunks. No one *ever* tells you about that in, like, school or at home or anything. You see those Playtex commercials and they've got this watery blue liquid and that's what you're expecting, and then one day you look at your pad and there are . . . *chunks* there. Gro*tac*ious."

Karla, ever logical, said, "I knew intellectually it had to be uterine lining, but I envisioned the lining as being thin, wispy . . . not like chunks of liver."

Dusty figured, "We, as women, also need to invent some alternative to that adhesive they use on pads. I wouldn't even wear them if it weren't for chunks. It rilly bothers me to think of these chunks that want to migrate south, but they can't because of this Tampon Roadblock. So I always wear pads on like the second day, but I hate them. It's like getting a drive-by waxing."

Karla suggested, "If they ever made 'chunky-style' tampons, we wouldn't need to ever wear pads."

Susan said, "I'll bet you anything Fry's doesn't carry tampons because they're misogynist and afraid of adult, *bleeding* women . . . they can't accept the non-Barbie, fully-functional female!"

Karla and Dusty: "Right on, Sister!"

Susan said, "Yet again men win: with condom hysteria and semen they monopolize the notion of sacred body fluids. Women lose *again*. I want pads to be to the 1990s what condoms were to the 1980s. Destigmatize the flow!"

Susan had the idea to start up a support group for Valley women who code. She's calling it Chyx and has put word out on the Net. She said, "I was going to spell it 'Chycks' but then 'Chyx' sounds more like a bioengineering firm, and that's kind of cool."

Prerequisites for joining Chyx (which makes you a "Chyk") are "fluency in two or more computer languages, a vagina, and a belief that Mary Tyler Moore as Mary Richards in a slinky pantsuit is the worldly embodiment of God."

Susan will probably be swamped. Karla and Dusty have Chyx member numbers 0002 and 0003 respectively. They have been given a full set of photocopied writings of Brenda Laurel.

This reminds me, the lower your employee number down here, the higher your status—and the more likely you are to hold equity.

Later on in the day, our lives devolved into an *Itchy & Scratchy* cartoon. We all decided we needed sunlight—we've all been working so hard lately and our internal clocks are somewhere in the Eastern Bloc nations— so we went for a drive in the Microbus up through Stanford, up to the linear particle accelerator that passes underneath the 280 by the Sand Hill Road exit.

It was the core team from the old Redmond geek house: Karla, Michael, Todd, Bug, and Susan—as well as Ethan. Dusty didn't come because everything makes her sick these days. She's set her workstation up by the bathroom door. She craves instant "Mr. Noodles," and is constantly sending Todd out for food runs to Burger King. Michael gave her his collection of international airline sickness bags as a "fertilization present."

Emmett left early, no doubt to groom himself. Anatole came by, but left. We're mad at him because he *still* hasn't organized an Apple tour for us, and he said he would, *weeks* ago.

Anyway, Bug and Susan and Todd and Ethan got in this arcane discussion on the relative merits of QWERTY versus Dvorak keyboards and it got U-G-L-Y. They were screaming, and I swear, the four of them were going to strangle each other with seat belts and burn each other's eyes out with the cigarette lighter and drag each other raw on the pavement, making sick red smudges along the neat and clean California State white lines.

Finally I booted them out at Pasteur and Sand Hill Drive, then drove a quarter mile up, letting them feel stupid and walk it off. I screamed out the window, *"Stop the madness!"*

Anyway, after "our coders" had their little walk, they were much better behaved. Then Todd yelled "Sh*o*gun," not "shotgun," to claim the front passenger seat, but then Susan said only the word *"shot*gun" counted, and it turned all *Itchy & Scratchy* again, and Bug ended up nabbing the shotgun seat.

We drove to the Sand Hill Road exit (location of the dreaded venture capital mall) west off the 280, into the paddocks and oaks and horsey area, parked the bus, and walked across a Christmas tree farm to a Cyclone fence surrounding the Stanford Linear Accelerator, a structure that resembles a mile-long rear side of a 7-Eleven—sandstone-tinted aluminum siding with tasteful landscaping. Not much to look at, but let me say, extremity of shape certainly *does* imply extremity of function. And whenever you see no windows, there's *some*thing scary or beguiling going on inside. No humans. Stepford.

Needless to say, there were FUCK OFF AND DIE warning signs from the Department of Energy bolted onto the wire fencing around the accelerator's perimeter. Ethan said, "Why is it that everything I'm truly interested in has the words 'Warning: U.S. Department of Energy' stamped all over it?"

Today was one of those anything's-possible days: blue skies and fluffy clouds; smooth-flowing freeways; all plant life on 24-hour chlorophyll shift after three days of rain. So alive! Two red-tailed hawks circled in the winds above, wings immobile for ten minutes on end (we timed, of course) hunting mice and gophers and squirrels. Serene.

And then we went into the mountains, into the greenery, so dense, with the sun dappling through, walking across a small wooden bridge and we had to remind ourselves we weren't dead and not in heaven. We came away from it feeling that life really is good, and with our circadian rhythms somewhat restored to Pacific Standard Time.

On the way back we drove past Xerox PARC on Coyote Hill Road, and Bug swooned only mildly. He now no longer foams when he imagines how Xerox could be the biggest company on Earth if they'd only understood what they had back in the 1970s.

After that, we pulled into the Stanford Shopping Center mall to cool off and shop for short pants. Amid the Neiman Marcus, the Williams and Sonoma, the NordicTrack, and the Crabtree & Evelyn franchises we discussed subatomic particles. At Stanford Laboratory they're hunting down the magic particles that hold together the universe. There's one particle that's still unfound. I asked the carload if anyone knew what it was.

"The Top Quark," answered Michael.

"Duct tape," answered Susan, scowling at Todd.

Stanford is so weird. They have bumper stickers like:

"I ♥ ANTARCTICA," "I ♥ Cellos," and "Calligraphy ♥ for letter or verse."

The day taught us one thing: We all agreed we need to take a bit more time out for personal development and simple rest. Even Ethan conceded this necessity, albeit by asking us if we could take shifts to do it. We had to tell him that leisure, like intelligence, doesn't scale.

Everyone immediately bailed out of work, but I headed to the office to play with *Oop!* for a while to work on my space station. Karla drove up to San Francisco to help Laura from Interval paint her apartment the same color yellow as Mary Tyler Moore's Mustang convertible. Bug was going to go help, too.

Around 1:30 A.M. the door opened and I thought it was Karla, but it was Bug, saying Karla and Laura had gone out for a stag night after they ran out of paint.

Bug came in and sat down in the chair next to me and we had a conversation. The lights were low—just a few monitors and a light by the coffee machine. Bug said—not even to me, I think, but to himself, "I was just in this nightclub downtown, Dan. I felt awkward. I'm not used to nightclubs and I don't like cigarette smoke or the way people pose and get phony in clubs."

I realized that Bug had dressed up for the night, or rather, had made an effort to coordinate his wardrobe. Also, Dusty has him signed up with a trainer at a gym, and he's not looking so much like he was assembled from the leftover bits of the Lego box as he used to. For that matter, Karla and I are both looking better assembled ourselves, these days. The gym.

"And so anyway," Bug continued, "there was this picture frame–shaped thing hanging from the ceiling—part of the club's decoration—and I thought

I was looking into a mirror and so I reached up my hand to move my hair, and of course, my image on the other side was doing the same thing. And then suddenly I realized—*we* realized—at the same moment, that we were two different people and both went *'Whoa!'*"

"And?"

"And I realized that maybe it's even possible, however briefly, and without even much say in the matter, to become someone else, or to be handed another body, in a blink of an eye. Is that called 'body invasion'? Karla would know."

There was a quiet patch here—just the hums of the computers; a *blink* sound from someone's system receiving e-mail. Bug continued: "And so I met Jeremy."

"Well good for you."

"It's not love," he added quickly. "But we *are* going to see each other again. But tell me, Daniel—I mean, I knew you before you knew Karla. Did you ever think then that love was never going to happen to you?"

"Pretty much."

"And when it did happen, how did you feel?"

"Happy. And then I got afraid that it would vanish as quickly as it came. That it was accidental—that I didn't deserve it. It's like this very, very nice car crash that never ends."

"And where are you now?"

I thought: "I think the fear part's leaving. I don't know what comes next. But the love hasn't gone, no."

Bug looked perplexed and happy, but sort of sad, too.

He said, "I used to care about how other people thought I led my life. But lately I've realized that most people are too preoccupied with their own lives to give anybody else even the scantiest of thoughts." He looked up at me: "Oh, not you and Karla and the rest of the crew. But people in general. My family's from Idaho. Coeur d'Alene. A beautiful place as ever there was, but believe me, Dan, it's *hard* to be different there."

As usually happens in our office, he began to fidget with Lego bricks.

"It starts out young—you try not to be different just to survive—you try to be just like everyone else—anonymity becomes reflexive—and then one day you wake up and you've *become* all those other people—the *others*—the something you aren't. And you wonder if you can ever be what it is you really *are*. Or you wonder if it's too late to find out."

I had no idea what to say. So I listened, which is often the best idea. And I realized Bug had driven all the way down from San Francisco just to find a person to tell this to.

"Anyway, I never talk about myself, and you guys never ask, and I've always respected that. But there comes a time when you either speak or forfeit what comes next."

He got up. "I'm driving back up the Peninsula. Home. I just wanted to talk to somebody."

I said, "Good luck, Bug," and he winked at me.

Sassy!

TUESDAY

Day of coding. It felt really Microsofty for some reason.

Midday, Karla went walking with Mom and Misty, and the two of them returned absolutely comatose with boredom. I have never seen two people with less chemistry. I just don't understand how I can love two people so much, yet have them be so indifferent to each other.

Oh, and Misty's getting really F-A-T, even though Mom has her on a "slimming diet." The neighbors are feeding her scraps because she's irresistible. So Mom had to have a dog tag made up that says, "PLEASE DON'T FEED ME, I'M ON A DIET." Karla said Mom should have millions of the things engraved and she could make a fortune selling them all over America, to *people*.

But, oh, does Misty *waddle* now!

Smoggy day down in the Valley. Rusty orange. Depressing. Like the 1970s.

Susan told us about her first date with Emmett last night, at a Toys-R-Us superstore in San Francisco. Emmett bought himself a *Star Trek* Romulan Warbird. Susan bought some infamous "softer, less crumbly Play-Doh" as well as an obligatory Fun Factory, a Bug Dozer as well as a container of "Gak"—a water-based elastic goo-type play object endorsed by Nickelodeon and called by all of us, "the fourth state of matter."

Afterward they parked on the Page Mill Road and monitored cellular phone calls.

Susan's still obsessing that Fry's doesn't sell tampons. I think Fry's had better look out.

Todd's given up on trying to be political because Dusty no longer cares about the subject and, it would appear, nor does anybody at the office. It was a fun ride while it lasted. He talks to his parents up in Port Angeles more now, too. You can imagine how his religious parents wigged out when he told them he was a Communist. They still believe in Communists.

Ethan and I went out for drinks to the BBC bar in Menlo Park after a "Trip to Europe" (ten hours of coding; so much for yesterday's leisure dictum). We both commented on a sense of unrest in the Valley. The glacial pace of the Superhighway's development is absolutely maddening to the Valley's citizens, their mouths fixed in expressions of relaxed pique amid the LensCrafters franchises, the garages, the S&L buildings, and the science parks. Nonetheless, Broderbund, Electronic Arts, and everybody else here grows and grows, so it's all still happening. Just more slowly than we'd expected.

I said, "Remember, Ethan, these are geeky, on-demand type people who suddenly have to spend their lives as if they're waiting for an Aeroflot flight out of Vladivostok—a flight that may or may never take off." Then I remembered that we're all "Russia'd out" after the political turmoil of the past few weeks and wish I'd not said that.

Ethan was glum: "CD ROM design is beginning to feel like aloe product sales chains and pyramid schemes."

"Ethan—you're our *money* guy. Don't talk like that!"

"No one wants to pay for the highway's infrastructure—it's too expensive. In the old days, the government simply would have footed the bill, but they don't do much pure research any more. Unless there's a war, but then it's hard to see how Bullwinkle and Rocky interactive CD products will help us crush an enemy. Fuck. We don't even have *enemies* anymore."

The music was playing a comforting old Ramones song, "I Wanna Be Sedated," and we were feeling maudlin.

"Companies want to be signposts, toll booths, rest stops—anything *except* actual asphalt. Everyone's afraid of spending heaps of money and becoming the Betamax version of the I-way. And I don't think a war is something that would speed up development. I don't think it's that kind of technology. This thing won't be real until every house in the world has had a little ditch dug up in its front lawn, and an optical fiber installed. Until then, it's all *Fantasy Island*."

I guess he was remembering how long it took for him to build his own Lego freeway in the office's Lego garden.

We reordered Harvey Wallbangers (1970s night).

"It's just so strange to see this sense . . . of *stalematedness*," Ethan continued, remembering the Atari boom era. "This was the land where all you ever asked for was all you were ever going to get—so everyone asked *Big*." He was getting philosophical. "This is the land where architecture becomes irrelevant even before the foundations are poured—a land of sustainable dreams that pose as unsustainable; frighteningly intelligent/depressingly rich." He twisted a cocktail napkin into a rope. "Well," he said, "the magic comes and goes." He chugged a Wallbanger. "But in the end it always returns."

Later on Ethan then became excited and pulled a crumpled sheet of thermal fax paper from his pocket. It was his list of "Interactive Hiring Guidelines" he had laser-printed and faxed throughout the Valley, like one of those "Thank God It's Friday" posters, and was returned to him, about 17th generation. He felt proud to have entered the realm of apocrypha and urban legendary.

The Eight Laws of Multimedia Hiring:

1)

Always ask a person, *"What have you shipped in the last two years?"* That's all you should really ask. If they haven't shipped anything in the last two years, ask, *"So what's your excuse?"*

2)

The "job-as-life phase" lasts for maybe ten years. Nab 'em when they're young, and make sure they never grow old.

3)

You can't trust a dog that's bitten you. You wouldn't want to employ someone who you could steal away from another company in the middle of a project.

4)

The industry is made up of either gifted techies or smart generalists—the people who were bored with high school—the sort of people the teacher was always telling, *"Now, Abe, you could get As if you really wanted to. Why don't you just apply yourself?"* Look for these people—the talented generalists. They're good as project and product managers. They're the same people who would have gone into advertising in 1973.

5)

One psycho for every nine stable people in the company is a good ratio. Too many maniacally-driven people can backfire on you. Balanced people are better for the long-term stability of the company.

6)

Start-up companies beware: kids fresh out of school invariably bail out after a few years and join the big tech monocultures in search of stability.

7)

People are most ripe for pilfering from tech monocultures in their mid- to late 20s.

8)

The upper age limit of people with instincts for this business is about 40. People who were over 30 at the beginning of the late 1970s PC revolution missed the boat; anyone older is like a Delco AM car radio.

I suggested he plug the text into the Net in `comp.hiring.slavery`, and see what other laws get tacked on, but he got offended and said that because he had the paper version that these were "THE LAWS," and I realized there was no fighting either it or him.

"Ethan," I said, "thermal paper, I mean, how 199*1*."

Another super-long day. It's 6:00 A.M. I think I see the sky pinking up. Oh God—*dawn*.

WEDNESDAY

Susan is tormenting poor Emmett now by ignoring him. Poor Emmett is feeling "pumped and dumped."

Susan's switched off her instant mail, and whenever moonstruck Mr. Couch visits her workstation she rations out her words, saying that she's too busy coding and/or too busy working on her Chyx 'zine, called *"Duh . . . ,"* to speak with him.

Susan set up a Chyx Internet address and forecasts at least a hundred Chyx signed up on the Net by next week. She wants to set up forums about Fry's not selling tampons being a metaphor for men's fear of women, new product ideas, Barbie cults, and so forth. She's obsessively into it.

"I could structure the forums and bulletin boards like an issue of *Sassy* . . . there'd be comments, and a place to ask other women for advice . . . what's that column called?"

"Zits and stuff," Karla promptly replies.

"Oh yeah. Well, I wouldn't call it that, but something like personal narratives: 'IT HAPPENED TO ME'."

"I was the best programmer in my division and that jerk Tony got a promotion!"

"It happened to me: I dated a marketing manager and he turned out to be an asshole!"

"It happened to me: I was the only girl in Silicon Valley and still couldn't get a date!" (Susan).

"It happened to me—I wrote a *Melrose Place* scriptwriting program that generated vibrant, nonlinear, marginally controversial plot lines and made a fortune!"

Susan's on a crusade. Or a rampage.

Karla printed out the following letters and posted them all on her cubicle. They're HAL 9000's letters from *2001*:

ATM	LIF	COM
HIS	FLX	NUC
MEM	CNT	VEH

Ethan flamed some of Bug's code this afternoon. "Jesus, Bug—what are you making here—hot dogs? You've put in everything including the snout . . . everything but the *squeal*."

Bug told him to piss off, and who does he think he is . . . Bill? The *old* Bug would have held a local McDonald's hostage with a sawed-off carbine. Good for Bug.

We were discussing computer-aided animation and we realized that it would have taken every computer in the world then in existence to morph Elizabeth Montgomery's nose into a *twinkle-twinkle* on *Bewitched*—"ENIACS and all that," said Karla. "You could do it on a Mac now. In two minutes."

Jeremy came over this afternoon, and he's Bug's double. Twinsville.

He showed up at the front door of the office and all seven of us stampeded foyer-ward like 101 Dalmatians to gawk out the front window as he and Bug walked away to Jeremy's Honda.

Karla said the relationship had to be somewhat serious because "you *know* how hard it is to lure anybody down here from San Francisco." She's right. You could offer San Franciscans a free Infiniti J30 and they'd *still* have some excuse not to drive 25 measly miles down to Silicon Valley.

Actually, there's a slight back-and-forth snobbery between the Valley and the City. The Valley thinks the City is snobby and decadent, and the City thinks the Valley is techishly boring and uncreative. But I can see these impressions starting to blur. This all sounds like that old Joan Baez song, "One Tin Soldier."

While taking Misty on a walk with Mom through the Stanford Arboretum, Mom was telling me about this conversation she heard between two people with Alzheimer's down at the seniors home where she volunteers:

> "A: How you doin'?
> B: Pretty good. You?
> A: How you doin'?

> B: I'm okay.
> A: So you're doing okay?
> B: How you doin'?"

I laughed, and she asked me why, and I said, "It reminds me of America Online chat rooms!" She demanded an example, so I gave her one:

> "A: Hey there.
> B: Hi, A.
> A: Hi, B
> C: Hi
> B: Look, C's here.
> A: Hi, C!
> B: CCCCCCCCCC
> C: A + B = A + B
> A: Gotta go
> B: Bye, A
> C: Bye, A
> B: Poo
> C: Poo poo

"This," I said, "is the much touted, transglobal, paradigm-shifting, epoch-defining dialogue to which every magazine on earth is devoting acres of print."

Oh—Misty's fur was covered in burrs, and it took us fifteen minutes to remove them.

Mom really has all of this new energy now that she swims every day. And her confidence has swelled enormously since winning the swim meet. She's been restacking her rock pile with extra vigor.

THURSDAY

Astounding gossip meltdown: Susan and poor, meek little Emmett Couch, our manga-phobic storyboarder, went nuclear. It was SO embarrassing—right in the middle of the office Emmett started bellowing, "You just think of me as a piece of meat, Susan—I'm not sure I like that."

And Susan said back, "I *don't* call you a piece of meat. I call you my fuck toy."

(Susan surveys room for rebuttal, we all sit there, pretending to work, our eyes like sad-eyed velvet painting waifs, staring at our keyboards.)

"Well, I'm not sure I like *that*," Emmett says.

"Well, what do you want—to take it further? You want a *relationship*?"

"Well . . ."

"Stop sniveling. I thought the deal was, we just have sex and leave it at that. Don't annoy me. I have to get back to work."

So Emmett went back to work. We, of course, were silent, but the instant-mail was flying on each other's screens. *Blink blink blink*. We were riveted. Poor Emmett's in love, and Susan doesn't want that. Or maybe she *likes* this type of relationship. People always get what they need. She's truly earned her stud medal on this one.

I went to Price-Costco. My weekly job is to purchase in-office snacks, all set up in an IKEA shelf unit in the kitchen. Everything costs 75¢.

> Mr. Noodles (for Dusty)
> Pop-Tarts
> hot chocolate mix
> Cup•A•Soup
> granola bars
> Chee•tos

Famous Amos cookies
Fig Newtons
microwave popcorn
BBQ potato chips

Karla, Bug, and I went on a tour of "Multi-Media Gulch" later in the afternoon. What a joke. There's nothing there! Or rather, there's lots of stuff around the north end of the Bay Bridge, in around the warehousey neighborhood—many companies doing cool things—but there's no public interface, so you might as well be in any warehouse district anywhere. No T-shirt stands.

We met up with Jeremy, who, as it turns out, is highly into body manipulation: tattoos, piercings, and (scary) *branding*. He's really political and he talks about queer-this and queer-that and the whole thing reminds me of our office's recent fling with Marxism, and I try and pretend it's fascinating, but my mind *does* wander off. Like when someone starts describing their stereo.

I couldn't help thinking, though, that it was a good thing Bug moved to San Francisco—being gay is such a nonissue here. You could be an ultrapolitical gay activist or a gay Republican; there's no overriding clique dominating. And fortunately for Bug, there seems to be a bigger dating pool to draw from than in Coeur d'Alene or Seattle.

Anyway, Bug, Jeremy, Karla, and I stopped by Body Manipulations on Fillmore Street. The guy in front of us was waiting to get a "Gigue"—a pierce inserted onto the strip of skin between the scrotum and the anus.

"But your body is your hard drive!" said Karla, to embarrassing withering stares of everybody in the store.

Karla, Bug, and I blanched and Bug asked Jeremy if his earring could wait. Jeremy was furious and stormed out. So the piercing's on hold, at least temporarily, and Bug is in the doghouse with Jeremy. Bug said, "I think there's a lot about this new culture I don't quite understand yet. I'm coming to it pretty late."

Whenever Abe e-mails me, he uses a fast-food-related tag line. I've compiled a list. Herewith:

Ample Parking
Ask Your Manager about Unionizing . . . No, Don't
Batter-fried Batter: Yum
Backlit Plexiglas Signs: Excellent BB Gun Targets
Cat Food: The Next Level
Customers Are Taking too Many Free Napkins
e coli. 157 Bacteria Colonizes Undercooked Patties
Elderly Employees Easier to Bully
Everybody Fears Clowns
Fishwich . . . Real Word . . . Yes or No?
Focus Grouping Deems Lamb-burgers Unpopular
Garish Color Schemes Discourage Loitering
Gift Certificates Make Shitty Presents
Hairnets
Hard to Envision Ronald McDonald Dating
More Orange Drink Machines at Birthday Parties
Muzak Discourages Loitering Teen Thugs
Pictures Instead of Words on Cash Register Buttons
Pseudo-randomly Shaped Beef Patties
Shamrock Burgers Unlikely
Swan Nuggets Tempt Yuppies
28 Dead in Random Sniping Bloodbath
Unhappy Meals—And That's Okay
Uniforms Must Affirm Asexuality
Younger Staff Exhibiting Insolence

FRIDAY

Susan and Emmett have made up, but Karla says that it's going to be tempestuous between them. Susan likes bullying, and Emmett likes to be bullied. They were down in the parking lot earlier on filling up partially rotted green bell peppers with red marine alkyd enamel paint which they will then hurl at sexually exploitative billboards later tonight. Emmett wears the same expression on his face that Misty wears whenever Dusty twirls her around like a Maypole. He's just frighteningly in love. I mean, *I* love Karla, but Emmett seems, what is the word . . . enslaved.

UH OH.

But then, Susan's the obsessive type, too. So they're a pair.

Mom and I took Misty for a morning walk today and Mom was chattier than usual. Her work at the seniors home has her thinking quite a bit, it seems. Between the seniors home, swimming, the library, and Dad, she's so busy nowadays.

In order to keep up with "us kids," Mom's been reading (and clipping) yet more articles about this @$&*%!! Information Superhighway. The enormity of her clipping enthusiasm seems to have made the issue penetrate her consciousness. She was asking me about brains and memories.

I wasn't about to go into Karla's theories of the body and memory storage because discussing my body with my mother is something I'm simply unable to do. But I did say, "There's one thing computing teaches you, and that's that there's no point to remembering *every*thing. Being able to *find* things is what's important."

"What about if you don't use a memory often enough, then. If a memory isn't used enough, does it become irretrievable?"

"Well—aside from proton decay and cosmic rays eliminating connections, I think memories are always there. They just get . . . unfindable.

Think of memory loss as a forest fire. It's natural. You shouldn't really be afraid. Think of the flowers that grow where the land had just been destroyed."

"Your grandfather had Alzheimer's. Did you know that? Maybe I shouldn't be telling you this."

"I already knew. Dad told me about it years ago. Was it fast?"

"Worse—slow."

Misty became instant friends with a passing jogger who had been taking her pulse. Dogs have it so easy.

Mom said, "I've been wondering if maybe our time here on earth has been protracted out for too long—by science—and wondering if maybe it's not a bad thing to expire *before* our government-waranteed 71.5 years have elapsed."

"Mom, this isn't one of those 'I-have-cancer' talks, is it?"

"God, no. It's just that seeing all those old people at work, so lonely and forgetful and all—it makes me have some dark thoughts. That's all. Oh listen to me natter. How selfish."

Mom was always taught that other people's problems were more important than her own.

"Anything else . . . ?" I asked.

"And now I'm wondering. That's all."

"Wondering what?"

"I seem to feel myself losing . . . my*self*. This sounds so bored-housewife. But I'm not bored. But I have problems, too." I asked her what they were, but she said that problems were best not spoken of, and this is, perhaps, my family's main problem. "I'm joining a metaphysical discussion group."

"That's *it*?"

"You don't think I'm nutty?" (I have never heard anybody use the word "nutty" unironically before, and there was a satellite-link pause before I could say, "God no!" Karla and I have a metaphysical discussion group between ourselves almost every night.)

"Of course not."

Spent the latter part of the day set on "WANDER," cruising this glorious Bay with Karla. The freeways—they're so gorgeous—the 280 cresting the big hill going north, past all the Pacifica and Daly City exits; the Highway 92 cloverleaf to Hayward and Half Moon Bay off the 101. So sensual, so infinite, so full of promise.

Walking through the paddocks—we did the running-across-the-field-in-slow-motion-toward-each-other thing; we toyed with the bioanimatronic singing vegetable booth at Molly Stone's on California Street. Then we looked for an Italian restaurant so we could reenact the classic *Lady and the Tramp* spaghetti noodle/kiss scene.

During dinner we discussed encryption. I got to wondering what a paragraph with no vowels would look like, remembering that when Ethan first met Michael, at the Chili's restaurant, Michael was busy deleting vowels on the menu. So later on I'm going to experiment with this.

Abe:
It stopped raining today, so I wnet out and bounced around on the trampoline. But it wansn't the same without Bug standing on the sidelines outlining quadripoligeia in exquisite detail.

I wonder if maybe I don't talk to enough humans in a given day... I have a few casual interactions, but nothing really. And people I'm technically close with, like my family...I don't discuss deep things with them, either.

Anyways, it seeems okay for us to talk abuout things. I've never really done this before. And sometimes I feel kind of lost. There- I've revealed too much. I'm going to send you this before I can stop myself.

Barbecue dinner tonight chez Mom and Dad.

We were discussing the Consumer Electronics Show (CES) held every January in Las Vegas and every July in Chicago, and Mom asked us why CES is so important, and Ethan, disdaining food, plucking a grapefruit from a tree beside the wisteria vine, replied pronto. He's so nice to my mother. They get along so well. But he's not Eddie Haskell nice. He's just *nice* nice. He's also an information leaf blower:

"The CES began as an annual Las Vegas car speaker and pornography trade show. It only incidentally began showcasing video games in the early 1980s. Games were considered a sideline novelty and have only recently been revealed as the passageway for the future of the human race. Editorials aside, in Las Vegas at CES you have what's called the 'Demo Derby.' Companies like us have to have a working demo of our products to show the outlets—Toys-R-Us, Blockbuster, and Target—as well as business plans and market research. As well you have what are called 'product sneaks'—you show the press your product so you can attract potential licensee software developers as well as drum up new business. I've been to eighteen CES shows. They make or break you."

After this, Susan said, "You'd think I was at Sea World and had asked Ethan about Shamu's feeding habits. How does he re*mem*ber this stuff? He just *reels* it off."

Bug has broken up with Jeremy, who he says is too politicized and too extreme. He was fairly open about it with Karla and me.

"Jeremy wanted me to be *just* like him, which wouldn't be so bad, except *he's* just like all of *his* friends. It's like Coeur d'Alene all over again—except with pasta and better defined pectorals. And it doesn't annoy me that Jeremy wants me to be just like him. That's actually kind of nice. But what bothers me is that Jeremy is just essentially not like me, and we're too disparate to ever be in sync. I thought, you know, *dating* would be a bit easier. It's *not*. And what's *truly* freaky is realizing I'm vulnerable to identity changes because I'm so desperate to find a niche. I feel like Crystal Pepsi."

In the middle of all this, Dad was putzing around in the background. He's building my space station I'm designing in real space and real time. He asked me where the box with 8-stud beams was. ("Over there by the bowl of plastic eyeballs." "Oh right—there they are.")

Bug continued, "I know I'm sort of a nerd and I don't dress nicely and I grouch out at times, but I still want to be *me*. I want to find somebody else, sure, but I also don't want to end up *harder* at the end of all of this." He went back to work.

Ethan sauntered through. "Milestones? Are we meeting our *milestones*, O content delivery system of mine?"

Susan, Emmett, Dusty, and about a dozen Chyx organized together over the Net, and decided to picket Fry's for fostering female de-intelligence by not selling tampons. The *San Jose Mercury News* interviewed them, took their picture, and left soon enough. Victory!

M m D d   m K   h d   f w scr p s nd st ff b t th y w sh d th m p nd th y r g
tt ng K   nd   c ght   c ld b t th y r g v ng m p lls f r t   nd st ff

m n t b ng st rv d r b t n r nn c ss r ly fr ght n d   v h rd s m pr ss r p
rts nd s   kn w th t St v   nd ll th n ghb rs r   K nd th t n   n w s r lly h rt

nd   ls kn w th th t th SL m mb rs h r   r v ry ps t b t pr ss d st rt ns f wh
t s b n h pp n ng Th y h v   n t b n sh t ng d wn h l c pt rs r sh t ng d wn nn c
nt p pl   n th str ts

m k pt bl ndf ld d   m n t g gg d r nyth ng   nd   m c mf rt bl

nd   th nk y   c n t ll th t   m n t r lly t rr f d r nyth ng nd th t m K

w s v ry ps t th   gh t   h r th t p l c r sh d n n th th s   n kl nd nd   w
s r lly gl d th t   w sn t th r   nd   w ld ppr c t t f v ry n   w ld j st c lm d wn
nd try n t t f nd m   nd n t b   m k ng d nt f c t ns b c   s th y r n t nly nd ng r
ng m b t nd ng r ng th ms lv s

m w th   c mb t n t th t s rm d w th   t m t c w p ns nd th r s ls   m d c l
t m h r   nd th r s n w y w ll b r l s d nt l th y l t m g s t w nt d ny g d
f r s m b dy t c m   n h r nd g t m   t b y f rc

Th s p pl   rn t j st   b nch f n t s Th y v b n r lly h n st w th m b t th y
r pr f ctly w ll ng t d   f r wh t th y r d ng

nd w nt t g t t f h r b t th   nly w y   m g ng t s f w d t th r w y nd
j st h p th t y   ll d wh t th y s y D d   nd j st d   t q ckly

v b n st pp ng nd st rt ng th s t p mys lf s th t   c n c ll c t my th ghts
Th t s why th r   r s m ny st ps n t

m n t b ng fr c d t s y ny f th s   th nk t s r lly m p rt nt th t y   t k th r
r q sts v ry s r sly b t n t rr st ng ny th r SL m mb rs nd b t f ll w ng th r
g d f th r q st t th l tt r

j st w nt t g t t f h r nd s   v ry n   g n nd b b ck w th St v

Th SL   s v ry nt r st d n s ng h w y   r t k ng th s D d   nd th y w nt t
m k s r th t y   r r lly s r s nd l st n ng t wh t th y r s y ng

nd th y th nk th t y   v b n t k ng th s wh l th ng l t m r s r sly th n th p
l c nd th FB   nd th r p pl   r t l st m

t s r lly p t y t m k s r th t th s p pl d n t j prd z my l f by ch rg ng
n nd d ng st p d th ngs   nd   h p th t y   w ll m k s r th y d n t d   nyth ng ls
l k th t k l nd h s b s n ss

Th SL p pl r lly h v b n h n st w th m   nd r lly m n f l pr tty s r th
t m g ng t g t t f h r f v ry th ng g s th w y th y w nt t t

nd   th nk th t y   sh ld f l th t w y t   nd try n t t w rry s m ch   m n
kn w t s h rd b t h rd M m w s r lly ps t nd th t   v ry b dy w s   th m   h p

o a I O I a a e   a e a   u   u   e   a e   e u a   e e e i O A I
au   a o   u   e e i i   e i   o i a   u

I   o ei   a e o   e a e o u e e a i   i   e e   I e   ea   o e   e   eo   a   o
I   o   a   e e a a   e e i   o   a e O a   a   o o e a   ea   u

A   I a o o   a   e   A e e   e e a e e   u e a o u   e   i o i o   o   a   e e
a e i   e   a e o   e e   o o i   o   e i o e   o   o o i   o   i o e   e o e i   e   e e

I   e   i o e I   o   a e o a   i   a I   o o a e

A   I   i   o u a e   a I   o   e a   e i i e o a   i a   a I O

I a   e u e   o u   o e a   a   o i e u e i o   a   o u e i   O a a   a   I a   e a
a   a I a   e e a   I o u   a e i a e i i e e o e o u   u   a   o a   o o i   e
a   o   e a i   i e i i a i o   e a u e   e   e o o   e a e i   e u e a e i   e e e

I   i a o a u i   a   a e   i   a u o a i   e a o   a   e e   a o a e i a   e a   e e a
e e   o a I i   e e e a e u i   e   e   e o o i   o   o a   o o   o   o e o   o o e i
e e a   e   e o u   o e

e e e o e a e   u a u   o u   e   e e e   e a   o e   i   e u   e a e e e
i i   o i e o   a   e a e o i

A   I a   o e o u o   e e u   e o   a I   o i   o i i   e o i   e i   a   A I u
o e   a o u   o   a e a   a a u   o i u i

I e e e   o i a   a i   i a e   e   o a I a o e   o u   a   e e
a e o a   o i i

I   o e i   o e o a a o   i   I i i   e a   i o a   a o u a e   e i   e u e
e   e i o u   a o u   o a e i   a o e   A e e   a   a o u   o o i   e i   o o   a i   e u e
o   e e e

I u   a   o e o u o   e e a   e e e e o e a a i a   e a   i   e e

e   A i   e   i e e e i   e e i   o   o u e a i   i   a a   e a   o a e u e   a
o u a e e a   e i o u a   i e i   o a   e a e a i

A   e   i   a o u e e   a i   i   o e i   a o   o e e i o u   a   e o i e a
e   I a   o e   e o e   O a   e a   I a

I   e a   u   o   o u   o   a e u e   a   e e e o e o   e o a i e   i e   a i   i a
o i   u i   i   a I o e   a o u i   a e u e   e o   o a   i   e e i e   a O a a
o u e   u i e

e   A e o e e a   a e e e   o e   i   e a   I e a   e a I e e   e   u e a I   o i
o e o u o   e e i e e   i   o e   e a   e a i o

A   I   i   a o u   o u   e e   a a   o o a   o o o   o u   I e a   I o i
a   u I e a   o   a e a   u e a   a e e o   a a   o e I o e   a   i u   o u a i
e i a e a e o   a   o u   o   a I e a   a a   i

I u   o e   a I a e   a   o e e   o   e a   o o

SATURDAY

$\mathbf{M}$ichael and Ethan broke down and told everyone the news—we have NO money. They made sure Dad wasn't around for the news, which was nice. We'd more or less suspected this all along, so in the end it came as no surprise.

Suddenly Microsoft doesn't look so bad. How could we have been so stupid to leave? Microsoft is a business first and only—not a social welfare state for 13,000 people who lucked in at the right moment.

Michael is petrified we might have to sell his Lego. "It's so pretty—it would be murder . . . a *sin* . . . to take it all apart. And last week *ID* magazine came in to take its picture."

The thing is, we agree about the Lego. It *is* too pretty to sell. Somewhere a few weeks ago, like a piece of DNA with just the right number of proteins added, it became alive. We can't kill it.

Suddenly it occurred to me that Ethan could sell his Patek Phillipe watch. That's 35 million yen right there. I said, "Ethan, sell your watch," and he said, "I can't believe you thought this was *genuine*," and dropped it into the coffee pot saying, "Six dollars. Kowloon. 1991."

We got nothing done in the afternoon. In fact we got drunk. We have no idea what we're going to do. Work some more, I suppose.

$\mathbf{A}$be looks like he's all set to go nonlinear. His e-mail is becoming telltale to an amazing degree:

At 21, you make this Faustian pact with yourself- that your company is allowed to soak up 7 to 10 years of your life- but then at 30 you have to abandon the company, or else there's something WRONG with you.

The tech system feeds on bright, asocial kids from dive- orced backgrounds who had pro-education parents. We

ARE in a new industry; there aren't really many older poeple in it. We are on the vanguard of adoldescence pro-traction.

As is common with Microsoft people I worked like a mental case throughout my 20s, and then hit this wall at thiry and went *SPLAT*.

But just think about the way high tech cultures puropose-fully protract out the adolescence of their employees well into their late 20s , if not their early 30s,. I mean, all those NERF TOUYS and FREE BEVERAGES! And the way tech firms won't even call work "The office:, but instead , "the campus".

It's sick and evil. At least down in California YOU"RE not working on a campus.

With youre 30s begins "the closing"...you realize that it' not going to be forever...the game becomes a lot more serious. People get more involved in their work.

Conundrum: I can't imagine not giving myself fully to a job...100% of me..but if I DO, I'd never "have a life" (whatever that means.) The problem is, who'd WANT to have a job that couldn't absorb you 100%??

SEE?

Back at the office, drunk, Susan demonstrated for us the Official Chyx handshake—all Chyx members greet each other by emulating the world-famous Farrah Fawcett simultaneous hair-flip-and-aim gesture, touching fin-gertips in mock gun-firing pose at the end of the gesture's completion. Dusty, Karla, Michael, and Susan were in the Lego garden practicing, and it was like boot camp:

"Make it fluid, kids—remember, you're sweeping twelve pounds of Texan corn-fed hair out of your eyes and readying a loaded Colt .45 almost simultaneously. There's a slight flip of the neck involved, and the left gun-holding hand must reach horizontal position at exactly the same moment the hair-flipping finger has swept the hair and is ready to pull the trigger. Michael—a bit more grace. Dusty, what would Kelly, Jill, and Sabrina say about that jerkiness between the hair and the trigger? Take aim, Chyx. *You are the world. Free your mind. Unplug. Plug in.*"

Thought: all PC-style consumer electronics are the same oyster-gray color of Macintoshes. The guy who makes the gray pigment must be one rich pigment maker. And all TV-style things are black. What will be the color when TVs and PCs merge?

SUNDAY

Abe has defected! Susan was on CNN! What a day! Exclamation marks!

First of all, Abe arrived with a U-Haul filled with 10,000 plastic drinking straws, Jif, a bed, and, hopefully, a Scrooge McDuck–like heap of money. He entered our Hamilton Street office around noon wearing his *Starship Enterprise* T-shirt. I said to him, "Hi, Abe, welcome home," and he said, "Hello, Daniel. I'm having my trampoline shipped down—even though it would probably be cheaper to buy one here."

He paused here and looked about the Lego garden. "It would be a shame not to bring the trampster with me, you know—*such* a useful metaphor for labor in the 1990s." He scanned the room further, seemingly unfazed by its colorful shock value, and pulled a plump-looking Costco bag out from underneath his armpit. "Oh, hello, Michael . . . I brought you some cheese slices to help us through those all-nighters. Now please tell me, just where is *my* space going to be?"

Abe had a brief meeting with Michael and Ethan ran out shouting, "We're liquid! We're liquid! We really *are* the liquid engineers. Daniel . . . how do you spell relief? Spell it, C-A-P-I-T-A-L."

Indeed, Abe is becoming an equity partner. He's going to help Michael out as a "senior" engineer and finish some core low-level code for him. Not only that but, in the interim until he finds a place to live, Abe is also moving in with Ethan up at the Dirty Harry house, and Ethan's overjoyed at the prospect of *cash*. Ethan was like that old cartoon dog character who, every time he received a bone, his ears would twirl up like a helicopter, his body would rise into the sky, and then he would float down to the earth in limp abandon.

Abe said, "People without lives like to hang out with other people who don't have lives. Thus they form lives." Even better, he'll have *company*.

CNN: we bootlegged a coaxial cable line in from the next office over and had it blasting on the monitor all day, watching "our Susan" every hour on the hour until around six o'clock, demonstrating for 137 countries around the world the Official Chyx handshake, discussing gender-blindness in the tech world, and, *best* of all, sneaking in her Net address.

It was very "TV." After 6:00, her segment was replaced by a segment on toilet training your cat.

Susan never even *told* us she did a CNN interview. But she came across so well. She's a star! And already her Chyx mailbox on our little *Oop!* node is jammed with responses. Susan, wearing a T-shirt portraying gender intelligence researcher Brenda Laurel that she had custom-made at Kinko's, was radiantly happy—not just at seeing her equity in *Oop!* saved at the last minute by Abe's money bin, but in seeing Chyx explode internationally. "*Quelle plug* for Chyx," she said, obviously thrilled. "And that Chyx handshake looked so *good* on TV. Best idea I ever had."

We celebrated all of the day's news with sundown drinks at the Empire Tap Room, and people were coming up to Susan and saying, "You're the *smart* one!" and Susan admitted that she, indeed, identified with Kate Jackson on *Charlie's Angels*.

Michael mixed Robitussin with his Calistoga water. We asked him if the drink had a name and he said, "I hereby christen this drink 'the Justine Bateman' after the lovely and talented sister character, Mallory, of TV's beloved mid-eighties sitcom, *Family Ties*."

Abe felt left out and wanted to invent a drink, too, so he put two Redoxon vitamin tablets into his diet Coke and rum and christened it a "Tina Yothers," "the smart, sassy younger sister of the above-mentioned TV sitcom."

We then tormented the staff by demanding those European layered drinks with all of the various liqueurs of varying specific gravities in tall, thin glasses. Dusty called the drinks "metaphor for the class system," and we were all weirded-out because we remembered she used to be so political and now she just changes the subject whenever it comes up.

Then, because so many people in the Bay Area have tattoos, we lapsed into a discussion of the subject. In the end, we all basically decided, "*Yuck*," all except for Bug who is still considering a lifetime of body mutilation with an earring appointment he has next week. Bug was actually being a bit mopey—the breakup, I suppose.

Anyway, we concluded that if we were forced at gunpoint to have a tattoo put onto us, the only acceptable tattoo we could think of was a bar code symbol.

We then tried to decide which bar codes would be coolest, and we decided the best ones would be products with high brand-name recognition: Kraft dinner, Kotex, Marlboro, Coca-Cola, and so forth.

And *then* we figured that bar codes will be obsolete soon enough, and having one on your shoulder or forehead would be like having a Betamax tattooed on your shoulder or forehead.

So in the end we couldn't decide on a tattoo.

There was this weird moment at the end of the night when everybody was pixelated. Ethan was carrying two flaming Sambucas, and tripped over a *Planet of the Apes* lunchbox somebody left on the floor next to a backpack, and the drinks sloshed all over the back of Susan's T-shirt, and she was on fire, like the "Flame On!" guy from the Fantastic Four.

Emmett leapt over to her from behind and smothered her flames with his body and Susan, who was so drunk she didn't even know about the Sambuca, said, "I forgive you, my love," and Emmett kissed her on the neck and then he whispered to Karla and me, *"She's on fire and she doesn't even know it. Poor baby."*

After the Tap Room, we were all far too drunk to drive—even the intake-conscious pregnant Dusty—so we wobbled back to the office (piss tanks, all of us) and we turned the lights down low, so that only the dimmer lights were glowing on our Lego garden, as though it were sunset. We were all just lolling about on the floor, feeling childish because we weren't coding for another few hours. Dusty and Karla were making hair accessories out of Lego bricks (*"Ooh, it's a Topsy Tail!"*) and Ethan, Emmett, and Michael were having a half-hearted (make that quarter-hearted) game of Nerf Wars across the Lego garden. Todd was lying on his stomach staring at Dusty's stomach (no visible baby yet) and Bug was taking apart and rebuilding a small house my father had built, and seemed lost in some other world.

Susan was building a striped, Dr. Seuss–like radio tower, and asked Bug what was on his mind, and Bug said, "1978."

Susan said, "Not the best year for music."

Bug said, "That was the year I fell in love. The year I got my heart broken."

Drunk or not, all ears, visibly or surreptitiously, turned to Bug.

"I wasn't supposed to *fall* in love. I didn't even *know* it was love. I didn't even know that *love* was some sort of option. All I knew was that I couldn't take my eyes off *him*. I wasn't even looking around, but somehow this guy drew my attention magnetically, and I was bewitched."

Unsolicited confession: *woah!*

"This guy . . . he worked at the SeaFirst on Sherman Avenue in Coeur d'Alene. I'm not saying his name—as if it matters now. No. I *will* say his name. His name was Allan. So I've said his name. I've never done that before." A pause. "*Allan*."

Bug removed the roof completely from the house and plucked out, brick by brick, the interior.

"I came in one day around lunch hour—just before lunch hour—and I asked if he was into a quick bite nearby. He said yes. We went to a Sizzler, and it was such a loser lunch. Anonymous food, but it didn't matter. Allan was acknowledging the fact I existed, and I was half crazy for him. Hell, I was *totally* crazy for him."

Bug asked Susan if she had some extra six-stud white beams, and she gave him some.

"I asked Allan what he did on Friday nights. He said he went to this one bar. I don't even think it had a name. A dive. Truck stop with grease burgers and piss beer. I went there three weekends in a row, and on the third weekend, *he* showed up, and I tried to be *so casual*. And we talked, and we got really deep really quickly—that scary kind of deep you experience when someone has you entranced.

"And he asked me to go for a drive with him. And so ask me, did I go?"

"Did you go?" asked Michael.

"Oh yeah. We drove around for an hour in his pickup and we talked and drank Bud Light, and I kept waiting for it to go somewhere, but my problem was I didn't know what *it* was, or where *it* was supposed to *go* . . . where *there* was.

He'd swig and wipe his mouth and wipe his hand on the upholstery and nothing seemed to happen. Finally we returned to the bar. Back there, at the bar, he said he had to go, back to his . . . *girlfriend*. But before he went he held my hand and he stroked it, and I thought I'd die of excitement."

Bug sighed.

"What happened next?" asked Susan.

"Me? I hounded him. Oh fuck, what a *loser* I was. I made all these need-less deposits and withdrawals at the bank. $20. $50. $10. The manager finally came over and pointedly showed me the ATM machine. Allan always managed to elude me, so I never talked to him again.

"Around the same time, I got a job offer at Microsoft and I took it—talk about escape hatch! And so there was never any closure with Allan. He's probably married now, and has 44 kids. I've been avoiding people ever since.

"But there was one final incident, though. The weekend before I left for Microsoft, I went back to the dive, and there was Allan. I felt something swell in my heart, that maybe I'd have a second chance after all to really find out what it was that I wanted to happen, and I bought two beers and was carrying them over when I saw him go out to the parking lot with some other guy, taking some other guy out for a drive, and my heart fell like a bowl of goldfish smashing onto a cathedral floor. I guess it's his gig—little drives that go nowhere, with lonely boys. Whatta sleazebag."

Total silence had fallen over our office, save for a few machines purring. Bug picked up his Lego house and held it and smelled it.

"Sure, I *know* I'm a geek, and I *know* that predisposes me to introversion. And Microsoft *did* allow me to feed the introversion. But as you're all notic-ing for yourselves, you can't retreat like that here in the Valley. There's no excuse anymore to introvert. You can't use tech culture as an excuse not to confront personal issues for astounding periods of time. It's like outer space, where the vacuum makes your body explode unless you locate sanctuary."

Ethan said, "You mean to say you haven't . . . done *anything* since the mid-1980s?"

Susan said, "What do you mean, *done*, Ethan?"

"You know—*made whoopee*, for Christ's sake."

Bug said, "More like *ever*, Eeth . . . I had my hand held once. Woo-*ee*! I'd be a lousy contestant on *The Newlywed Game*."

Michael had gone to the bathroom when this subject came up.

Susan asked, "Well, Bug, what about *now*?"

Bug said, "Now? I don't know if it's because I was afraid of being gay or because I was afraid of being rejected, but all I know is that *now* feels like the first chance at having some sort of go at being in love with someone else. I was so busy geeking out that I never had to examine my feelings about anything. I jumped into one of those little cartoon holes they use in old

Merry Melodies, and I just came out the other side, and the other side is *here*. Didn't you ever wonder where the other side was?"

This was actually a pretty good question, and I got to remembering that I *did* sort of used to wonder where the cartoon holes would take you if you hopped into them.

Bug got quiet and put his head on Susan's legs. "You know, Sooz, I would have come here for *nothing*. I never *had* to get paid." Bug looked up. "Oh God, Ethan, you *didn't* hear that." He relaxed. "Well you *know* what I mean. I just wanted to leave the old me behind and start all over again. It's not the money. It's *never* been the money. It rarely ever *is*. It wasn't with any of us—was it? Ever?"

I don't think it ever was. We lay around and were silent while Bug pulled himself together. I put on an old Bessie Smith CD and we sat, alcohol scrambling our codes, our thoughts, our lives, if only for the remaining darkness, until work made its claim upon us once more.

MONDAY

Today was one of those days where I was snapped awake by a bad dream and a hangover. Beware of those layered Eurodrinks—they're made with scary, bee-sting-filled liqueurs!

All of us received an e-mail from Bug:

Hi kids. Me here.
Remember back in high school, there were always those
peple who were in relationhips starting in eighth grade,
and they're still in relationships today? They know all the
logical sequnce of the way things are supposed to happen.
Like in the third week, they have a spat, and they say,
"Oh, well this is just the Third Week Spat," and it passes.
Never having had a relationship, I don't know how all the
steps in a relationship are supposssed to go. I have to
learn all the steps, decades later. But I'll do it.

Sorry I lost it last night. I'm off to a B&B in Napa for a few
days to think things through. Leisure and all of that.
Freaky but necessary. Live and love. Bye kids.

It appears we might be getting a publishing deal lined up—with Maxis, the Sim City people. Apparently the fish are biting at the bait: Broderbund, Adobe, and Alias have also shown a bit of interest, too. So I guess we're doing something worthwhile, or more to the point, possibly profitable. Uh oh! Am I losing my integrity, my One-Point-Oh sensibility?

I drove with Abe and Ethan to Electronic Arts up the 101 in San Mateo, on Fashion Island Boulevard—a geek party friend of ours was going to let us beta-play a new game—and we got to drive the Highway 92-101 cloverleaf I like so much.

Like most Silicon Valley buildings, EA's headquarters, the Century Two complex, are sleek and clean, a Sony-based aesthetic, where a sleek, machine-shaped object contains magic components on the inside that do cool shit. Susan says it's a "male" aesthetic. "If men could have their way, every building on earth would resemble a Trinitron."

EA's parking lot was so odd—entirely composed of brand-new cars. I felt like I was in the lot at Alamo. In the fountain out front there was a big plaza sculpture plus a bunch of rubber float toys in water crested with Joy dishwashing liquid bubbles.

"I smell nerds," said Abe.

The lobby had a vitrine containing a football signed by John Madden and a basketball signed by Michael Jordan, game licensees, both.

Played their new game all afternoon. It was almost completely bug-free and they'll be shipping within weeks.

Fashion Island, BTW, is really great—it's all these huge dead department stores that got marooned by new freeway ramp construction.

After we drove back down the 101 from San Mateo, I checked my answering machine at the office. Michael left a message to phone him, so I did—even though he was sitting in his own office just a spit away. No matter. I got his machine's message, cobbled together from old *Learn how to speak Japanese* tapes:

> [Resonant Berlitzian voice:]
> > *Japanese at a glance*
> [Befuddled U.S. tourist:]
> > *I can't find my luggage*
> [Japanese bimbette voice:]
> > *Nimotsu ga mitsukarimasen*
> [Candice Bergen–type female:]
> > *My luggage is here*
> [Studly Toho Studios leading male voice:]
> > *Nimotsu wa, koko desu*

> [Game show host voice:]
>> *Is there a good disco nearby?*
>
> [Japanese nerdy male voice:]
>> *Chikaku ni, ii disco ga arimasu ka?*
>
> [Game show host:]
>> *I have cramps*
>
> [Candice:]
>> *I have diarrhea*
>
> [Studly male:]
>> *There's something wrong with this camera*
>
> [Bimbette:]
>> *Cauliflower*
>
> [Game show host]
>> *Eggplant*
>
> [Candice:]
>> *Prosciutto with melon*
>
> [Studly guy:]
>> *Shrimp cocktail*

BEEP . . .

I told Todd to dial Michael's number and he did, and we had to agree that Michael's messages always indeed rocked the Free World.

Todd, I should add, like many 1990s people, equates his self-worth with the number of messages on his phone answering machine. If the red light's not blinking . . . YOU ARE A LOSER. Todd's almost cybernetic relationship with his answering machine (who am I fooling—this goes for *all of us*) seems a precursor of some not-too-distant future where human beings are appended by nozzles, diodes, buzzers, thwumpers, and dingles that inform us of the time and temperature in the Kerguelen Archipelago and whether Fergie is, or is not, sipping tea at that exact moment.

Todd says that at least with e-mail you have a "loser backup system" so if you didn't get a phone message, you can at least have text.

Anyway, three minutes later my phone rang and it was Michael, asking if he could take me out for a late afternoon snack, but his voice was so hesitant in an un-Michael-ish way. He was stuttering and I began to freak out, the way you do when you pass a customs guard at a border, even though you're not hiding anything. I said yes and braced myself for what seemed could only be terrible news.

We drove up the 101 to Burlingame, driving and driving and driving and driving and driving and I realized that in the Valley, the formula really is, NO CAR = NO LIFE. We arrived at the SFO Airport Hyatt Regency of all places, and I asked him why on earth we were there.

"Daniel, I *love* this building. It resembles the world's most piss-elegant nuclear power plant—look at the copper-oxide-colored roof, turret-like center structures, and the delightful Bayside location providing cooling waters for all those toasty transuranic fuel rods." His expression never changed during this ode.

We talked about the games at Electronic Arts, but in the back of my mind, I was trying to remember if I was pulling my weight with *Oop!*. Everybody's been doing such amazing work lately—the freedom and freefloat of intellectual Darwinism is bringing out the best in all of us—and maybe Michael doesn't think my work is as amazing as everybody else's. But I think it *is*. I mean, not only am I doing some really hot Object Oriented Programming, but I think my space station is going to be truly *killer*. The injustice of it all—especially after Abe made us liquid.

Michael was trimming his finger nails and nudging the keratoid crescents into his shirt pocket, and I was getting so PaRAnOId.

We arrived and were sitting in the Swift Water Cafe, and Michael ordered a decidedly non-two-dimensional piece of apple pie, flaunting in my face his betrayal of his Flatlander eating code. He seems to be abandoning it of late. It's like an alcoholic going off the wagon. He's changing.

And then, from nowhere, he asked me, "Daniel, do I seem alive?" I was so taken aback. I think this is the oddest question anybody's ever asked me.

I said, "What a silly question. I mean—of course you do—a bit machine-like at times, but . . ."

He said, "I *am* alive, you know. I may not have a life, but at least I'm alive."

"You sound like Abe."

"I always used to wonder, do machines ever feel lonely? You and I talked about machines once, and I never really said everything I had to say. I remember I used to get so *mad* when I read about car factories in Japan where they turned out the lights to allow the robots to work in darkness." He ate his apple pie, asked the waitress for a single-malt scotch, and said, "But I think, yes, I *do* feel lonely. So alone. Yes. Alone."

I said nothing.

"Or I *did*."

Did . . . "*Did?* Until when?" I asked.

"I'm—"

"What."

"I'm in *love*, Daniel." Oh man, talk about a gossip bomb. (And thank God I'm not fired.)

"But that's great, Michael. Congratulations. With who?"

"I don't know."

"What do you *mean* you don't know who."

"Well, I do and I don't. I'm in love with an entity called 'BarCode.' And I don't know who he-slash-she is, how old or anything. But I'm in love with . . . *it*. The BarCode entity lives in Waterloo, Ontario, Canada. I *think* it's a student. That's all I know."

"So let me be sure I understand this. You've fallen in love with a person, but you have no idea who the person is."

"Correct. Last night you were all talking about getting bar code tattoos, and you kept saying the word 'bar code' over and over, and I thought I was going to go berserk with love. It was all I could do to contain myself. And then Bug was so open and honest I thought I would die, and I realized things can't go on as they have been going."

Michael's scotch arrived. He rolled the ice around and gulped—he's shifted from Robitussin into the hard stuff.

"BarCode eats flat food, too. And she-*slash*-he's written a Flatlander *Oop!*-style product with immense game potential. BarCode is my soulmate. There is only one person for me out there, and I have found it. BarCode's my ally in this world *and* . . ."

He paused and looked across the restaurant.

"Sometimes when I'm loneliest, life looks the most dreadful and I don't want to be here. On earth, I mean. I want to be . . . out there." He pointed to the sun coming in a window, a beam coming down, and the sky over the Bay. "The thought of BarCode is the only thing that keeps me tethered to earth."

"So what are you going to *do* about it, Michael?"

He sighed and looked at the other businessmen in the restaurant.

"But what are you going to *do* about it?" I asked again. He looked up at me. "Is *that* why I'm here, Michael? Am I getting involved in this?"

"Can you do me a favor, Daniel?"

I knew it. "What."

"Look at me."

"I'm looking."

"No, *look*."

Michael put himself under the microscope lens: pudgy; eyeglassed; ill-clad; short-sleeve shirt the color of yellow invoice paper; pale complexion; Weedwacker hairdo—the nerd stereotype that almost doesn't even really exist anymore—a Lockheed junior draftsman circa the McCarthy era. But for his almost Cerenkovian glow of intelligence, he might be mistaken for a halfwit or, as Ethan would say, a fuck-wit. I said, "Is there something I should be seeing?"

"*Look* at me, Daniel—how could anyone be in love with *me*?"

"That's ridiculous, Michael. Love has almost nothing to do with looks. It's about two people's insides mixing together."

"Nothing to do with looks? That's easy for all of you to say. *I* have to work everyday inside our body-freak world of an Aaron Spelling production. You think I don't notice?"

"Point *being* . . . ? From what I can see, if one person is feeling something, there's usually a pretty good chance the other is feeling the same thing, too. So looks are moot."

"But then they see me—my *body*—and it's over."

In a way I was losing my patience, but then who am I to be an expert in love? "I think you're perfectly lovable. Our office is a freak show and no indication of the world at large."

"You say that like a father whose son just got braces and headgear."

"What do you want me to *do*, Michael."

He paused and looked both ways and then to me: "I want you to visit Waterloo for me. Meet BarCode. Offer . . . it . . . a job. BarCode's the smartest programmer I've ever conversed with."

"Why don't *you* go, Michael?"

He looked down at himself and clamped his arms around his chest and said. "I can't. I'll be . . . rejected."

Well, if there's one thing I know, it's Michael and his unbudgeability. "Michael, if I were to do this, under no circumstances would I be willing to pretend, even for one *micro*second, that I were you."

"No! You wouldn't have to! Just say that I couldn't make it and you came in my stead."

"What if BarCode turns out to be a 48-year-old man wearing a diaper—a diaper with spaghetti straps?"

"Such is love—though I *hope* that wouldn't be the case."

"How long have you and BarCode been e-mailing each other?"

"Almost a year."

"Does BarCode know who you are? *What* you are?"

"No. You know the joke: *On the Internet nobody knows you're a dog.*"

"Oh *God*."

"You'll do it!"

"BarCode could be *anybody*, Michael."

"I love their insides already, Daniel. We've already blended. I'll take what fate throws me."

"But tell me one thing—how can you talk to somebody for over a year and not even know their age or sex?"

"Oh, Daniel—that's part of the *thrill*."

Back at the office I went on a walk with Karla and told her about it right away and she said it was the most romantic thing she's ever heard of and she smooched me right there in the middle of a downtown street. "Michael is so brave to love so blindly."

When I told her that it was private and that Michael would prefer Dusty and Susan didn't know, her face expressed slight peevedness, but she understood. They can be merciless.

Susan showed me a dozen boxes of "Glitter Hair refill packs" she'd bought from the Barbie aisle at Toys-R-Us. It was so creepy—this dead fake hair inside a pink box. All Chyx are receiving an Official Chyx Wristband made of Pentium-grade knotted, liberated Barbie hair garnished with a small sliver of silicon lattice ingot made by a friend of Emmett's down in Sunnyvale. "Cool or *what*?" Susan already has over 3,500 Chyx "happening" on-line. So it looks as if Chyx is real. CNN really changed her world.

Time warp: it's been months since I've arrived here. How long have I been here? I can't tell. I leave for Waterloo in three days.

TUESDAY

I was with Mom in the car somewhere in Menlo Park and suddenly we were surrounded by, like, nine Porsches. It was just ridiculous. And Mom said, "When your father and I first moved here back in '86, and I saw all these cars, I said to myself, '*My*, there's a lot of drug dealers here in this area.'"

"Mom, did you buy drugs for Dad's IBM parties?"

It's fun teasing Mom. She smiled, "Oh, you *know* . . . I clip news clippings."

This quick chat served to remind me that while car status here is different than at Microsoft, it is no less hierarchical and fetishistic.

Ethan knows nothing of my matchmaking mission. He thinks I'm going to Waterloo to haggle over purchasing some subroutines and possibly to hire a new recruit. He came over to the house to tell me that he'll be accompanying me to Ontario—he has to speak with the people at CorelDraw in Ottawa. They're paying for him to go, so it's a different gig entirely.

I said that this was a truly random coincidence, except Ethan said I was not only being redundant ("random coincidence"), but that he didn't believe in randomness, which is, I imagine, a tacit admission of religiousness.

Ethan.

Odd.

He said he'd prove it tonight.

We then got into a discussion of Nerd Schools and the end of the era of "single-dose" education—and of course this led to a listing of schools that had the best nerd reputations.

> • Cal-Tec (Extreme nerds; the Jet Propulsion Lab is just up the hill and around the corner. The big rumor is that they had to institute pass-or-fail grading because there were too many GPA-related suicides.)

- CMU
- MIT
- Stanford
- Rensselaer Polytechnic Institute (for undergrads)
- Waterloo
- UC Berkeley
- Dartmouth
- Brown—"Hipster nerd school with a good undergrad comp-sci program."

We drove up to Redwood City and played electronic darts at a bodega there . . . Karla, Ethan, and I. Ethan and I grew up in suburbia, and we're both pretty good dart players (those nutty rumpus rooms). Karla's never played darts before tonight.

Anyway, it was three darts per person, per round. Ethan put in four quarters and selected a *four*-player round. We asked him why, and he said, *"You'll see."*

Karla went first, me second, Ethan third, and then for the fourth round we had what Ethan called, the "Random Round" where instead of any of us trying, we'd each huck a dart standing on one foot, gulping a beer, throw it backwards . . . as silly as possible. Ministry of Silly Walks.

Needless to say, the Random Round won every single game, and always by a minimum of 100 points. It was *scary.*

Ethan said randomness is a useful shorthand for describing a pattern that's bigger than anything we can hold in our minds. "Letting go of randomness is one of the hardest decisions a person can make."

Ethan!

Identity. I go by the Tootsie theory: that if you concoct a convincing on-line meta-personality on the Net, then that personality really IS you. With so few things around nowadays to loan a person identity, the palette of identities you create for yourself in the vacuum of the Net—your menu of alternative "you's"—actually IS you. Or an isotope of you. Or a photocopy of you.

Kinko's again—photocopy yourself!

Karla noted that when photocopy machines first started to come out, people photocopied their bums. "Now, with computers, we photocopy our very *being.*"

THURSDAY

Ethan was in business class and I was in coach. If it was *Oop!* paying, he'd be in the hold with all of the sedated pets.

Ethan vanished at the airport gate, and once in flight, the blue curtain came down and Ethan was gone until we arrived in Canada. I PowerBooked some code on ThinkC and so was able to remain productive. Batteries—the weight! They suck up gravity. They fellate the planet.

I got to thinking that nerds really like anything that smacks of teleportation: freeways; airport first-class lounges; hotel rooms with voice mail . . . anything that erases distance and makes travel invisible. Why don't airlines pick up on this?

Upon landing, standing in line at immigration in Toronto, Ethan asked me, "So, pal, how was life in the Egg Farm?" (referring to the chokingly full, cramped, and miserable realm of coach class; we can thank *computers* for perennially cramped planes). I said "*Lovely*, thank you, Ethan. I took complimentary salt-and-pepper packets as souvenirs. I'll trade them for your Reuben Kincaid sleep goggles."

"Get real, pal."

At immigration, Ethan pulled out his passport and a whole whack of Iraqi banknotes tumbled onto the carpet in a dervish of cash—Susan had bought them at a San Francisco stamp store and stashed them in his passport as a prank. It was great; it was delayed reaction for the time two months ago that Ethan left an inflatable hemorrhoid doughnut on Susan's chair while some Motorola guy Susan had a crush on was visiting. Ethan looked at the doughnut, then at Mr. Motorola and said, "*Oh—poor Susan. Such pain—you really can't imagine.*"

Back in Canada, Ethan was promptly whisked off to the cavity search room as *I* toddled off to catch my teensy connector flight to Waterloo. I had to pretend I didn't know him because I didn't want to visit THE ROOM either, thank you.

I was looking at the in-flight magazine, and at the end they had this map showing where the airline flies and it looked like a science-fiction map of how a virus transmits from one place to another. All these parabolic arches from city to city to city to city. If the Marburg virus ever does mutate and go airborne, we're DOOMED!

Canada: such a cold, cold country. In the plane I saw below me the blue moon's light on white snow; towers, poles, and lights and blinkings; a wide land that must be shouted across with electrons. And I got to thinking, towers are going to be obsolete, soon. All of these towers, dreaming of their own demise.

Out the hotel window, it was just miserable and there were these Zamboni scraping piles of the past winters' snows, all stacked up. It reminded me of those Antarctic ice-pack core samples where they drill into the ice and date the gases and pollens trapped back in time. Except outside my window there were two layers of soot, one of dog poo, another layer of soot, another layer of dog poo. God, winter is gross. I can't believe Eskimos just don't set themselves adrift on ice floes for the boredom of it all. Or move to Florida.

Karla sent me a fax saying IF YOU LIVED HERE YOU'D BE HOME RIGHT NOW. And I was so homesick.
    Watched CNN. Coded *Oop!*.

Thought: one day the word "gigabits" is going to seem as small as the word "dozen."

SATURDAY

Michael arranged for me to meet BarCode at a student union pub.

BarCode, given the possibility of making a flesh-to-flesh connection, admitted on-line that . . . *it* was, as Michael guessed, a student—so at least the 48-year-old-man-in-spaghetti-strap-diapers scenario was averted.

"Don't be so sure, Daniel," said Michael on the phone from California with not a touch of worry in his voice. "Mature students, you know. Well— we can only hope not . . ."

Waterloo's student pub is better than others I've seen. "The Bomb Shelter," with an all-black inside, a large bomb painted on the wall, big screen TV, video games, pool, and air hockey.

The outdoor temperature was about minus 272 degrees and the students wore thick, gender-disguising outfits to ward off the gales of liquid helium sweeping down from Hudson's Bay. I thought of how in-character it was of Michael to fall for someone's insides and not even know their outsides. I sat there in a seat next to the wall, drinking a few beers, wondering if whoever came by could be . . . *it.*

I was getting all mushy and lonely and missing Karla when suddenly a hand grabbed my throat from behind and yanked me toward the wall, like an alien from *Aliens.* Fuck! Talk about terror. It was a small hand, but God, it was like steel, and a voice whispered to me, a girl's voice: "Talk to me, baby. I know who you *aren't.* So speak—gimme a sign, send me a code—let me know that you're *you.*"

Oh man, I was meeting *Cat*woman . . . with an Official Chyx Wristband!

My head blanked. Only one word came into my head, Michael's code word for our meeting: "*Cheese slices,*" I squeaked out from my snared vocal cords.

The hand loosened. I saw a bare arm. I saw a bar code tattoo below the vaccination bump. And then I saw BarCode, revealed at last, as she let go of her grip and climbed down off the railing and into my view: smaller than

Karla, more muscular than Dusty, and dressed so tough that Susan looked like a southern belle in comparison: filthy down vest on top of an oily halter top; hot pants; gas station attendant's boots; haircut with a blunt Swiss Army knife; both eyes dripping with smudged mascara and melting snow . . . all underneath an ancient hand-knitted Canadian-type jacket with trout knitted into the front and back. She was small and tight and the natural embodiment that everything Karla, Dusty, and Susan self-consciously were trying to turn themselves into. She was the most aggressive female I'd ever seen and so young—and man, she was so IN CHARGE.

She looked both ways. She looked me in the eyes. She said. "You're Kraft singles's friend?" She narrowed her gaze. "*You're* here to interview me? Why didn't Kraft come himself/herself?"

"It's, uh . . . *him*self . . . and I'll be honest with you right now—I'm here because he didn't think you'd like him if you saw *him*."

She smashed a bottle on the ground and scared the wits out of me. "Man, what sort of pussy does he think I *am*? . . . that I give a shit whatthefuck he looks like?" But then her demeanor changed. She got sweet for a second: "He's a *he*? He cares what I think about him?"

"'Kraft singles,' as you call him, is stubborn. You should know *that*."

She relaxed a bit. "You're telling *me*. Kraft is one stubborn motherfucking entity."

She giggled. "She." Pause. "*He* . . ."

"You mean," suddenly I was beginning to understand, "you didn't know who he was . . . what he was? I mean, sorry for being blunt, but *you* didn't know, *either*?"

"Don't make me feel like a wuss." She picked up an empty 7-Up can, crushed it flat on her knee and then got sweet again. "Is Kraft, ummm . . . like . . . *married* or anything?"

"No."

I could tell she was relieved and it was beginning to dawn on me that Michael wasn't the only one who had fallen for an entity.

"Do you want to see a picture, BarCode . . . do you have another name?"

"Amy."

"Do you want to see a picture of Michael, Amy?"

Quietly: "You have one?"

"Yeah."

"His name is Michael?"

"Yeah."

"What's your name?"

"Dan."

"Can I see a picture, Dan?"

"Here." She greedily snatched the group picture taken at a barbecue at Mom and Dad's earlier on in the year. Nine of us were in the photo, but she spotted Michael right away. I think I had just transacted the most bizarre matchmaking transaction in the history of love.

"That's *him . . . there*."

"Yup."

"*Dan*, you're gonna think I'm an asshole, but I had a dream, and I knew that's what he looked like. I put a diskette under my pillow for weeks waiting for a sign, and it came to me, and here he is. I'm taking the photo."

"It's yours."

She looked at Michael's image. She was tentative and girly. "How *old* is he?" Her voice up-inflected at the end.

I was slightly drunk, and I laughed and I said, "He's in love with you, if that's what you want to know."

She got all cocky again.

She grabbed my right hand and shouted, "Arm wrestle!" and after a two-minute tussle (thank heavens for the gym), broken up only because a group of drunk engineers lollygagged up to our table and one of them barfed one table over, cutting the moment short, did we speak again. "It's a draw," she told me, "but remember, I'm younger than you and I'm only getting stronger. So tell me about . . . *Michael*." She paused to think this over—the *name*. "Yes. Tell me about *Michael*."

The waiter brought us both beers. She clinked mine so hard I thought it would shatter and she said, "Tell me again, what does Michael feel? You know—about . . . *me*?"

"He's in love."

"Say it a*gain*."

"He's in love. Love. L-O-V-E. Love, he loves *you*. He's going to go insane if he doesn't meet you."

She was as happy as I've ever seen another human being. It made me feel good to be able to say this with a clear heart.

"Go on," she said.

"He doesn't care who you are. He only knew your insides. He's smart.

He's kind and he's always been a good friend to me. There is nobody like him on earth, and he says that you're the only reason he stays tethered here to the planet." And then I told her the diaper-and-spaghetti-straps scenario.

She leaped backward into her seat.

"I'm gonna fuckin' explode! Dan! I'm gonna tell you, I'm in love, and I'm in love like an atomic bomb detonating over industrialized Ontario, so watch out *world*!"

I realized that Michael was BarCode's first love, and I realized that I was seeing something special here, as if all of the flowers in the world had agreed to bloom just for me, and just for once, and I said, "Well, I think it's mutual. Now could you relax just a bit more, Amy, because you're frankly scaring the daylights out of me, and I don't think my right arm can deal with another wrestle."

She gushed a bit, flush with happiness. She sat and smiled at the undergrads who, it seemed, regarded her with a no small tinge of fear. She surely must be some sort of campus legend.

"You're the bearer of hot news, and I'll always remember you for that, Dan," and she kissed me on the cheek and I thought of Karla, and my heart felt so happy yet faraway from her.

"Man, I'm so happy I could crap," she said, "Hey—over there—that table of engineers—let's go trash 'em!"

SATURDAY
(one week later)

Michael and BarCode—excuse me—*Amy*—are now engaged. Amy and Michael have been having a John-and-Yoko lovefest at the Residence Inn Suites down in Mountain View. Karla and I went to visit them, and their suite was all a-rummage with pizza boxes, diet Coke cans, dirty laundry, unread newspapers and gum wrappers. Michael has transformed from a lonely machine into a *love* machine.

People!

Amy, 20, is going to finish her degree in computer engineering, and is going to come work for us starting in May. We're all in love and awe and terror of her. She and Michael together are like the next inevitable progression of humanity. And the two of them are so happy together—seeing them together is like seeing the *future*.

Oh—here's something I forgot to write last week. At the bar, I asked Amy what it was—or rather, *how* it was that two people could not *know* each other and fall in love and all of that. She told me that all her life people had only ever treated her like a body or a girl—or both. And interfacing with Michael over the Net was the only way she could ever really know that he was talking to *her*, not with his concept of her. "Reveal your gender on the Net, and you're toast." She considered her situation: "It's an update of the rich man who poses as a pauper and finds the princess. But fuck that princess shit—we're both *kings*."

We both got drunker and she said to me, "This is it, Dan. This is the way I wanted to always feel. This is *it*."

"What?"

"Love. Heaven is being in love, and the love never stops. And the feeling of intimacy never stops. Heaven means feeling intimate forever."

    And I can't really say I disagree.

Later on tonight, Michael stomped into the office in a way he never has before, clapped his hands, and shouted, "Troops, let's make these machines do something they've never done before. Let's make them *sing*."

Melrose Voyager Melrose Voyager

"Press pound now . . ."

7
Transhumanity

EIGHT MONTHS LATER
Las Vegas, Nevada
Thursday, January 5, 1995

The Alaska Airlines captain said, *"Ladies and gentlemen, the city of Las Vegas is below us to your right. You will be able to see the pyramid of the Luxor Hotel . . ."*

The 727 lurched sideways as its human cargo chugged like Muppets to view a Sim City game gone horribly wrong: the Luxor Hotel's obsidian black glassy pyramid, and beside it, the Excalibur's antiseptic, Lego-pure, obscenely off-scale Arthurian fantasy. Farther up the Strip was the MGM's jade glass box with 3,500 slot machines and 150 gaming tables representing the largest single concentration of cash points on earth—"the Detroit of the postindustrial economy," Michael declared.

It was pleasing for me to see so many of the faces of the people in my life, lit by the glow of the cabin windows—Karla, Dad, Susan, Emmett, Michael, Amy, Todd, Abe, Bug, and Bug's friend, Sig—their faces almost fetally blank and uncomprehending at the newness of the world below into which we would shortly dip.

Sig is an ophthalmologist from Millbrae who convinced Bug that he wasn't stereogramatically blind. He's a vast improvement over Jeremy, and

Bug is suddenly so much more *himself*, relaxed and joking and just . . . glad. Back at SFO Airport Sig and Bug adopted a J. Crew fashion thing: instead of vogueing, they "Crew." When we shout the word *"Crew!"* they'd freeze into a rehearsed series of maniacally-smiling dorky male model poses. It was good for laughs the whole flight down. Also, Bug almost got whiplash from craning his neck halfway through the flight trying to catch a glimpse of the ultrasecret Groom Lake military facility. He told me, "They have UFOs and aliens cryogenically frozen there."

I said, *"Right*, Bug. As if Alaska Airlines is allowed to fly over a top secret base," and Bug replied, "Look down there, Dan—that's the place where they staged the fake moon landing back in 1969." I looked, and it *did* resemble the moon.

So I started to torment Bug about his new 3-cylinder Geo Metro, and Amy joined in, saying, "God, Bug, you couldn't even *kill* someone with that thing. You could maybe *nudge* them to death, or something . . ." And then she pretended she was at her doctor's office and her doctor was saying, "Amy, this rash you've got . . . have you had prolonged exposure to rodents, perhaps, or small dogs, maybe 3-cylinder cars?" and Amy says, "Well, *yes*, actually, I have noticed a Geo following me around and nudging me considerably . . . I just assumed it was maybe a lost student driver but now that I think about it, *that's* where my rash is coming from!"

Susan, Karla, and Amy have really Chyx'd out for the CES—bullet-proof vests over tiny little tube tops (Susan has declared that it's her responsiblity as a feminist media figure to singlehandedly revive the tube top), baggy jeans worn low on the hips, and black sunglasses. Susan continues to gain celebrity with Chyx (*New York Times* business section last week). All three of them decided to dress "Tough Love" because Ethan told them the fair is 99 percent male and they don't want to look "like dweeb bait."

I, as ever, am clad in my Riot Nrrrd staple: Dockers and Gap pocket-T. Dad was in Brooks Brothers, and now that his hair's turned snow white over the last year, he makes a singularly trustworthy impression as a representative for the company. (And he also finally speaks C++.) Todd was wearing a trench coat because he'd read in the *Chronicle* that it was raining in Las Vegas. We told him he looked like Secret Squirrel, the old cartoon character, and the coat soon vanished. Todd also unveiled his new "hockey hairdo" on the flight: short on the top and long in the back. I guess this is because of the hockey strike. Todd bought season tickets to see the Sharks.

Also on the plane was a company called BuildX which is doing an *Oop!*-like product, down in Mountain View, and there were eight of them and they had matching black sweatshirts with a futuristic BuildX logo on them and they looked like the Osmonds or the Solid Gold Dancers. We didn't talk to them the whole flight.

Ethan couldn't come. He's back in Palo Alto, staying with Mom while he does his chemotherapy, which appears to be going well, even though it makes him crabby. He's starting to lose a little hair, not too bad, and this is a terrible observation but his dandruff is finally clearing.

Dusty is still in disbelief that her baby wasn't a grapefruit and is also at Mom's house for a few days while we're at CES, nursing Lindsay Ruth and keeping Ethan company. Mom is giving her a crash course in motherhood, dragging out embarrassing baby photos of me and tiny little jumpers that I had no idea she kept. Dusty sits and stares at Lindsay for hours on end, saying to anyone who'll listen, *"Ten toes! Ten fingers!"* Lindsay was delivered on the evening of the final round of the Iron Rose IV competition, and Todd told me on the flight down that Lindsay Ruth was named after movie-of-the-week star and Bionic Woman Lindsay Wagner, as well as for a Bible person. He hasn't really talked about the baby yet—I think it's finally sinking in that he's a father, now that he's got the physical proof.

Luggage lost; luggage retrieved; Vietnam veteran taxi driver; Gallagher billboards. We checked into our hotel in a daze—a creakingly old hotel called the Hacienda. (Best not discussed. It's sole redeeming feature is its location right next door to . . . the extravagant-beyond-all-belief pyramid of the LUXOR.)

We left the hotel to register at the Convention Center, many football fields' worth of sterile white cubes, which are as attractive as the heating ducts atop a medical-dental center. The look on all the registrees' faces was great. You could tell that all they could think of was sex and blowing their money later that night. It was so transparent. Las Vegas brings out the devil in everyone.

Las Vegas: it's like the subconsciousness of the culture exploded and made municipal. I was so overwhelmed by it that I ended up reviving my old-style subconscious file from last year. Herewith:

vasectomy reversal billboard
breakfast
Siegfried & Roy
Compaq
NY Steak & Eggs $2.95

moccasins
Sahara
Nokia
47-Tek

control.
remote.

keno

social interface
cardboard IBM box
is it loud?
tanked girl
reflective surfaces

forgotten cocktails
name tag
cheddar
interactive virgin
Flamingo
dry ice

Moon
American
Floyd
Heywood

cities destroyed
win win win
Nam-1975
monster lab
air lock
Bob
orb
tatami
rings
object popping
lemon

fight
morphin mighty
VFX-1
colonize
thrust
boy game
64 bits
pods
Softimage
anti alias
BAR

trilinear MIPmap interpolation
Ultra 64

gravy

Samsung paper napkin cherry

synthetic
emotional
response

Nye County, Nevada
traffic lights
computer personal
Howard Hughes Parkway

Dept. of Energy
White Tigerzoid
floral carpeting
***69**

cinderblock walls
First Interstate
implant
strip
Big Endian

escort leaflets
00
beverage
bell
I Endian

When we returned to the hotel to change, Karla's and my room somehow became the party room. None of us except for Anatole, who's here to schmooze Compaq, have ever been to Las Vegas before, let alone a CES. (Amy called us "bad American citizens.") We were all giddy at the prospect of an evening's unchained fun; sleazy adventure divorced from consequences.

Anatole and Todd brought up vodka, mixer, and ice. Our ancient queen-size bed was as concave as a satellite dish—the same mattress must have been mangling the lumbars of low-budget gamblers since the Ford Administration—so we sat clustered in its recess like kangaroo babies inside Mom's pouch. Chugging V&Ts, we surfed through the channels, high on simply *being* in Las Vegas, even just watching TV in a hotel room in Las Vegas.

The TV began showing these three-minute pay-TV movie clips. (*"Hey, let's watch* Curly Sue*!"*) Then one came on touting the AVN Awards, the Adult Video News awards. Susan yelled, "The Stiffies!" It's an actual Academy Awards–style show for porn people. We had to pay. It was simply too juicy *not* to. People were sashaying up the aisles to collect awards for things like "Best Anal Scene" and they were getting all teary and emotional making acceptance speeches. It was unbelievable. Awards for, like, "Best Group Scene."

Dad was fortunately in his own room, talking on the phone with a friend from Hewlett-Packard he was having dinner with that evening. But really, the whooping we all made . . . we were just the sort of people you *don't* want staying in the room next to you.

Anatole said, "Oh *look*—that actress *there*—she was in the booth across from my old company six years ago—and now she's won an award!" Anatole actually seemed quite proud. "In the old days, you had 12 computer game geeks and 12 porn stars all crowded into the most remote corner of some remote convention building. We were the freaks of the convention. Now we *run* it. Ha!"

Amy and Michael went into the bathroom and emerged with Kleenex boxes on their feet: "We're Howard Hughes!"

We phoned Mom, and she said Ethan was woozy from today's treatment. Lindsay is pleasingly, Gerberishly plump, and former bodybuilding enthusiast Dusty is eating my family out of house and home. Misty, who hasn't shed an ounce since starting her diet last year, follows the "Madonna and child" everywhere. "Dusty's a sucker for dog-begging," says Mom, "and I keep trying to tell Dusty *not* to feed the dog, but it's not working." Mom sounds pissed, but she has to learn that her dog is never going to be slim. So, all in all, it sounds like things are fine there.

Mom asked, half-jokingly, but also for real, if Dad was pulling his weight as our company rep, but I said we wouldn't be able to tell until tomorrow.

The ten of us double-cabbed (20-minute cab wait) up the Strip (clogged) to a Sony party Todd had gotten us semi-invited to, and dropped Dad off at the MGM Grand along the way. All three Chyx in the two cars shouted in practiced tra-la-la voices, *"Good night, Blake Carrington, you hulking piece of man meat!"* Dad's ears turned bright red. I think the porno awards were a bad influence on them.

At the Sony party, we all got weirded out because suddenly all of the people at the party looked like they were porn stars, even though they were just real people. It was only because all of the Stiffie Award winners and their film clips were still in our brains that we were perceiving this. And then we realized that viewed from a certain perspective, *all* people can look like porn stars. So for a few minutes there, humanity seemed really scary indeed. I wonder how porn people's mind-body relationships are—I can't imagine. Their bodies must be like machines to them, or products to ship, but then they're not the only ones—Olympic athletes and geeks and bodybuilders and people with eating disorders.

But the Sony party . . . we checked out the live-action footage in the new Sony games, and the *ac*ting—it was so *cheesy*. It was like *porn* acting. This merely reinforced our collective impression that the real world is a porn movie. Talking to a Sony executive named Lisa, I asked her how they went about recruiting talent for games, without actually saying that their live action sucked. She told me that industry people aren't realizing yet just how unbelievably expensive it is to shoot any sort of game with live action. "Just say the words 'live action,' and the price goes up a million dollars," she said.

I then wondered out loud if starring in multimedia products is going to be the modern equivalent of appearing on the *Hollywood Squares*. Michael and Amy lapsed into a lovebird recital of questions from an old version of the *Hollywood Squares* board game they both had as children:

"Q: True or false: Frank Sinatra never
wears jewelry of any kind."
"A: False."

"Q: True or false: The average person
can hold their breath for 45 seconds."
"A: True."

"Q: According to Cats *magazine, should*
you tranquilize your cat before taking it
on an airline flight?"
"A: No."

The two of them irritated all the Sony people, because everyone was trying to be so smooth and Hollywoodish tonight, and not be geeky, and
Michael and Amy were destroying the illusion. And then they started
smooching, and this confused everybody further. Geeks smooching?

You could tell the LA people there—the attitude—they all looked like—
minifigs, I guess. Wait . . . am I being tautological? But really, Los
Angelenos are like a completely different *species* from Bay Area people.
There really is this whole North/South dichotomy in California. They truly
are two different states.

Michael said, "Los Angelenos dress like they've been focus-grouped."
We decided that in game shows in the future, contestants will win a free
focus-grouping, where they spend six hours with ten demographically prese-
lected focus-groupers commenting and criticizing all aspects of their lives.
Then, they get to watch the next winner get ripped apart behind a two-way
mirror. Forget year-supplies of Rice-A-Roni and bedroom sets.

We were talking with another woman, also named Lisa (which wasn't
hard to remember because every single woman we met there was named
Lisa). "Last year all of the studio executives were bluffing it about multimedia," she said, "but this year they're starting to panic—they don't have a
handle on what they're doing and it's starting to show, and mistakes are cost-
ing them a pile of money—trying to spooge Myst into a feature-length
movie; trying to spooge movies into CD-ROMs. It's a mess. And New York
still doesn't have a clue. Usually they're first, but with multimedia, they're

babies and it annoys the hell out of them. The people who really do know what's going on are the people who *aren't* posing as visionaries."

I thought about it and she's right—the geeks aren't flying down to LA to take studio executives out to schmooze dinners at Spago. Spago has to come to the geeks. Spago must *hate* that.

Amy suddenly piped up and said to the Lisa-unit, "Exactly. I'm working on the Tetris property for Castle Rock, and I can't believe how many bozos are calling the shots in a medium they have no expertise in! They're all faking it!"

The Lisa *believed* her—hook, line, and sinker! She obviously had never even *seen* Tetris. This was fun.

Amy continued, "In the history of games-into-movies, I think only *Tron* has begun to scratch the surface of what can be done . . . and that came out in '82. Just because a game has characters doesn't mean it can tell a story . . . Take *Super Mario Brothers*. Whoever okayed the $45 million budget for that lemon must have had a *lot* of explaining to do."

Lisa nodded and asked, "So what's your budget?"

Amy smiled and said, "The live action sequences are really going to add up—I think we're shooting for around 30 mil."

Lisa, "Do you have a card? Let me give you mine . . ."

Across the room, Anatole was busy chatting up a Lisa-unit, misguidedly trying to impress her with his "extreme knowledge" of Sony products.

"The good thing about Sony products," said Anatole, "is that they always say exactly what they are right on the front of them. For example, the CFD-758 CD-radio cassette recorder, or the TMR-IF310 stereo transmitter, or the 9-band ICF-SW15 FM/MW/SW receiver."

But evidently his *Frainch* accent made the above conversation sound alluring, and he and his Lisa were pair-bonded for the evening. Karla said, "Ever notice how when Anatole's around girls, his accent thickens?"

Susan was chatting with a male Lisa-unit solely to torment Emmett, but he's used to it by now. Susan was a real cachet addition to our party. She's become such a cult figure with Chyx. It was like Jim Morrison had entered the room, and she was swamped with admirers.

Then Amy said in a loud and unbelievably embarrassing voice, "What the fuck is with this place? Every single chick here is named *Lisa*."

Michael swam in to smooth things over: "She's from *Can*ada."

"Michael, you *promised* we'd have martinis and lose a hundred dollars at roulette. And the food here *stinks* and you know it."

"And right you are."

And the two of them vamoosed off to the MGM Grand.

Karla and I and a few Lisas tried to guess what the charades hand signal would be for "interactive multimedia product." A movie is where you turn a camera reel; a song is where you hold your hands up to your lips; a book is two palms simulating open flaps. All we could come up with for multimedia was two hands going fidgety-fidgety in space. A definitive interface is certainly needed, if only to make charades an easier game to play five years from now.

After we left the Sony party, we wandered around the grounds of the yuppie hotel, and I never realized it, but Todd's a mean drunk. Maybe his new haircut is bringing out "The Asshole Within." He went around the pathways kicking muffins into the hot tubs and sticking pilfered beta versions of Sony CD ROMs down the hotel's miniature fake rivers, and screamed at all of us, calling us geeks. Hel*looooo* . . . like, this is some big surprise, or something? I suspect that becoming a father and spending the last two months (as did we all, Dusty included, barely able to reach her keyboard over her watermelon stomach) pulling trip after trip to Kuwait while tweaking code for the *Oop!* beta version for Las Vegas—it all got to him and he's releasing the pressure. We all feel it. Tomorrow and Sunday we find out if *Oop!* (and Interiority Co.) have a strong future.

Todd was wearing his Secret Squirrel trench coat, but we dared not mock it. And then he vanished, probably to pick a fight at a sports bar.

We checked out the burning lava water show in front of the Mirage and the people in the city began weirding me out. Las Vegas must be the only place left where it's politically correct to wear a fur coat. They were just the sorts of people who would have gone to Las Vegas, not Boulder, in *The Stand*, and here they were.

We were standing next to this huge sculpture of post-human white lion tamers Siegfried and Roy not far from the lava, and then Bug and Sig got into this discussion about how Henry Ford made Model Ts for ten straight years without one change, and then GM came along with something spiffy, and Henry laid everybody off, retooled, came out with the Model A, and then built that without a change for another *five* years, and then Plymouth came out with something spiffy and Ford finally had to accept the notion of competition and styling.

We tried to imagine making a product without any changes for five years, but we couldn't. Then we noticed that all the cars on the Strip look the same: Chryslers and Tauruses and Toyotas . . . they all have "bubble-butts" that look like they came from the same mold. So by default we're right back to Henry Ford again. We figured that tail fins would come back in, simply because people are going to have a consumer revolt against how boring and blob-like cars are becoming.

At the mall in Caesar's Palace we bumped into the BuildX team at the Warner Brothers store. We bought our Marvin the Martian coffee mugs and house slippers, glared at the BuildX team, and left.

I wonder if Bill ever runs into John Sculley or Steve Jobs at a 7-Eleven.

We all wanted to go to the Luxor and play the games and do the rides there, inside the pyramid's interior. Emmett informed us that SEGA has its only showcase arcade there, where you can play the brand-new-almost-beta games. It's a brilliant marketing idea because normally arcade games don't enjoy the same kind of brand recognition and loyalty that home games do, but after visiting the SEGA arcade, the logo is burned into your brain permanently. It's like allowing a McDonald's orange drink machine at your child's birthday party. Later, we ran into Dad and we were gamed-out, so we all went to the Tut's Hut. We were starved.

The Tut's Hut kitchen was closed and we were begging for food—any sort of food—and the waitress brought over a plastic cup full of garnishes: pineapple wedges, maraschino cherries, and strawberries. I made a joke to her, that my Dad was an alcoholic barfly, and that growing up I ate garnishes as meals almost every night—but then the waitress got all weird, and Karla reminded me that people often move to Las Vegas to forget things, and she stopped coming to our table, and Dad, sitting two seats over, was embarrassed because he's not used to this kind of joke.

The Luxor has a laser beam of pure white light that shoots up from the tip of its pyramid and I'd never seen anything so tall, and never knew this beam of light existed. Pure and clean, and seen from the ground, it's so powerful that it really appears to puncture the atmosphere. I started rambling on about the laser, but everyone thought I'd gone loony and Abe told me to be quiet.

Ethan would have liked the light beam because the whole Luxor pyramid thing is sort of like the pyramid on the dollar bill, so I sent him a postcard. Instead of having a faux Egyptian theme, the Luxor should get to the point and have a U.S. Mint theme.

Todd was in the lobby of the Hacienda when we walked in, at around 2:30 A.M. He had a plastic container full of Kennedy dollars and was drunk on free drinks, but his meanness was gone. The casino noise was horrendous. It put Palo Alto's gas-fired leaf blowers to shame. As Karla and I were walking to the elevator bank, Todd came with us and did his impression of the machines: "Dollar slots go *koonk-koonk-koonk-koonk-koonk*; quarter slots go *kathunka-thunka-thunka-thunka*; dime slots go *nink-nink-nink-nink-nink*." He did a really good job as a machine. I think he bonded with the slots. We commended him on his performance and sent him wonkily tottering back onto the floor to lose his remaining coinage. He said, "It's an upperbody night!" and flexed his bicep at us.

Karla fell asleep quickly, but as ever, sleep eluded me, and I went downstairs to the casino and half-assedly played the slots until my $20 in quarters was gone.

Sands

stolen watches   abandoned wedding rings

buried cinderblocks full of $100 bills.

You want to surrender.

Subjected to the random, you acknowledge your inability to comprehend logic and linear systems.

21

**royal flush
barbecue sauce
garage door openers
antenna
La Quinta**

**three lemons
plastic bucket
woofer
touch-tone
calling card**

We generate stories for you because you don't save the ones that are yours.

FRIDAY

Todd made out last night with a Lisa-unit from the Sony party, which he returned to after screaming at us. This morning he burst into Karla's and my room and confessed, teary eyed, and carrying a basket of croissants. It was a bad start to a weird day. He was sick with remorse.

Anatole was in the bathroom borrowing Karla's blowdryer, so he heard everything through the door. Todd made me, Anatole, and Karla swear on a stack of Bibles that we would never say anything to Dusty. Anatole launched into one of his "een my couwntree . . ." tirades about how French men all had mistresses, but he stopped when he saw how sad Todd looked.

Todd was morose and silent all day. I thought about Dusty and Lindsay Ruth at home, and was glad he felt miserable, but he'd been in such denial over his new family unit that he was bound to explode. At least he didn't SLEEP with a Lisa.

Also, it was raining outside. *Raining*. It was so odd to think of Las Vegas having weather, like it was a real *place*. But since everyone's always indoors in the casinos, I guess it doesn't really matter.

There was once a *Twilight Zone* episode where adults were prisoners of the whims of a ten-year-old boy, Anthony, who could change the world simply by *thinking* the change into existence—he could make snow fall on crops— he could erase peopie—he forced everybody to watch TV that showed nothing but dinosaurs and cartoons. And all anybody could say, to prevent themselves from being erased themselves, was "That's *good*, Anthony, that's *good*." A focus group of one.

The CES is a trade show like all other trade shows: thousands and thousands of men, for the most part, wearing wool suits with badges saying things like: **Doug Duncan**, **Product Developer**, MATTEL . . . or NASA,

SIEMENS-NIXDORF, OGILVY & MATHER, and UCLA, and so on. Everyone loads up on free promo merchandise like software samplers, buttons, mugs, pins, and water bottles as they dash from meeting to meeting. The booths are all staffed by thousands of those guys in high school who were good-looking but who got C+'s; they're stereo salesmen now and have to suck up to the nerds they tormented in high school.

We *Oop!*sters were in and out of meetings all day, mostly earnest affairs held in little rooms above the convention floor. They look the same in every hotel: chrome & glass rental furniture, extension telephones, and a water cooler. All these people meeting inside, wearing the first good suit in their life, turning old right before your eyes.

We were really just there to schmooze and do PR, since our distribution's taken care of, and to approach people to develop *Oop!* starter modules. Standard stuff. We also did "seed plants" . . . *who* you give your hardware to prerelease is a high status issue.

But I must say, there's something timeless about the false sincerity and synthetic goodwill of meetings, the calculated jocularity and the simian dominant-male/subordinate-male body language. At least the presence of Karla, Susan, and Amy saved us from the inevitable stripper jokes. Karla pointed out how in marketing meetings at Microsoft, everybody was trying to be fake-perky, and trying to fake having ideas, while at CES, everybody's trying to be fake-sincere and trying to fake not looking desperate.

Also, later, during rare, quiet moments, I'd look through the windows at other people's meetings, and they looked like Dutch Master cigar box people, but modernized. Old, but new . . . like a cordless phone resting beside a bowl of apples.

We had a "hunch lunch" in the hallway outside the Intel theater to compare notes on how the meetings were going. The Convention Center has the worst food on earth, served in the most humiliating, chair-free, low-dignity manner possible. People looked like *dogs*, hobbled over, eating high-sodium, byproduct-enriched, grease-lathered guck. Convention Center food in your stomach is like having fifty chest X rays, it's so toxic. In fact for the rest of the day, the "chest X ray" became our official standard of measurement for something that is probably very bad for you, which shortens your life, but which won't take its toll until much later on. If we met someone really horrible, we said they were like "ten chest X rays," and we'll probably die three days earlier than if we had never met that person.

After lunch, we went to see the Pentium movie at the theater Intel put up in the main lobby. It was about how interactivity was going to make your life better in the future, and we couldn't stop giggling because of all the Pentium jokes about decimal points being spammed around the Internet. You knew that every single person watching the show was, too.

"0.999999985621," I whispered, setting everybody off into spasms again, and finally we had to leave because we were annoying too many people with our giggling.

I guess if you find jokes about decimal places interesting, then you truly *are* a geek.

In the afternoon, in between meetings, Susan spent most of her time in the SEGA-Nintendo building, and reconnoitered with her fellow Chyx at the Virgin Interactive mini-bar. There was a rumor that supermodel Fabio was signing autographs in another building, so Susan and Karla dashed over to check it out. Sure enough, His Hairness himself was signing calendars and paperbacks among the booming car stereos. Susan and Karla stood in line for an hour and finally they each got their "magic moment": a few snatches of intimate conversation, sealed with a kiss and, more important, a Polaroid. Susan's going to post hers on the Net. I asked Karla what he said to her and she said, "Stereos are my passion . . . but only after *you*." Gag.

Todd got sullen because Susan and Karla kept on discussing Fabio's pectoral muscles . . . "They're like beef throw cushions . . . they're like fifty-pound flank-steak Chiclets . . . they're like . . ." and Todd would say, "*Enough* already."

Went to about seventeen meetings altogether. At CES, everybody name-drops their hotel all the time. Hotelmanship is a big CES status issue—people kept on asking us during the day where we were staying. They'd say, "So, uh" (charged moment) "where are you *staying?*"

And we would casually reply, "Oh, the Luxor."

Las Vegas hotels are similar to video games—games and hotels both plunder extinct or mythical cultures in pursuit of a franchisable myth with graphic potential: Egypt—Camelot—the Jolly Roger. We found ourselves

feeling a little sorry for hotels that couldn't afford to lavishly re-create mythical archetypes, or were simply too stupid to realize that the lack of a theme
made them indistinguishable. It was as if the boring hotels couldn't figure
out what was going on in the bigger scheme of Western culture. Hotels in
Las Vegas need special effects, rides, simulators, morphings . . . today's
hotel must have fantasy systems in place, or it will perish.

Todd went to see Siegfried and Roy, and afterward made this big deal of
showing Karla and me his program when we were standing in line waiting to
go on the virtual reality theme ride. We were underwhelmed to say the most.
Todd was quite impressed, however, with Siegfried and Roy themselves as
proud examples of science and surgery combining in the name of entertainment and tanlines. He seemed wistful for his bodybuilding days of not even
a year ago. "Siegfried and Roy are very obviously at the extreme end of
some exciting new paradigm for the human body," said Todd. "'See
Tomorrow's Face, Today.'"

But then the big drama *du jour* was when Todd caught his parents gambling . . . right there on the main floor of the Luxor! They were at the quar-
ter-slot video poker machines, and talk about weird. They were *glued* to
their machines, really scary, like those mean old pensioners who smoke long
brown cigarettes and scream at you if they think you might be contaminating
their machine's winnability karma. Todd ran up and "busted" them, and it
was really embarrassing, but also too good to miss. I mean, they were all
screaming at each other. Todd was truly freaked out to see his parents so
obviously engaging in the "secular" world. And wouldn't you just know it,
his parents are at the Hacienda, too, and it really seemed like one of those
foreign movies that you rent and return half-wound because they're too con-
trived to be believed, and then real-life happens, and you wonder if the
Europeans understood everything all along.

Todd came to our room and ranted for a while about what hypocrites his
parents were, and it took all my restraint not to remind him that he had
"sinned" himself with a Lisa-from-Sony the previous evening. Karla
took him out on the Strip for a walk and I had some peace for the first time
all day.

I called Mom from the hotel during this period of peace. I'd turned out all
of the lights and closed the curtains in pursuit of sensory deprivation. It was

black and sensationless. All there was in the room was my voice and Mom's voice trickling out of the phone's earpiece, and this feeling passed through me—this feeling of what a gift it is that people are able to speak to each other while they're alive. These casual conversations, this familiar voice heard through a Las Vegas hotel room telephone. It was strange to realize that, in one sense, all we *are* is our voice.

SATURDAY

*B*ILL was in town launching a new product, and it was so bizarre, seeing his face and hearing his voice over the remote screens inside the convention floor. It was like being teleported back to eleventh-grade chem class. Like a distant dream. Like a dream of a dream. And people were *riveted* to his every gesture. I mean *riveted*, looking at his picture, trying to articulate the charisma, and it was so odd, seeing all of these people, looking at Bill's image, not listening to what he was saying but instead trying to figure out what was his . . . *secret*.

But his secret is, I think, that he shows *nothing*. A poker face doesn't mean showing coolness like James Bond. It means expressing nothingess. This is maybe the core of the nerd dream: the core of power and money that lies at the center of the storm of technology, that doesn't have to express emotion or charisma, because emotion can't be converted into lines of code.

Yet.

I kind of lost focus after a while, and I wandered around and picked up a copy of the *New York Times* lying next to an SGI unit blasting out a flight simulation. There, on the third page of the business section, not even the first, was a story about how Apple shares were going up in value as a result of rumors of an impending three-way buyout by Panasonic (Holland), Oracle (USA), and Matsushita (Japan). My, how things change. That's all I can think. Apple used to be the King of the Valley, and now they're getting prospected like a start-up. Time frames are so extreme in the tech industry. Life happens at fifty times the normal pace. I mean, if someone in Palo Alto says to you, "They never called back," what they really mean is, "They never called back within *one week*." A week means never in the Silicon Valley.

*T*odd was off all day having ordeals with his parents, and Bug, Sig, Emmett, and Susan walked around hoping they'd "accidentally" bump into Todd in order to eavesdrop a little, but to no avail.

MacCarran Airport is right next to downtown Las Vegas, and a plane flies over the city every eleven seconds. Karla and I were walking between pavilions and we saw Barry Diller in a gray wool suit (and no name tag). We sat down on a riser near the piled-up plywood freight boxes to rest our feet, and watched the planes fly by. We were both *overstimulated*.

Karla was fiddling with the Samsung shoelace holding her badge, and she looked up at a plane in the sky and said, "Dan, what does all this *stuff* tell us about ourselves as humans? What have we gained by externalizing our essence through these consumable electronic units of luxury, comfort, and freedom?"

It's a good question, I thought. I mentioned how weird it was that everybody keeps on asking, "*Have you seen anything new? Have you seen anything new?*" It's like the mantra of the CES.

Karla pointed out that there's really not that many types of things a person can have in their house in the end. "You can have a stereo and a microwave and a cordless phone . . . and the list goes on a bit from there . . . but after a certain point you run out of *things* to *need*. You can get more powerful and expensive things, but not really *new* things. I guess the number of types of things we build defines the limits of ourselves as a species."

Nintendo's Virtual Boy seemed the most advanced thing we'd seen here. SEGA won the Noisiest Booth award, and that's saying a lot at CES.

Bug, Sig, and Karla were all a bit annoyed by how "family-oriented" the city had become, and we yearned for traces of its proud history of sleaze and corruption. I mean, if you can't get lost in Las Vegas, then what's the *point* of Las Vegas?

During a 90-minute between-meeting lull, we decided to go to the Sahara to check out the porn component of the show, a highly secured second-floor salon room chockablock with the latest in, *errr* . . . cyber stimulation.

There were no empty cabs to be found so we ended up sharing a stray Yellow Cab with the worst transvestite on the planet, Darleena: great big hairy knuckles and five o'clock shadow like Fred Flintstone. Darleena kept on talking about the day last year when she met Pamela Anderson of *Baywatch* at the Hefner Playboy mansion. For half a mile she discussed breast augmentation with Sig (the doctor).

As a joke I told Darleena that Karla sometimes likes to dress up like a small Edwardian boy, and Darleena got all interested. It was a fun ride.

The porn pavilion itself was creepy. This weird porn energy and lots of women with breasts like basketballs. It sounds so great in that bachelor fantasy way, but then you see it, and you freak out. Actually, pornography really just makes sex look unappealing.

After about thirty minutes we'd reached our limit, and were heading toward the door when we saw the crowd surge in the direction of one particular booth, and we looked, and there was John Wayne Bobbit, dressed in Tommy Hilfiger, like a Microsoft employee, standing amid all of these silconized inhabitants of the planet Temptron 5.

Bug said, "Here it is, one day you're just a nothing buttwipe who cheats on his wife living in the middle of nowhere and then, *BAM!*, two years later you're wearing Tommy Hilfiger windbreakers surrounded by eleven women with seventy-inch breasts in Las Vegas, Nevada, with the whole United States of America wondering if your dick works."

The real world is a porno movie. I'm convinced.

I got to thinking about sin, or badness, or whatever you want to call it, and I realized that just as there are a limited number of consumer electronics we create as a species, there are also a limited number of sins we can commit, too. So maybe that's why people are so interested in computer "hackers"— because they invented a new sin.

McDonald's: "Paying homage to Ronald," said Amy, pulling into the driveway beneath the golden arches.

Everybody tried to remember the last time they ate a real vegetable.

"Pickles or iceberg lettuce don't count."

We were all stumped.

This McDonald's was offering a free 16-oz. soft drink if a student brings in a report card with an A. If they have two As, they get a drink and a small fries—three As, and they toss in a cheeseburger to boot. Amy said, "*Look out, Japan!*" But then she realized, "Las Vegas doesn't have schoolchildren, does it?"

Halfway through the meal, Michael said, over his Filet-o-Fish, "Las Vegas is perhaps about the constant attempt of humans to decomplexify complex systems."

"Huh?"

"Las Vegas was once seedy, but it has now evolved into a Disney version of itself—which is probably less fun, but certainly more lucrative, and *certainly* necessary for the city to survive as an entity in the 1990s. Disneyland presupposes a universe of noncompetitive species—food chains hypersimplified into sterility by a middle-class fear of entropy: animals who will not eat each other and who irrationally enjoy human company; plant life consisting of lawns sprinkled on the fringes with colorful, sterile flowers."

"Oh."

"Nonetheless, chaos *will* ultimately prevail, just as one day, all of this will be dust, rubble, and sagebrush once more."

"Oh."

"But you know, the *good* chaos."

I felt like my IQ had shrunk to one digit.

Amy and Michael began making out right there next to the McDonald's-world play station.

*O*op!, I might add, is going to be a hit. I think this has been lost on everybody in the Las Vegan blur, but it would appear that we're all still employed, and that our risk has become solid equity, but you know what? All I care about is that we're all still together as friends, that we're not enemies, and that we can continue to do cool stuff together. I thought the money would mean something, but it doesn't. It's there, but it's not emotional. It's simply *there*.

After dark Karla revealed to me that she, too, was fascinated by the laser beam, so we told everybody we were returning to the Hacienda next door, and instead drove our rented Altima sedan northeastward on Highway 15, to see how far away we could drive and still see the pyramid's laser beam. I had heard that air pilots reported seeing it from LAX. I wondered if astronauts could see the beam from outer space.

It was an overcast night. We drove and drove, and at forty miles out we realized that we hadn't been paying attention, and the laser beam was gone. We stopped in at a diner for hamburgers and video poker, and we won $2.25, so we were "a cheeseburger ahead for the evening."

We then got back into the car and drove back toward Las Vegas, and around twenty-six miles outside of Las Vegas we were able to see the

Luxor's beam of light up in the sky again. We pulled the car over onto the highway shoulder and gazed at it. It was awe-inspiring and romantic.

I felt so close to her.

Later, back at the hotel, I was PowerBooking my journal entry and I could feel Karla watching me, and I got a little self-concious. I said, "I guess it's sort of futile trying to keep a backup file of my personal memories . . ."

She said, "Not at all . . . because we use so many machines, it's not surprising we should store memories there, as well as in our bodies. The one thing that differentiates human beings from all other creatures on Earth is the externalization of subjective memory—first through notches in trees, then through cave paintings, then through the written word and now, through databases of almost otherworldly storage and retrieval power."

Karla said that as our memory multiplies itself seemingly logarithmically, history's pace *feels* faster, it is "accelerating" at an oddly distorted rate, and will only continue to do so faster and faster. "Soon enough all human knowledge will be squished into small nubbins the size of pencil erasers that you can pea-shoot at the stars."

I asked, "And . . . what then—when the entire memory of the species is as cheap and easily available as pebbles at the beach?"

She said that this is not a frightening question. "It is a question full of awe and wonder and respect. And people being people, they will probably, I imagine, use these new memory pebbles to build new paths."

Like I said . . . it was romantic.

SUNDAY

What happened was this: I was looking out the window and Todd was fighting with his parents out on the Strip, down below the Hacienda's sign. How long was this going to go on? I decided I had to help Todd and so I went down to see if I could "Stop the Insanity!" Just as I joined them, Karla came running out. We all turned, and I saw her coming, and I could tell something was very, very wrong.

She collected her breath and said, "Dan, I'm really sorry to have to tell you this, but there's been an accident."

I said, "An accident?"

She said that she had just spoken with Ethan in Palo Alto. Mom had had a stroke at her swim class, that she was paralyzed, and no one knew what would happen next.

Right there and then, Todd and his parents fell down on their knees and prayed on the Strip, and I wondered if they had scraped their knees in their fall, and I wondered what it was to pray, because it was something I have never learned to do, and all I remember is falling, something I have talked about, and something I was now doing.

plane window   green squares
towers   lights
telephone lines   baggage

The New World dream

The extended arm
The caravan traversing a million miles of prairie
Cross the uncrossable
Make that journey and build the road along the way.

You succeeded at memory-creation beyond all wildest dreams.

Two Weeks Later

TUESDAY, JANUARY 17, 1995

Hanshin Expressway

Stephen Hawking walking through quiet rooms pointing out things you've never seen before.

Mitsukoshi department store, Kobe, Japan, at a 45-degree angle, its contents smashed against walls

Western Washington State, minus Seattle's metro region, is assigned a new area code, 360, effective January 15, 1995

R U Japanese?

thin blood	rear-view mirror
Nirvana Unplugged	Hawaii
what I wanted	what really happened
Nikkei Index	Embolus
Cerebrovascular event	Possible reversibility

Monsterbreaker

Mothermaker	Kidnapper
System-beater	Codebreaker
Sharkprincess	Keypadburner
Skywalker	*Clot*

Godseeker

Braineater

This is the day of days, and so the telling begins.

Karla massaged Mom's back in Mom's new room beside the kitchen, a room that we filled with her rocks and photos and potpourri and Misty. Misty, buffered by dumbness, unaware of the traffic jams in the blood flow of her master's brain: carbon freeways of cracked cement and flattened Camrys and Isuzus and F-100s; neural survivors as well as those neural victims, all as yet unretrieved from within the overpasses of her Self. Mom's brain is crashed and inert, her limbs as stationary as lemon tree branches on an August afternoon, occasionally twitching limbs appended by a wedding ring and a Chyx wristband from Amy. Images of a crashed Japan on every channel, the newscaster's voice floating in the background. At least Japan can be rebuilt.

Karla spent the morning massaging the lax folds of Mom's skin. I wonder, is she *there*? It is what I . . . *we* have lived with for weeks, we who look into Mom's eyes and say, *Hello in there*, thinking, *We are here*. Where are *you*, Mom? Where did *you* go? *How did you disappear? How did the world steal you? How did you vanish?*

Actually, Karla was the first to cross the frontier between words and skin; speech and flesh.

Karla invaded Mom's body. Last week Karla removed her Nikes, took a plastic squeeze bottle of mineral oil from the bathroom, cut it with sesame oil, and crawled atop Mom's prone form on the foldaway rental bed. She told Dad to watch, told him that *he* was next, and so Dad watched.

Karla dug and sculpted into my mom's body, stretching it as only she knows how to do, willing sensation into her flesh, into her rhomboids, her triceps, her rotor cuffs and spaces where probing generated no reaction; Karla, laser-beaming her faith into the body of this woman.

Last week was the beginning, the Confusion, when everything seemed lost, the image of Mom lying frozen and starved of oxygen in the Rinconada swimming pool haunting us. Ethan meeting us at the hospital, his own skin the color of white fatty bacon embedded with an IV drip; Dusty and Lindsay, Dusty sucking in her breath with fear, and turning her head from ours, then returning her gaze and offering us Lindsay as consolation.

There had been discussions, a prognosis, pamphlets and counselors, workshops and experts. Mom's functions may one day be complete and may be one day partial, but as of today there's nothing but the twitches and the knowledge that fear is locked inside the body. Her eyes can be opened and closed, but not enough to semaphore messages. She's all wired up and gizmo'ed; her outside looks like the inside of a Bell switchbox.

What is *her* side of the story? The password has been deleted.

Karla would take Dad's hand over the last week and make it touch Mom, saying, "She is there and she has never left."

And it was Karla who started us talking to Mom, Mom's eyes fishy, blank, lost and found, requiring an act of faith to presuppose vivid interior dimensions still intact. Karla who made me stare into these faraway eyes and say, *Speak to her, Dan: She can hear you and how can you not look into these eyes that once loved you when you were a baby, and not tell her of your day. Talk to her, Dan: tell her . . . today was a day like any other day. We worked. We coded. Our product is doing well, and isn't that just fine?*

And so I told Mom these things.

And so every day, I hold the hand that once held me, so long ago.

And Karla gently guided Dad up onto the foldaway, saying, *Mr. Underwood, roll up your sleeves. Mr. Underwood, your wife is still here, and she has never needed you more.*

And there's Bug, reading Sunday's color comics to Mom, trying hard to make *The Lockhorns* sound funny, then saying to his unresponsive audience, "Oh, Mrs. Underwood, I understand your reaction completely. It's like I'm reading 1970s cocktail napkins out loud to you. I must admit, I've never liked this strip," and then discussing the politics of syndication, and which comic strips he finds unfunny: *The Family Circus, Peanuts, Ziggy, Garfield,* and *Sally Forth.* He's actually more animated than he is in conversations with *us.*

There is the image of Amy telling rude jokes to Mom and Michael trying to curb the ribaldry, but being swept away by the filth, and Michael responding with Pentium jokes.

There is Susan, washing and cutting my Mom's hair, saying, "You'll look just like Mary Tyler Moore, Mrs. U. You'll be a doll," and discussing new postings on the Chyx page.

There is Ethan, Ethan on the brink of erasure himself, saying, "Well, Mrs. U, who'd have thought that *I'd* be the one to monitor *you.* Don't tell me it isn't funny. Because it *is*, and you know it. I'd change your bandages for you, but you don't have any and that's a big issue here."

There are Dusty and Todd, demonstrating leg-stretching exercises, discussing physical therapy and how to keep her muscles in tone for the day they once again receive their commands.

And there is Abe, who brought in a tub of money, a tub full of coins, and said, "Time to sort some change, Mrs. U. Not much fun for you, but I'll try and be talkative while I sort . . . oh *look* . . . it's a peso. Woo!"

Last week there was a jolt. Last week Karla said, "You have to go further, Dan, you have to hold her body."

I looked at Mom's body—so long in not holding—and I thought of families who have had to watch a member die slowly and who have said all that can possibly be said to each other—and so all that remains is for them to sit and lie there and nitpick over trivialities or talk about what's on TV—and so I held Mom's body, and told her how my day had gone. I talked about stoplights on Camino Real, line-ups at Fry's, rude telephone operators, traffic on the 101, the price of cheese singles at Costco.

This afternoon, this afternoon of the day of days.

I, in this mood where this earthly kingdom was beautiful in spite of life's cruel bite, took the CalTrain and BART over to Oakland just to get out of the house, to thwart cabin fever. Sometimes we all forget that the world itself is paradise, and there has been much of late to encourage that amnesia.

Along a roadside I saw an unwound cassette tape, its brown lines shimmying in the sun—sound converted to light. I felt a warm wind's gust on the Oakland BART platform. I suddenly wanted to be home, to be with my family, my friends.

I was met by Michael, who opened the front door of the house. He told me about a story he had once seen on the news, a story about a boy with cerebral palsy who had been hooked up to a computer, and the first thing he said, when they asked him what he would like to do, was "*to be a pilot.*"

Michael said to me, "It got me thinking, that maybe your mother could be linked into a computer, too, and maybe the touch of her fingers could be connected to a keypad. So then she could speak to us." And then he saw my face and said, "She could speak to *you*, Dan. I've been doing some reading on the subject."

We entered the kitchen, where Bug and Amy were discussing an idea of Bug's, that "humans don't exist as actual individual 'selves'—rather, there is only the 'probability' of *you* being *you* at any given moment. While you're alive and healthy, the probability remains pretty high, but when you're sick or when you're old, the probability of you being yourself shrinks. The chance of your 'being all there' becomes less and less. When you die, the probability of being 'you' drops to zero."

Amy saw me and said, "Close your eyes right now, this very instant. Try to remember the shirt you're wearing."

I tried, and couldn't remember.

She said it would probably take me a lot longer than I'd think. "It's a cruel trick of nature that personal memory seems to be the first to go. You'll remember Alka-Seltzer long past the point where you've forgotten your children."

She then said to me, "Try *not* thinking of peeling an orange. Try *not* imagining the juice running down your fingers, the soft inner part of the peel. The smell. Try and you can't. The brain doesn't process negatives."

I walked onto the back patio, and looked over Silicon Valley, clear, but vanishing into a late afternoon fog, unexpected, fanning in from the west. Karla was wearing a sweater, and her breath was like the swimming pool's wafting heat, there in the coolness. I told her that it was always in the fall when the crops were in, that the wars were called.

She said to me, "We all fall down some day. We all fall down. You've fallen and we'll all pick each other up."

In the distance I saw the Contra Costa Mountains, and their silhouette was blurred as I confused the mountains for clouds, and Karla dried my eyes with fallen leaves and her sweater's hem. I told Karla about a Lego TV commercial I saw twenty years ago . . . a yellow castle and the camera went higher and higher and higher and the castle never ended. She said she had seen it, too.

Dad came by with Misty, and we all went for a walk. Down La Cresta we went, and Dad had brought along the electric garage-door opener, and we pushed its red ridged button, randomly trying to open strangers' doors.

When we returned to the house, my friends were gathered around Mom, in front of a monitor, their faces lit sky blue; they had forgotten to turn on the lights in the kitchen. Mom's body was upheld by Bug and Abe inside a kitchen chair, with Michael clasping her arms. On the screen, in 36 point Helvetica on the screen of a Mac Classic were written the words:

i am here

Dad caressed Mom's forehead and said, "We're here, too, honey." He said, "Michael, can she speak . . ."

Michael put his arms over Mom's arms, his fingers upon her fingers and assisted her hands above the keyboard. Dad said, "Honey, can you hear us?"

yes

He said to her, "Honey, how are you? How do you feel?"

;=)

Michael broke in. He said, "Mr. Underwood, ask your wife a question that only she and you would know the answer to. Make me sure that this isn't me doing the talking."

Dad asked, "Honey, what was your name for me, when we went on our honeymoon on Mt. Hood. Can you remember?"

There was a pause and a word emerged:

reindeer

Dad collapsed and cried and fell to his knees at Mom's feet and Michael said, "Let's push the caps-lock button. Capitals make easier words; consider license plates. You're a State of California vanity license plate now, Mrs. U."

The caps were locked and the point size lowered. The fingers tapped:

BEEP BEEP

Dad said, "Tell us how you feel . . . tell us what we can do . . ."
The fingers tapped:

I FEEL U

I cut through the crowd. I said, "Mom, Mom . . . tell me it's you. Tell me something I never liked in my lunch bag at school . . ."

The fingers tapped:

PNUT BUTR

Oh, to speak with the lost! Karla broke in and said, "Mrs. U., our massage . . . is it okay? Is it helping you?"

The fingers tapped:

GR8
I LK MY BDY

Karla looked at the words and, hesitating a second, declared, "I like my body now, too, Mrs. U."

Mom's assisted hands tapped out:

MY DOTTR

Karla lost it and started to cry, and then, well, *I* started to cry. And then Dad, and then, well, everybody, and at the center of it all was Mom, part woman/part machine, emanating blue Macintosh light.

Joy lapsed into silliness lapsed into relief and cocktails.

The kitchen lights went on. Amy said, "This is so first-contact!" Messages lost became messages found:

MIST'Z OVER ETING

DAN CT UR HAIR

GTTNG BETR

LUV U ALL

Here it is: Mom speaking like a license plate . . . like the lyrics to a Prince song . . . like a page without vowels . . . like encryption. All of my messing around with words last year and now, well . . . it's real life.

After an hour, the message, **GR8LY TIRED** came onto the screen and Dad said it was time to wrap it up for now. It was dark, and the fireplace had been lit by Todd. Amy came in with a pile of old horse blankets and flash-lights and a set of pen-size laser pointers from last Christmas, and said, *Michael . . . Dan . . . Susan . . . whoever, help me move the couch out beside the pool.*

She placed these things on the tired old Broyhill, and we carried it out next to the blue-green pool, and the sky above the Valley was filled with a cobalt-gray fog.

Amy turned on one of the portable lasers Abe gave us for Christmas, the ones we use to point at walls during meetings, and cut the sky with a thin red beam. Dusty carried Mom out and placed her on the couch, head skyward, and Dad lay down beside her on this couch, and wrapped her in blankets.

Amy said, "Mrs. U., you've probably always wondered what kids do on weekends. Well, the truth of the matter is, they smoke pot and go to Pink Floyd laser shows at the planetarium. Michael: hit the tunes . . ."

An art rock anthem from another era filled the air, and we turned on all of our lights and cast them into the sky, a chaotic symphony of lines and color.

The dozen of us stood out there on the patio, out in the January evening's foggy dark: Michael and Amy, still in their clothes, diving in the brilliant blue pool, rescuing the R2D2 pool cleaner from its endless serflike toil; Dad next to Mom on her bed, cradling her head in his arms, watching our lasers, positioning her head so that she could see the beams; Ethan, pale and feisty, testing batteries with a small device, arguing with Dusty over some small matter; Lindsay nearly asleep, lying next to Mom; Abe on his trampoline bouncing into the fog with Susan, Todd, Emmett, and poor, lum-bering, overweight, Misty, their four lasers cutting the heaven and joining my laser and Karla's laser and Dad's and Ethan's and Dusty's.

Karla and I lay down on the cement next to the pool atop a threadbare promotional towel for *Road & Track* magazine, its thin cotton insulating us from Earth's current lack of heat. I told her I loved her. Dad heard me say this, and so I guess Mom heard these words, too.

I remembered a friend of Mom's once told me that when you pray, and you pray honestly, you send a beam of light out into the skies as clear and as powerful as a sunbeam that breaks through the clouds at the end of a rainy day; like the lights on the sidewalk outside the Academy Awards.

And as Karla and I lay there, the two of us—the *all* of us—with our flashlights and lasers, cutting the weather, extending ourselves into the sky, into the end of the universe with precision technology running so fine, I looked at Karla and said out loud, *"You know, it's true."*

And then, I thought about us . . . these children who fell down life's cartoon holes . . . dreamless children, alive but not living—we emerged on the other side of the cartoon holes fully awake and discovered we were whole.

I'm worried about Mom . . . and I'm thinking about Jed, and suddenly I look around at Bug and Susan and Michael and everybody and I realize, that what's been missing for so long isn't missing anymore.

hellojed

About the author

About the book

Insights,
Interviews
& More . . .

Read on

A Q&A with Douglas Coupland

What is your idea of perfect happiness?

Right now. Where I am. At home.

What is your greatest fear?

That God exists, but doesn't care very much for humans.

Which living person do you most admire?

Vaclav Havel.

What objects do you always carry with you?

Earplugs.

What single thing would improve the quality of your life?

Everybody I like and love all living in the same city.

What is the most important lesson life has taught you?

We have time and we have free will. Otherwise, we're just animals.

Which writer has had the greatest influence on your work?

Jenny Holzer, an American artist whose work is text-based (what a dismal term). How tightly can you compress an idea? Where do ideas end and you, as a person, begin?

Do you have a favorite book?

Nonfiction, *The Andy Warhol Diaries*. Fiction, it's either Truman Capote's *Answered Prayers* or Margaret Drabble's *Ice Age*.

Which book do you wish you had written?

The Age of Extremes: The Short Twentieth Century 1914–1991 by Eric Hobsbawm.

What do you think of literary prizes?

They're wildly engaging, and they get people who normally don't discuss books discussing books. That's a hard thing to do.

Where do you go for inspiration?

Four-hour drives in my car, usually into the interior of British Columbia, into the desert cordillera that stretches down into Mexico. Believe it or not, Canada has cactuses/cacti. ∽

Life at a Glance

Name
Douglas Coupland

Born
December 30, 1961, on a military base in
Baden-Söllingen, Germany.

Education
Coupland graduated 1979 from Sentinel
Secondary School, West Vancouver.
Graduated 1984 from Emily Carr College
of Art and Design, Vancouver. Went to
European Design Institute, Milan, and
the Hokkaido College of Art and Design,
Japan. Completed course in business science
together with fine art and industrial design
in Japan in 1986.

Career
The first exhibition of Coupland's sculpture
took place at the Vancouver Art Gallery in
1987. He won two Canadian national awards
for excellence in industrial design. By 1988
he was a contributing journalist to *Vancouver*
magazine. St. Martin's Press, New York, asked
him to write a guidebook to Generation X,
a theme he had been exploring in his articles.
Instead he went to California and wrote a
novel—*Generation X*. This was published
in 1991.

Subsequent Fiction
Shampoo Planet (1992)
Life After God (1993)
Microserfs (1995)
Girlfriend in a Coma (1997)
Miss Wyoming (1999)
God Hates Japan (2001)
All Families Are Psychotic (2001)

Hey Nostradamus! (2003)
Eleanor Rigby (2005)
JPod (2006)
The Gum Thief (2007)

Nonfiction
Polaroids from the Dead (1996)
City of Glass (2000)
Souvenir of Canada (2002)
School Spirit (2002)
Souvenir of Canada 2 (2004)
Terry (2005)

On Location
In the Studio with
Douglas Coupland

Mutation Garden *Squeeze bottles, ikebana vases, and poured resin forms*

Photographs courtesy of the author.

Spike *Sculptural installation*

Gorgon 2003 *Aluminum fiberglass, approx. 1.25 × life size*
Kneeling Figures *Plastic, life size*

Headlining

"MICROSERFS could have been called *Life Under God*," quipped the *Scotsman*, "the role of the deity being played by Bill Gates." Some critics dug deeper into the Coupland back catalog for comparisons, and emerged with *Generation X*. "With *Microserfs*, he's up to the same sort of tricks," the *Observer* reckoned. "Indeed, the Microserfs could almost be the flipside to the Xers. The latter gave up work to have a life; the former give up on 'having a life' to work." "But whereas the young friends in *Generation X* take a slackly indifferent attitude to change," countered the *Guardian*, "*Microserfs* is much more positive, and its characters are full of energy. . . . In the first fifty pages there are more one-liners than in a decade of Woody Allen films."

The *Sunday Telegraph* reveled in Coupland's sharp eye for detail: "All nerd life is here: the quirky obsessions with appalling television shows, the revolting snacks, and the realization that your best relationships are on e-mail." "Yet there is more to Coupland than superficial 'nowness,'" the *Sunday Times* maintained. "His work is one long exploration for new meaning in a hollow modern world."

The *NME* gave a thumbs-up all around: "A hilarious, moving read. Brilliantly observed, sharply written, and constantly entertaining." "*Microserfs* is intelligent satire at its most inventive and witty," the *Independent on Sunday* agreed. "But read it firmly tongue-in-cheek," it warned archly. "For if you read it any other way you'll never go near a computer, a Barbie doll, or anyone under the age of twenty-five in that same unsuspecting way again." ∽

Backstage

IT IS JANUARY 1995, the month of Microserf Daniel's final dispatches from Silicon Valley. The prospects for Oop!, our geek heroes' software business, are looking up. "Oop!, I might add, is going to be a hit," Daniel tells us. Skip forward thirteen years— how would you rate the chances today of a group of low-level dissident Microsoft coders attracting investment for Digital Lego? About as good as finding the Justice Department on Bill Gates's Christmas card list.

With Michael's Oop! odyssey, Douglas Coupland captured the early nineties wave of geeky prospectors that made its way out to the West Coast for the Silicon Rush. By the late nineties, young, brash Internet start-ups were receiving seemingly limitless funding. Business reports carried the beaming faces of the latest reams of paper millionaires, who somehow found time to head up cutting-edge companies between snowboarding holidays and guitar jams. Normally sober share indices became a babble of Oops!, Boos!, and Yahoos!

So what went wrong? Well, here's the condensed version. It's all to do with investor confidence. Hundreds of dot-com start-ups around the world joined the stock markets. Most weren't turning a profit and had pitiful sales levels. But what they did have was the distinct whiff of revolutionary technology. Investors were desperate to get in on the ground floor, and banks would offer greenhorn companies huge borrowing levels (debt to you and me) to get them on their way. Share prices skyrocketed as investors ignored profits (there still weren't any) and instead used measurements such as website hits to measure success.

Then, in 2000, there were some high-profile casualties. In the U.K., online clothing retailer Boo.com was forced to shut down ▶

Backstage (*continued*)

just six months after it was launched. The £80 million of funding with which Boo.com had started was the largest ever in Europe for a retail internet venture, but it quickly ran out. Consumers shunned Boo's digital shopping experience with its epileptic array of pop-ups and unfathomable purchasing processes.

Another sufferer was online travel site Lastminute.com. On the day it floated onto the stock exchange in March 2000 its shares soared from 380p to 550p. Young cofounders Martha Lane Fox and Brent Hoberman became irresistible City pinups. However, although Lastminute.com has survived, by October 2001 its shares were worth less than 20p.

It is 1993 in *Microserfs* when a venture capitalist tells a deflated Ethan: "There's nothing the world wants as little as a new technology company. If you give a company $2 million, they'll spend it all and never ship a profitable product." Not for the first time, Douglas Coupland was ahead of the game, and it took another seven years for real-world investors to come to the same conclusion. By the end of 2000 the dream was over. Investors who had started getting impatient about their lack of financial return from the Internet now began stampeding toward the exit signs. Technology share prices collapsed, and so did the prospects of thousands of dot-com employees who had accepted equity packages in the companies they worked for. The geek's beloved desktop WinQuote window, for so many years a kaleidoscope of escalating share prices, now looked out onto a vista of tumbling numbers and corporate bloodshed. Venture capital firms, who two years before couldn't get enough of projects like Oop!, now couldn't run away fast enough from hexed technology start-ups.

66 Not for the first time, Douglas Coupland was ahead of the game. 99

Out-of-work geeks looked for people to blame, and they found them in the shape of stock market analysts. Henry Blodget was one of the more notorious. This wonderfully Dickensian-sounding character worked for Merrill Lynch, where analysts spend their long hours researching companies and crunching numbers, eventually coming up with investment advice. Buy it. Sell it. Sit tight. Blodget had made his name in 1998 with his now-legendary prediction that shares in online book retailer Amazon would jump from $243 to $400 within a year. Crazy talk, some yelled. But Blodget was proved right within a mere three weeks. The market was in the mood for this kind of gung-ho gambling.

The problem for Henry Blodget was that so many Internet stocks he looked at seemed to him, well, pretty great. The ominous-sounding Pets.com, which has long since gone to the dogs, famously got the Blodget thumbs-up. The other problem was that the media loved him. Here was a guy whose relentless optimism and magic touch were infectious, and journalists couldn't get enough of him. Blodget became one of the most prominent, and highest-paid, analysts on Wall Street, and his opinions alone could send shares soaring.

Sadly, what Blodget told the world didn't necessarily tally with his private opinions about certain stocks. An investigation uncovered embarrassing e-mails in Henry's inbox—in one, Henry famously deemed a stock he was publicly advocating to be "a piece of crap." And Blodget wasn't the only one at it. The roller coaster was out of control. Blodget quit in November 2001, and in 2003 U.S. financial institutions (including Merrill Lynch) paid out $1.4 billion to settle conflict-of-interest charges related to the dot-com boom.

In *Generation X*, Douglas Coupland identified a phenomenon where a body of people are forced to have memories they do not actually possess. He called this "legislated nostalgia." It's why those of us too young to have lived through the Sixties still get misty-eyed watching reruns of *The Wonder Years*. But Xer geeks don't need legislated nostalgia now. They've had the real thing, their very own recent revolution: the halcyon days of the *Microserfs* era, an era of economic and cultural upheaval, less than a decade ago, when fortunes were won and lost and the food remained forever fast.

So what would have happened to Oop! in the dot-com crash? Perhaps it would have survived, or perhaps the building blocks tumbled and the sons and daughters of Bill returned to the Seattle campus. One thing is for sure: *Microserfs* has already become a historical document, allowing us to peer through the Windows of history. ❧

If You Loved This, You'll Like . . .

THE CATCHER IN THE RYE by J. D. Salinger

Holden Caulfield is lonely and surrounded by phonies. Teenage alienation from the absent father of Zeitgeist fiction.

GOING OUT by Scarlett Thomas

Luke is allergic to the sun. At twenty-five, he's stuck in his bedroom where the world comes to him through TV, the internet, and Julie's nightly visits.

NUMBER9DREAM by David Mitchell

Episodic, fragmentary novel set in contemporary Japan.

MY TINY LIFE: CRIME AND PASSION IN A VIRTUAL WORLD by Julian Dibbell

A chronicle of the author's experience in LambdaMoo.

HARD, SOFT, AND WET by Melanie McGrath

Silvertown author's explorations in cyberspace. Humane, perceptive and bold.

Have You Read?
More by
Douglas Coupland

GIRLFRIEND IN A COMA (1997)

After making love for the first time, high school senior Karen Ann McNeil confides in her boyfriend Richard about the dark visions she's recently been suffering. It's only a few hours later on that snowy Friday night in 1979 that she descends into a coma. Nine months later she gives birth to a daughter, Megan, her child by Richard, the protagonist of this disturbingly funny novel.

Karen remains comatose for the next seventeen years. Richard and her circle of friends reside in an emotional purgatory throughout the next two decades, passing through careers as models, film special effects technicians, doctors, and demolition experts before finally being reunited on a conspiracy-driven supernatural television series.

Upon Karen's reawakening, life grows as surreal as their television show. With apocalyptic events occurring, Karen, Richard, and their friends explore the essential mysteries of life, faith, decency, and existence. Amid the world's rubble they attempt to restore their own humanity.

"To call Coupland the John Bunyan of his set would not be hyperbole, especially in light of his newest book, the monitory and fantastical *Girlfriend in a Coma*, which at times approaches an eccentric jeremiad worthy of Kurt Vonnegut." —*Washington Post*

"A message of hope and a challenge to . . . cynicism." —*USA Today*

Have You Read? *(continued)*

POLAROIDS FROM THE DEAD (1996)

Douglas Coupland takes his sparkling literary talent in a new direction with this crackling collection of takes on life and death in North America—from his sweeping portrait of Grateful Dead culture to the deaths of Kurt Cobain, Marilyn Monroe, and the middle class.

For years Coupland's razor-sharp insights into what it means to be human in an age of technology have garnered the highest praise from fans and critics alike. Coupland has at last assembled a wide variety of stories and personal "postcards" about pivotal people and places that have defined our modern lives. *Polaroids from the Dead* is a skillful combination of stories, fact, and fiction—keen outtakes on life in the late twentieth century which explore the recent past and a society obsessed with celebrity, crime, and death. Princess Diana, Nicole Brown Simpson, and Madonna are but some of the people scrutinized.

"Searing and unforgettable."
    —M. G. Lord, *New York Times Book Review*

HEY NOSTRADAMUS! (2003)

Pregnant and secretly married, Cheryl Anway scribbles her last will and testament—and eerie premonition—on a school binder shortly before a rampaging trio of misfit classmates gun her down in a high school cafeteria. *Hey Nostradamus!* tells the story of Cheryl's death and the knot of alienation, violence, and misguided faith from which her family and friends must untangle their lives.

"A pleasure to read: clever, affecting, effortlessly conceptual. The current

landscape, the mindless and endless
landslide of mass culture versus individual
vulnerability—no one sees these or gets to
the heart of them quite like Coupland."
—Ali Smith, author of Hotel World

ALL FAMILIES ARE PSYCHOTIC (2001)

In a cheap motel an hour from Cape
Canaveral, Janet Drummond takes her
medication and reflects on her children.
Wade has just been in jail, Bryan's suicidal,
and Sarah's an astronaut waiting to board the
shuttle this Friday. Where did it all go wrong?

"Heartbreakingly bittersweet. . . . This
book will make you want to phone your
own psychotic family and tell them how
much you love them." —The Telegraph

MISS WYOMING (1999)

Meet Susan Colgate—Miss Wyoming.
Winner of a hundred teen pageants, child
TV soap star, daughter of a hideously pushy
mother. Now she's reduced to small, brainless
parts in small, brainless movies. She is also
the sole survivor of Flight 802. If she were
to walk away from the wreckage now, before
the emergency crews get here, she could
disappear and nobody would ever know. . . .

"Astonishing. . . . Coupland creates
concepts that allow us to get to grips with
our unimaginable, real-life, end-of-the-
world news." —Literary Review

LIFE AFTER GOD (1993)

This collection of eight entwined short
stories showcased a starker style to Coupland
fans reared on the freewheeling prophecies of
Generation X. Characters search for meaning

and chinks of spiritual value within the mundane routine of everyday life.

"Plainly, even beautifully written, in an achingly nostalgic present tense."
—*The Times* (London)

"A wizard at cataloging our lives."
—*The Observer* (London)

SHAMPOO PLANET (1992)

Tyler Johnson, twenty-two, shampoo collector. Resident of a rundown town on the Pacific Northwest, he's burdened with a hippie mom, a drunk stepfather, and a love life split between his girlfriend and a French summer fling. Only one thing to do—escape to Hollywood. Coupland's X-files continue. . . .

"A snappy analysis of modern consumer culture in all its paradoxical surreality."
—*Mail on Sunday*

GENERATION X (1991)

Andy, Dag, and Claire reject the fast-lane pressures of modern life, moving to Palm Springs for a life of minimum wage McJobs and disillusioned storytelling. In *Generation X*, the book whose title gave a name to the sons and daughters of the baby boomers, Douglas Coupland unleashes an entirely new vocabulary for modern living.

"A new age J. D. Salinger on smart drugs."
—*Time Out*

"Fiercely comic."
—*The Sunday Express* (London)

Don't miss the next book by your favorite author. Sign up now for AuthorTracker by visiting www.AuthorTracker.com.